His mouth covered hers with a groan of pure primal satisfaction that drove her pleasure all the way to her toes. She could feel it pulsing through her, spreading over her limbs like a wave of pure molten heat.

His lips were soft but strong, his breath warm and spicy, as he crushed his mouth to hers.

His hand splayed against her back, possessively drawing her closer, bending her into the hard curve of his body.

For a moment she felt him yield. Felt his body envelop hers. His kiss grew more insistent. His lips dragging, kneading, opening her mouth.

Oh God.

She startled. Her heart fluttered like the wings of a butterfly. His tongue was inside her mouth, plunging, thrusting, circling. Tasting her deeper and deeper, as if he couldn't get enough.

The sensation was incredible. She moaned and circled her arms around his neck, wanting to get closer. His chest was so hot. So hard. She wanted to melt against him. She could feel her body soften, and the heat between her legs start to pulse and dampen.

The explosion of passion was so intense, so sudden, that she barely had time to savor it before it was gone. He broke away with a harsh, guttural curse, thrusting her from him as if she were plagued.

But it was the look of loathing on his face that cut her to the quick.

BY MONICA McCARTY

The Saint
The Viper
The Ranger
The Hawk
The Chief

Highland Warrior
Highland Outlaw
Highland Scoundrel

Highlander Untamed
Highlander Unmasked
Highlander Unchained

Books published by The Random House Publishing Group
are available at quantity discounts on bulk purchases for
premium, educational, fund-raising, and special sales use.
For details, please call 1-800-733-3000.

THE
Saint

A HIGHLAND GUARD NOVEL

MONICA McCARTY

BALLANTINE BOOKS • NEW YORK

The Saint is a work of fiction. Names, characters, places, and incidents are the products of the author's imagination or are used fictitiously. Any resemblance to actual events, locales, or persons, living or dead, is entirely coincidental.

A Ballantine Books Mass Market Original

Copyright © 2012 by Monica McCarty
Excerpt from *The Recruit* copyright © 2012 by Monica McCarty

Published in the United States by Ballantine Books, an imprint of The Random House Publishing Group, a division of Random House, Inc., New York.

BALLANTINE and colophon are trademarks of Random House, Inc.

This book contains an excerpt from the forthcoming book *The Recruit* by Monica McCarty. This excerpt has been set for this edition only and may not reflect the final content of the forthcoming edition.

ISBN 978-0-345-52840-7
eISBN 978-0-345-53211-4

Cover lettering: Iskra Design
Cover Illustration: Franco Accornero

Printed in the United States of America

www.ballantinebooks.com

9 8 7 6 5 4 3 2 1

Ballantine Books mass market edition: April 2012

"Ginger" hair doesn't necessarily bode trouble. Right, Maxine (my soon-to-be-teenage daughter)?

ACKNOWLEDGMENTS

A huge thank you to my editor, Kate Collins, who should be the poster girl for quick feedback. Of the eight (!) books we've worked on together, I think she's batting a two- or three-day average response time. Pretty impressive—especially given her workload. As an author, I can't tell you how wonderful it is not to sit on pins and needles waiting. And as always, thank you for helping me make my stories so much better with your insightful, thoughtful comments.

Where would I be without Junessa Viloria, "gatekeeper" extraordinaire? Thank you for keeping everything running so smoothly. You are the best!

To the entire Ballantine team for taking my manuscript from raw to polished in a gorgeous cover sitting prominently on shelves everywhere. Especially to Lynn Andreozzi and the Art Department for not one but two covers! I appreciate how hard you all work to get this done so quickly. Thank you.

To my wonderful agents, Annelise Robey and Andrea Cirillo, for the constant and unwavering support. Annelise, I still smile when I think about the message you left for me after reading this book. Wish we still had answering machines so I could hit replay when I need a pep talk!

Emily Cotler, Estella Tse, and the entire team at Wax Creative, thank you for keeping my website beautiful and up-to-date.

I'm fortunate to have a large group of writer friends who are always ready to brainstorm, talk industry, and meet for lunch. Bella Andre, Barbara Freethy, Carol Grace, Anne Mallory, Tracy Grant, travel-buddy and fellow "Onica," Veronica Wolff, and Jami Alden, who goes above and beyond the call of duty as my alpha (never beta) reader.

Finally, to my husband, Dave, who has become quite good with the grill and has even been called on to pinch hit on the stove. Necessity is indeed the mother of invention. And to Reid and Maxine who prove the point: if they're hungry enough, they'll eat.

FOREWORD

The year of our lord thirteen hundred and eight. After two and a half years of war, Robert "the Bruce" has waged one of the greatest recoveries in history. Against nearly insurmountable odds, with the help of his secret band of elite warriors known as the Highland Guard, he has defeated both the English at Glen Trool and Loudoun Hill and the powerful Scottish barons who stood against him—namely, the Comyns, the MacDowells, and the MacDougalls. In October, the Earl of Ross is finally brought to heel, submitting to Bruce, who now holds Scotland north of the Tay.

With England's new king, Edward II, busy trying to rein in his troublesome barons, and his brother Edward Bruce keeping watch over the troublesome south, King Robert enjoys a well-earned reprieve from battle. But Bruce's hold on the crown of Scotland is anything but certain, and in a realm filled with enemies both named and unnamed, peace is merely an illusion. Soon, Bruce will face the greatest threat to his life yet, and once again, he will call upon the legendary warriors of the Highland Guard to save him.

The Saint

Prologue

Inverbreakie Castle, Ross, Scottish Highlands, August 1305

Magnus MacKay caught the movement out of the corner of his swollen eye, but it was too late. He couldn't get the studded leather targe around in time to shield himself, and the war hammer landed with full, bone-crushing force across his left side, sending him careening headfirst into the dirt. Again. And this time with at least a few broken ribs.

Behind his own grunt of pain, he heard the collective gasp of the crowd, followed by the anxious silence as they waited for his next move. If he had one.

A broad shadow fell across him, blocking out the bright sunlight. He gazed up into the menacing visage of his enemy.

"Had enough?" the Sutherland henchman taunted.

Every inch of him had had enough. Magnus hurt in places he didn't know he could hurt. He'd been bruised, battered, and hammered to a bloody pulp, but he wouldn't give up. Not this time. For five years he'd suffered defeat at the hands of Donald Munro, the Sutherland champion. But not today. Today the prize was too important.

Magnus spit the dirt out of his mouth, wiped the blood

and sweat from his eyes, and gritted his teeth against the
pain as he dragged himself back to his feet. He wobbled,
but through sheer force of will steadied and shook the stars
clear from his vision. "Never."

A cheer went up from the crowd. Or half the crowd, that
is. Like the rest of Scotland, the clans gathered to watch the
Highland Games were divided. It wasn't Robert Bruce and
John Comyn that men took sides with today, however
(though both of Scotland's claimants to the throne were
present), but the parties to an even older and bloodier feud:
the MacKays and the Sutherlands.

"Stubborn whelp," the other man said.

Magnus didn't necessarily disagree. He lifted his targe in
one hand and his hammer in the other, and prepared for
the next blow.

It came. Again and again. Like a battering ram. Munro
was relentless.

But so was Magnus. Every time the fierce warrior
knocked him down, he got up. He refused to surrender.
He'd be damned if he'd come in second to the braggart
again.

The Sutherland henchman had been a thorn in his side
since the first Games in which Magnus had competed, five
years before. Magnus had been only eight and ten, and
besting the heralded champion, who was five years older
and already in the prime of his manhood, had seemed an
impossible task.

Then.

But Magnus was no longer a stripling lad. In the last
year, he'd added considerable bulk and strength to his lean,
muscular build. And at a handful of inches over Munro's
six feet, Magnus had the advantage in height. The scales
were no longer so unbalanced.

He'd already acquitted himself well at these Games, winning the foot race and sword challenges—although the best
swordsman in the Highlands, Tor MacLeod, was absent—

and placing among the top three in the other competitions with the exception of swimming, which was to be expected. Magnus hailed from the mountains of Northern Scotland, and the Islanders dominated the water events.

But this was the challenge Magnus had to win. The hammer event belonged to Munro. He'd dominated it for nearly ten years. It was his pride and dominion. And wresting the crown from his nemesis's head to claim victory for the MacKays would make it all the more satisfying. Hatred ran deep between the two clans, but Munro's arrogance and disdain had made it personal.

Still, it was far more than hatred and clan pride fueling Magnus's determination to win. He was deeply conscious of one set of eyes on him. One big and crystal-blue set of eyes. Helen. The girl—nay, woman—he intended to marry. The thought of losing to Munro in front of her . . .

He couldn't. Damn it. He *wouldn't*. How could he ask her to marry a man who came in second?

He blocked another powerful blow with his shield, his muscles flexing to absorb the shock. Steeling himself against the burning in his side, he took the full weight of his opponent's momentum on the shield and managed a swing of his own hammer. Munro twisted away, but the blow that Magnus landed on his shoulder was more than glancing.

It was the first crack. The look of fury on his opponent's face couldn't mask his frustration. Munro was tiring. The fierce attack and repeated swings of the heavy weapon had taken their toll.

This was it. The opening he'd been waiting for.

Magnus caught the scent of something that revived his aching body like nothing else: victory. With a sudden, inexplicable burst of strength from the very bowels of his determination, he took the offensive. Pummeling with his hammer and thrusting with his targe, he drove his surprised opponent back.

Munro stumbled, and Magnus seized the advantage, wrapping his foot around the henchman's ankle to knock him completely to the ground. Kneeling on his chest, he thrust his shield against his enemy's throat and lifted the hammer high above his head.

"Yield," he bit out forcefully, his words carrying across the silent arena. The stunning reversal had struck the crowd dumb.

Munro tried to fight back, but Magnus was in control. He dug the edge of the targe deeper, crushing his opponent's throat and cutting off his breath.

"Yield," he repeated. Rage surged through his veins, the brutality of the fight having taken its toll. The urge to finish it rose up hard inside him. But these were the Highland Games, not the life-and-death Games of the Gladiator.

For one long heartbeat, however, it might have come to that. Munro refused to yield and Magnus refused to let him go until he did. Despite the temporary truce of the Games, the hatred raging between the two proud Highlanders threatened to destroy it.

Fortunately, the decision was taken from their hands.

"Victory to MacKay," a man's voice rang out. Baron Innes. The holder of Inverbreakie Castle and the host of these games.

A cheer rang out. Magnus lowered his hammer, pulled back his targe, and released Munro. Standing, he thrust his arms out wide, basking in the cheers and savoring the rush of victory.

He'd done it. He'd won. *Helen.*

A swarm of people gathered around him. His father, younger siblings, friends, and a fair number of pretty young lasses.

But none was the lass he most wanted to see. Helen couldn't come to him. And as much as he wanted to see her right now, he dared not seek out her gaze.

For his Helen, the lass he intended to marry, was none

other than Helen Sutherland of Moray, the daughter of his greatest enemy, the Earl of Sutherland.

Thank God it was over! Helen didn't think she could bear another minute. Sitting there, watching Magnus get beaten to within an inch of his life, and not being able to react, being forced to smother every flinch, every gasp of horror, every whispered prayer for him not to get up, as the man who was like a brother to her pummeled him to the ground, had been pure agony.

Magnus was too tough for his own good. The stubborn ox didn't know when to give up!

She was going to kill him herself for putting her through that. He knew she didn't enjoy the violent competitions in the Highland Games—why men beat each other senseless in the name of sport, she would never understand—but for some reason he'd made her promise to be here.

"Are you all right?"

Helen tried to force her heart back down to her chest, but it seemed lodged permanently in her throat. She turned mutely to her brother.

Kenneth's concerned gaze flickered over her face and down to her hands, which were still clenched in the soft wool folds of her skirts. "You seem distressed. I thought you were going to faint for a moment."

Her pulse quickened. He was far too observant. She *was* distressed, but she dared not let him suspect the reason. Her brother despised the MacKays, and Magnus most of all. The two were close in age, but Magnus had gotten the best of him in the competitions since they were lads. If Kenneth found out about them . . .

He wouldn't. He couldn't. It would be a disaster if he discovered she was consorting with the enemy. Sutherlands hated MacKays. MacKays hated Sutherlands. That's just the way it was. But not for her.

"I didn't expect it to be so . . . *intense*," she said, which was the truth. Belatedly she recalled her family loyalty. "And of course, I'm disappointed."

Kenneth eyed her suspiciously, as if he didn't quite believe that was all there was to it. He knew her too well. She held her breath, but then the crowd roared again, distracting him. His face darkened as he took in the glee of the MacKays. "I can't believe he won." He shook his head. "Father is going to be furious."

A different kind of alarm shot through her. "Perhaps it would be best if we did not tell him? Not right away, at least."

Kenneth's eyes met hers, his expression instantly grave. "Is it that bad?"

"He will be fine," she said firmly, assuring herself as much as her brother. Of course he would. It was the only possibility she would consider. "But I do not want to distract him. He needs all his strength to fight the illness."

But each time the lung ailment came back it seemed worse. She probably shouldn't have come, but Magnus had made her promise. And the thought of not seeing him for another year with the threat of war swirling all around them . . .

She couldn't stay away.

It was only a week. Her father would be fine without her for a week. She'd left precise instructions for Beth, the serving lass who helped her care for her father, and Muriel had promised to check on him. It was she who'd taught Helen everything she knew about healing.

Kenneth held her gaze, the concern and fear in his eyes for their father mirroring her own. "Then perhaps you are right, it's better not to upset him." He took her elbow and nodded in the direction of their fallen champion. "Come, you'd best see to Munro. Although it appears it's mostly our champion's pride that has taken a beating." A wry smile turned his mouth. "Perhaps he will learn a little humility."

If her brother didn't sound altogether displeased by Donald's loss, Helen didn't wonder why. He'd suffered many defeats at the hand of their champion, and Donald loved to remind him of every one. Kenneth would have his day—as Magnus had just had his. But she knew how difficult it was for her proud brother, who was itching to step out of their shadows and prove himself.

As soon as her brother looked away, Helen stole one last glance toward Magnus. But he was surrounded, lost in the crowd of cheering admirers, his enemy's daughter undoubtedly far from his mind.

She sighed. Soon he'd have crowds of ladies following him about like Gregor MacGregor and Robbie Boyd. The famed archer with the face of Apollo and the strongest man in Scotland had taken on a godlike status at the Games and had their own retinues of starry-eyed young women hanging on their every move.

She followed her brother and pretended not to let it bother her. But it did. She wasn't jealous—not really. Well, perhaps more of the freedom the women had to talk with Magnus in public than of the women themselves. Although the curvaceous blonde attached to his arm was quite pretty, she recalled with a pang.

Why did everything have to be so complicated?

At first she hadn't given a second thought about sneaking away to meet him. The feud hadn't mattered to her. All she'd been thinking about was that she liked him. That for the first time she'd met someone who seemed to understand her.

When she was with him she felt unique, not different. He didn't care that she didn't like sewing or playing the lute. That she spent more time in the barn than she did in church. That watching animals give birth held an unmaidenly fascination for her. He thought it was funny when she pointed out to Father Gerald that bleeding seemed a strange way of restoring humours when all it seemed to do was make the patient weak and pale. He didn't care that she'd rather wear a simple woolen kirtle (more often than not tied up between her legs) than a fancy court gown. He hadn't even laughed the one spring she'd decided to cut her hair because it kept getting in her eyes.

But the constraints of the feud had begun to chafe. Stolen moments for the week of the Highland Games every year—and if they were lucky, perhaps a council meeting or two—were no longer enough. She wanted more. She wanted to be able to stand by Magnus's side instead of those women and have him smile down at her the way he did that made her insides melt.

If a little voice in the back of her head that sounded like her father said, "Perhaps you should have thought of this in the beginning, Helen lass?" she quieted it. It would be fine. Somehow they would make it work.

She loved him, and he loved her.

She gnawed on her lower lip. She was almost certain of it. He'd kissed her, hadn't he? It didn't matter that barely had their lips touched, and her heart finished slamming into her chest, when he'd set her harshly away from him.

Part of her sensed his feelings ran just as deeply and passionately as hers. And despite the danger, despite the knowledge that her family would consider her actions a betrayal, she couldn't stay away. It was foolish—impossible. But also exciting. When she was with Magnus she felt freer than she'd ever felt in her life.

How could she not take what they had and hold on tight? As the famous ancient Roman poet Horace said, "*Carpe diem, quam minimum credula postero.*" Seize the day, trusting as little as possible in the future. She might not have been much of a student when her father had brought in tutors for her, but she remembered that. The words had resonated.

It seemed to take forever to tend Donald's wounds, if not his tattered pride, but at the first opportunity she snuck away and waited for Magnus to find her. It didn't take him long. Usually, making him work to find her was part of the fun. But she was so anxious to see him, she made it easy on him.

The snap of a twig was the only warning she had before two big hands circled her waist from behind and snatched her down off her perch.

She gasped as her back met the hard planes of his chest. Her cheeks flushed with heat. By saints, he was strong! The lean frame of youth was now stacked with layer upon layer of hard, steely muscle. The changes in him had not gone unnoticed, and being plastered so intimately against those changes sent a strange warmth shimmering over her and a flutter of awareness low in her belly. Her heart quickened.

He spun her around to face him. "I thought we agreed no more climbing trees?"

Agreed? Ordered was more like it. She wrinkled her nose. Sometimes he could be just as bossy and overprotective as her brothers. "Ah, Helen," they'd say with an indulgent sigh, ruffling her red hair as if it were to blame. "What have you gone and done now?" They meant well, but they'd never understood her. Not like Magnus did.

Helen ignored his frown and gasped, as she gazed up into the familiar, handsome face. The boyishly strong, even features had been bruised and battered almost beyond recognition. He'd bathed and made some attempt to tend his wounds, but there was no washing away the big red and purple mass covering his jaw, the split lip, the broken nose, and the large cut near his eye. She traced the area around it lightly with her fingers, seeing that someone had already tended it. "Does it hurt horribly?"

He shook his head, capturing her hand in his to draw it away. "Nay."

"Liar." She pushed him away, hearing the grunt of pain and realizing she'd forgotten about his ribs. She put her hands on her hips. "It's no more than you deserve after what you did."

His brows furrowed in befuddlement. "I won."

"I don't care if you won, he nearly killed you!"

He folded his arms across his chest, a decidedly cocky grin on his face. For a moment her gaze snagged on the bulging display of muscle in his arms. Lately it seemed she was always noticing things like that at the most inopportune times. It flustered her. *He* flustered her. Which was disconcerting, since from the first she'd always been comfortable around him.

"But he didn't," he said.

The arrogance of his pronouncement distracted her from her distraction. Her eyes narrowed. Men and their pride. Nay, *Highlanders* and their pride. They were a special breed of proud and stubborn. "You don't have to sound so pleased with yourself."

He frowned. "Aren't you pleased for me?"

Helen nearly threw up her hands. "Of course I am."

The frown deepened. "Then why are you so upset?"

Were all men obtuse? "Because I don't like seeing you get hurt."

He grinned again, snagging her around the waist as she tried to spin away from him. It was a playful move—something he'd done many times before—but there was something different this time when he dragged her up against the long length of his powerful body. Something hot and dangerous crackled in the air between them.

She gasped at the contact, feeling every solid inch of the steely chest and legs plastered to hers.

He looked down at her, his warm, golden-brown eyes darkening. "But I have you to take care of me, don't I, *m'aingeal?*"

The huskiness in his voice sent a shiver running through her. *My angel.* He'd called her that since the first day they'd met, but today it sounded different. She blinked up at him, surprised at the change that had come over him. He never flirted with her like this. It was strange, exciting, and a little intimidating. He was a man. A warrior. A champion. Not the tall, lanky lad she'd first met. And suddenly she was achingly aware of it.

She tilted her head back, her lips parting in some instinctive response. She could see the desire swimming in his eyes and sucked in her breath in anticipation.

He was going to kiss her. God, he was *really* going to kiss her.

Finally!

Her heart hammered in her ears, as he lowered his head. She could feel his muscles tighten around her. Feel the pounding of his heart against hers and sense the passion surging inside him. Her knees weakened as desire shot through her in a wave of melting heat.

She sighed with pleasure at the first contact, at the sensation of his soft lips pressing against hers. Warmth and the faint tinge of spice infused her, flooding her senses with the heady taste of him.

He kissed her tenderly, dragging his lips over hers in a gentle caress. She sank into him, unconsciously seeking more.

Show me how much you care for me. She wanted throes of passion. She wanted heartfelt declarations of love. She wanted it all.

He made a pained sound, and for a moment she wondered if she'd hurt his ribs. But then his arms tightened around her. His mouth hardened, pressing against her more fully. The taste of spice grew deeper, more arousing. She could feel the tension in his muscles, feel the power surging through him, and her body melted in anticipation. Then suddenly he stiffened and pulled away with a harsh curse.

He released her so abruptly she had to catch herself from stumbling. Her legs seemed to be missing their bones.

Her eyes widened, shocked and not a little disappointed. Had she done something wrong?

He dragged his fingers through silky-straight, sandy-brown hair. "Marry me."

She gaped at him in astonishment. "W-what?"

His gaze locked on hers. "I want you to be my wife."

The spontaneity of the proposal was so unlike him, at first she thought he must be jesting. But one look at his face told her differently. "You're serious?"

"Aye."

"But why?"

He frowned. It was obviously not the response he'd hoped for. "I would think that would be obvious. I care for you."

Not "I love you." Not "I can't live without you." Not "I want to ravish you senseless."

There was a tiny pinch in the vicinity of her heart. Helen told herself she was being ridiculous. This was what she wanted, wasn't it? He'd told her how he felt—even if it wasn't exactly with the flourish she'd hoped for.

He was so confoundingly *controlled*. Not cold and unfeeling, but calm and even-tempered. Steady. A rock, not a volcano. But sometimes she wished he'd explode.

When she didn't respond right away, he added, "Surely this can't come as a surprise to you?"

Actually it did. She bit her lip. "We never talked about the future." Perhaps because they'd both been trying to ignore the realities.

Marriage. It was the only option for a woman in her position. Then why did the very idea strike fear in her heart?

But this was Magnus. He understood her. She loved him. Of course she wanted to marry him.

But what he was asking was impossible. "Our families will never allow it. The feud."

"I'm not asking our families, I'm asking you. Run away with me."

She sucked in her breath. A clandestine marriage? The notion was shocking. But also, she admitted, oddly appealing—

and undeniably romantic. Where would they go? Perhaps the continent? How exciting it would be to travel across the countryside with only each other to please! "Where would we go?"

He looked at her strangely. "Strathnavar. My father will be angry at first, of course, but my mother will understand. He'll come around eventually."

Northern Scotland, not the continent. The MacKay lands were in Caithness, which bordered Sutherland. Arguments over land for the neighboring clans had started and fueled the feud for years.

"And where would we live?" she asked carefully.

"At Castle Varrich with my family. When I am chief, the castle will be yours."

Of course. Silly lass, how could she have thought differently? His mother was the perfect lady of the castle. Naturally, he would expect as much from her. Her lungs squeezed, and her heart raced. "Why now? Why can't we wait and see—"

"I'm tired of waiting. Nothing will change." His jaw hardened, an unfamiliar glint of steel in his eye. He was growing impatient with her. For a moment she thought he might lose his temper. But Magnus never lost his temper. Sometimes she even wondered whether he had one. "I'm tired of sneaking around, not being able to speak or even look at you in public. You are eighteen now, Helen. How much longer before your father finds you a husband?"

She blanched, knowing he was right. She'd escaped a betrothal this long only because her father was ill and needed her.

Her heart stopped. Oh God, who would take care of her father? She looked at him helplessly, the enormity of the decision making her hesitate. She loved him, but she loved her family, too. How could she choose between them?

He must have read her indecision. "Don't you see, this is the only way it can be. What we have . . ." His voice dropped off. "What we have is special. Don't you want to be with me?"

"Of course, I do. But I need some time—"

"There isn't time," he said harshly. But he wasn't looking at her. A moment later, she knew why.

"Get the hell away from her!"

Her heart dropped. Helen turned around to see her brother flying toward them.

Magnus saw the blood drain from Helen's face and wished he could spare her from this moment. But it had been inevitable. They'd been fortunate to escape discovery for so long.

Although if they were going to be discovered by anyone in her family, he would rather it had been her eldest brother, William, the heir to the earldom. He at least wasn't a complete arse. If there was anyone he disliked more than Donald Munro it was Kenneth Sutherland. He had all the arrogance and all the snide mockery of Munro, with a hot temper to boot.

Instinctively, Magnus moved around to block Helen. He knew she was close to her brother, but he wasn't taking any chances. Sutherland was unpredictable at best, rash at worst.

Magnus caught the other man's fist before it could slam into his jaw and pushed him back. "This isn't any of your business, Sutherland."

Her brother would have come at him again, but Helen stepped between them. Next to her oaf of a brother she looked as diminutive as a child. Her head barely reached the middle of his chest. But she wasn't a child. For two long years Magnus had been waiting for her to turn eighteen. He wanted her so badly he couldn't breathe. This impish, fey creature, with her big blue eyes, freckled up-turned nose, and wild mane of glorious deep red hair. Hers was not a conventional beauty, but to him, there was no one more breathtaking.

"Please, Kenneth, it's not what you think."

Sutherland's eyes sparked with outrage. "It's exactly what I think. I knew there was something wrong at the competition, but I didn't want to believe it." His gaze softened as he met his sister's. "Good God, a MacKay, Helen? Our clan's most reviled enemy? How could you be so disloyal?"

Helen flinched with guilt, and Magnus swore. "Leave her out of this. If you want to take your anger out on someone, take it out on me."

The other man's eyes narrowed. "With pleasure." He reached for his sword. "I'm going to enjoy killing you."

"A bold claim for someone who has never bested me in anything."

Sutherland snarled with fury. Helen cried out and launched herself at her brother. "No, please," tears were sliding down her cheeks, "don't do this, I-I love him."

Magnus had been reaching for his own sword, but her words stopped him. His heart slammed in his chest. She loved him. She'd never said so before, and after their recent conversation he hadn't been so sure. Warmth settled over him. He'd been right. They were meant to be together. She felt it, too.

With more gentleness than Magnus would have thought him capable, her arse of a brother said, "Ah, Helen." He stroked her cheek fondly. "You're too young, love. You don't know what you are saying. Of course you think you're in love with him. You're eighteen. That's what young girls do, they fall in love."

She shook her head fervently. "It's not like that."

"It's exactly like that," he said. Had Magnus not seen it himself, he would never have imagined Kenneth Sutherland could be so—God forbid!—*tender*. But maybe Helen had a way of bringing out the softer side in everyone. He just hadn't realized Sutherland *had* a softer side. "You love to love," Sutherland continued. "God chose the first of May for your saint's day for a reason. Every day is like May Day to you. But how well can you know him?" Helen bit her lip, and Sutherland's expression narrowed. "How long have you been meeting like this?"

She flushed, looking down at her feet. Magnus felt his anger rise, seeing her guilt.

"We met at the Games at Dunottar," Magnus interjected. "By accident."

Kenneth spun on her. "Four years ago?"

He swore when Helen nodded.

"By God, if he's disgraced you, I'll string him up by his bollocks and see him gelded—"

"He's done nothing," Helen interrupted, putting her hand on her brother to hold him back. Remarkably, it seemed to work. "He's treated me with perfect courtesy."

Magnus frowned, hearing something odd in her voice. It almost sounded like disappointment. "Have care what you say, Sutherland. You have a right to your anger, but I will not allow you to impugn your sister's honor or mine."

It might have taken every last shred of his control, but Magnus hadn't done more than kiss Helen. He wouldn't dishonor her like that. He'd wait until they were married, and then he'd dishonor her plenty. The sweet taste of her lips on his still haunted him. But it had been as much care for her innocence as lack of confidence in his own control that had caused him to pull away.

Sutherland's face darkened, as if he knew exactly what Magnus was thinking. "It'll be a cold day in Hades before you get the chance." He shot Magnus a look that promised retribution and folded his sister under his arm as if to protect her from something repugnant. "Come, Helen, we're leaving."

Helen shook her head and tried to pull away. "No, I—"

She looked to Magnus helplessly. His mouth tightened.

She had only to say the word, and he'd claim her right now. He'd defeated the Sutherland champion—her brother would not stand in his way.

Sutherland put his cheek on her head, talking to her as if she were a child. "What were you thinking, lass? Your eyes are so filled with sunshine, you think it shines as brightly for everyone else. But you aren't going to be able to make this have a happy ending. Not this time. Surely you didn't think anything could come of this?"

Magnus had had enough. "I asked her to be my wife."

Sutherland's face turned so red, he appeared to choke. "God's blood, you must be mad! I'd sooner see her married to old longshanks himself than a MacKay."

Magnus's hand closed around the hilt of his sword. Feud or no feud, nothing would stand in their way. "It's not you I've asked."

Both men's eyes fell on Helen, whose pale face was ravaged by tears that looked so out of place. Helen never cried; that she was doing so told of her deep distress. She looked back and forth between them. Magnus knew she loved her brother, but she loved him, too. She'd just said so.

Magnus clenched his jaw, knowing how hard this was on her. He knew what he was asking of her. But she had to decide. It was always going to come down to this.

Sutherland did not show such restraint. "If you marry him it will renew the war between our clans."

"It doesn't have to," Magnus said. He didn't like Sutherland any better than Sutherland did him, but he'd do his best to put the feud behind him for Helen's sake. But his father . . . he couldn't be so sure.

Sutherland acted as if he hadn't spoken. "You would turn your back on your family? On Father? He needs you."

His voice sounded so certain. So bloody *reasonable*.

Her tear-filled eyes grew enormous in her pale face. She

looked at Magnus pleadingly and he knew. His chest started to burn.

"I'm sorry," she said. "I can't . . ."

Their eyes met. He didn't want to believe it. But the truth was there in stark, vivid blue.

Jesus. His gut twisted. He couldn't believe . . . He'd thought . . .

He stiffened and turned brusquely away, holding himself perfectly still so he wouldn't do something to shame himself like beg. The worst part was how badly he wanted to. But he had his pride, damn it. It was bad enough that Sutherland was here to witness his rejection.

Sutherland folded Helen into his arms and petted her hair. "Of course you can't, sweetheart. MacKay couldn't have expected you to agree to this. Only a romantic fool would have thought you'd agree to run away with him."

Magnus could hear Sutherland laughing at him. He clenched his fists, wanting to smash the taunting grin off the bastard's face.

Had he really expected her to run away with him?

Aye, fool that he was, he had. Helen was different. Helen wasn't bound by convention. If she'd loved him enough, nothing would have stopped her. Knowing that was the worst part.

He would have given up everything for her, if she'd only asked.

But she never did. The next morning he watched the Sutherland tents coming down. They were leaving. Her brothers weren't going to give her any chance to change her mind.

Robert Bruce, the Earl of Carrick, approached him with Neil Campbell just as Helen exited the castle. Her face was hidden in the hood of her dark cloak, but he would know her anywhere.

Magnus barely listened to their proposition. Barely heard the details of a secret band of elite warriors being formed by Bruce to help defeat the English. He was too caught up in Helen. Too busy watching her leave him.

Turn back. But she never did. She rode out of the gate, disappearing into the morning mist, and never once looked back. He watched until the last Sutherland banner had disappeared from view.

Bruce was still talking.

He wanted Magnus for his secret army. It was all he needed to hear. "I'll do it."

He'd do anything to get away from here.

One

❧

Dunstaffnage Castle,
December 1308

He could do this, damn it. Magnus could withstand almost any kind of physical torture and pain. A tough bastard, they said of him. He needed to remember it.

He kept his gaze fastened on the trencher before him, concentrating on his meal and not what was going on around him. But the ham and cheese intended to break his fast stuck in his throat. Only the ale went down easily. Still, it wasn't strong enough to quiet the tumult eating him up inside. If it weren't an hour after daybreak he would have asked for whisky.

Although given the celebratory mood around him, he doubted anyone would notice if he did. The festive atmosphere reverberated from the wooden rafters laden with fragrant boughs of pine to the stone floor strewn with fresh rushes. The massive Great Hall of Dunstaffnage Castle was lit up like Beltane, with hundreds of candles and a roaring fire blazing in the fireplace behind him. But the warmth of the room couldn't penetrate the icy shell around him.

"If you keep looking like you want to murder someone, we'll have to change your name."

Magnus turned to the man seated at the trestle table beside him and shot him a warning glare. Lachlan MacRuairi had an uncanny ability to find a man's weak spot. Like the viper his war name professed him to be, he struck with deadly precision. He alone of the other members of the Highland Guard had guessed Magnus's secret, and he never wasted an opportunity to remind him of it.

"Aye," MacRuairi said with a shake of his head. "You look decidedly *un*saintly. Aren't you supposed to be the calm and reasonable one?"

During the training for the Highland Guard, Erik MacSorley, the greatest seafarer in the Western Isles, had taken to calling him Saint in jest. Unlike the rest of them, Magnus didn't spend his nights around the fire discussing the next woman he wanted to swiv. Nor did he lose his temper. When it had come to choosing war names to protect their identities, Saint had stuck.

"Sod off, MacRuairi."

The impervious bastard just smiled. "We weren't sure you were going to make it."

Magnus had stayed away as long as he could, volunteering for any mission as long as it would keep him far from here. But he'd left Edward Bruce, the king's brother and newly created Lord of Galloway, two days ago to join the other members of the Highland Guard at Dunstaffnage for the wedding of one of their own. The wedding of William Gordon, his best friend and partner, to Helen Sutherland.

My Helen.

Nay, not his. She'd never belonged to him. He'd only thought she had.

Three years ago he'd joined Bruce's secret guard in the attempt to escape his memories. But fate had a cruel sense of irony. Not long after arriving, he'd learned that his new partner had been recently betrothed to Helen. The Sutherlands hadn't lost any time in ensuring she didn't change her mind about marrying him. Magnus had anticipated a quick betrothal; he just hadn't anticipated it would hit so close.

For three years he'd known this day would come. He'd come to terms with it. But if it were anyone other than Gordon, Magnus would have found an excuse to stay away. Despite his appellation, self-flagellation was not something he succumbed to willingly.

"Where's Lady Isabella?" he asked by way of a response.

MacRuairi's mouth curved. It was still strange to see such a black-hearted bastard smile, but these past few weeks since MacRuairi had won Lady Isabella MacDuff's freedom a second time—as well as, it seemed, her heart— the sight had become more frequent. If a bastard like MacRuairi could find love, he supposed there was hope for anyone.

Except for him.

"Helping the bride get ready," MacRuairi replied. "She'll be here soon enough."

Bride. That pricked. Even knowing that MacRuairi was watching, he flinched.

The smile left MacRuairi's face. "You should have told him. He deserves to know."

Magnus shot an angry glare back at the man who made it hard as hell to like him—though somehow Magnus did. "Back off, Viper," he said in a low voice. Gordon didn't need to know anything. Helen had made her choice well before their betrothal. "There is nothing to tell."

He pushed back from the bench, not wanting to listen to any more of MacRuairi's prodding, when he noticed a group of men entering the Hall.

Ah hell. He muttered a curse, seeing the impending disaster and knowing there wasn't a damned thing he could do to stave it off.

His partner in the Highland Guard and closest friend, William Gordon, broke into a wide smile and headed straight for him. "You made it. I was beginning to wonder."

Magnus didn't have a chance to respond. The other man he'd noticed—the one who'd provoked his reaction—prevented it.

"What the hell is *he* doing here?" Kenneth Sutherland demanded angrily.

Magnus held very still, but every battle instinct flared. Sutherland's hand had gone to the arming sword at his waist. The moment he moved, Magnus would be ready. MacRuairi, too, having sensed the threat, had tensed with readiness at his side.

"He's my guest, as well as my friend," Gordon said to his foster brother and soon-to-be brother-in-law—what the hell Gordon saw in the bastard, Magnus couldn't fathom. It wasn't often that the good-humored Gordon sounded angry, but there was a distinct edge of steel in his voice now.

"Your friend?" Kenneth said, aghast. "But he—"

Realizing he was about to say something about Helen, Magnus got to his feet and slammed his flagon on the table. "Leave it. What is between us has no bearing on today." He eyed his old enemy intently, and then forced himself to relax. "The feud is in the past. Just like imprudent alliances," he added, unable to resist prodding him.

The Sutherlands had aligned with the Earl of Ross and England against Robert Bruce. But after Bruce's victory over the MacDougalls at the Pass of Brander in August, the Earl of Ross had been forced to submit. The Sutherlands had reluctantly followed suit a month ago. Magnus knew Sutherland's pride must have still been smarting.

From what Gordon told him, Sutherland had acquitted himself well in battle and was considered a formidable warrior—equal to if not surpassing Donald Munro and his elder brother, William, who'd become earl on his father's death two years ago. But to Magnus's mind, Sutherland had one fatal flaw: his temper. And if the angry flush on

Sutherland's face was any indication, it hadn't lost any of its volatility.

"Bastard," Sutherland growled, taking a step forward. But Gordon held him back.

The air, which only moments before had been light with celebration, was now charged with strife. Swords had been drawn, if not in fact then in spirit. In response to the threat, two sides had formed. Sutherland's men had gathered behind him and the members of the Highland Guard who'd been nearby had come to stand beside MacKay, with Gordon caught in the middle.

"Let him come, Gordon," Magnus said idly. "Mayhap the English have taught him something."

He and Sutherland were of a similar height and build, but Magnus had no doubt he could still best him in a sword fight—or with any weapon, for that matter. It seemed that most of his youth had been spent with the purpose of besting Sutherlands. If it wasn't Munro, it was one of Helen's brothers.

Sutherland bit out a crude oath and tried to break free from Gordon's hold. He might have succeeded if a new group hadn't entered the Hall. A group not armed in leather and steel but in silk and satin.

Focused on the threat before him, Magnus hadn't seen the women approach until one woman stepped forward. "Kenneth, what's wrong? What's happening here?"

Magnus froze at the sound of her voice. The muscle slid from his limbs. For a moment he felt boneless, empty but for the fire burning in his chest. The fire that it seemed would never die.

Helen stood before him. Every bit as breathtaking as he remembered—yet different. There was nothing unconventional about her beauty now. The freckles that had once been smattered across her nose had vanished in the creamy perfection of ivory skin. The rich auburn hair that had tumbled about her shoulders in wild disarray—when it hadn't been chopped indiscriminately—had been tamed into a maidenly coronet of braids. The tiny, pixie features were no longer quirked with laughter and mischief but were soft in repose. Only her eyes—a clear crystal blue—and lips—the reddest he'd ever seen—were the same.

But it wasn't her beauty that had drawn him to her, it was the irrepressible good humor and untamed spirit that made her different from any other woman he'd ever known. A lively sprite who was as hard to catch as quicksilver.

He saw no evidence of that girl in the woman standing before him now, but it didn't change the fierceness of his response. His chest felt as if it had been put in a vise of longing.

He'd thought he was prepared, damn it. Thought he could do this. But nothing could have prepared him for the shock of seeing her after three long years. Three years of war and destruction. Three years when he didn't know whether he'd live or die. Three years of telling himself he was over her.

Three years of delusion.

Realizing that Gordon was looking at him with a frown, he quickly got himself under control, schooling his features in a blank mask. But calm deserted him.

It was then that she noticed him. He heard her gasp a dozen feet away. Her eyes widened and her face lost every bit of color. Her expression reminded him of the men he'd seen in battle after they'd taken an arrow to the gut: startled, shocked, and pained.

Instinctively, he made a move toward her, but MacRuairi held him back. Gordon was already at her side.

Gordon his friend.

Gordon her betrothed.

Gordon the man who would be her husband in a few short hours.

His stomach knifed.

"It is nothing, my lady," Gordon said, taking her arm.

"A minor misunderstanding. I believe you've met my friend Magnus MacKay?"

His words had shocked Helen out of her trance. "Aye, my lord." Because she couldn't avoid it, she turned to him. But he hadn't missed the slight stiffening of her shoulders, as if bracing herself. For one long heartbeat their eyes met. The lance of pain through his chest stole his breath. She nodded her head in acknowledgment. "My lord."

"My lady." He bowed politely. Formally. Marking the distance that must now be between them. This wasn't the Helen of his youth, but a woman who belonged to another.

Lady Isabella saved the moment from further awkwardness. She was in the group of women who'd entered the Hall with Helen and rushed forward to greet him. "Magnus, you're back!" Grabbing hold of his elbow, she turned him back to the table. "You must tell me all that is happening in the south." She pursed her mouth in Lachlan's direction and gave an indignant toss of her chin. "He tells me nothing."

MacRuairi lifted a wry brow. "That's because I don't want you grabbing a sword to join them."

She reached over to give the infamous mercenary a gentle pat on the arm as if soothing a naughty child. "That's ridiculous. I don't have a sword." She winked up at Magnus and whispered. "I have a bow."

"I heard that," MacRuairi snapped.

Magnus smiled, grateful for the distraction. But it was only temporary. He was acutely aware of the two people walking arm-in-arm down the long aisle to the dais.

Bread. Chew. Cheese. Chew. Smile at William. Laugh politely at the king's joke. Don't look across the room.

Helen sat at the dais between her betrothed and the King of Scotland and tried to go through the motions of normality. Tried to quell the firestorm of emotions reverberating inside her. Tried to breathe.

But she felt as if she'd taken a blow to the chest and nothing would put air back into her lungs. Magnus. Here. On her wedding day.

Dear God.

The shock of seeing him after so long had been like an explosion, shattering the very foundations of her carefully constructed façade. Just when she'd reconciled herself to this marriage, just when she'd convinced herself that she could go through with it, just when she'd given up hope that she would ever see him again, he appeared and blew it all apart.

For a moment she thought he was there to put a stop to the wedding. "Silly lass," she could almost hear her father say. Magnus was no more likely to fall to his knees and beg her to come with him now than when she'd wished him to do so all those years ago. Proud Highland warriors didn't beg.

And he was certainly that. Big. Hard. Every inch the powerful warrior. He was six and twenty now, she realized with a pang of longing at the differences forged by time. In the prime of his manhood, and it showed. There was no hint of boyishness left in his handsome face; it was all rugged, dangerous warrior. His features had hardened, his hair was darker and shorter, his skin had tanned from hours in the sun, and the wide mouth that had often been pulled in a grin fell in a flat line.

All those confusing, unsettling feelings came rushing back to her in a hot wave.

"Would you care for more cheese, Lady Helen?"

She startled at the question. Cheese? At a time like this? "No, thank you," she managed with a small smile.

William grinned back at her, completely unaware of the calamity swirling around him.

What was she going to do? In a few hours she was to be married.

It was the day she'd dreaded from the moment her father had announced her betrothal. She had known William Gordon only through the recollections of her brother Kenneth. The two had been fostered together under the Earl of Ross and had been like brothers. Indeed, Kenneth was closer to William Gordon than he was to their own brother of the same name.

She'd protested the alliance to no avail. Her father was determined that she would marry. But then war had come, and miraculously she'd been granted a reprieve. Her betrothed had split from his family—and hers—to take up the sword for Robert Bruce. Her brother Kenneth had convinced her father not to break the betrothal, and indeed it had worked to their advantage. Her father had an ally in the Bruce camp should the war go against them, and she had the ideal situation of a fiancé without the prospect of a wedding.

For a while she'd convinced herself the wedding might never take place. But with Bruce's victory and her family's submission, it could no longer be delayed.

She'd thought she could go through with it. William was every bit as wonderful as her brother had promised. Charming, lighthearted, gallant, and certainly pleasant enough to look upon. But seeing Magnus . . .

His presence had to mean something. God could not be that cruel. He could not intend her to marry another, while the man she loved looked on?

Somehow she made it through the meal, escaping to the sanctuary of the room that had been set aside for her in the donjon tower as soon as she could.

Unfortunately, she was not alone. Since she'd arrived at Dunstaffnage the week before, she'd been welcomed with open arms by Lady Anna Campbell, the lady of the castle, and her friends, Christina MacLeod, Ellie MacSorley (formerly a de Burgh—making her sister to Bruce's queen and daughter to the English loyal Earl of Ulster), and most surprisingly, Lady Isabella MacDuff (soon to be MacRuairi), the famous patriot who was supposed to be imprisoned still in an English convent. The ladies had taken one look at the motherless, sisterless girl and had tucked her under their very large collective wing.

Helen wasn't used to female companionship. Except for Muriel, there were few women of her age at Dunrobin Castle. But even when the opportunity did arise—such as when visitors arrived or when they traveled for the Games—her interactions with other ladies were awkward and uncomfortable. She usually ended up saying or doing the wrong thing, and never seemed to share their interests. Her gaffes did not seem quite as bad with these women. And it was nice to not hear whispers every time she walked in the room.

There was an unusually strong camaraderie among the women that she didn't quite understand, but couldn't help admiring—and perhaps envy a little. Usually, she didn't mind their company, but today their pleasant laughter and conversation prevented her from doing what she needed to do.

She had to see him. This was her chance to correct the biggest mistake she'd ever made in her life.

Ironically, when she'd had the chance to seize the day she'd faltered. It was the one time in her life she'd tried to do what was right. Instead of following her heart, she'd let her brother persuade her to do her duty to her family and return with him. She knew Kenneth thought he was doing what was right, and perhaps given the circumstances it was. Rationally. But love wasn't rational. Love had its own rules, and she'd been too weak to follow them. She'd been confused. Unsure of Magnus's feelings for her and, truth be told, of hers for him. The enormity of the decision had overwhelmed her.

Her family had been so convincing. A youthful folly, they'd told her. "You know how you are, Helen, you love to love." It was the excitement. The illicit nature of their relationship. She would see. Give it time. She would forget about him.

But it didn't take her long to realize her feelings weren't going away. That what she felt for Magnus was special. He saw her differently than anyone else and loved her for it. Her longing for passion had been misplaced. She'd taken for granted his calm solidity. The security in knowing that he was there for her.

She'd begged and pleaded for her family to reconsider, but an alliance with the hated MacKays was unfathomable. And then it was too late. Magnus had disappeared and her father had betrothed her to William.

She'd never thought it would be forever. She thought Magnus would come for her. But he hadn't. War broke out, and nothing had ever been the same.

But maybe it wasn't too late after all. Maybe—

"Is everything all right, Helen?" Helen turned to see Lady Isabella—or Bella, as she insisted on being called—watching her. She smiled. "Or is the comb not to your liking?"

Helen looked down and blushed, realizing she'd been staring absently at the comb in her hand for some time. She shook her head and put it down. "I think perhaps I should not have broken my fast. My stomach is a bit unsettled."

"It's your wedding day," Bella said. "It's normal to feel as if you have a few butterflies fluttering around in your belly. Perhaps you would feel better if you lay down for a while?"

Helen shook her head, the means of escape suddenly coming to her. She stood up. "A spot of fresh air is all I need."

"I shall go with you," Lady Anna volunteered, overhearing the last part of their conversation.

"Nay, please," Helen said quickly. "That isn't necessary. I shall only be a short while."

Bella came to her rescue a second time this morning. "Anna, weren't you going to fetch some earrings . . . ?"

The recently married young bride jumped to her feet, the soft roundness of her belly just visible beneath the folds of her gown. "That's right. Thank you for reminding me. They will go perfectly with your eyes," she said to Helen.

"Your dress will be ready for you to put on when you get back," Christina said with a bright smile. The formidable MacLeod chief's wife was easily one of the most beautiful women Helen had ever seen.

Helen felt a stab of guilt, seeing how eagerly everyone was looking forward to this wedding. Everyone but she.

Bella followed her to the door. "I've always enjoyed the path through the forest to the chapel," she suggested. "I believe what you are looking for is there." Their eyes met. The hint of compassion in the other woman's eyes told her she'd guessed at least some of the truth. "I love them both," the former Countess of Buchan finished quietly.

Helen nodded, understanding. No matter what happened, someone would be hurt.

But unlike Bella, Helen loved only one of them. She raced down the stairs and out of the tower into the frigid December morning. The thick blanket of icy mist had yet to lift from its moorings and hung like a silty sea of gray across the large courtyard.

Thankfully, no one remarked upon the oddity of seeing the bride make her escape out the gate mere hours before her wedding. Moments later, Helen found herself walking down the small, rocky rise upon which the castle sat and into the shadowy darkness of the forest to the south.

It was a short walk through the trees to the small chapel, which served the spiritual needs of the castle and the surrounding village. The stone building sat on a small rise in the middle of the small woodland. It was quiet as she approached. Eerily quiet. A whisper of trepidation slid down her spine.

She slowed, for the first time considering what she was doing. Her brothers would be furious. Her betrothed . . . angry? She didn't know him well enough to guess his reaction. Her father, gone now for two years would have given her that look that he always did when she'd done something that seemed perfectly logical to her, but incomprehensible to him. It was the same look Will had perfected, often accompanied by some comment about her hair. As if red were some explanation for all the trouble she caused.

But it didn't matter. She knew what she was doing. She was following her heart. What she should have done all those years ago.

The chapel was only a few feet away when she saw him. Her heart caught in a gasp in her throat. He sat with his back to her on a rock a few feet from the chapel door, staring at it as if he couldn't decide whether to go in. The mere sight of him swelled her chest. If there was even the slightest chance that they might be able to find happiness, she had to seize that chance.

"Magnus." Even saying his name invoked too much emotion, and the simple word came out as a strangled cry.

He turned and blinked once, as if not sure whether she were real or an apparition. The hardening of his jaw told her he'd figured it out. "You're early."

The sarcasm and flatness of his tone unsettled her. She searched his gaze for the man she remembered. But the warm, caramel depths of his eyes seemed hard and unfamiliar.

Ignoring the do-not-approach aura that seemed to radiate from him, she took a tentative step toward him. "I came to find you."

He stood up. "Why? To rehash old memories?" He shook his head. "It would serve no purpose. Go back to the castle, Helen. Where you belong."

That was just it. She didn't belong anywhere. She never had. Only with him had she felt the possibility.

Helen searched for the slightest hint of anger, the slightest touch of pain. But his tone gave no hint of any emotion other than the vague sense of weariness she heard in her father's voice when she'd done something "wayward."

Three years was a long time. Perhaps the feelings he'd once had for her were gone. She felt a twinge of uncertainty but pushed it aside. This was Magnus. Calm, steadfast Magnus.

"I made a mistake," she said softly.

If she'd hoped for any reaction to her words, she was to be disappointed. Taking a deep breath, she forged on. "I should have gone with you. I wanted to, but I couldn't leave my family. My father was ill, and he needed me to help care for him. It was happening so fast." She gazed up at him, pleading for understanding. "I was surprised— scared. You'd never mentioned marriage before. You'd barely even kissed me."

His gaze pierced hers, his mouth a thin line. "What purpose does this serve, Helen? It is all in the past. You have no need of absolution from me. You owed me nothing."

"I loved you."

He stilled. "Obviously not enough." The soft parry sent a blade right through her heart. He was right. She hadn't trusted her feelings. Then. She'd been eighteen. She hadn't known what she wanted. But she did now. She knew in her heart that he was the man who'd been meant for her. She'd been given a rare chance to have love, and she'd failed to grasp it. "I still—"

"That's enough." He crossed the distance between them in a few strides and grabbed her by the arms. The feel of his big hands on her was like a brand. For a moment, her heart had leapt, thinking that he'd snapped. That the calm indifference of his response had proved to be an act. But as he held her up so that her toes dragged on the ground, he looked perfectly in control. "Whatever you have to say, it's too late." He released her and took a step back. "For Christ's sake, you are about to marry a man who is like a brother to me."

The blasphemy, the small hint of emotion, urged her on. She moved closer to him—much closer—and put her hand on his arm, feeling a jolt of awareness as the muscles leapt at her touch. She looked up into the handsome face that had haunted her dreams, locking her gaze on his. "And it means nothing to you?" She moved her hand to cover his heart; beneath the hard shield she felt the thump against her palm. "It doesn't bother you *here*."

He looked down at her completely still and achingly silent, his expression unreadable. She looked for a sign that it mattered. Instinctively, her gaze went to the small muscle below his jaw. But beneath the shadow of dark stubble, there was no tic to betray him. He was perfectly controlled—as always.

Carefully, he extracted himself from her touch, setting her away from him. "You are embarrassing us both, Helen."

She sucked in her breath, feeling the knife of shame cut through her heart.

He looked into her eyes and said, "I feel nothing."

He turned on his heel and left her standing there, watching as her chance for happiness slipped silently away. This time she could not delude herself that he would come back for her.

Two

⁂

Helen didn't know how long she stood there in the woods, frozen with heartbreak. Of course it was too late. What could she have been thinking?

By the time she returned to the castle, the women were in a mild panic. Bella took one look at her face and took charge.

"Are you sure you want to do this?" she asked quietly.

Helen stared numbly at her. No. Yes. She didn't care. What difference did it make?

She must have nodded because she soon found herself gowned, perfumed, and coiffed, with a circlet of gold upon her head, retracing the steps she'd taken only hours before.

Only once did she falter. As her brother Will, now the Earl of Sutherland, led her to the place where her betrothed waited for her outside the chapel door, she took in the crowd that had gathered to stand witness to the ceremony. There, in the front, standing beside a handful of other warriors, she saw him. Magnus had his back to her. The once familiar form was broader, more muscular, and much more formidable, but she would know him anywhere.

Disappointment sank like a stone to her gut. His presence did away with any lingering doubt she might have had that this mattered to him—that she mattered to him.

"Is everything all right, Helen?"

She blinked up at her eldest brother. "You stopped," Will pointed out.

"I . . ."

Every instinct clamored *stop, do not do this*.

"She's fine." Kenneth had come behind them. "Come, sister, your betrothed is waiting."

Though he said it gently, there was a look in his eyes that cautioned her against doing something "wayward." It was too late to change her mind.

For once, he and Magnus were in accord.

Swallowing through the hot ball of longing and regret that seemed lodged in her lungs, Helen nodded. When her brothers stepped forward, she moved along with them.

If her hand trembled as her brother placed it in her betrothed's, she did not notice. In a trance, she stood to the left of William—as women had been formed from the left side of Adam—and faced the church door. As was tradition, the first part of the ceremony would be conducted outside, with the final blessing to take place inside the chapel before the altar.

Thus it was that she was married to William Gordon in the same place she'd made a fool of herself earlier, with the man she'd thrown herself at not five feet away.

She was aware of Magnus the entire time, a solid, dark presence, hovering on the periphery of her vision, as she responded to the vows that would bind her to another man forever. He did not move, did not voice an objection when the priest asked if anyone knew of any reason this couple should not be married (had she really hoped he would?), and did not once look in her direction.

With William's betrothal ring firmly on her finger, she followed the priest inside the dark chapel and knelt beside William as the marriage was solemnized before God. When it was over, William kissed her lightly on her dry lips, took her hand, and led her out of the chapel as his wife to a roar of cheers.

She barely noticed. It was almost as if she weren't there. The pale, serene figure standing beside him wasn't her. The shy smiles and murmured pleasantries in reply to the storm of congratulations heaped upon her did not come from her. That woman was a stranger.

It was as if part of her had died. The part with hopes and dreams. The part that thought everything would work out in the end. What was left was a shell of the woman she'd been before. In her place was the woman who did what was expected. The woman who sat beside her new husband throughout the long wedding feast and pretended that her heart had not broken. Who ate from among the endless platters of food and jugs wine and celebrated with the rest of the clansmen in the Great Hall of Dunstaffnage Castle.

She fooled them all.

"It's about time."

Helen turned to the king, who'd spoken. As in the morning, she'd been given the seat of honor to his right. Robert the Bruce, who'd won his crown on a battlefield, cut an impressive figure. Dark-haired and sharp-featured, he would have been considered handsome even if he were not a king and one of the greatest knights in Christendom. "About time for what, Sire?"

He smiled at her. "It seems your wedding feast is a great success. Everyone is having fun."

William, who was on her right, must have overheard. He leaned forward and grinned. "Highlanders know how to celebrate as well as they know how to fight."

Bruce laughed. "Aye, that they do." He nodded toward a table to the right. "I've just never seen *that* Highlander do *that* kind of celebrating."

Helen was smiling as she turned in the direction of his gaze. But the smile froze in a mask of horror. She could feel every ounce of blood drain from her face as pain stabbed like a knife of fire through her chest, claiming her breath.

In the midst of dancing clansmen and drunken revelers, Magnus sat on a bench with a serving maid in his lap. He had one big hand on her hip, holding her firmly against him, as the other gripped the back of her head and held her face to his. He was kissing her. Passionately. Every bit as passionately as Helen had longed to be kissed. The woman's enormous breasts were crushed against his powerful chest. Helen couldn't look away from her fingers. The way they dug into his wide, muscular shoulders as if she couldn't get enough transfixed her.

The lash of pain that sliced through her was white hot, slicing the flesh from her bone. Nay, slicing was too clean. This pain was jagged, crudely wrought pain with little finesse.

"We might need to change his name, eh, Gordon?"

The king's words snapped her out of her stupor. He obviously hadn't noticed her reaction. She turned to her new husband. Perhaps, he hadn't either—

She stopped. Their eyes met. One look at William's face and she knew she'd not been so fortunate. He'd seen her reaction. His gaze shot to Magnus. She could see the fury in the white lines around his mouth.

Oh God, he *knew.*

When William answered the king, however, he hid his reaction with a tight smile. "Aye, I think you are right." His gaze locked on hers. "I wonder what could have caused such a change."

Her heart hammered in her chest. She tried to cover her anxiety with a question. "Name, Sire?" Her voice barely trembled.

The king smiled. "A wee jest," he said, patting her hand. "That's all. It isn't much like our friend to uh . . . celebrate so enthusiastically. I'd begun to think we really might have one of the Templars hidden in our ranks," he said with a mischievous wink to William.

It was rumored that Bruce had given sanctuary to many of the Templars when the order had been disbanded and excommunicated by the pope—the same pope who'd excommunicated Bruce for the killing of his rival John "The Red" Comyn before the altar of Greyfriars nearly three years ago.

"I always thought there was a woman," William said slowly. His gaze pinned hers.

Me. Oh, God. Had Magnus avoided other women because of me?

"Well, if there was," Bruce said, "I guess there isn't anymore." He chuckled and, thankfully, changed the subject.

With William temporarily engaged by Lady Anna on his other side, Helen ventured one more look in Magnus's direction. The woman was still on his lap, but to her relief they were no longer locked in a passionate embrace.

He was looking at her. His gaze shifted away, but for one moment their eyes caught. And in that instant of connection, in that hard stab of pain, she knew the full horror of this day.

A muscle twitched under his eye. Something she'd seen only once before. And in that one small betrayal, she knew: *He still cares for me. He lied.*

But it was too late.

Dear God, what have I done?

Lady Isabella—Bella—set the comb down on the small table beside the bed. "You look very beautiful."

"Your hair is exquisite," Anna added. "The way it catches in the candlelight. It looks like liquid fire shimmering down your back."

Not even the rare compliment about her hair could rouse her. Magnus had loved it, too, she remembered.

"William will think himself the luckiest man alive," Christina said with a broad smile.

Helen doubted it. She wanted to thank them, but feared if she opened her mouth, she would "baa" like a lamb to the slaughter. Instead she nodded with a smile that she hoped they interpreted as shy and not panicked.

The women had escorted her from the feast to the chamber she would share with William to prepare her for her bridal night. She'd changed from her gown into the fine linen chemise that had been richly embroidered for the occasion, and her hair had been released from the intricate crown of braids and combed until it was smooth and glossy.

She saw Bella exchange a look with Christina, who nodded. A moment later, Bella sat down beside her on the edge of the bed. "Your mother passed when you were a child, did she not?"

Helen's brows drew across her nose. "Aye, not long after my first saint's day. She died after giving birth to a stillborn babe." She hated that she had no memories of her. Her father had said they were much alike. She felt a wave of sadness. Even after two years, the sadness of her father's death still felt fresh. She missed him so much. Although he'd recovered from the lung ailment he'd been suffering from at the time Magnus had asked her to marry him, even with her help and Muriel's considerable skill, they hadn't been able to save him when it recurred six months later. "Why?"

Bella bit her lip. "How much do you know about what is to happen tonight?"

Helen blanched.

"There is nothing to be scared about," Anna quickly assured her. "Congress with one's husband can be quite . . ." She blushed adorably. "Nice."

Christina gave her a bawdy grin. "It can also be quite wicked."

Bella shot her a look that said she wasn't helping. "What

we mean is that it's natural to be nervous. If you have any questions—"

"Nay," Helen cut her off, unable to take any more of this. She didn't want to think about what was to come. She wasn't nervous because she didn't know what was going to happen, she was nervous because she did. If there was a moment she'd dreaded more than the wedding, it was the bedding. And now she had even more cause for dread. William had barely spoken to her after discovering her secret. She knew he was angry but didn't know how he would react. Would he confront her or pretend it hadn't happened? "I know what happens between a man and a woman."

Another unmaidenly curiosity that Muriel had finally been the one to alleviate a number of years ago.

Bella nodded. "Sometimes there is pain the first time."

"It's like a sharp pinch," Christina added.

"But it goes away quickly," Anna assured her.

Helen knew they were trying to be helpful, but the discussion was only increasing her anxiety. Bella seemed to understand. She stood up. "We will leave you, then."

"Thank you," Helen managed. "Thank you all. You have been very . . ." her voice choked a little, ". . . kind."

In other circumstances—in the right circumstances—she would have laughed and smiled along with them, while peppering them with questions they probably wouldn't want to answer. But these weren't the right circumstances.

A few minutes later she was alone. Though it was the last place that she wanted to be, she scooted back and slid under the bed linens. It was common for the groom's friends to accompany him to the bedchamber, and Helen didn't want to be sitting in her embarrassingly thin chemise if they did.

Her fingers were like ice as she gripped the sheets to her chin and stared at the door as if at any moment the bogeyman were going to come bursting through.

Baaa.

Helen knew she was being ridiculous, but she couldn't quiet the frantic flutter of her heartbeat or the panic surging through her veins. How was she going to do this? How was she going to quietly submit to her wifely duty when in her heart she belonged to another man?

Magnus cared for her. She still couldn't believe it. But the small twitch had betrayed him. She'd seen it only once before. It was the first time they'd met. The memory was as fresh as if it were yesterday.

The Games were being held at Dunottar Castle that year, near Aberdeen. At four and ten, it was the first time Helen had been permitted to attend. It was also the first experience she'd had with large groups of girls her own age, which had dampened the excitement of the adventure somewhat.

All they seemed to be interested in was discussing who was the most handsome competitor, who had the richest coffers, and who was likely to be looking for a wife. With all the giggling and mooning over Gregor MacGregor—who Helen had to concede was heart-stoppingly handsome— she looked for the first opportunity to slip away.

Deciding to search for shells along the beach to add to her collection, she crossed the narrow bridge of land that joined the castle to the mainland and started down the path on her right. The castle was one of the most dramatically situated that she'd ever seen. Perched on a small piece of land, surrounded by magnificent sheer cliffs that rose out of the sea over 150 feet, it was virtually impenetrable. Descending the cliffs even along the walking path was treacherous, as she discovered. More than once her foot slipped out from under her on the slippery rocks. She glanced down after one of these near mishaps and caught sight of something below.

A young lad knelt on the beach with a big pile of fur

cradled in his lap. A dog, she realized, and she could tell by their position that something was wrong.

Her pulse jumped. The dog must have slid off the cliff. Helen loved animals and her heart squeezed with trepidation. She hoped the poor thing wasn't hurt too badly and hurried her step to see if there was something she could do.

The lad—who was actually older than she'd initially thought, probably close to her brother Kenneth's age of nine and ten—was facing in her direction but had yet to notice her. She was just thinking that she hadn't seen him before—he was handsome enough to remember—when she saw a silvery flash above his head. Nay, not silver. The steel from a blade. Oh God, he was going to . . .

"Nooooo!" she shouted, racing toward him.

He glanced up, the dirk high in his hand, and the look of raw anguish on his face cut her to the quick. But by time she'd closed the remaining distance between them, the emotion was gone, hidden by a mask of control, but for the slight twitch below his eye. It was as if the sheer force of emotion he was trying to contain had found one small crack through which to escape.

Her heart melted. The small vulnerability at an age when it seemed so important for men not to have any—let alone show any—touched her. Why being a man meant you couldn't have any emotion, she didn't know. But toughness seemed to be some prerequisite to Highland warriorhood. And from his size, breadth of shoulder, and clothing, she could tell he was a warrior.

She came to a sudden stop before him and was relieved to see his hand come down.

"You shouldn't be down here, lass. The path is dangerous."

He spoke kindly, which, especially given the circumstances, impressed her. If she needed any proof of his words, all she had to do was look at the poor animal in his lap whose soft, whinging cries tore at every string in her heart.

She knelt down beside him, her eyes falling to the dog. It was a deerhound, and from the looks of him, one who'd been loved for many years. He had a large cut on his side, but it was his right rear leg that had provoked the dirk. It was bent at a hideous angle, the bone poking through the black and gray fur. A large pool of blood had gathered in the sand around it. But blood had never bothered her.

She wanted to reach out and pet its head, but she knew better than to touch an animal in pain. Unlike the lad before her, it would lash out.

"He fell?" she asked, gazing up at the young warrior.

He nodded. "Go now, lass. There's no help for him. He's in pain, and you . . ." His voice caught. "You shouldn't see this."

"You care for him?"

He nodded again, as if he didn't trust himself to speak. After a long pause, he said, "I've had him since I was seven. My father gave him to me when I was sent away to foster."

The dog made another pained sound, and he flinched. She could see the fingers around his dirk tighten. She reached out, putting her hand on his wrist as if to stop him. But the solid muscle under her palm told her she would have little chance of that. "Please, I think I can help."

He shook his head. "Tail is beyond help." Tail? What an odd name for a dog! "It's too badly broken, lass. There's nothing to be done but put him out of his misery."

But what about yours? Helen wanted to ask. "Will you allow me to at least try?"

He held her gaze and something passed between them. He must have sensed her earnestness because after a moment, he nodded.

She raced back to the castle to gather what she needed, after making him promise to do nothing to the dog while she was gone, and told him to gather all the wood he could find that had drifted onto the beach.

She was gone no longer than half an hour and was relieved to see him waiting with the dog where she'd left him. After explaining what she wished him to do, he placed one of the sticks in the dog's mouth to prevent him from biting and held him down while she went to work.

She'd watched Muriel and her father do this only a handful of times on human bones, but somehow she seemed to know what to do. She applied what she'd seen, followed her instincts, and managed to reposition the bones, fashion a leg brace from the sticks, and hold them in position by wrapping strips of her chemise around them.

The hardest part was listening to the animal's sounds of pain and keeping him still. But Magnus—that was the young warrior's name, as she had learned in their quick exchange of names before she'd left—was strong.

He watched her in growing disbelief as she worked. After she'd finished telling him how to tend the injuries, and what herbs to mix in a tincture that would keep the dog sleepy while it had time to heal, he looked at her in wonder. "How . . . ? You did it."

He was looking at her with an expression on his face that made every part of her insides feel warm. "He did well. Tail, you called him?"

Magnus nodded. "My friends started to call him that because he followed me everywhere. He was my tail, they said. I called him Scout originally, but Tail stuck."

She smiled and was surprised to see him smile back at her. "Thank you," he said gruffly.

He held her gaze, and she felt something shift in her chest. With his golden-brown hair, soft brown eyes, and tanned skin, he was a startlingly handsome young man. For the first time, she understood how the other girls could act so silly about a lad.

Perhaps he read her thoughts. "How old are you, lass?"

She sat up straight, looking him in the eye. For some reason it was very important to her that he not think of her as a child. "I'm four and ten," she said proudly.

He smiled. "All that, eh? But since you're too young to be a healer, I think you must be an angel."

She blushed. Hadn't he seen her hair? Of course he had. She hated veils and "forgot" them as often as she could.

"Tell me, how is it, wee Helen, that you have such skill?"

She shrugged, embarrassed. "I don't know—I've always been interested in it, I suppose."

He would probably think her as odd as her father and brothers did. She ventured a glance up at him from under her lashes. But he wasn't looking at her as if she were odd at all. He was looking at her as if . . .

Her breath caught. As if she were *special*.

"Well, it's fortunate for me and Tail here that you are so talented."

She beamed. She'd never met anyone like him. This bronzed young warrior with the kind eyes and dazzling grin. She knew right there and then that he was special, too.

"Helen!"

She heard her father's impatient shouts from above and realized her absence had been noticed.

"I think someone is looking for you," he said, helping her up.

She glanced down at the dog, still curled by his feet. "You'll be able to carry him from here?" she asked.

"We'll be fine. Now."

"Helen!" her father shouted again.

She cursed under her breath, not wanting to leave him just yet.

Perhaps he was feeling the same reluctance to part. He took her hand, bowing over it as gallantly as any knight. Her heart actually strummed like the strings of a harp.

"Thank you, Lady Helen. I look forward to our next meeting."

Their eyes held, and Helen felt the squeezing around her chest tighten, knowing he spoke the truth. There would be more meetings between them.

And there were. The next time she'd seen him—six months later, when she'd learned his identity at the negotiations to end the feud between their clans—the dog had been right at his heels, a small limp the only sign of his ordeal. There had been no question of them ever being enemies. Their bond had already been forged. First in friendship, and then in something much more.

She'd never seen the twitch below his eye again.

Until the wedding feast.

God, why hadn't he stopped her? Why had he let her marry another man?

The door opened.

She gasped—actually, she feared it sounded more like a squeak. William strode into the room and closed the door behind him. Alone. At least she would not have to endure the added discomfort of others watching him get into bed beside her.

He eyed her wryly, his gaze skimming over the sheet that had made its way even higher under her chin. "You can relax. Your virtue is safe for the moment." His eyes hardened. "Or perhaps it is too late for that?"

It took her a moment to realize what he meant. Though she knew he had cause to wonder, the accusation still stung. She lifted her chin, a spot of heat burning on each cheek. "My virtue is perfectly intact, my lord."

He held her gaze and shrugged. "Of course it is. He's a bloody saint."

The hint of bitterness in his voice tugged at her conscience.

He strode over to the table where a jug of wernage had been set out for her and poured himself a drink. He grimaced at the sweetness of the wine, but drank it nonetheless.

He hadn't changed for bed, she noticed. He still wore the fine tunic and hose he'd worn to their wedding. He sat down in the chair beside the brazier and studied her over the rim of the glass.

Some of her tension eased.

"So you are the woman he's been pining for all these years." He shook his head disgustedly. "I should have known. How could I not have known?"

He didn't seem to expect her to say anything.

After a moment, he looked at her again. "What happened? Did your families prevent a match?"

"That was part of it." She explained how they'd met secretly for years until the fateful day when Magnus had asked her to run away and her brother had discovered them.

"I can imagine how that went," he said. "Your brother has always had a particularly virulent streak when it comes to MacKay."

She didn't disagree with him. "I was scared. My father was ill and needed me to care for him. I let them persuade me it was nothing more than a youthful transgression. By the time I realized my mistake, Magnus was gone and you—" She stopped.

"And your father had betrothed you to me."

"Aye." She realized she'd sat up in the bed, and the sheets were now in her lap being twisted in her hands.

"You didn't know he'd be here?"

She shook her head. "I haven't seen him since that day. You never mentioned that you knew him."

"Do you love him?"

There was something in his voice that bothered her. A niggle of guilt wiggled its way into her consciousness. She'd been so caught up in her own misery, she hadn't thought much about William's feelings. Unlike Magnus, he seemed much more adept at showing them. He was angry, yes, but also, she could see, disappointed. "I—"

He held up his hand, stopping her. "You don't need to answer. I saw your face." He dragged his fingers through his hair. "What I don't understand is why you didn't say anything. Why you went through with it."

Heat crept up her cheeks. "It didn't seem to matter."

He stared at her for a long moment. "You tried to talk to him."

She nodded, shame heating her cheeks.

"And that's what he told you?"

She nodded again.

He swore. "Stubborn arse."

She didn't disagree.

He leaned back in his chair again and seemed to contemplate the contents of his glass quite thoroughly. When he was done, he looked back up at her. "So what are we to do now?"

She looked at him uncertainly. "Do?" What could they do?

"It's a fine mess."

"Aye, that it is."

"Unlike others, I'm not a saint."

Her brows furrowed. "My lord?"

He shook his head with a laugh. "I will not share my wife." His gaze intensified. "Nor do I care for bedding a martyr. When I make love to my wife, she will not be thinking of another man."

There was something dark and promising in his voice that sent an unexpected shiver down her spine. In another time, in another place, she might have been quite content to be married to William Gordon.

He smiled, perhaps guessing the direction of her thoughts. Leaving his drink on the floor beside the chair, he stood. "It appears I'm giving you a choice, my lady."

She startled. "A choice?"

"Aye. Come to my bed willingly or don't come at all."

"I don't understand."

"It's quite simple. The marriage is not consummated—yet. If you wish to have it declared invalid I will not stand in your way."

"An annulment?" Her voice barely sounded above a whisper.

He nodded. "Or if one cannot be procured, a divorce. It is not pretty, but it is a solution."

It would cause a scandal. Her family would be furious. She looked at William. He would be shamed. And Magnus . . .

William seemed to read her thoughts. "He will never change his mind." She stilled. "You married me," he said softly.

Helen's heart stopped. He was right. Dissolved or nay, Magnus would never be hers. She'd married his best friend. His pride and loyalty to his friend would keep him from her. To his mind, she belonged to William, and that was a line he would not cross. She knew that as well as William did. Mangus was lost to her.

"I'll return in an hour and expect your answer." He shut the door softly behind him, leaving her alone to the tumult of her thoughts.

He had to get out of here. It had been hard enough watching the women lead Helen from the Hall, but if Magnus had to watch Gordon leave—or God forbid, be forced to go along with him to witness him sliding into bed with his bride—he was going to kill someone. Probably MacRuairi, who kept looking at him as if he were the biggest fool in all of Christendom, or Kenneth Sutherland, whose knowing smirk told him that he'd guessed exactly how much this was torturing him.

Magnus couldn't believe she'd actually gone through with it. She'd married someone else. And in another hour—maybe less—she'd be consummating those vows and lying in the arms of another man. Nay, not just another man, the closest friend he'd ever had.

Jesus. The burning in his chest exploded as he made his way out of the Hall, relieving one of the serving maids of a large jug of whisky on the way.

He couldn't think about it. He'd go mad if he thought about it. It had taken everything he'd had to stand silent witness as she married Gordon, but the mere thought of her readying herself for bed . . .

Letting down her long, silky hair . . .

Removing her clothes . . .

Waiting in bed, those big blue eyes wide with maidenly nervousness . . .

She should be mine. He swore. The knife of pain bent him over. He took a long swig from the jug and stumbled out into the black, misty night.

He headed for the boathouse, where he and the other members of the Highland Guard without wives were sleeping. He intended to get good and drunk, so they wouldn't have far to move him when he passed out.

First women, now drink. Today began a bloody new chapter for him. He took another swig. All hail the fallen Saint.

Moonlight filtered through the wooden planks and small window in the large building constructed just beyond the castle gates to house the MacDougall chief's *birlinns*. But since the MacDougall loss at the Battle of Brander a few months ago, it belonged to Bruce.

A few torches had been lit, but Magnus didn't bother with a brazier. Cold had become his comfort. Like the drink, it kept him numb.

"I feel nothing," he'd told her. God, how he wished it were true!

A small part of him had thought she wouldn't be able to do it. That despite what he'd said, she would not bind herself to someone else forever. That she loved him enough to do what was right.

But she didn't. Not then and not now.

He sat on his pallet, leaning his back against the wall with his legs stretched out in front of him, and drank. He drank to find peace, to reach the mindless oblivion where the torture of his thoughts wouldn't find him. Instead he found hell. An angry, black hell where the fire of his thoughts raged and burned in the farthest reaches of his soul.

Was it happening right now? Was Gordon taking her in his arms and making love to her? Was he giving her pleasure?

The torture went deeper, became more explicit, until he thought he'd go mad with the images.

How much time had passed, he didn't know, before the door opened. A man strode in.

When he saw who it was, blood raged through his veins. "Get the hell out of here, Sutherland."

Despite the slur of drink, there was no mistaking the warning in his voice.

The blasted fool ignored it. He crossed the room with his usual arrogant swagger. "I was wondering where you'd disappeared to. Gordon was looking for you. I think he wanted you to accompany him to the bridal chamber. But he left without you."

Nothing could have dulled the stab of pain that hit him then. It was happening right now. Oh, Jesus.

The bastard smiled. Magnus's hand squeezed around the neck of the jug until the blood fled from his knuckles. But he wouldn't give Sutherland the satisfaction of showing him how well his dagger had stuck. "Is that all you wished to tell me or is there something else?"

Helen's brother stopped a few feet away from him, looming over him. Despite the obvious intent, Magnus wasn't threatened. The disadvantage of his position on the floor wouldn't last long if he didn't want it to. Sutherland didn't know just how much danger he was in. This wasn't the Highland Games. Magnus had three years of war behind him, fighting alongside the best warriors in Scotland. Sutherland had fought with the English.

"I think they're going to be quite happy together, don't you?"

Magnus flexed his hand. God, how he itched to smash it through Sutherland's gleaming-white sneer!

"Or maybe you don't want that at all? Maybe you still fancy yourself in love with my sister? Maybe that's the reason why you never told Gordon about your illicit little romance?"

"Have care, Sutherland. Your friend isn't here to protect you this time."

He was rewarded with an angry clench of his enemy's jaw.

"I wonder whether he'll still be *your* friend when he hears the truth."

Magnus was on his feet with his hand around the other man's neck before he could react. "You'll keep your damned mouth shut if you know what's good for you." He shoved him up hard against a wooden post. "It's in the past."

In a move that would have made Robbie Boyd proud, Sutherland pushed up with the back of his arm, breaking Magnus's hold, and twisted out of the way. "Damned right it's in the past, and there's not a blasted thing you can do about it. I'll bet right now he's—"

Magnus snapped. He let his fist fly right into the bastard's sneering grin. He heard a satisfying crunch. The force of the blow would have felled most men, but Sutherland absorbed the shock with a snap of his head and returned the blow to Magnus's gut with enough force to exact a grunt.

Either Sutherland had become a much better warrior or

the drink had taken more of a toll than Magnus realized. Or perhaps both. The result was that in the exchange of blows that followed, Sutherland gave him more of a battle than he expected. It had been a long time since Magnus had brawled with only fists for a weapon, but it didn't take him long to get the upper hand. He let off a barrage of blows that would have knocked Sutherland senseless if someone hadn't pulled him back.

"Stop! Damn it, MacKay, that's enough!"

He was grabbed from behind, an arm around his neck. He reacted instinctively, twisting and intending to use the momentum and leverage to throw the other man over his head, but recognition broke through the haze.

It was Gordon. What the hell was he doing here?

From the look on Sutherland's face, he was wondering the same thing.

"What is this about?" Gordon looked back and forth between them. His eyes narrowed with an intensity that gave Magnus an uneasy prickle. "Or perhaps I don't need to ask? If you two want to kill each other, do it someplace else. This isn't the time."

He was right. Magnus was ashamed he'd let the bastard get to him. He didn't try to offer an excuse.

He and Sutherland exchanged a look. Despite his taunts, it was clear Sutherland had no intention of telling Gordon about Helen. His intent had only been to torment Magnus with what he knew.

Gordon looked at them both in disgust. "Leave us," he said to Sutherland. "There is something MacKay and I need to discuss—alone."

Magnus suspected Sutherland was more concerned by Gordon's pronouncement than he let on. But he ceded to his demand with a curt nod to Gordon and a look toward Magnus that promised this was not over.

Magnus poured some cold water into a basin and dunked his face, as much to clean the blood left by Sutherland's fists as to shock the whisky from his blood. He suspected he was going to need a clear head for what Gordon was about to say.

He wiped the water away with a drying cloth and turned to face his friend.

His trepidation spiked. Now that they were alone, he could see the rare signs of fury in Gordon's normally cheerful face. Even before he spoke, Magnus knew.

"Why didn't you tell me?"

He didn't pretend to misunderstand. "There was—is—nothing to tell."

Gordon's eyes flared with anger. "You didn't think I might be interested to know that my closest friend was in love with my betrothed?"

"Whatever existed between Helen and me was over before I met you."

"Is that right?" Gordon challenged. "So you are telling me that you no longer have feelings for her?"

Magnus clenched his teeth so hard his jaw hurt. He wanted to deny it, but they both knew it would be a lie.

Gordon shook his head. "You should have told me. I would have stepped aside."

"So that she could marry someone else? It wouldn't have mattered. Her family hates me. You see how well her brother and I get along. I'd rather see her with someone who deserves her. Someone who could make her happy."

"How bloody noble of you," Gordon said, not hiding his bitterness. "But how in the hell is that supposed to happen when she's thinking about another man each time I make love to her?"

Magnus flinched. Was that how it had happened? Was that how Gordon had discovered the truth? God, he felt ill.

Gordon was about to say something when the door opened, and MacRuairi burst into the room. He looked back and forth between them, obviously wondering what was going on, but duty overruled curiosity. "Pack your things," he said to Magnus. "We're leaving."

He didn't bother with questions; if they were leaving in the middle of the celebration it was serious. Snapping into warrior's mode, he immediately began to gather his things.

"What's happened?" Gordon asked.

"The new Lord of Galloway is in trouble."

Gordon swore, knowing that if the king's proud brother Edward was sending for reinforcements, it must be bad. "Who's going?"

"All of us."

Gordon nodded. "I'll get my things."

"Not you," MacRuairi clarified. "No one expects you to leave your bride on her wedding night."

"I know," Gordon said. "But I'm coming all the same. You may need a distraction." He exchanged a look with Magnus. "My bride probably won't even have a chance to miss me."

Three

*

"Gone?" Helen echoed, stunned.

Bella frowned. "Aye. The men were called away late last night on a mission for the king. Did William not tell you?"

Helen fought to control the rise of heat to her cheeks but failed. She shook her head. "I . . . I must have been asleep."

Christina ascribed her reaction to maidenly modesty. "He probably didn't want to wake you. You must have been exhausted after such a long . . . day." She smiled.

"Aye, no doubt he was just being considerate," Bella agreed, although it was obvious she was concerned.

Helen took another piece of bread from the platter and smothered it with butter to cover her embarrassment. She'd stayed awake most of the night anxiously waiting for the door to open to give William her answer. She must have fallen asleep, because the next thing she remembered was waking to an ice-cold room. The young maidservant who came to light the fires in the morning must have been told not to disturb them. A consideration that had proved unnecessary.

Why hadn't William returned? Was he giving her more time to decide or had something prevented him? Fearing the reason might have something to do with Magnus, Helen had hesitated to leave her room. But hunger and curiosity had gotten the better of her, and she'd made her way down to the Great Hall to break her fast.

The success of the celebration was evident in the number of guests still sprawled out on the floor sleeping. Bella and Christina, however, were awake, and—much to Helen's surprise—had immediately expressed how sorry they were on her behalf that the men had been called away right after her wedding.

"Did your husbands go as well?" Helen asked.

"Aye," Bella answered. "A number of the men were called away."

Her heart jumped. Magnus? Did he go, too? Bella must have guessed the direction of her thoughts because she nodded in response.

"Where did they go?" she asked.

The women exchanged looks. "I'm not precisely sure," Christina said carefully.

Too carefully. Helen sensed there was something they were not telling her.

"They never tell us exactly where they are going," Bella added dryly.

Helen frowned. "Does William usually fight with your husbands?"

"Not all the time," Christina offered in another vague response.

"When will they be back?"

"A week," Bella said. "Maybe longer."

Helen knew she shouldn't feel so relieved, but she was. William's departure gave her plenty of time to prepare herself for what was to come. For she did not delude herself—if she took William's offer, it would make all her previous "wayward" decisions pale in comparison.

"It seems odd that they would be called away in the middle of the celebration like that," she said. Especially the groom. According to Kenneth, William had been a man-at-arms for his uncle Sir Adam Gordon—the head of Clan

Gordon. When they'd had a falling-out, he'd joined Bruce, then the Earl of Carrick, in his rebellion. That William had distinguished himself on the battlefield was evidenced by the king's insistence that the wedding be held at his recently acquired castle of Dunstaffnage. But beyond that, she knew little about his place in Bruce's army. "What is it exactly that William does for the king?"

Both women appeared decidedly uncomfortable—even nervous—about her question. "It's best if William explains it to you," Bella said.

Christina leaned closer, so as to not be overheard. "I know you have questions, but try to keep them until William returns. It's safer that way. Questions sometimes have a way of reaching the wrong ears."

Helen didn't understand the warning, except to know that she'd been given one. She decided to let it go—for now.

She would recall it, however, a short while later when her brothers and Donald Munro entered the Great Hall. Dreading their questions, she would have tried to avoid them by accepting Bella's offer to join the women with their children in Lady Elyne's chamber—apparently her husband, Erik MacSorley, had gone as well—but then she caught sight of her brother's face.

She rushed forward to intercept them before they sat at one of the trestle tables that had been set out for the meal. Her hand went to Kenneth's bruised and battered cheek. "What happened?"

It was obvious that he'd been struck—repeatedly. He had an enormous bruise on the left side of his mouth and jaw, a split lip, a bruised and swollen left eye, and a large cut on his cheek.

He wouldn't meet her gaze. "It's nothing."

"You were fighting." It wasn't unusual for her quick-tempered brother. He was quick to take offense and quicker to exact retribution.

"Aye, he was," her eldest brother replied. Unlike she and Kenneth, Will and she had never been close. He'd always seemed a stranger to her. At ten years her senior, he was being fostered with the Earl of Ross when she was born. By the time he'd returned to Dunrobin, he was more concerned with improving his battle skills and learning the duties that would be his as earl than troubling himself with a ten-year-old sister who clearly baffled him. He was not unkind or uncaring, but simply preoccupied. Stern and more than a little intimidating, he'd assumed the duties of the earldom upon her father's death with the ease of a man who'd been trained for the role since birth. "It seems that young MacKay hasn't learned any discipline in the past few years. But what can you expect from a cur—young or old."

Helen gasped, covering her mouth with her hand. "Magnus did this to you?"

Will's gaze sharpened; he didn't like being reminded of her "ill-conceived" acquaintance with their enemy.

"Aye," Donald said. "He attacked your brother without cause."

That didn't sound like Magnus. The frown Kenneth sent in Donald's direction seemed to suggest there might be something more to the story. She hoped that something didn't concern her. She knew that Donald, too, hated Magnus—even more so since his defeat that fateful day.

"Being forced to abide the usurper is bad enough, but MacKays? Your new husband keeps unfortunate company, my lady," Donald added.

Will shushed him harshly under his breath, looking around as though the walls might have ears, though they stood to the side of the Hall a good distance from anyone. "Have care, Munro. I like it little more than you do, but 'the usurper' is now our king."

Donald had been vocal in his objections to submitting to Bruce, and his continued disgruntlement was plain in his face. But he clenched his jaw and nodded. Donald's loyalty to their father had passed to his son. As had his sword. He'd retained his position as the *An Gille-coise*, the chief's personal henchman, for her brother.

"Where is your new husband?" Kenneth said, scanning the room behind her. "I should have thought to find him here with you."

There was something pointed in his question that caused her to flush. Recalling Christina's warning, she said, "He was called away for a few days."

"Called away?" Will repeated, voicing the surprise evident on all the men's faces. "What do you mean 'called away'?"

She gave a careless shrug. "The king had need of him."

"The day after his wedding?" Kenneth didn't hide his incredulity.

She forced a smile to her face. "He will be back soon."

"Where did he go?" Will demanded.

"He did not say, and I did not ask," she answered truthfully, neglecting to mention that he'd never given her the opportunity.

Donald was clearly outraged on her behalf. He'd always been protective of her. "I wonder what could be so important to take a groom from his bed and send a dozen men sailing out in a *birlinn* in the middle of the night?" he asked.

How would he know that? Her brothers had a solar in the main donjon, away from the boathouse and the barracks.

Seeing the frown on her face, he explained. "I thought I saw something on my way back from the garderobe—I assume it was he and the other men leaving."

"Perhaps you should ask the king," she suggested.

"That I will, sister," Will said. "Although I'm not sure the Bruce is ready to take us in his confidence."

He was right. The king might be eager to welcome the earls and powerful magnates, such as Sutherland and Ross, back into the fold in the interest of a united realm, but that did not mean he trusted them. The Sutherlands were in a precarious position, and Helen hoped her decision to dissolve her marriage didn't make it worse.

Will and Donald joined the rest of her brother's large retinue at the trestle table. Helen would have returned to her room, but Kenneth held her back. Blue eyes, so like her own, bored into her. Though Kenneth shared her father and Will's penchant for treating her with a mixture of fond befuddlement and exasperation, he had always had a knack for sensing when she wasn't telling the truth. And though he rarely lost his temper with her, Kenneth didn't show the same exaggerated patience, as if he were a shepherd tasked with minding a constantly straying lamb, that her father and Will did. "Are you sure you are telling us everything, Helen?"

"I'm telling you all I know."

He stared at her until she felt like shifting her feet. When their father died, it was Kenneth who'd stepped into the role of shepherd to her straying lamb. But he wasn't her father—although he certainly sounded like it.

"I hope this doesn't have anything to do with why I saw your husband in the boathouse looking for MacKay last night not an hour after he left the Hall to be with you."

He'd surprised her, and her expression showed it.

He dropped her arm and swore. "What did you do, Helen?"

She hated to see the disappointment on his face, but the worst part was that it was only going to get worse. "I didn't do anything."

His temper flashed. "Don't be a fool, sister. Gordon is a good man. He will make you a good husband. MacKay has known about this betrothal for years. If he'd wanted you, he would have told him. But he didn't."

She knew he was right. But no matter what Magnus had said—or whatever his feelings—she'd been wrong to marry

William when she loved another man. She would always love Magnus. Whether he wanted her or not.

William deserved a wife who would love him. A woman who would come to his bed without thinking of another. She would never be able to give him that.

She just hoped that some day her family would be able to forgive her.

Galloway Forest, Two Nights Later

"Any questions?" Tor MacLeod scanned the blackened faces of the men circled around him in the darkness. The ash—like the dark nasal helms and armor—helped them blend into the night. "I don't need to tell you how important this is. If you don't know exactly what you are supposed to do, now is the time to speak up. There isn't any room for mistakes."

"Hell, if there was room for mistakes, I'd think I was in the wrong place," Erik MacSorley quipped. The brash seafarer could always be counted on to lighten the mood. The more danger, the more jokes. He'd been making jests all night.

The Highland Guard had been formed for the most dangerous, seemingly impossible missions. The rescue of the king's brother was going to test those limits. Fifteen hundred English soldiers stood between them and Edward Bruce. With the addition of James Douglas's men, their forces would number about fifty. Daunting odds for even Scotland's most elite team of warriors. But they were at their best when the odds were against them. They never considered failure. The belief that they would be victorious under any situation is what made them succeed.

MacLeod, the leader of the Highland Guard, usually ignored MacSorley. That he didn't perhaps more than anything underscored the severity of the situation. "Aye, well, try not to abduct any lasses this time, Hawk."

MacSorley smiled at the reference to the "mistake" that had led to his absconding with Lady Elyne de Burgh from her home in Ireland last year. "I don't know, Raider could use a wife. With his surly disposition it might be the only way he finds one."

"Sod off, Hawk," Robbie Boyd replied. "Maybe I'll just take yours? The poor lass must be tired of you by now. God knows we are." Boyd's exaggerated weary sigh elicited quite a few laughs and murmurs of agreement, succeeding in dissipating some of the tension.

"Be ready, then," MacLeod said. "We leave in an hour."

Dismissed, Magnus started to break away like the others, but MacLeod stopped him. "Saint. Templar. Hold back a minute." He waited for the rest of the men to leave before he turned to Magnus and Gordon, the steely gaze that missed nothing flickering back and forth between them. "Is there anything I should be worried about?"

Magnus straightened, not needing to look at Gordon to know he did the same. "Nay, Chief," he said, Gordon's voice echoing his.

Tor MacLeod was lauded as the fiercest warrior in the Highlands, and right now he looked it. He scrutinized the two men with withering intensity. Few men gave Magnus pause, but the leader of the Highland Guard was one of them. They all had a little bit of Viking in them, but MacLeod had more than most. "Discord is poison in an army. Whatever is going on between you two, put it aside."

MacLeod walked away, not waiting for them to respond. He didn't need to; they understood what was at stake.

From the moment MacRuairi entered the boathouse with word of Edward Bruce's crisis in Galloway, the only thing that mattered was the mission. He and Gordon were too experienced as warriors to let personal matters interfere with the job Bruce sent them to do. Their lives, and the lives of their Highland Guard brethren, depended on it.

But the tension was there, lingering under the surface,

waiting but not forgotten. The fact that MacLeod had picked up on it shamed them both.

Gordon looked as grim as Magnus felt. "Come," he said. "We'd best get something to eat. I've a feeling we're going to need all our strength for the night ahead."

"Not to mention a few miracles," Magnus said dryly.

Gordon laughed, and for the first time since Magnus arrived at Dunstaffnage for the wedding, the knot of tension twisting in his gut dissipated. He'd already lost Helen; he'd be damned if he lost his friend, too.

They walked back to camp to join the others, reviewing the details of the daring plan to rescue the king's proud, headstrong, and at times reckless brother. Edward Bruce was not a favorite among the Highland Guard, but he was the king's trusted lieutenant in the troublesome south and, significantly, his sole remaining brother. Edward's death or capture would be a personal blow to a king who'd already suffered too many since the war began: three brothers executed in less than a year; a wife, two sisters, and a daughter imprisoned in England—one of those sisters in a cage.

If they had to get through fifteen hundred Englishmen to save Edward Bruce's damnable hide, they would do so. *Airson an Leòmhann.* For the Lion. The symbol of Scotland's kingship and the battle cry of the Highland Guard.

For the past two days, the eleven members of the Highland Guard had worked together with one purpose in mind: reaching Edward in time to avert disaster. They'd sailed as far south as Ayr, then headed east on horseback into the wild and untamed forests and hills of Galloway.

Although the war in the north had been won, the war in the south waged on. The English controlled the borders, with large garrisons occupying all the major castles, and in Galloway—the ancient Celtic province in the isolated southwest of Scotland—pockets of rebellion flared by those loyal to the exiled King John Balliol and his kinsman, the powerful clan chief Dugald MacDowell.

Operating from his headquarters in the vast and impenetrable forests, Edward Bruce had spent most of the last six months putting down those rebellions with a vengeance, especially toward the MacDowells, who were responsible for the deaths of two of the Bruce brothers in the disastrous landing at Loch Ryan the year before.

Young James Douglas, dispossessed by the English of his lands in nearby Douglasdale, had made a name for himself in Edward Bruce's army, his black hair and fearsome reputation earning him the epitaph of the "Black Douglas."

Most of the members of the Highland Guard had spent some time in Galloway over the past six months with Edward Bruce—especially Boyd, Seton, MacLean, and Lamont, who had ties to the area. Magnus himself had left the area only a few days ago to attend the wedding. But this was the first time the entire Guard had been called into Edward's service.

The situation warranted it. According to the messenger who'd arrived from Douglas, Edward Bruce had received word that his nemesis Dugald MacDowell had returned to Galloway from exile in England. He'd gone after him with a small force while Douglas was on a raid.

When Douglas returned and discovered Edward gone, he'd followed him, only to to find fifteen hundred Englishmen blocking his way. Edward had been lured from the forest into a trap and had been forced to take refuge at Threave Castle, which he'd wrested from the English only a few months before.

The ancient stronghold of the Lords of Galloway, most recently held by Dugald MacDowell, was located on an islet in the middle of the River Dee, connected to the grassy marshland by a rocky causeway. The castle should have been highly defensible. But like William Wallace before him, Bruce's strategy was to scorch the earth behind him, leaving nothing for his enemy to use, including destroying castles and befouling the wells. That meant Edward Bruce was defending himself from a burned-out shell of rock with no fresh water.

The English army, according to Arthur Campbell, the Highland Guard's vaunted scout, was laying siege on the eastern banks of the river. But without fresh water, the siege would not last long. An assault by sea would make it even shorter.

Two hours before dawn, Magnus and the rest of the Highland Guard gathered with Douglas's men around MacLeod. "Are you ready?" he asked.

"Aye," the men replied.

MacLeod nodded. "Then let's give the bards something to sing about."

They left the cover of the forest, riding hard for the castle. Timing was everything. They needed to be in position at the flank of the English army right as dawn was breaking. While Edward Bruce and his army distracted the enemy from the front, the Highland Guard and the rest of Douglas's men would mount a surprise attack from behind.

Eoin MacLean, or Striker as he was called, was the master of the bold strategies and daring tactics for which the Highland Guard had become known. But this plan was bold and daring even for him.

MacLean's plan was calculated for maximum impact, taking advantage of the light and mist to mount a quick, fierce surprise attack to unsettle the enemy, to take away the advantage of superior numbers, weaponry, and armor, and most of all, instill fear in the enemy heart. It had worked before—albeit never with so few against so many.

In the cloak of heavy mist that blanketed the valley of the River Dee, the black-helmed, dark-cloaked members of the Highland Guard would appear out of the misty dawn suddenly and undetected, their numbers shrouded, like the phantom band of marauders some proclaimed them to be. In the ensuing chaos and panic, they hoped to create enough of a break for Edward and his men to escape.

They followed the river south for about an hour before reaching a small woodland in a bend on the northern bank just opposite the island. From here, MacSorley and MacRuairi would make use of their water skills by swimming across the murky black waters of the river to sneak into Edward Bruce's camp and prepare them for the plan. Assuming they could sneak past Edward's guards first.

"Wait for the signal," MacLeod said.

"Aye, Chief," MacSorley said, and then turned to Gregor MacGregor with a grin. "Just make sure you don't miss." The famed archer would light a fiery arrow to send over the causeway when it was clear.

"I'll aim for your head," MacGregor said. "That's a big target."

MacSorley smiled. "If you want a big target, aim for my cock."

The men laughed.

"This smells like shite," MacRuairi said, smearing the black seal grease over his naked skin. They'd bundled their armor and weapons in a pack to keep them dry when they crossed the river. The seal grease would not only help them blend into the darkness, it protected them from the cold December waters.

"You'll be grateful for it in a few minutes." MacSorley grinned. "The water will freeze your bollocks off."

"Which shouldn't be a problem for you anymore," MacRuairi said dryly.

"Damn, cousin, was that a joke?" MacSorley shook his head. "It does snow in hell."

MacRuairi muttered something under his breath as he finished applying the grease.

When it was time to go, MacLeod gave a few further instructions before giving their traditional parting: *"Bàs roimh Gèill."* Death before surrender. To Highlander warriors there was no other choice. They would succeed or die trying. Death held no fear for them. To Highlanders there was no greater glory than dying on a battlefield.

Leaving the two warriors to their icy swim, the rest of the party rode east, skirting the sleeping English army camped along the eastern bank of the river to block the causeway. When they reached a small wooded hill—the site of an ancient ring fort—MacLeod gave the signal to stop. From here they would launch their attack.

Stretched out between them and the river-bound castle lay a wide expanse of boggy marshland, the ground hardened and grasses browned by the cold breath of winter. Though darkness and mist shrouded the English army from view, their presence—sleeping or nay—was evident in the sounds and smells that carried through the night. Piss and shite from fifteen hundred men left its mark.

The enemy was close. No more than a furlong away. But every man there knew the importance of silence. For their plan to have any chance of succeeding, they must have surprise on their side.

For nearly a half-hour no one said a word as they waited for dawn to break and MacLeod to give the signal. Like a horse chomping at the bit, Magnus could feel his heart pounding in his chest, his blood surging as every instinct clamored to begin.

At last it came. When the first rays of dawn pierced the darkness, MacLeod raised his hand and motioned forward. Magnus and the other members of the Highland Guard took their positions in the front and slowly made their way downhill, using the thick curtain of mist to shield their approach.

The English were rousing. Magnus could hear the sounds of voices, punctuated by the clamor of mail and men moving about. He felt the familiar dead calm come over him. His mind cleared, his pulse slowed, and everything seemed to move at half the speed of normal.

MacLeod signaled for them to stop. Again they waited.

More anxiously this time, as every minute the cold light of day strengthened all around them. Worse—disastrously worse—the mist that had seemed so thick only moments before, the mist that could be counted on to stay till mid-morning, started to lift. The shield that would hide their presence and their numbers was about to disappear. In a few minutes they would be exposed.

Their dangerous plan had been shot to hell. They were about to become target practice for thousands of English soldiers.

Magnus could see from the look exchanged by MacLeod and MacLean that they were thinking the same thing: how much longer could they wait to see whether MacSorley and MacRuairi had succeeded?

Finally, they heard the surprised shouts from the English as Edward Bruce's army began to fire arrows on them, engaging them from the front.

MacSorley and MacRuairi had done it! They had their distraction. As the English rushed to get into position, the Highland Guard attacked. But without the mist to hide them, they had to rely on the one thing that they had left: terror.

With a battle cry to chill the blood of any mortal man, they drove into the flank of the English army with a savage ferocity, cutting down everything in their path. The startled cries reverberated through the icy morning. Before the English could mount a defense, the Highland Guard, with Douglas's men behind them, had turned around to charge again. They sent the knights reeling and bored through the foot soldiers like a stake, splintering the carefully positioned army into chaos. The English army had broken.

Christ, MacLean's plan had worked! Magnus felt a jolt of victory surge through him, as he saw the causeway left unprotected.

MacLeod shouted to MacGregor to light the signal, and

a moment later an arrow shot across the sky in a flaming arch.

As soon as the English started to scatter, the Highland Guard moved into position near the causeway, creating a line of defense for Edward Bruce's men to leave the island, while Douglas and his men kept up the terrifying assaults on the fleeing English.

But something was wrong. Bruce's men weren't coming.

He heard Gordon shout beside him. "The river!"

In between thrusts and blows, Magnus glanced toward the castle.

Ah hell. The mist that had shrouded their attack had also shrouded another: The sea assault they feared had arrived. Three—nay, four—English galleys were approaching the sea-gate, raining a stream of arrows down on any man who tried to venture out of the castle gate. In a few minutes English soldiers would be pouring off those galleys, able to block any attempt by Edward Bruce to escape. There was the added danger of the fleeing English soldiers realizing what was happening and turning around. Fear would no longer obscure their smaller numbers.

"Chief!" Gordon shouted. "Over there."

MacLeod had seen the same thing they had. "Go," he said to Magnus and Gordon, understanding the unspoken request. "Take Ranger and Arrow with you."

They didn't hesitate. The four men shot across the causeway, heading for the castle, situated on the far side of the islet.

The boats had already started to pull into the jetty under the partially dismantled sea-gate. Ironically, Edward Bruce's slighting of the castle a few months ago left him in the position of being unable to defend his position.

But as the sea-gate was located on the far side of the castle, the English arrows were now out of range of the causeway, giving them a small chance of escape. MacRuairi and MacSorley had realized the same thing. Magnus could see them ahead, ordering Edward's army to run.

The burned-out shell of the castle loomed in front of them. Most of the wooden outer buildings had been burned to the ground, including large sections of the wooden palisade that surrounded the bailey. Only part of the stone tower remained.

The English started to pour into the bailey from the sea-gate, stalling the efforts of MacRuairi and MacSorley to get Edward's men out.

"The tower," Gordon said. "The wall will block them."

Magnus took one look and understood. If Gordon placed his powder under one of the partially destroyed walls, it would crumble right into the path of the English. Even if it didn't block them entirely, it would give MacSorley and MacRuairi added time to clear all of the men from the island trap.

Magnus nodded, and quickly told Campbell and MacGregor what they intended to do while Gordon removed an ember from one of the braziers and used it to light a torch.

"The vaults!" Gordon shouted above the din of battle, as they fought their way past a few of the invading Englishmen.

They raced into the cool, damp stairwell. Without its roof, the stone had been left open to the elements, and the stairs were damp and slippery with moss as they made their way into the vaults.

Magnus didn't need to ask what Gordon intended. It was nothing they hadn't done many times before. They'd worked for so long together, they communicated without speaking.

Gordon headed for the far wall that was directly under the precariously perched tower wall. "It may take more than one," he said, removing a few small sacks from a leather bag he wore slung across his shoulder. He handed four of them to Magnus. "We don't have much time, so fire them all at once. At the arch," he said, pointing Magnus to the side nearer the stairwell. He used the torch to light two small candles he'd removed from his bag for such occasions. "I'll tell you when."

Gordon went to the far side of the wall, packing his bags along the arch near the top of the wall. Magnus did the same on his.

"Ready?" Gordon asked.

Magnus nodded.

Gordon wedged his candle between the bags and started to run. "Now!" he yelled.

Magnus secured his candle and did the same.

There should have been plenty of time to make it up the stairs and out of the tower before the first explosion. But something went wrong. Magnus was a few feet from the door—Gordon a few feet behind him—when the first shattering boom exploded beneath them, the concussion of sound and earth knocking him to the ground. The ground was still moving as the second one sounded.

He covered his ears and tried to get to his feet. The explosions were too loud. Too powerful. What the hell had happened?

He couldn't hear a damned thing, but somehow he knew Gordon was saying something. He turned around, seeing him shout—"Run!"—but it was too late. The walls were coming down, and they were trapped.

He tried to fight his way to the entry, attempting to dodge the falling stone that crashed all around him. One big stone hit him in the shoulder, sending a crushing blast of pain through his entire left side. He staggered. His ears were still ringing, but he could hear Gordon shout behind him and knew he'd been struck, too. He turned around to try to help him, but at that moment the tower collapsed around them.

Magnus put up his arm, trying to shield himself from the

rain of stone pelting him mercilessly, driving him to the ground.

He was certain he was dead. But somehow, when it stopped, the tower was gone, and he was still alive.

He extracted himself from the pile of rubble and looked around for Gordon, blinking against the acrid smell of the black powder and the heavy cloud of dust and ash swirling all around him.

Through the ringing in his ears he heard a moan. Gordon! He crawled through the pile of rocks toward the sound. At first he couldn't see him. Then he looked down and felt his stomach heave.

His friend was sprawled out on the ground in a sickly position, buried under a pile of enormous stones, the largest of which—part of one of the massive pillars of the vault—had fallen across his chest, pinning him and crushing his lungs.

Magnus swore, trying to pull the rocks off. But he knew it was useless. It would take three or four men of Robbie Boyd's strength to lift that pillar—and he had only one good arm. His left arm had been crushed badly, at the shoulder and forearm. He tried to cry out for help, but the others had to be too far away.

But he wouldn't give up.

"Stop," Gordon wheezed. "It's no use. You have to go."

Magnus didn't listen. He gritted his teeth against the pain and redoubled his effort with both hands.

"Stubborn . . ." Gordon's voice dropped off. "Go. They're coming. You can't let them capture you."

Suddenly, Magnus was aware of the voices behind him, coming from the sea-gate. He staggered to the collapsed wall and looked over, seeing the English climbing up. They'd been slowed, but not blocked. In a minute or two they'd be filling the bailey.

He swore and returned to his friend. "Try to press up, while I pull."

Gordon shook his head. "I can't move." He held Magnus's eyes. "I'm not going to make it."

The sickly liquid sound of his voice punctuated his words. Blood was filling his lungs.

"Nay," Magnus said furiously. "Don't say that."

"You know what you need to do. I can't do it myself. My hands are pinned."

Oh God, no. He shook his head. "Don't ask that of me."

Gordon ignored him. "Helen," he breathed. "Promise me you'll watch over her."

"Damn it, Templar," Magnus growled, his eyes stinging.

"Promise me."

Magnus couldn't find the words, but he nodded.

Their eyes held. "You can't leave them to find me," Gordon said. "I'm not sure how long this will take. I won't take the chance that anyone can identify me. You know what's at stake. The Guard. My family. They will be at risk."

Helen would be at risk. Gordon didn't need to say it. There was little the English wouldn't do to discover the names of the Highland Guard. It was why they were so careful. Why they used war names to cover their identities. MacRuairi had been uncovered, and he had such a bounty on his head that all of England and half of Scotland were hunting for him.

Magnus didn't have a choice. He did what he had to do.

Four

Helen did not let the difficulty of what she had to do dampen her spirits for long. She was confident she was doing the right thing in ending her marriage before it had begun to William, and that it would all work out for the best in the end. It was getting to the end, however, that would be hard.

But she wouldn't let her brothers change her mind—not this time. Which meant she had to do her best to avoid them until William returned.

It wasn't easy. The day after the men left, an unusually heavy winter storm descended over Lorn, burying the castle and surrounding countryside in nearly a foot of snow and delaying the departure of most of the wedding guests. The icy blast of winter also left the men—including her brothers—unable to train and confined to the Great Hall.

Thus, Helen spent most of her time with the women and children in the small second-floor solar occupied by Lady Anna and her husband, Arthur Campbell, who'd been appointed keeper of the castle.

After four days of nothing to do but sew (which Helen dreaded even in the best of circumstances) and listen to Christina MacLeod do her best to instill excitement in Pliny (the library at Dunstaffnage was limited to a few scholarly works), while trying to keep the six-month-old Beatrix MacLeod away from the brazier (she'd just learned to crawl) and quiet the four-month-old Duncan MacSorley (who seemed to cry at the barest provocation), they were all going a little crazed.

Ellie most of all. The new mother looked close to tears as she bounced the screeching infant in her arms. "I don't know what's wrong with him," she groaned, clearly overwhelmed. "He won't stop. His father does nothing but grin like the devil, but all he does is cry."

"My daughter did the same thing," Bella said. "I think she screamed for two months straight when she was his age."

Helen didn't miss the note of sadness in her voice. Bella's daughter was in England, living in exile with her father's family. She didn't know the exact circumstances, but it was clear Bella missed her terribly.

"The yarrow and mint seems to help a bit," Ellie said with a look of gratitude to Helen. "But how I wish Erik were here! He seems to be the only one who can make Duncan quiet."

"He'll be back soon," Bella said firmly.

The women had been trying to hide it from her, but Helen could sense their worry. She felt it, too. For Magnus— and for William, of course. It was the curse of women, being forced to stay behind to wait and worry as the men went off into battle. The reality of her fate unsettled her.

"Why don't you give him to me for a while," Christina offered, holding out her hands for the baby. "The snow seems to have stopped for a—"

Bella jumping to her feet and racing out of the room, her face a sickly gray, interrupted her.

Helen stood. "Perhaps I should see if she needs anything. That's the second time this week she's not felt well after breaking her fast."

Christina, Ellie, and Anna exchanged smiles. "She's

fine," Christina said. "I suspect she'll be feeling much better in a few months."

"A few months?" Helen asked.

Ellie shook her head, gazing lovingly at her son, who'd miraculously fallen asleep in Christina's arms. "I felt ill the entire time. Perhaps I should have guessed he'd be trouble. But he's a cute little devil. You are fortunate, Anna, that you have escaped the malady."

Anna unconsciously rubbed her stomach. "On the contrary, all I seem to want to do is eat. I dream about my next meals."

Finally, Helen understood. "She's expecting a child?"

Christina nodded.

Helen flushed, realizing Bella must have anticipated her impending marriage to Lachlan MacRuairi by at least a few weeks.

"Go," Christina said to Ellie. "Get a bit of fresh air. I'll watch him for a while."

Ellie bit her lip uncertainly. Helen's heart went out to her. Christina was right. They all needed to get out of this castle. Helen, too. All the talk of marriage and babies made her feel anxious. The walls seemed to be moving closer. But with all the snow . . .

Suddenly, a broad smile spread over Helen's face. She had the perfect way to take advantage of the wintry weather and put a smile back on Ellie's face.

"I have a better idea," she said. "But you're going to need to bundle up."

Ellie had looked skeptical at first, and Helen had the feeling that she'd suggested something silly again.

"Ride down the hill on *what*?" Ellie had said. But an hour later she was sliding down the small hill behind the castle, screeching with laughter.

The daughter of the most powerful earl in Ireland and sister to Scotland's imprisoned queen came to a magnificent stop, flying off the targe and landing in a deep puff of powdery white. When she finally managed to extricate her-self from the bank of snow they'd built to cushion their landings, she was covered in white. She dusted the snow from her gown, wiped her face with the back of her hand, and shook the rest from her hair.

"Did you see that?" she asked excitedly. "I was going so fast I felt like I was flying. You were right—rubbing the wax on the leather was a great idea." Her eyes twinkled. "Although I doubt Arthur will be happy when he sees what we have done to the targes hanging in the Great Hall."

Helen bit her lip. Oh no, she'd done it again. "I didn't think—"

Ellie laughed. "I was teasing. He won't mind. And if he does, it was worth it." She pulled the shield out of the snow. "Ready to go again? The only bad part is climbing back up the hill in all this snow. These boots are slippery."

Helen laughed. "Aye. But I think we're going to have a little company."

She pointed to the castle gate, where a small crowd had gathered. It wasn't just young children, she noticed, but a number of squires as well. Soon it seemed they had half the castle out with them, sliding down the hill in targes.

Helen was standing beside Ellie atop the hill, laughing as two of the children tried to slide down on one targe, when Ellie suddenly stopped. Her laughter turned into a gasp, and her cheeks, red from the cold, paled.

"What is it?" Helen asked.

Ellie shook her head, her gaze locked on the horizon. "Something's wrong."

Helen followed the direction of her stare, seeing at once what had caught her attention. A *birlinn* had just made the elbow turn around *Rubha Garbh*, the rocky promontory of land upon which the castle was situated, traveling faster than any ship Helen had ever seen.

"Is it . . . ?"

Ellie turned to her, eyes wide with fear. "Aye, it's Erik's ship. He's going too fast and they're back too soon."

They raced down the hill, entering the main gate just as the men rushed into the courtyard from the sea-gate opposite them. A mixture of fear and panic clutched her chest when Helen saw a man being carried into the castle, an arrow protruding from his neck.

Not Magnus! She sighed with relief. *Thank God.*

Ellie let out a cry that made Helen's heart clench right before she leapt into her husband's arms. "You're all right?" she said, just loud enough for Helen to hear.

The big Norseman didn't look all right. He looked as though he'd been through hell. All of them did.

Helen didn't wait to hear his reply. She scanned the crowd of men, heart pounding in her throat. Finally she saw him. He was slowly making his way up the beach from the jetty.

Oh, no! Her heart knifed. He was hurt.

She pushed through the crowd, reaching Magnus just outside the castle gate. She would have rushed into his arms just as Ellie had done to her husband, but his left arm was bound in a sling of linen at his side. He was covered in dirt, soot, and blood.

He stopped when he saw her, his eyes hard with something dark and forbidding that sent an icy chill through her veins.

"You're hurt," she said softly.

"I'm fine."

"You're not fine." Gently, she placed her hand on his arm. "Your arm—"

He jerked away from her, gritting his teeth against what must have been a blast of pain. "Leave it, Helen."

Tears of concern filled her eyes. What was wrong with him? Why was he acting like this? "Is it broken?" She placed her hands on him again. "Let me see it."

He flinched as if her touch scalded. "Damn it, Helen. Have you no care?"

Helen blinked up at him, taken aback by the fury in his voice. By the passion. Indeed, she'd never heard such passion from him. "Of course I care. I've been so worried. I was so scared when I saw you—"

"Me?" he boomed. "I don't want or need your concern. But what of your husband, Lady Helen? What of the man you married not four days ago? Have you no care for him?"

Helen stepped back, the lash of vitriol so unexpected. "William?"

An icy drop of trepidation slid down her spine.

His soft golden-brown eyes turned as hard and black as onyx, pinning her to the snow-covered ground. "Aye, William. Remember him? Your husband. My friend. The man you took to your bed a few nights ago."

"I didn't—"

"He's dead."

She let out a gasp of horror, her eyes widening with the shock of his harsh pronouncement. *Dead?*

She murmured a prayer for his soul.

The look he gave her was full of such hatred and pain it seemed to burn her insides. He turned away, but not before she saw the disgust. "He deserved more from you than prayers. But you've never been very devoted in your affections, have you?"

Helen felt a stab of guilt and despair that drained the blood from her body, leaving her as cold and empty on the inside as she was on the outside.

He was right.

For nearly eighteen hours—since he'd stumbled out of the collapsed tower from one hell into another—Magnus had existed in a state of barely repressed anger and torment. Seeing Helen had been the final blow. He'd snapped, giving way to all the emotions lashing inside him.

She'd married Gordon, damn it. It was he who deserved her compassion and concern.

Perhaps it wasn't fair, but it didn't matter. Gordon's death had finally succeeded in severing the connection between them. Magnus would never be able to see her without thinking of his friend. His dead friend. She belonged to Gordon. Not him.

Magnus pushed aside his anger, knowing he needed to focus on doing for MacGregor what he'd been unable to do for Gordon: saving his life.

By necessity if not inclination, Magnus had become the de facto physician of the Highland Guard. A rudimentary knowledge of healing coupled with "gentle" hands (laughable, given their size and strength) had earned him the position. But it was one thing to press some moss in a wound and wrap it, boil a few herbs for a tincture, or even press a hot iron on a wound that wouldn't stop bleeding; it was another to remove an arrow from the neck of a man who'd taken it to save your life.

When Magnus had emerged from the collapsed tower, it was to find that the English had overtaken the bailey. Only MacRuairi, MacSorley, Campbell, and MacGregor remained. Waiting, it seemed, for Gordon and him.

Leave no man behind. Part of the Highland Guard creed. At least it had been—until Gordon.

Magnus tried to fight his way toward his friends, but the injury to his arm hampered him. Unable to hold a targe or a second weapon, he couldn't adequately defend himself, and his left side was left vulnerable to multiple attackers. When the English surrounded him, he knew he wouldn't be able to hold them back for long.

Recognizing that he was in trouble, MacGregor and Campbell had come to his aid. They'd almost made their way back to the safety of the gate when MacGregor had gone down, ironically felled by an arrow from a longbow. Magnus had seen the arrow protruding from his neck and thought he was dead. He'd let out a roar of pure rage, attacking the English around him with the half-crazed vengeance of a berserker.

He heard the murmurs of "Phantom Guard" rolling through the enemy soldiers, saw the fear in their eyes beneath their helms, and eventually he also saw their backsides as they turned and ran. "Tail" was a slur often directed at the English—and it was well earned.

The English, realizing their prey had already been lost (Edward Bruce had escaped), had decided that taking the slighted castle wasn't worth dying.

From the moment Campbell realized MacGregor was still alive, Magnus's only thought was getting him to safety. Riding was out of the question. MacGregor needed to be kept as still as possible. Somehow a small boat had been procured, and with MacSorley at the helm they'd raced back to their own ship, and then on to Dunstaffnage.

Edward Bruce was safe, but at what cost?

Gordon, and now MacGregor? Magnus would be damned if he'd lose another friend this day. It seemed inconceivable that the team could survive intact through two and a half years of war, major battles where hundreds had lost their lives, and even exile, only to lose two of the greatest warriors in Christendom—hell, in Barbariandom as well—in a skirmish.

Every warrior knew that death was part of war. To their Norse forebearers it was the ultimate glory, a philosophy that had lived on in the successive generations. But in his years fighting alongside the other members of the Guard, seeing what they could do, and then hearing the stories of their feats, which had taken on almost mythical proportions, Magnus had started to believe their own legend. Gordon's death was a brutal reminder that they weren't invincible.

As soon as they arrived at Dunstaffnage, Campbell sent some men to fetch the healer from a nearby village. But Magnus knew what they needed was a skilled surgeon—something they'd be hard pressed to find even in a major burgh like Berwick, where the guilds would be found. Most surgeons were barbers—as crude at cutting off a limb as they were at trimming a beard. Their training was one of exigency, by trial and error.

The placement of this arrow left no room for error. It had pierced through the mail coif and entered the front left side of MacGregor's throat at an angle, coming to a stop at the back of his neck. The arrowhead was lodged inside.

Magnus had managed to stop the bleeding, but he knew if he attempted to pull the arrow out, one wrong move would kill MacGregor.

"Can you remove it?"

He lifted his head from his extensive examination of the wound to look over at Arthur Campbell. He stood with the rest of the Highland Guard around the trestle table they'd requisitioned from the Great Hall and set up in the adjoining laird's solar. The only other people present were the king and Campbell's new bride, who was coordinating water, fresh linens, and whatever else they might need with the servants.

"I don't know. I've never seen anything like this. It's in a dangerous location. I fear that if I try to pull it out . . ."

He didn't need to finish.

"What other choice do you have?" MacLeod said somberly.

"None," Magnus admitted. "It has to come out." He just didn't know if he had the skill to do it. "Perhaps the healer will have another idea," the king added.

But the old woman who arrived a few hours later had no more expertise than he. Nor did the priest, who advocated bleeding the opposite side of MacGregor's neck to restore his humours, praying for his soul, and then leaving it to God's will.

To hell with God's will! Magnus wasn't going to let him die.

"Is there anyone else?" MacRuairi asked Lady Anna. Campbell's wife was a MacDougall and had been raised at Dunstaffnage. "Perhaps you know of someone in the area?"

Magnus stood. "I know someone."

Helen. She wasn't a surgeon, but she seemed to have an unusual gift for healing. He'd seen her perform a miracle once. God knew, MacGregor was in need of another one.

So Magnus swallowed his anger and asked Lady Anna to send for her.

After the way he'd lashed out at her, he knew he had no right to ask for her help. But he would, just as he knew she would give it.

Only a few minutes passed before he heard the door open. He felt a stab of guilt, seeing her red-rimmed eyes and blotchy, tear-stained face. If his harsh relating of Gordon's death had been intended to make her conscience suffer, it appeared to have worked.

He felt a second stab, this one more of a cinching in the region of his heart, when he saw the caution in her eyes as she approached.

He clenched his jaw and met her gaze. "My lady, I'm sorry to disturb you in your grief, but I thought . . . I hoped you might be able to help."

She looked so tiny and young in the room crowded with the big warriors. For a moment, the fierce urge rose inside him to protect her. To tuck her under his arm and tell her everything was going to be all right the way he'd used to do. But it wasn't. And it never would be again.

Though her chin trembled, she lifted it determinedly and nodded her head. For the next few minutes the room was deathly silent as she examined the fallen warrior.

"I've never seen anything like this," she said, when she'd finished. "It's a miracle he survived."

"Can you take it out?"

Without killing him. Their eyes held; the unspoken words passed between them in silent understanding. "I don't know, but I can try."

The quiet note of determination in her voice did much to soothe the frayed edges of his tightly wound nerves.

She straightened, shedding the pale, uncertain, grief-stricken girl as easily as she would shrug a cloak from her shoulders. And just as she'd done the first time they'd met, when she'd boldly stopped him from ending his dog's life, she snapped into action. Claiming the room was too stuffy, she ordered everyone from the small solar—even the king—except for Lady Anna, whom she sent about procuring her the items she would need.

When Magnus started to follow the rest of the guardsmen out, she stopped him. "Not you. I may need your help." She looked at his arm. "But if I do this, you must promise to let me see to your arm as well."

He bit back the automatic refusal, knowing he was in no position to argue, and nodded. Curtly. He didn't like being coerced.

She murmured something under her breath that sounded suspiciously like "stubborn ox" and resumed her tending of MacGregor.

"I need you to lift his mail coif, while I look at the entry wound."

Magnus came up to stand beside her, ignoring the soft scent of lavender that rose from her hair. It had dried, he noticed. He'd seen the group of children sliding down the hill from the water, and somehow had known she was involved. It was something she would do. His suspicions had been confirmed when she'd appeared in the bailey, drenched with snow. Her unrelenting joy in the face of his own misery didn't seem so wrong now. She hadn't known. *Every day is May Day,* he recalled her brother saying. Sometimes he envied her that.

"The entry wound is small and round, so I think it must be a needle bodkin."

He nodded, returning to the moment. "Aye. That's what I thought as well." To pierce mail at such a close distance, the long, thin, pointed arrowhead was more effective. The flat, broadhead arrowhead would have done much more damage, particularly had it been barbed.

"Do you have an arrow spoon?"

He shook his head. He'd seen them used before, but had never had need of one himself. It was a thinned piece of shaft with a wooden spoonlike end to cup around the arrowhead and help ease it out in one piece.

"Then we shall hope the English soldier glued this arrowhead on with something stronger than beeswax. But if not, I shall need something to pull it out."

"I have a few instruments." He unfolded the items he carried with him in a piece of leather that he'd fashioned with pockets and held them out for her inspection.

She looked pleased by what she saw and removed a long, thin pair of iron pincers. "These will work well." She paused. "All right, here it goes."

He knew from the way her cheeks flushed and her hand shook as she grasped the shaft that she was much more nervous than she appeared. But her concentration was as fierce as any warrior's on the battlefield as she unhesitatingly started to pull the shaft out.

She's good at this, he realized. She seemed suited for this and more comfortable in her own skin than he'd ever seen her before.

The arrow came out easily. Unfortunately, it was without the tip. But the removal of the shaft didn't appear to have caused any extra bleeding.

The small frown between her brows was her only reaction to the dangerous complication. "I would use a trephine to make the entry wound wider, so that I might be able to see the arrowhead. But with this location, I'm reluctant to try." She picked up the pincers. Their eyes met. "Be ready to press that cloth on the wound as soon as I have it out."

He nodded.

She inserted the pincers into the hole created by the arrow shaft. MacGregor moaned, but Magnus didn't need to call for help to hold him down. The wounded warrior was so weak, he was able to keep him still with one hand. She bored the instrument steadily through his neck, taking care to follow the exact path of the arrow. Magnus heard the strike of iron on iron. With a deft, delicate touch she squeezed the pincers, attempting to grasp the arrowhead. It took a few tries, but finally, she stopped. Slowly, she began to pull it out.

Each second was agony. He kept waiting for the telltale burst of blood that would indicate something had gone wrong. That she'd struck one of the deadly veins that ran through the neck.

Even when he saw the arrowhead, he still didn't believe she'd done it.

"Now," she said, "Press the cloth to his neck."

They both stared at MacGregor, watching for any sign of a change.

"It's Gregor MacGregor," she said suddenly.

He frowned. "You know him?"

She gave him a bemused look. "From the Highland Games. But I should know him anywhere. Every woman over five has heard of that face."

Magnus knew well of MacGregor's reputation—God knows they loved to needle him about his "pretty" face— but hearing it from Helen didn't impart quite the same level of amusement.

He clenched his mouth and turned away, concentrating

on his friend while Helen found Lady Anna and gave her instructions on how to make a salve.

By the time the salve was prepared, the wound had stopped bleeding enough to remove the cloth.

"I'll need to cauterize it with an iron," she said.

He removed one of the tools made for such a purpose—a long, thin piece of metal with a wooden handle at one end, the other end bent at a right angle with a flat nub on the tip—and heated it in the fire. He held MacGregor down firmly as Helen placed the hot metal on the wound, searing it closed. She never flinched from the smell. Finally, she spread the salve and bound the wound with a fresh cloth, before turning her attention to him.

With help from Boyd and MacRuairi—the sadistic bastard seemed to enjoy watching Magnus bite back his pain—she forced the broken bones back into position. The shoulder where the first stone had hit wasn't that bad, but his forearm where he'd tried to block the falling walls had been snapped nearly in two. The only good part, according to Helen, was that the bone hadn't broken through the skin.

When she had finished, Helen braced Magnus's forearm arm between two thin pieces of wood just like she'd done with his dog, and wrapped it with linen bandages soaked in egg white, flour, and animal fat to harden. His shoulder had to be kept immobilized in a sling. And miraculously, MacGregor was still alive.

Because of Helen, one of his friends had been saved tonight.

But his happiness was tempered by the loss of the other. When Helen met his gaze, he turned away.

The death of William Gordon cast a dark pall over the castle that not even Gregor MacGregor's continued improvement could lift. The guests who'd celebrated their wedding only a week before now listened to the same priest pray for the groom's immortal soul.

Helen sat on the first bench in the chapel beside her brothers, listening to the priest drone on in Latin, still unable to fully comprehend the horrific turn of events. It seemed inconceivable that the handsome, lighthearted young man who'd stood beside her in this chapel a week ago could be gone.

She didn't belong here, sitting in this place of honor due his wife. The knowledge that she'd intended to dissolve the marriage with the husband she now mourned ate at her mercilessly. The sadness she felt for his loss seemed insufficient in the face of the suffering of those who truly loved him. Magnus. Her brother. Even Lady Isabella had been devastated.

She should feel more, shouldn't she? She wanted to, but how could she muster the grief he was due when she'd barely known him?

She kept her gaze down-turned, fixed on her hands shaking in her lap, afraid that everyone would see the truth. She was an impostor, suffering from her own selfish guilt and not for the man who'd died . . .

She didn't know how he'd died. An attack, they said. His body lost at sea.

Suddenly, Helen felt her brother tug on her arm, helping her to her feet. The funeral was over, she realized.

Kenneth kept hold of her, propping her up like a poppet, as he led her out of the dark chapel. She couldn't meet the sympathetic gazes of the people who watched them pass. She didn't deserve them. Magnus was right—William had deserved more.

Magnus. Her heart stabbed. He couldn't even look at her. Since the day she'd pulled the arrow from Gregor MacGregor's neck, he'd assiduously avoided her. He hadn't even thanked her for removing the arrow or for tending his arm. She shuddered, recalling how badly his arm had been broken and how stoically he'd weathered what must have been excruciating pain. He might have been maimed for life if she'd not insisted on tending it. As it was, she couldn't be sure how well the bone would mend.

They made their way back to the castle through the snow, a path forged two hours earlier by the footsteps of the many mourners who'd come to pay their respects to the fallen warrior.

A light repast had been prepared for them in the Great Hall. As they passed the laird's solar, she removed her hand from the crook of Kenneth's arm. "I will join you in a moment," she said. "I need to check on MacGregor."

Her brother frowned. "Right now? I thought a nurse had been brought in to tend him."

"I shall only be a minute."

She left before he could argue with her. She ducked into the darkened room and heaved a sigh of relief to escape the oppressive weight of the day, if only for a moment.

The nurse stood as soon as she entered. The girl from the village was young, but Lady Anna assured her, quite capable.

"How is he?"

"Sleeping, my lady."

She managed a half-smile. "That's the best thing for him now." He'd regained consciousness, but only for a few minutes each day. It was to be expected; he'd lost a lot of blood. He would have lost more had she not insisted the priest be prevented from bleeding him again.

"Any signs of fever?"

The girl—Cait—shook her head. "I've made him swallow a few sips of the beef broth, just as you said."

Helen smiled. "That is good. And the medicine?"

Cait wrinkled her nose. "Aye, a bit of that as well. But he doesn't seem to like it much."

The way she said it made Helen laugh. "I'm not surprised. It is quite bitter. Perhaps he is feeling better than we realized if his tastes are so discriminating."

The girl smiled back at her. "I hope so, my lady." She cast a shy gaze toward the man stretched out across the table. "He sure is a handsome one."

"The most handsome in Scotland, it is said," Helen agreed with a grin.

"Am I interrupting something?"

Helen spun around at the sound of Magnus's voice behind her, not having heard him enter.

Her cheeks flushed, embarrassed to have been caught . . . laughing, smiling, if only for a moment. "I was just checking on him." She turned to the girl. "Thank you, Cait, you're doing wonderfully."

The girl blushed with pleasure and bobbed a curtsy. "Thank you, my lady."

Helen exited the room and was surprised to realize that Magnus was still behind her. For a moment, her heart caught, thinking that his anger might have abated. But one look at his rigid jaw cured her of that notion. Her heart ached for him. She wanted to give him comfort, but it was clear it would not be welcome. Not from her.

"Is there something you wanted?" she asked.

Me? She let herself dare hope.

He shifted his gaze, not meeting her eyes—almost as if he'd heard her silent plea. "I should have thanked you. For what you did. You saved his life, and," he motioned to his sling, "the use of my arm."

"You must not try to use it—"

"I know. I heard you the first time." One side of his mouth curved. "I never knew you could be so bossy."

She lifted her chin, ignoring the heat that rushed to her cheeks. "Only when I anticipate the patient will be stubborn and pigheaded by trying to resume activity before the bones are fully healed."

His mouth quirked. "I didn't say it wasn't warranted."

Their eyes caught for an instant, before he quickly looked away. The small exchange was so reminiscent of how things used to be between them that it made her heart tug with longing. Yet the uncomfortable silence that followed made clear it was no longer that way. It would never be that way again.

He could barely stand to look at her.

If marrying William had been unforgivable, what chance did she have now that he was dead? Unlike marriage, death was a bond that could never be dissolved. In Magnus's mind, she and William were forever connected, and his loyalty to his friend would never let him forget it.

Nor would he forget what would only add to his belief in her lack of loyalty. To him all those years ago, and now to his dead friend.

He cleared his throat. "You are leaving?"

She stilled. "Tomorrow."

Say something.

He gave a curt nod of acknowledgment. "Safe travels."

Is that all, then? Her chest throbbed painfully. But it was clear he wanted nothing to do with her. "Magnus, I—"

He stopped her with a hard look. "Goodbye, Helen."

Helen sucked in her breath against the hot stab of pain. Like a knife, his words severed any threads of hope. He'd cut her out of his life. The one person who'd always made her feel like she belonged no longer wanted her around.

"Get away from her."

Helen gasped at the sound of her brother's voice. Dread flooded her, anticipating the confrontation to come. Kenneth had made no secret who he blamed for William's death, and nothing she'd said could convince him otherwise.

Helen grabbed her brother, holding him back. Aware that they were in a corridor where anyone could hear them, she said in a low voice, "I was only saying farewell, brother. You have no cause for concern."

Helen could see the dangerous flush of anger in her brother's face and knew he would not be so easily pacified. Kenneth wanted answers, and so far he'd had none.

"You do not even wait until Gordon is cold in his grave before panting after my sister. Oh, that's right," he said sarcastically. "There is no grave to go cold. You took care of that."

Though Magnus gave no outward sign that the words had affected him, she sensed him tense. "What are you trying to suggest, Sutherland?"

"I'm suggesting nothing. You've made no secret of your feelings for my sister."

Mortified heat crept up her cheeks. "You're wrong, Kenneth. Magnus doesn't feel—"

"I know exactly how MacKay feels." He gave her one of those patronizing brotherly glances and set her to the side, squaring off against Magnus. "He might have fooled you, but he didn't fool me. He was half-crazed the night you married Gordon. He wants you. He still wants you. The only question is how far he'd go to have you."

Helen blanched in horror at what her brother implied. Magnus would never have had anything to do with William's death. Her gaze flew to Magnus's. His face had gone white. Horribly white. But it was the pained, haunted look in his eyes that struck her cold.

She threw herself in front of her brother, expecting Magnus to strike. It was no more than her brother deserved.

What she didn't expect was for Magnus to turn and walk away.

The next morning Helen left with her family, certain that she would never see him again. Her heart was breaking a second time. She wanted to go after him but knew she could not. It was over. She felt the finality she'd never felt the first time.

Five

❧

The sun beat down upon Magnus's bare head and torso, his chest slick with the sweat of exertion. The truce negotiated between King Robert of Scotland and King Edward II of England in January had provided temporary peace from war but not from MacLeod. "Peace" for MacLeod only meant more training.

The leader of the Highland Guard and famed trainer of warriors came at him again, wielding the two-handed great sword as if it weighed no more than a stick. Striking first to the right high above Magnus's head and then to the left, MacLeod forced Magnus to move his arm and shoulder in every direction to deflect the powerful blows.

It hurt like hell, but Magnus gritted his teeth and forced his body to fight through the pain, fending off every strike. Not any easy feat against the greatest swordsman in Scotland, especially for a man whose arm and shoulder had been severely broken only months before. But he was tough enough to withstand anything MacLeod threw at him.

Magnus knew he should be grateful that his arm had healed as well as it had, but the forced weeks of inactivity had been its own kind of pain. Eight wall-crawling weeks before he could remove his arm from the splints and sling. Another four before he could even think about picking up a sword.

His arm had been as weak as a damned Englishman's! For the past two months, he'd thrown himself into a training regimen to rebuild his strength with the single-minded purpose of a zealot. He didn't have time to think about . . .

He stopped himself, irritated by the lapse. *Focus.*

Now that his arm was healed, it was just a matter of pushing through the pain. Something that MacLeod seemed intent on maximizing.

Chief swung again with a crushing force that would fell most men. Magnus blocked the blow with his own great sword. The shattering clash of metal reverberated in the air and down the entire left side of his body. MacLeod pressed down so hard, Magnus could read the inscription on his sword: *Bi Tren.* Be valiant. Be strong. The motto of the MacKays, and fitting as hell right now. The pain was excruciating, but he pushed the fierce swordsman back.

"I think he's getting tired, MacLeod," MacGregor observed from the gallery—in this case a bale of hay, turned-over crates, and an old barrel that were set out near the section of the castle yard where they practiced every morning. A few other warriors had gathered around to watch as well. Other than offer the occasional encouragement, however, they were content to watch the two men battle in reverent silence. Except for MacGregor: he wouldn't shut up. "You probably should go easy on him."

Magnus shot him a nasty glare. "Go to hell, MacGregor. I didn't hear you volunteer."

But MacGregor was used to his foul temper, having borne the brunt of it for the past five months.

Like Magnus, MacGregor was fully healed from the arrow that should have killed him. Other than the angry red scar where the hole had been burned shut—which eventually would lighten—he bore no signs of his ordeal. He'd even managed to avoid a fever.

Because of Helen.

Damn it, don't think about her.

Magnus's jaw clenched against the reflexive surge of emotion. When he thought of Helen, inevitably he thought of Gordon. The two were forever linked in his mind. The shock of Gordon's death had faded, but not the guilt. Helen was caught up in that guilt.

He was grateful for what she'd done for him—and for MacGregor—but there was nothing left between them.

Watch over her.

The promise he'd made to Gordon haunted him. He had nothing to feel guilty for, damn it. No link had been made between Gordon and the already legendary attack of the Highland Guard at Threave.

He wasn't breaking his vow to Gordon. There was no threat. No *real* threat, at least. And there wouldn't be any at all if her brothers would keep their mouths shut. The earl and Kenneth Sutherland had made trouble at the king's first Parliament in St. Andrews a couple of months ago with their dangerous questions about the circumstances of Gordon's death. Questions that were also being raised by Gordon's English-loving family in the south.

It was the timing of the mission with the wedding that had created problems. Too many people were aware of exactly when they'd left. Usually the Highland Guard missions were undertaken with few people aware of their comings and goings. Admitting to being in Galloway would be too risky, so they'd claimed to be in Forfar laying siege to the castle, which had been taken for Bruce. Supposedly, Gordon had been killed in an attack by freebooters on the way home.

Helen was perfectly safe.

But Magnus wasn't. He was distracted when MacLeod came at him again, nearly taking off his head.

"He'll get his turn," MacLeod said, referring to MacGregor. "Once I'm done with you. Again."

For the next thirty minutes—forty minutes? It felt like forever—MacLeod worked him until his eyes burned with agony and every muscle in his body shook with exhaustion. It was almost as if he were trying to get him to quit. When it became clear Magnus wasn't going to do that, that he would fight until he collapsed, MacLeod finally relented.

"That's enough. You're ready. Get cleaned up and meet me in the king's solar in an hour." He smiled at MacGregor. When Chief smiled like that it didn't bode well. "Your turn."

"Have fun," Magnus said to MacGregor as he started toward the barracks to retrieve soap and a drying cloth. He looked back over his shoulder at MacLeod. "Watch his face. The serving lasses from the village were upset the last time you bruised him up a little."

The men sitting around watching snickered.

"Sod off, MacKay," MacGregor said.

"Too bad that arrow wasn't a little higher," Magnus added. "You might actually look like a warrior."

The man renowned for his handsome face let off a string of ugly oaths.

Magnus actually smiled as he walked away, a rarity of late. It was a source of constant annoyance to MacGregor—and thus a constant source of amusement among the Highland Guard—that no matter how many battles he fought, his face came out unscathed.

For a warrior, scars were expected. A badge of honor and impossible to avoid, especially on the face. But it was almost as if MacGregor's mother had dipped him headfirst in the protective waters of the River Styx like Achilles: no matter how hard he tried, his face healed smooth and unmarked.

Poor bastard.

It didn't take Magnus long to gather his belongings and

make his way to the river behind the castle to bathe. Though it was a warm spring day, the river of melted snow from the mountains retained its wintry chill.

The numbing effect on his muscles drove away the pain almost as effectively as the mandrake, poppy, and vinegar concoction Helen had left for him. He'd taken it—at first. But dulling the pain also meant dulling his thinking and reactions. So when he resumed training, he'd weaned himself off the foul-tasting brew.

He took his time in the water, allowing the cold to restore his aching muscles. But as the hour drew close, he became anxious to return to the castle.

MacLeod had been testing him, he realized. And if "you're ready" was any indication, he'd cleared Magnus at last to rejoin the others in the west. MacRuairi and MacSorley were in the Isles, keeping watch over John of Lorn, who was stirring up trouble again from Ireland. Seton, Boyd, MacLean, and Lamont were in the southwest, keeping the peace in Galloway with James Douglas and Edward Bruce. Campbell had been with Magnus, MacGregor, and MacLeod, but had returned to Dunstaffnage the month before for the birth of his first child. A son named William, named after their fallen friend.

Magnus was tired of infirmity and eager to rejoin the others. He needed action. A mission. Here with the king's court he had too much time to think. It was harder to escape the memories. Memories that hung over him like a dark cloud and were far more painful and raw than any broken bone.

The guard posted at the solar must have been expecting him. He opened the door as soon as Magnus approached.

He was greeted with the hearty sound of laughter. The king sat in a large, throne-like chair before a small fireplace, a goblet of wine in his hand and a broad smile on his face.

Peace suited the Bruce. For the first time in over three

years, since he'd stabbed his nemesis John "The Red" Comyn before the altar of Greyfriars Church, the king looked at ease, the lines of suffering and defeat on his battle-weary face less noticeable. After all he'd been through, God knew he'd earned it.

"MacKay, there you are," he said. "Come, have some wine. MacLeod was just telling us about your training today. It seems our fair friend didn't fare as well." The king chuckled. "Nor does he look so fair."

It didn't surprise him. Only a handful of them could keep up with MacLeod. Although MacGregor was highly skilled with a blade—they all were—his weapon was the bow.

MacLeod shrugged, a rare smile curving his mouth. "I'm sure he'll heal."

The men laughed. In addition to MacLeod, a handful of the king's closest companions and favored members of his large retinue had joined them. Among them were the venerable knights Sir Neil Campbell, Sir William De la Hay, and Sir Alexander Fraser, MacLeod's young brother-in-law.

"I'm sending MacLeod west." The king's face darkened. "The Lord of Lorn is making trouble again. MacSorley said he's gathering a fleet. Even in exile the bastard manages to defy me, and now his treasonous father has joined him!" The king stiffened with fury, no longer looking so relaxed. "Six months after he submitted and not two months since he attended Parliament, the Lord of Argyll has fled to Ireland."

Magnus could understand the king's anger. The MacDougall chief's submission had been an important coup, a sign of the reconciliation of enemies to form a united Scotland. The quick defection of the powerful clan who were closely tied to the Comyns was bound to cause unrest in Argyll. Arthur "Ranger" Campbell would have his hands full at Dunstaffnage.

It would have been better had Campbell gotten rid of

Lorn when he'd had the chance. Magnus understood why he hadn't—he'd married the man's daughter, after all—but Lorn and his father wouldn't get a second chance.

Magnus felt a little bit of the dark cloud hovering over him lift. He couldn't wait to get back to action. He'd be too busy to think about her. But sometimes it felt as if it would be easier to forget a missing limb.

"When do we leave?"

MacLeod shook his head. "You aren't going."

Magnus stiffened. "But I'm ready—you said so yourself."

"Aye, but you and MacGregor have a different mission. You will be guarding the king."

"I've decided to make a royal progress through the Highlands to thank the chiefs who offered shelter in those dark days after Methven." King Robert's face clouded as the memories struck of his days as an outlaw. Men like William Wiseman, Alexander MacKenzie of Eilean Donan, and Duncan MacAulay of Loch Broom had saved his life. "As well as ensure that those who have recently given me their pledge are not inclined to follow the example of the Lord of Argyll."

Meaning the king wanted to ensure he didn't have any more defectors.

"With the truce and the country at peace," MacLeod interjected, "there is no better time."

Magnus swallowed his disappointment. A peacekeeping jaunt through the Highlands didn't sound like a mission for the illustrious Highland Guard. The king had a large retinue of knights. Even were trouble to arise, he would be well protected. With trouble brewing out west, wouldn't Magnus be better utilized with MacLeod? Why did he feel as though he was being given this mission because of his injury?

"I'm putting you in charge," MacLeod said. "The king

will travel north through Ross and Cromarty before turning west through the mountains to the coast."

Magnus's mountains. He'd grown up ranging those hills. But the knowledge that MacLeod might have reason to have appointed him bodyguard—or guide—didn't ease the sting of disappointment.

"We will finish in August at Dunstaffnage, where I will hold the first Highland Games in four years," the king added enthusiastically. "What better way to mark the continuity of the realm and celebrate our victories?" He winked at Magnus. "Perhaps I will find some men to recruit for our army."

Magnus stiffened. The subtle reference to his recruitment for the Highland Guard, which wouldn't be understood by those not privy to their identities, was not lost on him. MacLeod had been hinting for weeks about finding him a new partner. But his partner was dead. He didn't need or want another one.

"When do we leave?" Magnus asked.

"After the feast of Pentecost," the king said. "I should like to be at Dunrobin Castle by the end of the month."

Magnus stilled, carefully schooling his features into a mask of indifference, but every nerve-ending in his body flared in rejection. "Dunrobin?"

Helen's home.

He could feel MacLeod's heavy gaze on him, but it was Bruce who answered. "Aye. As the Sutherlands are the newest members to our fold, I thought it best to start with them."

"I trust that won't be a problem?" MacLeod asked.

Magnus clenched his jaw. Dunrobin Castle was about the last place he wanted to go and Helen the last person he wanted to see. His feelings where she was concerned were still too much in turmoil.

Hurt. Anger. Gratitude. Guilt.

After all that had happened between them—she'd married his best friend, damn it—he still couldn't erase her from his mind.

Gordon couldn't have known what he was asking. But he'd made a promise to his dying friend. A promise that so far he hadn't kept. This journey would give him the opportunity.

Once he'd assured himself that she was safe, his task would be done.

"It won't be a problem," he answered. "For me."

But he was damned sure it would be a problem for the Sutherlands. They wouldn't relish having to play host to a MacKay.

He smiled. Perhaps he might see a bit of action on this journey after all.

As she'd done almost every morning since her return to Dunrobin, Helen traipsed along the grassy shoreline from the castle to her friend's cottage. Many times she'd asked Muriel to take a room at the castle after Muriel's father had died, but her fiercely independent friend always refused, claiming she enjoyed the privacy when she could find it—which wasn't very often. As the best healer for miles around, Muriel was rarely alone. Besides, she pointed out, at only a few furlongs up the coast from the castle she was close if anyone needed her.

Helen admired the other woman's determination and courage. It wasn't easy for a young woman to live on her own—especially a pretty, unmarried one. But her friend had done it, heedless of what anyone said. Helen was surprised that Will hadn't attempted to find a husband for her. It seemed strange. But then again, when it came to Muriel, much of what her brother did was strange. She'd never known him to be so hard on anyone—even her.

A light breeze swept up from the sparkling waters of the firth to Helen's right, ruffling her hair and filling her nose with the tangy, briny scent of the sea.

It was a spectacular day, the sun already bright and hot in the cloudless blue sky. After the cold, dreary May they'd had, the hint of summer as the first week of June came to a close was a welcome reprieve.

She waved to some of the villagers as she passed. The stone and thatched houses were more sporadic along the coast, belonging to the fishermen and kelpers. Most of the clansmen lived closer to the castle or the crofts in the glen where the small black cattle typical in this part of the Highlands grazed.

A few young children, the eldest no more than three, screeched with laughter as they tried to catch a butterfly in an old piece of hemp net, no doubt discarded from one of their father's boats, not realizing the weave was too big. She laughed along with them, feeling more like herself than she had in months.

Slowly, she was coming back to life, taking pleasure in the simple things she'd always loved. A beautiful spring day. The sound of children's laughter. A cool ocean breeze.

But pain and regret were lasting companions. She wished . . .

God how she wished she'd done things differently. If she'd married Magnus all those years ago, none of this would have happened. He wouldn't be angry with her. He wouldn't hate the sight of her. He'd look at her the way he used to. With love, though she'd been too young and foolish to realize it.

Now it was too late. Her smile slid. She should never have married William. And now it was a mistake that could never be undone.

"None of that," a familiar voice said. "It's so good to see you smiling again, lass."

Helen glanced up, not surprised to see Donald approaching along the path in front of her with a few of her brother's men. It seemed as if at least a few times a week, their paths crossed as she made her way to Muriel's cottage and he returned to the castle from patrol.

Her brow furrowed. He seemed to ride out on patrol quite often of late. Although with the king's visit, perhaps it was to be expected. Will wanted to ensure that nothing went wrong when the king was here. Roaming war bands weren't as common in the past few months, but there were still plenty of people who opposed Robert Bruce and "renegades" like her brother who'd turned on his compatriots to come to Bruce's side.

And there was always the MacKays. Her heart tugged. It seemed there was always trouble with the MacKays. Feud or not, disputes over land broke out frequently between the neighboring clans. Descendants of the Moarmers of Caithness, the MacKays refused to answer to the Sutherlands for their lands.

When they'd first received the king's missive, her foolish heart had leapt, wondering if Magnus would be with him. But of course he wouldn't. He could barely stand to look at her.

Don't think of him.

Focusing on healing had been a boon in more ways than one.

She forced a smile back to her face and greeted the men. To Donald she said, "You rode out early this morning; I did not see you at the morning prayers."

He broke out into a broad smile, clearly pleased by her observation. "Aye, with the usurper arriving any day, the earl has us covering a lot of land this morning."

Before she could remind him that he shouldn't be calling the man her brother was trying to curry favor with a usurper, one of the other men added, "The captain insisted on being back for—"

"That's enough, Angus." Donald hopped off his destrier. The enormous mail-clad warhorses were scarce in this area—and impractical in the mountainous Highlands—but her brothers and Donald took their roles as knights seriously. "Take the horses back. I'll escort the lady the rest of the way."

"That won't be necessary," she protested. But the men had already hastened to do his bidding.

"I insist," he said with a wink.

Helen couldn't help but laugh. Donald had always been protective of her, from the time she was a young girl. He didn't approve of her walking about unescorted. Fortunately her father, and now Will, didn't mind as long as she stayed within the castle environs.

They walked a few minutes in companionable silence before he spoke again. "You've been spending a lot of time with Muriel."

She caught the note of disapproval in his voice and sighed. Truly, it was like having another brother. "I like spending time with her. I'm learning so much."

Since she'd returned from Dunstaffnage, Helen had thrown herself into learning as much as she could from her friend. She'd never before attempted anything as dangerous as removing the arrow from Gregor MacGregor's neck. She might have appeared confident, but in truth, she'd been terrified.

But when it was over, she'd also been proud.

She was good at healing, she realized. And with Muriel's instruction she would be even better. Muriel's father had been a university-trained physician in Berwick-upon-Tweed, and he'd taught his daughter everything he knew. Even though the guilds of physicians were closed to women, the Earl of Ross had offered to sponsor her. But Muriel had refused the rare opportunity, claiming that the only recognition she needed was from the local clansmen she cared for. Helen was happy that she'd decided to stay, but wondered if there was something else keeping her here.

Whatever the case, working alongside Muriel gave Helen something to do and kept her mind from straying to painful places.

From the expression on Donald's face, she could see her reason hadn't impressed him. She thought of another way to do so. "Is it not my responsibility as lady of the keep to tend to our guests?"

Donald frowned, unable to argue her point. "Aye, but Muriel is not a proper companion for an unmarried lady—"

"A widow," Helen reminded him firmly. "And just because Muriel has decided not to marry does not mean she's improper."

"The lass is young and fair of face. She should be married with a handful of children nipping at her heels. Not roaming the countryside alone."

The way he'd expressed it, it sounded like a pack of pups would suffice just as well. Helen tried to remain patient, knowing Donald spoke as most of the others felt, but it infuriated her that some believed Muriel must be of questionable morals because she chose not to marry. "She is my friend," she said. "And I would caution you to remember it."

For Helen, friends were a rarity, so she valued her all the more highly. Muriel never judged her. Muriel didn't think she was odd. Perhaps because she was as "wayward" as Helen. And she didn't even have red hair as an excuse, Helen thought with a laugh.

Donald must have realized he'd gone too far. He took her hand and patted it as if she were a child. "Of course she is. She's lucky to have a loyal friend like you." He stopped, Muriel's small stone cottage having just come into view, the ruins of the old broch looming in the distance beyond. He turned and tipped her chin to him. "You know I only want what's best for you, don't you?"

Helen met his gaze, thinking his voice sounded somewhat gruff. Perhaps he was catching a chill?

She nodded uncertainly. "Aye."

He smiled, dropping her chin. "Come, don't be cross

with me." He pointed to a patch of grass along the cliff-side. "Look, a primrose! Rare this late in the season."

Helen's heart caught. The delicate purple flower native to the far north coast of Scotland stirred cruel memories.

It was a year after the first time she'd met Magnus. The games were being held at Freswick Castle that year, and she'd been weaving a chain of the beautiful purple flower that grew only along the coast of Scotland's far north when Magnus had found her. She was only fifteen, and Magnus, at twenty, had just learned that he'd drawn the unfortunate position of facing the legendary Tor MacLeod in the first round of the sword challenge. Helen knew it must have seemed impossibly daunting to a young warrior and had desperately wanted to do something to boost his spirits. She'd plucked a large primrose and pinned it to his *cotun* with one of the pins from her dress.

"A talisman," she'd said. "For luck."

His face had turned a little red, but Helen hadn't thought anything of it at the time.

It was only later when she'd caught sight of him with a group of young warriors, which included her brother Kenneth, that she realized he'd been anticipating their reaction to the flower.

"What's that, MacKay? A favor from your lady?" one of the men said.

"He must think he's a bloody English knight," someone else said.

"Or maybe it's meant for his grave," the first man countered. "MacLeod is going to kill him."

"How sweet," her brother said. "It really brings out the rosiness in your delicate complexion."

The men all laughed, and Magnus stood there taking their taunts without saying a word. She knew how proud he was and seeing him forced to endure their laughter because of her . . .

She wanted to rush over there and tear the offending

flower off his *cotun* herself. But he left it there the entire time. *To please me,* she realized. It was at that moment she knew how different he was—how special—and she'd lost her heart to him.

Her chest squeezed. How could she have been uncertain in her feelings? Why hadn't she trusted herself? How could she have been so weak and failed to seize the chance given her?

Donald dropped her hand to bend down, snapping the stem in half. Heat gathered behind her eyes as he tucked the stem behind her ear, wishing with all of her heart that he was someone else. "You look like a May Queen."

Not knowing what to say, she was glad when she heard the sound of a door opening. Seeing Muriel standing in the doorway watching them, she thanked him and hurried to join her friend.

It wasn't until much later, when she and Muriel were returning from visiting one of the crofters who had tripped on a spade and had fortunately only twisted rather than broken his ankle, that Muriel made a comment on what she'd seen. "Your brother's henchman has been around often of late."

"Donald?" Helen shrugged. "Aye, Will has him patrolling our borders to the north."

Muriel's mouth twisted as if she were trying to hold back a smile. "I very much doubt a sudden fear of raiders from the north is the cause."

Her brows furrowed. "Then why?"

Muriel shook her head, this time unable to hold back her smile. "He's wooing you, Helen."

Helen came to an abrupt stop. Her body pulled back in surprise. "Wooing me? Don't be ridiculous."

But even as she made her denial, she realized it could be true. Since William Gordon's death, she'd sensed a shift in Donald's attentions to her. He'd always been protective, but lately that protectiveness had seemed more intense. More personal. More intimate.

Muriel watched as understanding dawned.

Horror drained Helen's face. "Oh God, is it true?"

"Is the idea so unpleasant?"

Helen bit her lip. "Yes . . . No . . . I've just never thought of him that way."

She'd only thought of one man that way.

"It would not be an advantageous alliance, but it would not be a bad one either."

Helen felt the reflexive burst of panic at the thought of marriage. She knew her friend was only trying to be helpful, but she couldn't even think of marriage right now. Or maybe ever.

"You must have loved him very much," Muriel said compassionately.

"I—" She stopped, nodding as if in agreement. She *had* loved him very much, just not the man her friend thought. Though they'd spent virtually every day together since Helen had returned from Dunstaffnage, she had not confided the details of the nightmare that had been her wedding. Muriel assumed her unhappiness was the result of losing her husband. Helen's shame prevented her from confiding the truth.

They started to walk again. The square keep of the castle perched on the cliffside overlooking the kyle loomed ahead of them.

"Have you ever regretted not taking a husband?" Helen asked.

Muriel shook her head. "I love what I do, but it does not leave much time to be a wife."

"No man has ever tempted you to want both?"

With her fair hair and skin, it was impossible for Muriel to completely hide the heat that rose in her cheeks. Though she was five and twenty, her delicate features and big blue eyes gave her an appearance of a girl much younger.

"Nay," she said firmly. "I'm not sure it is possible to have two lives—one as a wife and one as a healer. And no one has ever made me an offer that I was tempted to try."

It was an odd way of phrasing it, but Helen thought of something else. "What of children? I've seen how much you love them. Do you never want any of your own?"

The look of raw pain that flashed in Muriel's eyes disappeared so quickly, Helen wondered if she'd imagined it.

Muriel looked straight ahead and shook her head. "Nay. God has given me another path. I will never have children."

There was a finality to her voice Helen didn't understand. Muriel rarely talked about her past, but Helen suspected she had one. She and her father, the famous Nicholas de Corwenne, had arrived at Dunrobin about ten years ago. It had seemed a boon to have such a venerable physician agree to move from Edinburgh to the wilds of northern Scotland—even if it was to be the personal physician of an earl. Now, Helen wondered if there had been another reason.

"And what of you, Helen? What will you do?"

The question startled her. It made it seem as though she had a choice. But women in her position had a duty to marry to further the interests of the clan. The only other "choice" was a convent. She couldn't do what she wanted, even if she knew what that was. She wanted . . . everything.

Silly lass. What was wrong with her? Why couldn't she be content with her lot like other women in her position? She had wealth and position, a family who cared about her, a man who would marry her and give her children . . . it should be enough. But the subject made her feel restless and anxious.

She shrugged. "I don't know. Stay here, I suppose, until Will marries." Though her brother was nearing his thirty-second saint's day, he still had not married. She thought Muriel stiffened at her side, but when Helen glanced over she realized she had been mistaken. "Then . . . I don't know."

"The earl is planning to marry?"

Something in her voice made Helen look at her. Was her face a little pale? She frowned. "Not that I know, but I would not be surprised if that is one of the reasons for the king's visit."

Marriage alliances were one of the ways in which the king was ensuring the support of his barons. He was fortunate to have many sisters.

They were close enough to the castle to hear the first shout go up from the guard along the wall.

"Riders approach! 'Tis the Lion Rampant!"

The king! Helen looked around to the south, seeing the dot of riders appear on the horizon. "Come," she said, gripping her friend's arm. "We must go inside to properly greet him." She looked down at her plain woolen dress, wrinkled from being tied between her legs as they stomped through the marshy heather. Instinctively, her hands went to her hair. She'd tied it haphazardly in a knot at the top of her head, but most of it had come loose.

Not much of an impression for the lady of the keep. Her appearance today would certainly encourage Will to take a wife, if that was what the king intended.

Muriel tried to beg off. "I think I will just return—"

"Nonsense," Helen said, taking her arm and pulling her alongside her. "Don't you wish to see the king?"

She didn't give her an opportunity to argue. They entered the *barmkin* just as her brothers and Donald were making their way down the stairs. Will had called Kenneth back from Skelbo, their stronghold at the mouth of Loch Fleet ten miles south, as soon as he'd received the king's message.

She saw Will stiffen as soon as he saw them. She could see his disapproval as he took in her disheveled appearance, but she knew there was more to it than that. It was Muriel. The tension in the air seemed to go up a dozen notches whenever they were together. It hadn't always been that way, she realized. But lately, Will became stiff and cold whenever she was around—even more so than usual. Saints, he could be austere and imposing!

Helen didn't understand why he'd taken such an active dislike to their healer. They were lucky to have her, and if he kept acting like this they were going to lose her.

"Good God, Helen, what have you been doing?" He ignored Muriel completely.

Helen lifted her chin, refusing to be bullied by her stern older brother. "Tending to the ankle of one of your clansmen."

He shot Muriel a glare as if this were her fault. "I'll thank you to remember that my sister has her own duties to attend." His gaze could have cut ice. "She will be lady of the keep."

Muriel flinched as if he'd struck some kind of invisible blow. "I am well aware of that, my lord."

Though there was nothing outwardly disrespectful in her tone, Helen heard it nonetheless. "This is part of my duty, as you well know, Will. Do not blame Muriel; it was I who insisted I stay when she urged me to return."

"Leave her alone, brother. She doesn't look too bad," Kenneth said. Helen suspected there was supposed to be a compliment in there somewhere. "The flower is a nice touch."

Helen felt her cheeks redden, conscious of Donald, who stood in his familiar position at Will's right shoulder.

"Aye, it looks quite fetching," Donald said with a laugh that was a little too intimate.

Helen bit her lip, realizing Muriel was right.

"They're here," Muriel whispered excitedly as the first of the mail-clad riders came streaming through the gate. It was an impressive sight: the gleaming mail and colorful tabards of the knights and men-at-arms on their enormous warhorses, carrying banners, pikes, and all manner of weapons, followed by the carts carrying the king's household plate and personal attendants. Her brother was right to have anticipated so many: there must be over fifty men.

"Is that the Bruce?" Muriel whispered.

Even were it not for the gold crown forged into his helm or the red rampant lion on the colorful yellow tabard, Helen would have known the king by the regal aura that surrounded him. She nodded.

The men started to dismount and remove their helms. She was so focused on the king that it took her a moment to realize who stood beside him.

A gasp escaped from between her lips.

"What is it?" Muriel asked, noticing her reaction.

But Helen couldn't speak. Her heart had leapt and was lodged in her throat.

Magnus! He was here. What did it mean? Was it possible . . .

Had her prayers been answered? Had he forgiven her?

Six

Helen was so happy to see him, she forgot everything and everyone else around her. For a moment it was one of those times years ago when she'd been hiding, and he'd caught her by surprise. Her heart jumped in an excited burst, and she almost yelped in girlish pleasure. Unconsciously, she took a step toward him. "You're here!"

Magnus turned at the sound of her voice. Their eyes met, and all at once she realized her mistake. The smile fell from her face, her hopes crushed before they'd a chance to rise. Whatever reason Magnus was here, it wasn't for her. He was looking at her aghast, as if he would rather be anywhere but here, as if she'd done something to . . .

Suddenly, she looked around, realizing the men had stopped talking and everyone was staring at her.

Heat crawled up her face as she realized the cause for that look. She'd embarrassed him. Again. Although this time, she was old enough to know better.

The king came to her rescue. Robert Bruce gave her a courtly bow, as if he were the one to whom she'd been speaking. "And it's nice to be here after so long on the road. I thank you for your gracious welcome, Lady Helen. I hope we have not put you to too much trouble?"

She shook her head like a simpleton, too embarrassed to manage more than something like "of course not."

But the king had earned her undying gratitude with his gallantry. She'd been impressed with "the Bruce," as his men called him, at Dunstaffnage. It wasn't hard to see why so many had been willing to risk so much to rally to his banner. A gallant knight in the prime of his manhood, a formidable warrior and shrewd commander, Bruce was good-natured, charming, and charismatic. Her brothers (and most of Christendom) had not believed it possible to best Edward of England. The Bruce had proved them wrong.

"We are honored to have you, Sire," Will said with more graciousness than she would have thought possible. A year ago, the two men had been facing each other across a battlefield. But her eldest brother was pragmatic and would not let his considerable pride stand in the way of doing what was best for his clan. If that meant making friends with his former enemy, he would do it. Grudgingly.

With one former enemy, at least.

Her brothers did not hide their animosity when they saw Magnus. Will and Kenneth, as well as Donald, all looked ready to draw their swords. The challenging look Magnus was giving them wasn't helping matters any. He was just as bad as they were. The feud ran deep between the two clans. It was difficult to push aside years of hatred, distrust, and suspicion. But she prayed that day would come. Unfortunately, it wasn't today.

Helen stepped forward to defuse the tension, presenting Muriel to the king, a few of the other knights standing nearby, and Magnus.

Unable to avoid it, he nodded stiffly in her direction after greeting Muriel. "My lady."

His curtness hurt. She looked at him, willing something from him that was no longer there.

"Your arm," she said. "It has healed well?"

Their eyes met, and for an instant he was her Magnus again, looking at her with his soft caramel-brown eyes full of the gentleness and tenderness that she'd always taken for granted.

"Aye," he said gruffly. "It's as good as new."

"What he means is 'thank you.'" Another man came forward. When he removed his helm, she gasped in surprise. Gregor MacGregor took her hand and bowed. "Lady Helen, I'm delighted to see you again."

Helen beamed at him, her eyes pricking with heat. Six months ago, he'd been close to death. But look at him! And the change was because of her. "As I am you, my lord. You are well?"

He gave her a roguish grin that would fell half of the hearts of Scotland—the female half. Helen was not immune, and her heart skipped a little beat. Gregor MacGregor was the most dazzlingly handsome man she'd ever seen, with his bronzed skin, golden-brown hair, sparkling white teeth, brilliant blue eyes, and divinely chiseled features that even Adonis would envy. Tall, broad-shouldered, and muscular, he looked ready to take his place on Mount Olympus.

"Very well, my lady. Thanks to you." His expression sobered for a moment. "I owe you my life. If there is anything I can ever do for you, you have but to ask."

Helen blushed, both pleased and embarrassed. To cover her embarrassment, she introduced Muriel. "Lady Muriel is the best healer in the North. She has taught me everything I know."

Gregor flashed one of those gorgeous grins in the direction of her friend, who seemed to be in something of a stunned trance. Helen could hardly blame her. Gregor MacGregor tended to have that effect.

"My lady," he said, bowing over her hand. He looked back and forth between the two women. "Had I healers as beautiful as you, I should have always been ill." His magnificently blue eyes actually twinkled when he smiled. "In fact, I have every intention of coming down with a chill while I'm here."

Helen giggled like a simpering maid and was surprised to hear her serious friend doing the same.

"Helen," her brother Will said sharply, causing her to startle. From his dark expression, she gathered Will was annoyed with her again. Except he was looking at Muriel. "The king has had a long journey."

Her cheeks burned at the reminder of her duty. "Of course. I shall show you to your chamber, Sire, and send some wine and bread with cheese before the evening meal."

"That sounds perfect," the king said, trying to ease her discomfort once again.

Magnus, who also looked irritated for some reason, and a few of the other men started to follow, but Will stepped in front of him to block him.

He addressed Bruce, not Magnus. "Munro will show the rest of your party to the barracks. I'm sure they will be quite comfortable there."

"I'm sure they will," Magnus said calmly. "But we go with the king." He didn't bother to hide his amusement, lifting a brow with a not-so-subtle taunt. "I assume there isn't a problem with me staying in the tower?"

Will, Kenneth, and Donald all glanced in her direction. They weren't much for subtlety either. Will's jaw was clenched so tightly, she was surprised he could talk. "Nay," he managed. "No problem."

Why did Helen suspect one of them would be sleeping outside her door?

"Glad to hear it," Magnus said. "I shall look forward to partaking of the famous Sutherland hospitality."

Will, trying not to choke on the sarcasm, let him pass.

Helen sighed, leading the king and a few of his men— including Magnus—into the tower. She had no doubt that the king's stay was going to be filled with tension between her brothers and Magnus. But she didn't care. She wasn't going to let her family interfere. Not this time.

She knew why her future had looked murky when she was talking to Muriel earlier. She couldn't imagine one that didn't include Magnus. He was the only thing that had ever made any sense to her.

He was here, and she intended to do everything in her power to do what she'd failed to do before: fight for him. The king's missive had said he planned to stay two weeks. She wasn't going to waste one minute of that time.

She would seize every day. Even if he could barely look at her.

Magnus was at war.

With himself.

In the middle of the damned feast.

From where he was seated, he couldn't avoid looking at the couple . . .

Munro put his hand on Helen's arm, and Magnus nearly shot off the bench. The urge to slam his fist into the smug bastard's jaw was almost overwhelming.

He clenched his teeth, trying to ignore them. But it was impossible. Which was probably intentional. No doubt this torturous seat was Sutherland retribution.

Magnus might have forced his way into the tower, but the Sutherlands had seated him as far away from Helen as they could without giving offense. His position as the king's personal bodyguard and henchman earned him a place on the dais, but he was at the far end of the table while Helen was near the middle, seated between the king and Munro. Giving him a perfect view . . .

The Sutherland henchman leaned over and whispered something in Helen's ear that made her smile.

God's blood! Magnus tamped down the flare of anger with a long drink of ale. One week. Thank God it had taken them longer to leave Kildrummy than anticipated, and that was all of *this* he would have to endure.

It hadn't taken him long to realize what was happening. Munro obviously had decided that Gordon's death had opened the bloody floodgates to include him as a potential suitor for Helen.

The irony was not lost on him. The man who Magnus had made a hurdle to conquer before he could ask Helen to marry him now thought to marry her himself.

Magnus clenched his jaw. Oh, it was ironic all right.

But why the hell was he letting this bother him? He should be glad of it. Whatever else he thought of Munro, he couldn't fault his warrior's skills. Munro would protect her. He would keep her safe, and Magnus would have no reason to feel guilty. A husband would absolve him of his promise to Gordon. There was probably no cause for concern as it was. Gordon's identity as a member of the Highland Guard hadn't been compromised.

But Munro, damn it. He couldn't stand the thought of them—

"Is everything to your liking, my lord?"

Hell no! Magnus stopped the thought from becoming words and turned to the woman seated to his left. Realizing he was scowling, he forced a smile to his face. "Aye, thank you, Lady Muriel. Everything is delicious."

It was the truth. However awkward their arrival yesterday, Helen had acquitted herself well as hostess today. The feast was magnificent, offering nothing to find fault with the young lady of the keep.

He wasn't surprised. Helen's enthusiasm and *joie de vivre* were contagious. She made every day feel like a feast day. A prized quality for a chatelaine. Ironically, the role had never seemed to interest her much. But she'd matured.

In some ways.

But when he thought of yesterday, the way her face had lit up with happiness when she'd seen him, how she'd blurted out the first thought in her head, it was exactly how she'd been as a girl.

She'd even looked like the Helen he remembered. Her fiery auburn hair pinned haphazardly atop her head, her skirts muddy and wrinkled. Hell, he'd even noticed a few freckles smattered across her nose. And that smile . . .

It had lit up her whole face.

His chest grew tight. Damn it. Did she have to wear her emotions so plainly? Why couldn't she be a little circumspect just once?

But that wasn't her. It never had been. Helen's openness was one of the first things he loved—

He stopped the thought. He *had* loved about her.

"Don't mind him," MacGregor said from Lady Muriel's other side. "Surliness is part of his charm." He grinned. "I blame it on the arm."

The lady immediately grew concerned. "Helen spoke of your injury. The bones in the arm, especially near the shoulder, can cause pain for a long time—"

"I'm fine," Magnus said with a glare to MacGregor. "The bones have healed well. Lady Helen did a fine job. You've taught your pupil well."

She shook her head, a wry smile curving her mouth. "Helen gives me too much credit. She is a natural healer—her instincts are pure. Her optimism is a great gift for a healer; it helps her get through the difficult times. She has an unusual aptitude for what I call blood and gore—the trade of a barber surgeon on the battlefield. My father would have been beside himself. I was a much slower learner."

Magnus held her gaze. "Aye, I've seen what you speak of. She has a gift."

He could tell she wanted to question him further, but politeness prevented her from doing so. "I will give Helen something to rub on your arm after you—"

Good God! "Nay!"

The thought of Helen's hands on him . . .

He'd been in too much pain to notice when she'd treated his wounds, but the memories were enough to drive him mad. In the middle of the night, when his thoughts had nowhere to hide.

When his body grew tight, hot, and hard. Painfully hard.

Lady Muriel's eyes widened at the intensity of his reaction.

The blood had leeched from his face, but returned quickly when he realized how loudly he'd spoken. A number of eyes were turned in his direction, especially those on the dais.

MacGregor was staring at him with a strange expression on his face—as if he'd just made a connection Magnus didn't want him to make.

"Thank you, my lady," he said, attempting to smooth the gaffe. "That isn't necessary."

She nodded, eyeing him cautiously.

He'd scared her, he realized. Feeling like an arse, he would have attempted to put her at ease, but MacGregor had already drawn the lass's attention back to him—where in Magnus's experience it was likely to stay. Once MacGregor let his interest be known in a lass, it wasn't often that it wasn't returned.

The healer wasn't as flamboyantly beautiful and young as the women MacGregor usually flirted with, but she was pretty in a reserved fashion. And she seemed to be enjoying the attention. He heard her laugh at something no doubt outrageous that MacGregor whispered in her ear.

But Magnus made the mistake of turning his head and caught Munro doing the same thing to Helen. Their blasted shoulders were touching.

Magnus's fist clenched his goblet. He fought the reflexive surge of anger and forced his gaze away, only to meet that of another.

Kenneth Sutherland was watching him, and if his narrowed gaze was any indication, he hadn't missed Magnus's reaction. But instead of the taunting smile that Magnus expected, Sutherland appeared surprised, apparently noticing for the first time what had taken Magnus only a few minutes to conclude: Munro wanted Helen.

And Sutherland didn't look happy about it.

Magnus recalled that he hadn't been the only one to suffer the sting of Munro's arrogant taunts and humiliations. Sutherland had as well. Probably more so, since Magnus had only had the misfortune of seeing Munro at the Highland Games.

They might not agree about anything else, but apparently he and Sutherland were of one mind when it came to Donald Munro.

It was damned unsettling. He didn't like to think he and Sutherland had anything in common.

Although, of course, there had been Gordon. Sutherland was the friend of his boyhood and Magnus of his manhood. Magnus tried not to think about it.

He returned his attention to the conversation next to him. The healer and his friend were talking about MacGregor's miraculous arrow. That particular battle wound had already earned the famed archer an endless supply of feminine appreciation. Lady Muriel, however, was more sophisticated than his usual audience. Rather than ooh and ah, and flutter her eyelashes at him as if every word from his mouth were gilded, she told him that he was very lucky in the Englishman's aim.

"What is the most dangerous surgery that you've performed?" MacGregor asked her.

Lady Muriel paused for a minute, considering. When Helen did that, she had a tendency to bite her lip.

He was doing it again, damn it.

"It was about a year ago, after the battle at Barra Hill."

"You were there?" Magnus asked, surprised. Though it wasn't uncommon for a tent or castle near the battle site to be set aside to tend the wounded, he wouldn't have thought a man of Lord Nicholas de Corwenne's repute would allow his daughter to be so close to danger.

Barra Hill had been one of the most deadly battles in Bruce's war. He'd chased John Comyn, Earl of Buchan, from the battlefield and laid waste to the countryside with thoroughness that was still talked about today. It would be some time before the "hership of Buchan" was forgotten.

"Aye, my father usually brought me along when he was attending the earl. He believed the best learning was done by experience. He was right." Her eyes grew distant and a wistful smile played upon her lips. He could tell she was remembering her father fondly. He must have died not long ago, Magnus realized.

"What happened?" MacGregor asked.

"A man took a war hammer to the head, breaking a bone in his skull and causing blood to build up underneath. I had to bore a small hole into his skull to relieve the pressure."

"He survived?" MacGregor asked.

She nodded. "He returned to his wife and five children with a dent in his head and a story to tell."

Crushed skulls were a common injury in battle, Magnus knew. As was trepanning, the method to treat them. It just wasn't often that it was a success.

"A fine feast, Lady Helen," the king said loudly, drawing their attention to the center of the table. "Your brother is fortunate to have a sister who is not only a skilled healer but also an admirable chatelaine."

Helen dimpled with pleasure at the praise, her flawless ivory skin tinged a becoming pink. "Thank you, Sire."

Bruce returned her smile. "Though perhaps your brother won't be calling upon those skills much longer."

Magnus knew of what Bruce spoke, but Munro did not. Assuming the king spoke of Helen's marriage, the Sutherland henchman stiffened with offense. Munro hid it well, but Magnus was watching him carefully and saw the flare of barely concealed animosity leveled at the king. Magnus knew exactly how much the proud warrior must hate to have to bow to his enemy—he would hate it, too.

"The lady has suffered a recent loss," Munro said pointedly, a protective hand on her arm that Magnus wanted to rip off.

"I'm well aware of the lady's loss," the king said sharply. "But Lady Helen wasn't of whom I spoke." His gaze slid to the earl.

Sir William didn't seem surprised by the king's suggestion, but the tight smile on his face indicated it was not a welcome one. For some reason, the earl's gaze flickered to Magnus's. Nay, not his, he realized, but to Lady Muriel's. But she didn't notice, as her head was down-turned and her gaze fixed on her lap. He'd noticed the tension between the earl and the healer on their arrival, but he wondered if there was something more to it. From the death glare the earl was shooting at MacGregor, Magnus suspected there was.

"There will be plenty of time over the next week to discuss such matters." Having planted his seed, Bruce changed the subject. "Lady Helen, I believe you said there would be dancing?"

Helen nodded, looking troubled. "Aye, my lord." She motioned for the pipers and harpist to ready. "But a week? I understood you would be at Dunrobin a fortnight."

Magnus pretended not to notice that her gaze kept flickering to him.

"Aye, that was our original intention, but we were delayed in leaving Kildrummy and thus must shorten our stay. I've many stops to make before the Games at Dunstaffnage. I hope that you will be attending this year, Sir William?"

It was more of a command than an invitation. The earl gave a short nod. "Aye, my men are looking forward to it."

"Very much," Munro added. "After four years without a

new champion, the men are eager to take their rightful place."

Magnus didn't react to the challenge that he knew had been issued to him. Munro's defeat had been festering for four years; he would want to come after Magnus with everything he had.

"A rather bold boast, Munro, given the level of competition." The king's gaze met Magnus's; he was obviously amused. "I hope your men are prepared to defend your words?"

"More than prepared," Munro said with his usual arrogance.

"Will you be competing, my lord?" Helen asked.

Magnus realized she was speaking to him.

He was forced to look at her. Their eyes met. He knew exactly what she was thinking about. The same thing he was thinking about. What had happened the last time he'd competed. How he'd foolishly thought she'd wanted the same thing he did. How he'd handed her his heart, and she'd thrown it back in his face.

"I'm sorry." He heard her words again. *"I can't . . ."*

His mouth tightened, and he shook his head. "Nay, my duties will not permit it this year."

None of the Highland Guard would be competing. Bruce and MacLeod thought it would invite too many comparisons and questions.

"Oh," Helen said softly. "I'm sorry to hear that."

Munro's gaze bit into him like acid. He put his hand over Helen's. The fact that she didn't look very happy about the possessive gesture didn't do anything to calm the blood surging to Magnus's temples.

"Perhaps MacKay is not so anxious to lose his crown?" Munro said. "If he quits now, he will never be forced to give it up."

The slur demanded retribution. Magnus knew it as well as Munro did. He wanted Magnus to challenge him. And

Magnus would have liked nothing better than to give him
his wish. But Bruce prevented him. "I believe your henchman is still sensitive about his last loss, Sir William," the
king said with a laugh. "As I recall, MacKay beat you
rather handily, didn't he?"

Munro's face turned an unhealthy shade of red. Before
he could respond, Helen stood. "Come, the music is starting."

Helen barely managed to avert disaster by leading
Donald in the first reel. For a moment, she thought he
might challenge the king himself. Will had been so relieved,
he'd actually shot her a look of gratitude.

But no sooner had the dance ended than she threaded her
way back through the crowd of celebrating clansmen to
find Magnus.

One week! How was she supposed to win him back in
one week?

It seemed impossible, especially with the way he'd been
looking at her during the meal. It was as if she'd done
something wrong. Made yet another mistake. She'd wanted
to impress him in her temporary role as lady, and instead
she felt as if she'd done something to anger him. She'd
thought everything had gone so well. Donald had been a
bit of a bother, but it was nothing she couldn't handle.

She returned to the dais, finding the table empty. Taking
advantage of the raised platform, she looked around the
room. Her brothers were standing with the king and a few
of his knights near the enormous fireplace watching the
dancers while the servants kept their goblets full. The rogue
MacGregor had convinced Muriel to join him on the dance
floor, but Magnus was nowhere to be seen. She scanned the
room again.

Her heart dropped when she finally found him. He was
near the entry to the Hall with his back toward her, looking
as if he'd been about to leave. But his path had been

blocked. By Donald. She didn't need to hear what he was saying to know that it wasn't good. Every muscle in Magnus's body was coiled and ready to strike.

She muttered Kenneth's favorite oath under her breath. Good lord, she'd barely left them alone for a few minutes, and they were going at each other's throats again!

Keeping the peace between her family and Magnus was going to take all of her effort. How was she going to find time to convince Magnus to give her another chance? To prove to him that she'd changed?

By the time she made it across the Hall, the men had disappeared. Seeing Donald's dark auburn head winding through the crowd toward the fireplace, she dashed out of the Hall into the corridor that had been built to connect the Hall to the donjon, catching sight of Magnus just as he entered the stairwell.

"Magnus!"

Her heart squeezed when he stiffened at the sound of her voice. Very slowly, like a man preparing for battle, he turned around.

She hurried toward him, trying to think of what she was going to say. Especially when he looked so . . .

She bit her lip. *Forbidding.*

Her pulse spiked and a shiver spread over her skin. The big, fearsome warrior wasn't the strapping youth of her memories. The contrast was unsettling, and she had to remind herself this was the same young warrior she'd given her heart to—just with a lot more muscle and a few more scars.

She came to a sudden stop before him, winded from racing to catch up with him. Flustered, she fumbled with her skirts. "Is everything all right . . . um, with the king's rooms?"

"Everything is fine," he said brusquely. "Return to your guests, Helen."

She stared up at him, not knowing what to do—how to

reach him. How to penetrate this icy wall he'd built between them. "But don't you want to dance?"

She'd always dreamed of dancing with him, but the feud had always prevented it.

A strange look crossed his face. "Nay, but I'm sure you won't have difficulty in finding someone who does."

She frowned, puzzled by his tone.

She placed her hand on his arm, feeling a pinch in her chest when he flinched. "Don't you remember? You said one day you'd be proud to lead me out in a reel, and no one would be able to stop you."

"I was a boy," he said, shrugging her off. "I said a lot of things I didn't mean." He gave her a pointed look. "We both did."

"Why are you acting like this? Why are you acting as if there was never anything between us?"

"Why are you acting as if there still is?"

She sucked in her breath, feeling as if he'd hit her square in the chest.

Something in her stricken expression must have moved him. The tension seemed to ease out of his rigid muscles. He raked his fingers through his hair the way he'd used to do when he was frustrated. "I don't want to hurt you, Helen."

She gazed up at him, her eyes filling with tears. "Then why are you?"

"Because what you want . . . the way you are looking at me . . . it's not possible."

"Why—?"

"Helen!"

She cursed under her breath, hearing her brother Will's voice behind her.

But she didn't turn; she kept her gaze on Magnus, watching as his mouth fell in a hard line. "Do you need to ask?"

Her family? Was that what he meant?

"Helen!"

Hearing the sharpness in his voice, she whirled around in frustration, seeing Will's furious face glaring at her. "Where is she? Did you see her?"

She blinked. "Who?"

"Never mind," he said, stomping off in the direction of the courtyard.

Whoever she was, Helen felt sorry for her. Her imposing brother looked ready to kill someone.

For once it wasn't Magnus. But when she looked back around, she realized why. Magnus was no longer standing there.

Seven

❧

Muriel raced out of the Hall the moment the dance was over.

Oh God, oh God, oh God! The desperate plea echoed through her head.

Married.

Her step faltered as a wave of hurt heaved inside her, filling her chest and pressing against the back of her eyes before she could push it back again.

No! She would not cry for him. He did not deserve her tears.

But *married*?

A dry, burning sob shuddered through her. Why did it have to hurt so much? How could she have let this happen? She knew better. She was no wide-eyed innocent that believed in happy endings and faerie tales. Her eyes had been opened to the cruelty and unfairness of the world a long time ago. She'd never wanted to lose her heart to a man. She hadn't thought it possible.

She'd chosen a different path.

It wasn't fair. Hadn't she suffered enough?

"Muriel!"

God, no! She ran faster. Out of the gate. Beyond the realm of his power.

But he'd never been one to show restraint. "Damn it, Muriel." He grabbed her arm, jerking her to a stop. "By God, you will listen to me."

She bristled, pain turning to anger. She hated when he talked to her like that. The cool, imperious Earl of Sutherland to her insignificant minion.

How could this stern, harsh man have won her heart?

Because he wasn't always like this. In those rare, unguarded moments, he could be funny and tender and passionate and—

"*I love you, Muriel.*" But not enough. She caught her heart and forced it back into position. In her chest, not in the clouds.

Lifting her chin, she met his gaze. "Do not touch me."

Never again would she give him the right to touch her.

If only the memories were so easy to push away.

He dropped her arm, something in her tone penetrating his icy fury. He was the one person left in this world to know exactly why a man's forceful touch was so repugnant to her.

Trying to maintain as much of her dignity as she could, she resisted the urge to walk away and faced him. "Was there something you wanted?"

His eyes narrowed at her cool, indifferent tone. "I did not object when my sister seated you at the dais." She tried not to flinch, but the cruel reminder of their different stations stung. His face darkened, oblivious or uncaring of the pain he caused her. "But I will not have my Hall turned into a bordello."

She was so shocked, she didn't know what to say. She could only stare at the handsome face of the man who now seemed a distorted stranger to her. What he insinuated wasn't possible—not for the man she'd known.

How had it come to this? How had something so wonderful become so twisted?

Because she hadn't given him what he wanted?

"You'll have to forgive me," she said stiffly, trying to hold on to the shreds of her flagging dignity. "I do not understand to what you refer!"

He leaned closer, his dark-blue eyes flashing with a dangerous emotion she didn't recognize. "I refer to the way you conducted yourself with a guest in my house."

It took her a moment. "Do you mean Gregor MacGregor?" she burst out in astonishment.

His mouth tightened.

A gurgle of laughter rose inside her. The idea was so ridiculous. MacGregor was a handsome rogue, and she'd been flattered by his attentions, but it had never crossed her mind—

She gasped, understanding striking like lightning. *He's jealous.* This man who'd shredded her heart to pieces was jealous. That was why he was acting like this.

He was a fool. An arse *and* a fool.

She drew up all the hurt he'd caused her into a ball of disdain. He didn't deserve another moment of her time. He'd made his choice, and she'd made hers. "Next time I shall be more circumspect."

She turned, dismissing him, and started to walk away.

But he stopped her, latching her arm again. "You aren't going to deny it?"

If she weren't so angry, she would have laughed at his boyishly incredulous tone. Her heart pounded, but she refused to look down at the hand wrapped around her arm. Refused to let him know how much it affected her. How she could feel the imprint of his fingers burning into her skin. How the hairs on her arms stood on end. How with every fiber of her being she wanted to curl against his powerful chest and let those arms wrap around her one more time. How her lips burned with the memory of his kiss.

"I love you, Muriel." She heard the voice in her head again, but shut it down.

"I do not believe I have to explain myself to you. You are not my chief, my father, or . . ." *My husband.* Her chest squeezed. She drew a deep, ragged breath. "I do not answer to you."

She should have known better than to challenge the power of a powerful man. Sir William, Earl of Sutherland, didn't like being denied. His eyes flared dangerously, not unlike his hot-tempered brother's. "While you reside on my land, you will answer to me." His voice was as unyielding as steel, with no room for disagreement.

"Is that what you are going to do, bend me to your will? Would it make you feel better to have me under your thumb where you can control me? I would not give you what you want, so now you will bully me and order me about?"

"Jesus." He dropped her arm as if she'd scalded him. "Of course not."

For a moment she saw a glimpse of self-loathing before the cold, imperious mask dropped back into place.

They stared at one another in the fading daylight. The powerful man who wasn't used to being denied and the insignificant woman who'd dared to deny him.

"I do not want you spending so much time with my sister," he said after a moment. "It is . . ." He stopped. "It might give her the wrong ideas."

How easy it was for him to hurt her. He didn't even have to try. A few carelessly uttered words and she was skewered. How could he claim to love her, if he didn't respect her?

The strength left her. She sagged, the fight gone out of her. Her voice barely rose above a whisper. "Just because you think I'm a whore doesn't make it true."

He swore, his icy facade cracking like the surface of a pond in the spring. "God's blood, Muriel, I don't think you are a whore."

"No, you just wanted me to be your leman. A home, jewels, a lifetime of security, isn't that how you put it?

Everything I could wish for." *Except for the one thing that mattered.* She looked up at him, this time unable to blink back the tears that slid down her cheeks. "You know the irony, Will? You didn't need to make me your whore, I would have given you everything you wanted for free."

She'd loved him so much. He'd learned the worst, and miraculously, had returned that love. She'd never thought it was possible. She would have given him anything. But then he'd ruined it.

He stiffened. "I wouldn't dishonor you—"

She laughed then. The reasoning of men was such an anathema to her. Taking what she offered of her own free will was dishonorable, but setting her up in the position of his leman was not? Could he not see how badly his offer had hurt her? He'd put a name on what they had together and made it ugly.

"Damn it, Muriel. I'm an earl. I have a duty." A tortured look crossed his face, a glimpse of the emotion that he kept so well hidden. So much so that she almost forgot it was there. "What else could I do?"

I can't marry you. I need a son.

The unspoken words passed between them. It was wrong of her to want something that was impossible. She knew it. But she couldn't stop the longing.

"Nothing," she said. "As you said, you are an earl and I'm . . ." Her voice dropped off. *I'm flawed. Damaged.*

She couldn't look at him again. The reality of what could never be hurt too much.

This time when she turned to leave, he did not stop her.

I can't do this, she thought. *I can't stay here and watch him marry someone else. It will kill me.*

Muriel returned to the cottage that had become her home. The home that had been a place of refuge from the depths of hell. The place where she'd healed.

But this healing place was a refuge no longer. She had to leave before it became a prison.

Eight

❧

Helen couldn't have heard her right. She stared at Muriel in stunned disbelief. "You are leaving? But why?"

Muriel stopped placing her belongings in the wooden trunk long enough to look up at her, a wry smile on her mouth. "I thought you of all people would understand. Haven't you been urging me to accept the Earl of Ross's offer of patronage for the past year?"

Muriel was right. Every since she'd mentioned Ross's offer to help her enter the Physicians Guild in Inverness, made after he'd seen her skill following the Battle of Barra, Helen had been encouraging her to try—despite the certain resistance because of her being a woman. "Aye, but you said you didn't need the approval of a group of old men to make you a better healer. What changed your mind?"

"My mind was never made up." Muriel sat on a bench near the largest window in the cottage and drew Helen down beside her. Sun streamed through the open shutter, catching her blond hair in a bright halo of light. "When we were talking the other day, I realized I was allowing my fear of what might happen prevent me from taking a chance. But I shall never know whether they will accept me until I try."

Helen bit her lip, seeing the determination on her friend's

face and imagining some of the difficulties she would face. "They would be fools not to welcome you with open arms." Her eyes shimmered with unshed tears. "I've admired you for years, Muriel, but never more so than right now."

With a tremulous smile and misty eyes, Muriel took her hand. "You have been a good friend to me, Helen. I—I shall miss you." She stood, brushing aside the wave of emotion with an overly bright smile. "But if I do not finish my packing, I shall miss my cart."

Helen glanced at the two leather bags on the bare mattress and the large wooden trunk packed almost to the rim with the rest of Muriel's household belongings. "Must you leave so soon?"

"Aye, if I don't want to carry all this myself. It was my good fortune that old Tom could squeeze me in amongst the woolen cloth that he is taking to market."

"I'm sure Will could find some guardsmen to accompany you at a later—"

"Nay!" Muriel cried. Realizing she'd overreacted, she said, "I am eager to begin. Besides, long farewells have never been one of my fortes. It will be better this way, trust me."

Helen frowned, seeing how upset her friend looked. There was something wrong. Something going on beyond Muriel's desire to attempt to enter a guild. She was eager to leave, Helen realized, but why?

Helen watched Muriel finish her packing, still stunned by the sudden turn of events. She was torn: proud of her friend but selfishly not wanting her to go. "What will we do without you?"

Muriel shook her head, her smile no longer strained. "You don't need me anymore, Helen. You haven't for a long time. You are more than capable of taking care of your clansmen on your own."

A wave of trepidation rolled over her. "Do you think so?"

"I know so."

Despite her friend's confidence, Helen wasn't so sure. The role and responsibility seemed daunting. But it was also, she had to admit, exciting. Something about it felt right. Almost. "Will won't be happy. He thought I was spending too much time tending to the clansmen as it was. What did he say when you told him?"

Muriel had her back to her. When she spoke, her voice had an odd tightness to it. "I . . . I haven't told him. The earl has been busy with the king, and I did not wish to interfere. I hoped that you might tell him for me?"

Helen couldn't blame her. There'd been something bothering Will for the past few days—since she'd seen him in the corridor during the feast. Had she not been seeking any opportunity to see Magnus, Helen would have been attempting to avoid her irritable brother as well. Not that she'd had much luck in that regard. It seemed that except for meals—where Magnus took care to avoid her— the men had been locked in her brother's solar for the past two days. Focused on Magnus, and her quickly disappearing time, she hadn't given much thought to her brother's poor humor. But she suspected it was a result of their discussions.

"Will has been distracted with all the talk of his marriage," Helen said.

Muriel appeared to flinch. Her narrow shoulders trembled as she paused in her packing. "It has been decided, then?"

Helen shook her head, watching her closely. "Not formally. But according to Kenneth, the king has offered his twice-widowed sister Christina as a bride once she is released from the convent in England. An alliance my brother would be hard pressed to refuse even should he wish to."

"And why would he wish to."

It wasn't a question but a statement. There was something vaguely unsettling about Muriel's dull voice. For a moment, Helen wondered—

No. It wasn't possible.

She frowned, the idea refusing to let go. "I'm sure he would wish to know of your leaving. Will owes you so much for what you have done—we all do. But I will tell him, if that is what you wish."

Muriel turned around to face her, and the calm evenness of her expression relieved some of Helen's fears. "Thank you. I've been happy here, Helen. After my father died, you and your family made a place for me. I owe you much for that. I will never forget it."

"You will always have a place here," Helen said. "Promise me you will come back if Inverness is not to your liking."

Muriel smiled, knowing what she meant. "I promise, but I am not easily intimidated. Especially by a group of cantankerous old men. But you must promise me something as well."

Curious, Helen nodded.

"Don't let anyone force you down a path you do not wish to take. If you have a chance at happiness, take it. No matter what anyone says."

The intensity of her words made Helen wonder how much of the truth her friend had guessed.

A wry smile curved her lips. "You do realize what you are advocating is tantamount to heresy. As a woman—a noblewoman in particular—I have no path other than that which is chosen for me. Duty has very little concern for my happiness."

"But you don't really believe in that, do you?"

Helen shook her head. Perhaps that was her tragedy. She sought a life of happiness in a world that did not value such emotion.

"I almost forgot." Muriel crossed the short distance from the bed to the kitchen. The stone cottage was warm and cozy, but small—perhaps ten feet by twenty. The bed was built into the far wall. In the middle there was a table, bench, and chair set out before the brazier. At the other end was the small kitchen. Muriel reached up on one of the open shelves and pulled down a small pot. "Take this," she said.

Helen pulled off the lid and sniffed, smelling the strong scent of camphor. Though it was usually used for sweets, Muriel's father had learned from an old crusader that the Infidels used it to relieve aches. "A muscle salve?"

Muriel nodded. "It might help. MacGregor mentioned that MacKay's arm was still giving him some pain. I was going to bring it to him, but I thought perhaps you would like to instead?"

Helen stared at her, knowing Muriel had guessed quite a lot. Including how desperately she'd been trying to find a way to see him. "What if he doesn't want it?"

What if he doesn't want me?

Muriel gave her a solemn look. "Then you'll have to convince him he does."

Helen nodded. If only it were so simple.

After two long days of being locked in a room with three men it had been Magnus's duty to despise since the day he was born—who made that duty bloody easy on him—it felt damned good to be outside with a sword in his hands again.

Two days of listening to the earl find countless ways to avoid committing to an alliance by diversion, excuse, or condition, of enduring the endless questions by the surprisingly tenacious Kenneth Sutherland about the circumstances of Gordon's death, and of pretending he didn't hear Munro's barely concealed slurs had taken its toll. Magnus was ready to take off someone's head. As the truce made that impossible, he settled for a good, hard sword practice in the yard.

With MacGregor standing watch by the king, who had uncharacteristically retired to his chamber to rest rather than join Sir William and his men falconing, it was left to Sir Neil Campbell—Ranger's eldest brother—to help Magnus get the lead out of his muscles and exorcise the demons from his blood.

Exorcising one particular demon had proved harder than he'd anticipated. Being near Helen, seeing her every day, even if only from across the dais, stirred painful memories, reminding him of feelings he wanted to forget and proving far more of a temptation than it should.

He'd loved her once with his entire soul. Though that love had been crushed, vestiges of it still remained. A laugh would remind him of an afternoon spent sitting in the grass, watching as she plucked flowers for a chain—he could almost feel the warmth of her hair on his shoulder; a mischievous smile would remind him of how she'd used to try to hide from him, making it a game to find her; an absent tuck of an errant strand of hair behind her ear would remind him of the day she'd showed up with her hair chopped around her face so it wouldn't get in her eyes.

Style and fashion were irrelevant when it came to practicalities. If her skirts dragged in the mud or got in the way of her climbing, she tied them up without thought or artifice. How could he not have been enchanted?

There had been only a dozen or so meetings between them, but every minute had been firmly imprinted on his mind. No matter how many times he told himself she'd changed, that even if he thought he'd known the girl he did not know the woman, he couldn't force himself to believe it. The things he'd fallen in love with—her openness, her verve for life and thirst for happiness, her strength and passion—were still there.

But she was no longer his to love.

He drove the venerable knight back in a relentless attack, putting all his anger and frustration behind every swing of the sword.

Though Sir Neil was one of Bruce's greatest knights, he had trouble keeping up with Magnus today.

When one particularly violent swing landed a little too firmly, the other man put down his sword. "Damn, MacKay. Take it easy. I'm on your side."

Magnus lowered his sword, the heaviness of his breath and pain in his shoulder telling him exactly how hard he'd been going.

God's bones, it felt good!

He smiled. "All this peace has made you soft, old man. Perhaps I can find a nice Englishman for you to practice with?"

"Bloody hell, I'll show you soft." The knight attacked, coming damn close to taking Magnus's mind off his problems.

Until the source of those problems appeared out of the corner of his eye, distracting him just enough to suffer a blow to his arm—his bad arm.

He swore as the flat of the steel landed with full force on his exposed shoulder, causing his sword to fall from his hand.

Campbell looked stunned. It wasn't often Magnus gave an opponent an opening like that, and to be the recipient of such a lapse surprised him. "Christ! Sorry about that. Did I hurt your shoulder?"

As Magnus was grabbing the offending shoulder he could hardly deny it. "Just give me a moment," he said, furious at himself.

But it only got worse. Helen rushed up to him, putting her hand on his arm and setting off every nerve-ending he'd fought so hard to contain. "Oh Magnus, are you all right? Your arm—"

"My arm is fine," he lied, his arm stinging as sharply as his pride. "What do you want?"

Campbell had moved away, but Magnus could feel him watching with unabashed interest.

"I didn't mean to disturb you."

Her cheeks heated when he didn't say anything, but just continued to scowl at her. Summer was less than two weeks away, but she looked as fresh and sunny as a warm summer day. With her fair skin, blue eyes, and dark red hair, yellow shouldn't look so good on her. But the buttery shade brought out the warmth of her complexion, and made him think of bread fresh from the oven that he couldn't wait to sink his teeth into.

Damn.

He apparently growled.

She took a step back, eyeing him uncertainly. "Muriel gave me some salve for your arm. She said it might be giving you some pain."

It sure as hell was now. For a man who was known for his even-keeled temperment, he sure was having trouble keeping a grip on it right now. "Please thank Lady Muriel for her thoughtfulness, but—"

"If you like," she interrupted, "I could rub some on you when you are finished. Or if you'd prefer, after you bathe?"

Agony. That's what the images were. If she only knew how her innocent words wreaked havoc on his body! But she didn't. Nor could he ever let her know.

He gritted his teeth together. "That won't be necessary. My arm is fine. I'm fine. I don't need—"

"What's going on here?"

Perfect. Magnus looked over his shoulder to see that the Sutherlands and Munro had chosen this exact minute to return from falconing. Sir William was glaring daggers at his younger sister.

Surprisingly, Helen was glaring them back. "If it's any of your business, Muriel gave me some salve for Magnus's arm."

Magnus's brows lifted in surprise. He'd never heard her challenge one of her brothers like that before. Nonetheless, he added, "And I was just telling Lady Helen that the salve was unnecessary."

Magnus tried not to grimace as Munro hopped off his horse and sauntered toward them.

"How thoughtful of you, Helen. As a matter of fact, I took a blow to the side yesterday from your brother. Every now and then he manages to land one." Kenneth Sutherland pricked at the slur. "Perhaps you could try the salve on me?"

Magnus met the gaze of his enemy over her head. He knew he wasn't imagining the amusement there.

The slight tightening of Helen's mouth—probably noticed only by Magnus—was the only sign that she didn't necessarily welcome the change of patients.

Magnus suspected the lines around his own mouth were much deeper.

Helen glanced at Magnus as if begging him to intercede, but he clenched his jaw, forcing it not to open. He pretended not to see the dejection on her face, but his chest pinched nonetheless.

"Of course," she said brightly. "Come with me into the Hall, and I shall take a look at it." She glanced at her brother. "Will, if you have a moment, I need to speak with you." The earl looked about to argue, but Helen cut him off. "It's about Muriel."

The sudden flash of alarm in the earl's expression betrayed him. "Is she all right?"

Helen had noticed the reaction as well and seemed confused by it. "She's fine. At least I think she is."

The earl's face darkened, but he followed his sister and Munro—who'd taken her arm, blast him!—into the Hall. If Magnus was relieved to know that there would be a third person present when she rubbed the salve on Munro, it didn't do anything to take the edge off the much more powerful emotion surging through him.

Nine

✿

Panic had started to set in. Time was running out, and Helen was nowhere nearer to convincing Magnus to give her another chance than she had been the day he arrived. Three days had passed since Muriel left, and between the meetings, hunting, falconing, and his duties attending the king, she'd barely had a chance to exchange a few words with him. Worse, it seemed that whenever a chance might occur, Donald appeared by her side.

It wasn't by accident. She suspected a conspiracy by her brothers and Donald to keep her far away from Magnus. If only they would do so themselves. It seemed every time she turned around, the three of them and Magnus were arguing or exchanging not-so-subtle barbs.

The constant tension between her family and the man she loved was wearing on her. Naively, Helen had thought the end of the feud and the recent alliance with Bruce would make her brothers more amenable to Magnus. But every time she saw them together, her doubts of ever being able to reconcile these two important sides of her heart grew. It was clear the hatred and distrust between the men ran deep.

But she would not let that hatred stand in her way. She'd tried to do her duty to her family, allowing them to persuade her not to marry Magnus, but she would not do so again. If only the men in her life—*all* the men in her life—weren't so pigheaded. An alliance between the two neighboring clans could be a benefit, but how could she convince them of that?

Of course, first she had to convince Magnus. She needed time alone with him. She saw her chance when her brothers and Donald left after breaking their fast to hunt with some of the king's men. The king himself had begged off at the last minute, claiming he had to attend to some correspondence before resuming his progress the day after tomorrow.

At first she feared Magnus would be locked up in the room with him the entire time. But when he and MacGregor headed toward the practice yard, she knew this was it. She'd watched him enough to learn that when he finished practicing, he headed down to the beach to bathe in the icy waters of the North Sea. She pursed her mouth, knowing that it wasn't just cleanliness driving him but soreness in his arm. Yet the proud warrior was too proud to admit it troubled him.

Rather than attempt to follow him—which he'd demonstrated a frustrating ability to detect—she decided to wait for him down by the beach. Perhaps she should hide to make sure he didn't see her and turn right back around?

If she weren't so desperate, she might have found it rather humiliating to be chasing after a man who so obviously wished to avoid her. But she was determined not to let him go this time without a fight.

The sun was still high in the sky as Helen crossed the *barmkin,* waved at the guards positioned at the gate, and followed the path that led from the castle to the beach. Dunrobin was strategically positioned to overlook the sea, with the curtain wall running along the edge of the cliff. The steep walls made it easy to defend but impractical to descend. Instead, access to the beach was by a path that wound around the forested cliffside.

She had just turned off the main road when she heard a startled voice say, "Lady Helen!"

Her heart dropped. She glanced up to see Donald approaching on foot along the very path down which she was headed. He looked just as surprised to see her as she was him.

Forcing a smile of greeting to her face, she said, "Donald. I thought you'd gone hunting with the others."

He shook his head. "I changed my mind."

More likely he and her brothers had decided not to leave her alone with Magnus. But why had he been at the beach? The jetty was at the other side of the castle. All that was on this side was a long stretch of sandy white beach and a few sea caves.

"Where are you coming from?" she asked. Rarely did the men venture down here.

He grinned. "If you hoped to catch me bathing, you are too late."

Helen blushed, embarrassed by the very thought. "You shouldn't say such things. It isn't . . . right."

He took a step closer, backing her up to a tree. The scent of the sea enveloped her. It wasn't wholly unpleasant, but she didn't feel that overwhelming warmth come over her that she did when Magnus stood near her.

Actually, she felt a little wary. She'd felt comfortable around Donald her entire life, but for the first time she realized what an imposing man he was. Tall, thickly built, his rough-hewn features implacable and, she had to admit, attractive, with his dark blue eyes and thick auburn hair that fell in short waves around his bearded jaw. He was around Will's age, she knew. Older than she by a decade but still in the prime of his manhood.

She frowned, noticing that his hair had dried rather quickly.

"Why not?" he said huskily. "Surely you can see where this is headed, Helen?"

Her eyes widened. He was staring at her so intently, his eyes heavy with something that set off whispers of alarm.

Desire, she realized. *He wants me.*

Her pulse spiked. She felt him leaning closer to her. Like a rabbit who sensed a trap, she looked around for an easy way to escape, but he put his hands on either side of her, bracing himself against the tree and blocking her in.

"Please, Donald, I don't want—"

Her voice caught in a gasp. He leaned in so close she thought he was going to kiss her. His hand cupped her chin, and he tipped her face to his. "Perhaps not now, but you will." His thumb traced the bottom of her lip. "I can wait. But don't make me wait too long."

Helen's heart was pounding in her throat. How had this happened? She tried to shift free, but he'd wedged his body to hers. She pressed against him, but he blocked her efforts by drawing her into his arms in a firm embrace.

"Please, Donald, you're scaring me."

He let her go, as if he'd only just realized she wasn't welcoming his attentions.

"Forgive me," he said with a bow. "I vowed not to rush you."

Suddenly, a sound coming from the road drew his attention. A strange look crossed his face. "We'd best get back. Your brothers will return from the hunt at any time." His eyes narrowed. "What were you doing out here by yourself?"

Irritation replaced her fear. "I am collecting some flowers for the feast tomorrow. I hope that meets with your approval?"

He laughed at her outrage. "I'm only worried about you, lass."

Some of her anger dissipated. The brotherly Donald had returned. "You don't need to worry, I'm perfectly capable of taking care of myself."

"But you don't have to."

Their eyes held. She knew what he was offering—and she was flattered—but how could she explain she didn't think of him like that?

Almost as if he could read her mind, his face darkened. "He's not worthy of you." She didn't pretend to misunderstand of whom he spoke. The look of rage that flashed on his face chilled her blood. But it was gone so fast she wondered whether she'd imagined it. "And I'll prove it to you."

Before she could ask him what he meant, he stormed off to the castle. Helen waited until he'd disappeared from view, and then heaved a deep sigh of relief. The incident had shaken her more than she'd realized.

And she feared it had probably upset her plans. If Donald saw Magnus heading this way, he would guess—

Her heart stopped. Oh God, would he do something? Abandoning her plan, she spun around, intending to return to the castle to try to avert disaster: *"I'll prove it to you."* What would Donald do?

She'd barely taken a few steps, however, when someone moved out from a tree to block her path.

"Magnus!" she cried out, startled but also relieved.

Her relief at seeing him, however, dissipated when she saw his expression.

She took an unconscious step back. He had a drying cloth looped around his neck and his hair hung in loose, sweaty chunks around his face. Though he'd removed his armor, wearing only leather breeches and a linen tunic, she'd never seen him look more fierce. His muscles—of which there was an impressive amount—were bunched up, flexed and taut. His eyes glared with fury, his mouth curled in a cruel line, and his jaw was hard and unyielding.

His boyishly handsome face didn't look boyish at all, but very dark and very menacing.

"I-I . . ." To her amazement, she stuttered.

"Surprised to see me?"

She could hardly claim that, as she had come out here for exactly that purpose.

But he didn't give her time to answer. "I didn't mean to interrupt your little . . ." He nearly spat the word. "Liaison."

Good lord, what was wrong with him? "It wasn't a liaison. I was walking toward the beach—"

"Spare me your explanations. I know what I saw."

Her eyes widened. "What you saw?"

Suddenly, she realized that from his vantage, with her pressed up against a tree and Donald's broad shoulders blocking her from view, what he'd seen would have looked . . .

She blushed. It would have looked like Donald was kissing her.

Her blush seemed to confirm it for him. His mouth turned stark white.

My God, he's jealous! The realization hit her like a battering ram.

She decided to test her theory. She thrust her chin up and boldly looked him in the eye. "He wants to marry me."

His eyes narrowed with predatory intent. "Is that so?"

If hope wasn't rushing through her, she might have felt a wee bit of trepidation. But instinctively, she sensed how far she could push him. It was rather exhilarating to see him angry.

She nodded, and heaved a false maidenly sigh of contentment.

His fists clenched. "And this is what you want?"

She took a step closer to him, the warmth of his body spreading over her just as she'd remembered it. He smelled of sweat, and leather, and sun. But there was something deeply arousing—almost primal—about it. Her body flushed with heat. The shock of sensations made her gasp as frissons of pleasure rippled through her.

"What I want? What do you care about what I want?

You've made your feelings toward me clear. Why should you care who I kiss?"

He flinched, and she felt a wicked sense of feminine power surge through her. She leaned closer, until the hard tips of her breasts brushed against his chest.

He made a pained sound low in his throat. She felt the tension radiate around him like a drum as he fought for control. She sensed the danger but felt drunk, with a new kind of power. "At least when he kisses me, it makes me feel like a woman, not a nun." The muscle below his jaw jumped. "Aye, there is nothing chaste about his kiss," she added for good measure.

He moved so fast, she barely had time to process that she'd done the impossible: snapped the powerful bonds of his control. She was in his arms, breasts crushed against the muscular wall of his chest and hips plastered to his. And God, it felt incredible! Every nerve-ending in her body flared at the contact.

His mouth covered hers with a groan of pure primal satisfaction that drove her pleasure all the way to her toes. She could feel it pulsing through her, spreading over her limbs like a wave of pure molten heat.

His lips were soft but strong, his breath warm and spicy, as he crushed his mouth to hers.

His hand splayed against her back, possessively drawing her closer, bending her into the hard curve of his body.

For a moment she felt him yield. Felt his body envelop hers. His kiss grew more insistent. His lips dragging, kneading, opening her mouth.

Oh God.

She startled. Her heart fluttered like the wings of a butterfly. His tongue was inside her mouth, plunging, thrusting, circling. Tasting her deeper and deeper, as if he couldn't get enough.

The sensation was incredible. She moaned and circled her arms around his neck, wanting to get closer. His chest was so hot. So hard. She wanted to melt against him. She could feel her body soften, and the heat between her legs start to pulse and dampen.

The explosion of passion was so intense, so sudden, that she barely had time to savor it before it was gone. He broke away with a harsh, guttural curse, thrusting her from him as if she were plagued.

But it was the look of loathing on his face that cut her to the quick.

He still blames me, she realized. For not marrying him, and for marrying his friend. And bound up with that blame was guilt. He thought his feelings for her were a betrayal of his friend's memory. "Will you ever forgive me for what happened? I made a mistake, Magnus. I'm sorry. If I could go back and do it differently I would. I shouldn't have refused you. I shouldn't have agreed to the betrothal with William. But you left and never came back. Never sent word. I thought you'd forgotten all about me." Her hands twisted furiously in her skirts. "And then at the wedding . . ." She gazed up at him, begging for understanding. "You said you didn't care."

"I don't."

He had that hard, stubborn look on his face that infuriated her. "How can you say that after what just happened?"

"Wanting is not the same thing as caring, Helen. Surely you know the difference?"

It horrified her to realize she didn't. How would she? The only man she'd ever kissed was he—and William, but the chaste peck in the church didn't seem to count.

No, she wouldn't let him confuse her. She might be innocent, but she could tell when a man cared for her. And she'd seen his face at the wedding. The tic betrayed him. She thrust her chin up. "I don't believe you."

He shrugged. "I've never liked Munro. But marry him, if that's what you wish."

Her heart dropped. "You don't mean that." Her voice

sounded raw and dry. It wasn't just competitiveness that had made him jealous . . . was it?

"He can protect you."

What did that have to do with anything? Why did she need protection?

"But I don't love him. I love you."

Magnus stilled, trying to not let himself react to her words, but feeling them reverberate inside him like a drum.

She didn't mean it. And even if she did, it wasn't enough. He'd traveled down this road before. He wouldn't do it again.

She'd made her decision four years ago. She didn't love him enough then; nothing had changed. Whatever chance they might have had died the day she married Gordon.

He was furious at himself for losing control and kissing her. But he'd been out of his mind with jealousy, and when she'd taunted him with her body and her words, he'd lost control—which around her was becoming an appallingly frequent occurrence. The temptation to take what she offered . . .

He needed to get the hell out of here.

I love you.

Damn it. He couldn't stop hearing the words.

She didn't mean it. Her brother was right. She loved everything around her. She didn't love him. If she had, she would never have refused him, and she sure as hell wouldn't have married another man.

"Did you figure this out before or after you married my best friend?"

She flinched, perhaps as he intended. He knew it was wrong, this lashing out. But something about her—something about this situation—made him want to hurt her as badly as he'd been hurt. As he still hurt.

"That was a mistake. I never should have married William. He knew it as well as I—"

He didn't want to hear this. "It doesn't matter."

But the reminder of his friend hardened his resolve and reminded him of why he'd come here. Now that he'd assured himself she wasn't in danger, he could put this all behind him. He could put *her* behind him.

One more day. He could make it through one more day.

At least he thought he could. But then she closed the distance he'd put between them. She was so small and feminine. The overwhelming urge to take her in his arms again rose inside him. Her soft, alluring scent taunted him. He could still taste her on his mouth, the sweet honey of her lips ambrosia to a starving man.

He'd never lost control like that. Never. He'd wanted to ravish her senseless. Press her up against that tree, wrap her legs around his hips, and do what he'd been wanting to do to her for years. She wasn't a girl any longer. Nor the virginal maid he'd thought to take for his bride.

"What must I do? Get down on my hands and knees to beg your forgiveness?"

Oh hell. For that was where he was surely going. The image of her on her knees before him . . .

It wasn't begging that he was thinking about, but her mouth wrapped around him. His hands sinking through the soft silk of her hair as she took him deep into her naughty mouth and milked him. Heaviness tugged in his groin, his cock thickened.

Damn it, he was losing all rationality. Her nearness was like a sensual drug. She had no idea what she did to him. How one look, one touch, one whiff could send him into a mindless, lust-induced stupor.

Suddenly, one more day seemed like forever.

"There is nothing to forgive." Their eyes met and seeing her earnestness, a little of the hardness inside him softened. "You don't even know me anymore, Helen. I'm not the same man I was four years ago."

It was the truth. They couldn't go back to the way things were, even if he wanted to.

"Neither am I. I'm stronger. I would never let my family persuade me to go against my heart. Won't you give me—us—a chance?"

He was more tempted by her words than he wanted to admit. But guilt was a powerful antidote. *She's not yours, damn it.*

The sound of footsteps behind him proved a welcome interruption. He turned, surprised to see MacGregor racing toward him through the trees.

His instincts flared, immediately sensing that something was wrong. He reached for his sword.

"What is it?" he asked as MacGregor came to a hard stop before him, the heaviness of his breath testament to how fast he'd run.

The look on his face made Magnus brace himself for the worst. But still it wasn't enough.

"It's the king," he said. His gaze shot to Helen. "You'd better come, too, my lady. He's ill. Terribly ill."

Ten

❧

Helen had never been more scared in her life. The realization that the King of Scotland's life rested in her hands was terrifying, to say the least. A messenger had been dispatched to try to find Muriel, but the situation was too dire to wait. Robert the Bruce was dying.

She worked tirelessly through the day and night, doing everything in her power to halt the deathly plague that had overtaken him. Feverish, violently ill, and unable to keep anything down, the king came close to dying so many times she lost count.

Magnus was by her side the entire time. He told her of the king's illness the winter before last, where he'd nearly died after a similar malady. He'd suffered a few recurring bouts since then of fatigue, weakness, and aches, but nothing like this violent vomiting and flux.

Magnus's description matched a common malady that typically affected sailors and nobles. Farmers and peasants, however, rarely suffered from the sickness. Some suspected certain foods were the cause; poorer folk couldn't afford as much meat and subsided on less expensive foods like fruits, vegetables, eggs, and pottages.

She'd asked Magnus to describe the king's diet and found

that like most noblemen, he favored meat, cheese, fish, and bread.

But so far, her efforts to combat the illness with pottages and mashed-up vegetables and fruits had not worked. It wasn't surprising, as the king couldn't seem to keep anything in his stomach. But part of her wondered whether it was something else.

Late on the second night—or early the third morning— the king became delirious. Helen mopped his brow, squeezed drops of whisky in his mouth, and tried to keep him calm, but she didn't know what to do. She was losing him, and never had she felt so helpless.

She gazed at Magnus, who had taken a position opposite her at the king's bedside. The stress of the situation had caught up to her, and tears of frustration and exhaustion gathered in her throat. "Where is Muriel? Why isn't she here?"

Magnus detected the threat of hysteria lurking behind the despair. He took her hand in his as he used to do when they were young, and gave it an encouraging squeeze. It was so firm and strong. The king's illness had toppled the wall Magnus had erected between them—at least temporarily.

"The king can't wait for Muriel, Helen. He needs you. I know you're tired. I know you're exhausted. I am, too. But you can do this."

There was something about his voice that calmed her fraying nerves. It was how he'd been the entire time throughout his own ordeal. It was as if the direness of the situation, the pressure, the stress, never reached him. He knew the king was dying, but his confidence in her never wavered.

God, had she really thought him too temperate? He was solid—a rock. An anchor in a stormy sea.

She nodded. "You're right."

With a burst of renewed energy and determination, she

asked him to describe the king's previous illness for her again, wondering if she could have missed something.

He spoke of the king's pallor and weakness, the sunken eyes, the violent nausea, and the lesions on his skin. All common characteristics of the sailors' illness.

Helen could still see the scars on the king's legs where those lesions had been. But so far, no new ones had appeared.

"Was there any swelling of his limbs?" she asked.

He shook his head. "There could have been; I don't remember."

Helen knew that was a common trait of the sailors' illness.

"What is it?" he asked.

She shook her head. "Nothing." Or nothing she could put her finger on. But the absence of the skin lesions and swelling bothered her.

Other maladies ran through her mind, but the one that made the most sense was the sailors' illness. The only other time she'd seen something like this was when one of the villagers had accidentally been poisoned by handling monkshood.

Poison. Here at Dunrobin? Even the suspicion could have horrible ramifications for her family, whose recent submission made them of suspect loyalty as it was. She quickly pushed the thought away.

"There must be something else you can do? Something you haven't tried?"

She hesitated, and he immediately jumped on that hesitation. "What is it?"

She shook her head. "It's too dangerous." The finger-like plant foxglove was poisonous in certain quantities, causing violent vomiting not unlike what the king was experiencing now. Except that sometimes, Muriel said it could effect a cure of the same. The difficulty was in determining the quantity.

He held her gaze, steady. "I think we are past caution, Helen. If there is something you can do—anything you can do—try it."

He was right. Dunrobin village was too small for an apothecary, but Muriel had always kept the castle well provisioned. "Keep giving him the whisky and try squeezing some of the juice from the lemon," she said. Fortunately, the trading routes from the East had opened again with the truce, and the availability of foreign fruits had become more plentiful. "I'll be back in a moment."

She returned in less than a quarter of an hour with the tincture of foxglove, vinegar, and white wine. Her brothers, Gregor MacGregor, and other high-ranking members of the king's retinue who were standing vigil in the Great Hall and wanted to know whether there was any improvement had delayed her a few additional minutes. Magnus had given strict instruction that the news of the king's illness must be kept quiet—Bruce's hold on the throne was still too precarious. There would be some who would try to take advantage. Undoubtedly he counted her family in that group.

When she saw the king's stilled body, she feared the worst. "Is he . . . ?"

Magnus shook his head. "He's alive." *Barely*, she heard the unspoken word. "But exhausted," he finished.

The delirium had weakened him even further. Helen knew she had no other choice. Praying that she hadn't used too much, she poured the medicine in a small pottery cup. Her hand shook as she held it to the king's mouth. Magnus lifted the king's head and she poured it between his chapped lips. His face was as gray as a death mask.

Some of the liquid dribbled out of the corner of his mouth, but most of it went down.

She and Magnus sat in silence, anxiously waiting for a sign. Helen was beset by self-doubt, wondering if she'd done the right thing. For a while nothing happened. Then the king woke and started to writhe. Her fear increased. He started to lash out, calling her Elizabeth—his queen still imprisoned in England—and demanding to know why she hadn't bought him marzipan for his last saint's day. He loved marzipan. Was she still angry with him about the woman? She didn't mean anything. None of them did.

Magnus held the king down, and their eyes met. He looked at her in question.

"Sometimes it makes people see things." She explained the king's vision of his imprisoned wife, ignoring the private conversation they'd overheard. But the king's love of the lasses was well known.

Still, Helen held out hope. But a short while later the vomiting and flux started again. The king was more ill than ever. When at last the terrible barrage ended, his breath was so shallow as to barely come at all.

She looked at Magnus and shook her head. Tears streamed down her cheeks. "I'm sorry," she said. It hadn't worked.

He walked around the bed and drew her into his arms. She collapsed against him, letting the warmth and solidness of his embrace wrap around her. "You tried," he said softly. "You did everything you could." She thought she felt his mouth on the top of her head, but she was so exhausted she'd probably imagined it.

He sat in the chair she'd just vacated and drew her down on his lap. She put her head on his shoulder the way she used to do when they were young. And just like then, his solid strength filled her with a sense of contentment and warmth. A sense of belonging. It was the last thing she remembered until she woke to gentle shaking.

She opened her eyes to bright sunlight and winced, immediately shutting them again. "Helen," he said. "Look."

Blinking the sleep from her eyes, she became aware of Magnus before her. She was no longer in his lap, but was curled up in the same wooden chair with a plaid draped over her.

Suddenly, she realized what he was looking at. Bruce was still unconscious, but his face was no longer so pallid and his breathing was stronger. He looked . . . better.

"What happened?"

He shook his head. "I don't know. I kept giving him the whisky and the lemon." A look of shame crossed his face. "I must have dozed off a few hours ago. I woke and found him like this."

Had the remedy for the sailors' illness worked?

Her first reaction was relief. *Thank God, it wasn't poison.*

She hoped. But a niggle of doubt lingered. Could it have been the foxglove? Some thought the foxglove a remedy for poison. It was impossible to know for certain.

She quickly began an examination, placing her hand on the king's head, feeling that it wasn't so clammy, then on his stomach, relieved to not feel the twisting underneath, and on his heart, which beat remarkably steadily.

"Well?" Magnus asked expectantly.

She shook her head. "I don't know, but I think . . . I think . . ."

"He's getting better?"

She drew in a deep breath and sighed. "Aye."

He bowed his head, murmuring, "Praise God." He looked back up. "You did it."

Helen felt a swell of pride but knew he wasn't correct. "Nay, *we* did it."

And just for a moment when she looked into his eyes, time slipped away. She saw the lad she'd fallen in love with and felt the force of the connection between them beat as strongly as ever.

Under the cover of darkness, the *birlinn* approached the shore. He waited anxiously—eagerly—as John MacDougall, the exiled Lord of Lorn, made his way up the rocky beach, his feet once more treading solidly on Scottish soil. It was a moment to celebrate.

Lorn had been forced to take refuge in Ireland after the MacDougall loss at the battle of Brander last summer, but the once powerful chieftain hadn't conceded defeat. He'd been planning his retribution against the false king every day since.

Now, the time was at hand. Robert Bruce may have made a near miraculous return from ignominy and defeat, but his run of good fortune was about to come to a deadly end. Ironically, by a sword of his own making.

The two men—allies in the quest to see Bruce destroyed—clasped arms in greeting.

"The team is ready?" Lorn asked.

"Aye, my lord. Ten of the greatest warriors from Ireland, England, and those loyal to our cause from Scotland are waiting to attack on your command."

Lorn smiled. "The perfect killing team. I would thank Bruce for the idea but do not believe I shall have the chance. The next time I see him, the bastard will be dead. I trust you will not disappoint me?"

Lorn had recognized his skills and picked him to lead his killing team. He would not let him down. "Bruce might have his phantoms, but I have my reapers. He will not escape my scythe, my lord."

Lorn laughed. "Fitting, indeed. What is your plan?"

"We shall wait to attack until he takes to the mountains, when he is far from help."

"How many men protect him?"

"A handful of knights, and a few dozen men-at-arms. No more than fifty warriors in total. A number that should be easily handled in a surprise attack."

Again they would use Bruce's own tactics against him. Bruce had proved the effectiveness of small numbers in quick, surprise attacks launched in darkness in places of their choosing.

"And what of his phantom army? Have you managed to identify any of them?"

MacKay's face sprang immediately to mind. He was almost convinced his old nemesis was part of the famed group. He gritted his teeth. "I have a few suspicions, but I think you are keeping most of them busy out west."

Lorn smiled. "As I shall continue to do. How soon do you think it will be done?"

"Bruce has a few more castles that he plans to visit before turning west. I should think sometime in late July. He plans to hold the Highland Games in August."

He decided not to mention it would be at Dunstaffnage, which was Lorn's stolen castle.

Lorn frowned, not bothering to hide his impatience. "What is this I've heard of Bruce falling ill again at Dunrobin?"

"Rumors, my lord," he assured him, surprised the news had reached Lorn's ears in the west, when such an effort had been made to contain it.

The poison had been his one miscalculation. One he would not make again. He was fortunate that Helen was a better healer than he'd realized. Bruce dying at Dunrobin would have brought scrutiny and criticism to the clan.

It was the last thing he wanted. What he did, he did for the Sutherlands. The honor of the entire clan had been impinged when they'd been forced to bow to the usurper, but he would get it back by defeating Bruce and restoring Balliol to the throne. Will's hand had been forced by Ross, but he would thank him in the end.

Conscious that every moment he spent on Scottish soil he was in danger, Lorn did not linger. "In July, then." They shook hands, and Lorn started toward his *birlinn*. He'd nearly reached the water's edge when he turned back. "I almost forgot. You were right—there were reports of a strange explosion last December."

He stilled. *Gordon.*

"But not at Forfar," Lorn said. "At Threave, when Bruce's phantoms were said to have defeated two thousand Englishmen."

It was the confirmation he'd been waiting for. William Gordon had been a member of Bruce's famed guard, which made MacKay almost certainly a member as well.

And then there was Helen. What had she known of it? He intended to find out.

Eleven

❧

The connection didn't last. If Helen hoped that the bond forged in those long, desperate hours while caring for the king marked a new beginning with Magnus, she was to be disappointed.

In the intervening days as the king continued to improve, Magnus displayed the same steady, matter-of-fact disposition that she remembered so well. And just as before, the inability to decipher his true feelings proved frustrating. He was polite to a fault, but distant and remote. He displayed none of the fierce longing and attraction that rose in her chest and nearly suffocated her with its intensity whenever she looked at him. She could almost imagine he hadn't lost control and kissed her—really kissed her.

His duties to the king and hers as healer ensured that for the first time since arriving at Dunrobin Castle he could not avoid her, but any attempts at personal conversation were instantly quashed. As the king continued to improve, Magnus's duties tended less toward personal bodyguard and more toward captain of the king's guard. Duties that took him away. More often, Gregor MacGregor, Neil Campbell, or Alexander Fraser could be found at the king's bedside.

But Helen knew the king's illness had given her a reprieve, and she did not intend to squander the opportunity. Her declaration of love had fallen on deaf ears. Obviously, he didn't believe her. She would just have to prove it to him, showing him how she felt by boldly tempting him with the one weapon she had: desire.

The only problem was that she didn't know how to be bold. With little female guidance—even less since Muriel had gone—flirting and seduction were not an art she'd perfected. So she took to observing the servants. But unless she intended to start wearing gowns from which her bosom spilled out, and pick up a pitcher of ale to bend over and pour (displaying those bosoms to their full advantage) while men fondled her bottom, she didn't know how to proceed.

But he was not as immune to her as he wanted her to think. Never far from her mind was that kiss. He wanted her. Of that he was willing to admit. It was a start. An opening through which she could attack. If lust was the sword that would penetrate his shield, she intended to do what she could to pierce his defenses.

With Donald gone it should have been easier. Will had sent him to Inverness in search of Muriel when the first messenger had returned empty-handed. But of course, there were still her brothers with whom to contend.

She grimaced. They were making it exceedingly difficult on her. Will was in a foul temper, which Kenneth blamed on the king's illness. When she wasn't attending the king, her eldest brother the formidable earl ensured her duties kept her too busy to do anything else. Kenneth was worse. Except for the blissful (and far too short) two days while he was at Skelbo Castle, it seemed as if every time she turned around, her unnecessary and unwanted "protector" was there.

"Where are you off to this beautiful morning, sister?"

She stiffened. He followed her so closely he was lucky she hadn't stomped on his nose. It would serve him right if she did. Her brother was nearly as handsome as Gregor MacGregor but far more arrogant. Attention from women was the one thing he'd never had to fight for. Women fell at his feet, and he let them enjoy the view.

Helen gritted her teeth and tried to smile. "I thought I'd check with the cook to see if the shipment of lemons has arrived. The king enjoys a bit of the juice with his ale."

She wondered whether he even heard her answer. Kenneth's eyes narrowed as he scanned her gown.

"Interesting dress," he said slowly. "But some of it seems to be missing."

Helen felt the heat rise to her cheeks but ignored his comment—and his obvious disapproval. She took the fine silk in her hands and spread the skirt wide, swishing it around a little for effect. The silvery pink threads caught in the light streaming through the high windows of the Great Hall where he'd caught her. "Isn't it beautiful? The latest style from France, I'm told. Lady Christina was wearing one just like it at the wedding."

Helen had lowered hers by an inch in the bodice, but she wasn't going to point that out. What difference did an inch make?

Quite a bit, it seemed, if her brother's reaction was any guide. "Lady Christina is a married woman with a husband who would kill any man for looking at her."

"And I'm a widow," she pointed out. She thrust her chin up, refusing to let him cow her. "I shall wear what I like, brother."

She could tell that Kenneth didn't know whether to be amused or annoyed by her sudden assertion of independence.

He considered her for a moment, and then seemed to decide. A wry smile turned his mouth. "It won't work, you know. You won't change his mind. MacKay is one of the most proud and stubborn men I know, and damned if I'm not happy about it right now. You refused him and married his friend; it will take more than a low gown to change his mind."

Furious, Helen met his amused gaze with a glare. "I don't know what you are talking about." But the heat in her cheeks belied her claim; she was embarrassed that her ploy had been so obvious.

Brothers could be so infuriating. Especially when he only laughed and tweaked her nose in response as if she were two. "Ah, Helen, you are still such an innocent." He had that even more infuriating "silly Helen" look on his face. If he looped her under his arm and mussed her hair, she might sock him in the stomach the way she used to do when she was younger. "One night as a married woman does not make you a *coquette*."

Not even one night, but she wasn't going to tell him that. It would only bolster his argument, and her "widowhood" imparted a certain amount of freedom that she was reluctant to lose.

"Hell, that bastard's so stubborn you could probably crawl into his bed naked and he wouldn't notice you."

Kenneth was laughing so hard he didn't see the flare of possibility in her widened eyes. Climbing into his bed naked . . . good God! . . . was that what women did? It seemed rather extreme, but she added it to her mental list of weaponry.

She thought about thanking her brother for the suggestion, but didn't think he'd be as amused by the irony. "If we are done, then I should see to the king's meal."

"Ah Helen, don't get all prickly. I'm sorry for laughing." He tried to look chastened, but his deep blue eyes, so like her own, sparkled with laughter.

Brothers! Her mouth thinned. Sometimes she wished she were five years old again and she could just kick him—even if he was twice her size.

As if he knew what she was thinking, he took a step back. He crossed his arms, clearly not done with her yet.

"You've taken quite an interest in the king's food. The cook mentioned that since Carrick—I mean, the king—has resumed eating, you've insisted on overseeing his meals personally."

Helen thought she covered her reaction, but Kenneth had always been irritatingly perceptive. All signs of his previous humor vanished. "What is it?"

She shrugged. "The king nearly died under our roof. It is prudent to have care."

He watched her until she felt like squirming. Sometimes he could be just as stern and intimidating as Will.

"But that's not all is it?"

She shook her head. She hadn't given voice to her fears, but the urge to confide in someone was overwhelming.

With a harsh curse, Kenneth looked around, took her firmly by the elbow, and pulled her into the small store-room behind the stairs that smelled of ale and wine. Although the hall wasn't crowded, there were always people milling around to overhear.

"Tell me," he insisted in a low voice.

She bit her lip. "It's probably nothing. But there were things about the king's illness . . . things that reminded me of monkshood."

She mouthed the last word, but the flare of alarm in her brother's eyes told her that he'd understood. "I thought you said the king suffered from the sailors' malady."

"I did. He did. Probably. But I can't be certain."

He swore again and stormed around the room restlessly. She feared that he would be angry with her, but it pleased her to realize that he trusted her skills as a healer enough to accept her suspicions without comment.

It was also clear he was shocked—which relieved her more than she wanted to admit. Her brothers wouldn't be involved in something so dishonorable. It hadn't been easy for them to swallow their pride and submit to Bruce, but they'd warmed to the king . . . hadn't they?

"You mustn't say anything to anyone until we are sure."
He grabbed her arm and forced her to meet his gaze. "Do
you hear me, Helen? No one. And sure as hell not MacKay.
No matter what you think of him or his feelings for you, be
clear of one thing: his duty is to the king. If he thinks the
king is in danger, he will act first and ask questions later.
They don't trust us as it is. Even the suspicion of something
like that would jeopardize our clan. That's all it is, isn't
it—a suspicion?"

She nodded. "I probably shouldn't have mentioned it.
The king seems to be improving with the change in diet."

He nodded. "Then we shall hope he continues to improve. But promise me to tell no one."

"I promise."

"Good. I will tell Will. It will be up to him as to whether
to inform the *meinie*"—her brother's closest warriors, who
formed his retinue. "But I doubt he'll risk it. The fewer
people who know of this, the better."

Kenneth left to find Will, and Helen made her way down
to the kitchen vaults to see to the king's meal. She thought
she probably shouldn't have said anything, but then again,
under the circumstances perhaps it was better to err on the
side of caution.

Robert the Bruce was the king, whether her brothers
liked it or not. He'd won the people's hearts by his defeat
of the English at Glen Trool and Loudoun Hill, and he was
on his way to winning most of Scotland's barons as well. If
he'd come to harm under their care, there would have been
repercussions.

It was her other problem, however, that weighed upon
her now. Kenneth was right. The dress had been a silly
idea. Magnus was not the type of man to be tempted by
something so obvious. She vowed to change before the
midday meal. And then . . .

She sighed. Then she'd have to think of something else.

* * *

Magnus lingered at the beach. From his rocky seat by the sea, he watched the waves crash against the dark cliffs below the castle, hurling great plumes of water into the air. A few gannets dipped and soared over the water, hunting their next meal.

He savored the rare moment of peace. But the sharp glare of the sun high in the sky reminded him of the hour. He should get back for the midday meal.

Where he would see Helen.

"I love you."

He pushed the words away and jumped off the rock. It didn't matter, damn it! Hadn't she said as much before? Look how well that had turned out for him—three and a half years of misery. She'd left him standing like an arse while she rode away with her damned brothers only to dig her knife even deeper by marrying his closest friend.

But the words had affected him more than he wanted to admit. After nearly three weeks at Dunrobin, including two by her side while she nursed the king, seeing the way she looked at him he could almost believe she meant it—that she regretted what had happened and wanted to make it right.

But it could never be right. Excising Helen from his heart had cost him too much.

Yet no matter how much his body wanted to forget, he flared up like a stallion with a mare in heat whenever she was near. Hiding his reaction in the king's small chamber had become impossible.

Fortunately, Bruce's improving health allowed him to spend more of his time away from his bedside—and from Helen. Unfortunately, that meant he was spending more time with her brothers in the training yard.

He grimaced. Kenneth Sutherland was proving to be annoyingly tenacious. He refused to let go of the matter of Gordon's death. His questions were growing increasingly dangerous, and increasingly closer to the truth. The only way to shut him up, it seemed, was to distract him in the yard.

His boyhood competitor had proved to be distracting to him as well. He frowned, admitting that Sutherland's skills had improved more than he'd expected. Mindful of the king's admonition to the Guard not to draw too much attention to their skills, Magnus had kept to sparring and light competition. But ignoring the challenges was getting harder and harder to resist. He longed to shut Sutherland up once and for all.

There was a bright side. At least he wasn't being forced to endure Munro's blatant wooing of Helen. The Sutherland henchman had been gone for well over a week searching for the healer. If he stayed away another week or so, he and the king's party would be gone.

The king was recovering swiftly under Helen's care. Bruce said he felt better than he had in years, and only Helen's threats kept him in bed. Hell, Magnus had no liking for vegetables, but perhaps there was something to this peasant diet she'd implemented. The king's color was healthier than it had been in a long time.

He made his way back to the castle. Unfortunately, the path took him right by the place where he'd come upon Helen and Munro. Seeing the tree where Munro had kissed her sent a primal surge of anger running through him. He should chop the damned thing down.

But the reminder of his weakness only served to further infuriate him. He never should have kissed her. He'd been jealous, he admitted. Blind with jealousy. He hadn't been thinking rationally.

He wasn't fool enough to think she would not remarry. It was just Munro, he told himself. He couldn't stand to see the man who'd humiliated him too many times when he was young—and never missed the opportunity to remind him of it—win her.

It wasn't a competition. But it sure as hell felt as if he were losing.

The man known for his cool, level-headed temper was in

a foul mood by time he entered the castle. A mood that only got worse when he entered the tower and saw Helen standing by the stairwell.

She wasn't alone. Munro—the whoreson—was back. But something was wrong—or right, depending on your perspective—the Sutherland henchman had a fierce look on his face and seemed to be fighting for control.

"Don't be silly," Helen said. "I'm perfectly capable of carrying a tray—"

"I insist," Munro said, relieving her of the king's meal. "You should return to your room and get some rest. You look tired."

Helen sounded as though she was trying to contain her impatience. "I'm not tired. I told you I'm fine. I need to check on the king."

"Is there a problem?" Magnus said, making his presence known. His teeth gnashed together; apparently they were too busy to notice him.

Helen turned at the sound of his voice and let out a gasp. A gasp that he very nearly echoed.

Jesus! He'd taken hammer blows across the chest that had packed less of a wallop.

All he could see were two delicious mounds of creamy white flesh rising above a tight square bodice.

He'd never realized how big . . .

He'd never imagined how perfect . . .

How could he? The gowns she usually wore were fashionable, as befitting a lady of her station, but never more than well-made afterthoughts. This gown hugged every inch of her body, revealing curves he hadn't known existed.

But he knew now. He knew their exact shape and size. He knew that if he cupped her breasts to bring them to his mouth, the soft flesh would spill over his big palms. He knew the depth of the sweet crevice between them and that her nipples rose in delicate little points not half an inch from the edge of the fabric.

And he knew all this because the pink silk gown did very little to hide any part of her.

The watering in his mouth went dry. Suddenly, the reason for Munro's anger became crystal clear.

A vein Magnus didn't know he had started to throb by his temple. *Not yours,* he reminded himself. But damn it, if she was, he'd take her to their room and rip the blasted thing in two.

Only the suspicion that the dress was calculated to elicit just that kind of reaction kept him in control. "I'll take it," he said. "I was on my way to see the king anyway."

"That isn't necessary—" Munro started to say.

"I insist," Magnus said, an edge of steel in his voice. "The king isn't seeing visitors."

Munro didn't miss the slight. His smile was tight. "Of course." He handed over the tray.

But on one subject he and Munro could agree. Neither man wanted anyone seeing Helen like this, and for reasons of their own they didn't want her to know it. "Munro is right," he said. "Perhaps you should go to your chamber and rest." *And change that blasted dress.*

Averting his eyes from danger, he kept his gaze firmly on her face and saw the small furrow appear between her pixie brows. Thin and delicately arched, the velvety, dark-brown wisps framing her eyes held only a hint of auburn.

"I'm not tired. I assure you I've had plenty of sleep." She looked back and forth between them as if sensing something else at play. "I will rest later this afternoon. *After* I have seen to the king and the midday meal."

Magnus's jaw tightened, as did Munro's. Giving them no opportunity to object further, she lifted the skirts of her indecent gown and flounced up the stairs. Magnus exchanged a look with Munro and stomped up behind her.

It was going to be a very long meal.

Twelve

✀

"More ale, Your Grace?"

"Aye, thank you, Lady Helen," the king said eagerly.

Helen bent over the reclining king to pour the ale into the goblet. The king smiled appreciatively, and she turned to the expressionless man beside him. Holding the jug to her chest in blatant offering, she asked, "Magnus?"

"Nay." She thought his voice snapped, but then he added pleasantly, "Thank you."

She looked for any sign that he'd noticed the gown or the swell of flesh threatening to slide out every time she leaned forward, but his face remained perfectly impassive. Her brother was right—she could be naked and he probably wouldn't notice. The dress had been a foolish waste of time. She'd felt a little nervous donning it—it revealed far more of her bosom than she'd ever shown before—but apparently there had been nothing to worry about. She might have been wearing a monk's robe for all the notice Magnus took of it.

Or of her.

She was tempted to dump the blasted pitcher of ale on his head. He might notice that!

Mouth pursed, she set the jug back down on the tray. Picking up a plate, she inhaled the rich, buttery perfume.

But the deep breath she intended to take was cut short by the tightening of fabric across her chest. Lud, the silly dress was too tight to even take a deep breath!

"Tarts?" she said, holding the plate out.

"Please," the king said, appearing to be holding back a laugh.

Helen frowned and turned to Magnus. He shook his head, made a grumbly sound low in his throat, and shifted in his seat.

She wrinkled her nose at his curtness and slid one of the tarts from the plate. They smelled divine.

Plopping down on the bench beside Magnus, she sunk her teeth into the flaky strawberry tart, unable to hold back a groan of pleasure. "These are heavenly." She sighed with a flick of her tongue, catching the rivulet of juice before it dribbled down her chin.

Bruce laughed. "I don't think I should mind all the new foods you insist I eat if they could all taste like this." He made a face. "A king forced to eat carrots and beets, it's a disgrace."

She returned his laugh, and then turned to Magnus with a concerned frown when she noticed he was shifting again. "Is something wrong?"

His face was perfectly placid. "Nay, why do you ask?"

"You keep shifting in your seat." The frown between her brows deepened as she realized what might be the cause. "Do you need a cushion? I know you've been spending many hours by the king's bedside." Her cheeks heated. "It is not uncommon to have swelling—"

"Piles? Good God!" If Helen hadn't been so taken aback by the vehemence of his reaction, she might have found the look of outrage on his face comical. "I don't need a blasted cushion! And I sure as hell don't have swelling *anywhere*."

The king was making a choking sound that immediately drew her attention. She jumped to her feet and leaned over him, concerned. "Sire, are you all right?"

The coughing subsided, but this time she was sure there was laughter behind the innocent facade. "I'm fine," he assured her after a moment.

Confused, Helen looked back and forth between the men, but neither seemed inclined to illuminate her. "Sit down," the king said. "Finish your tart."

Helen complied, and she could feel the king's eyes on her while she ate. "MacKay says you knew one another as children?"

Helen cast a surreptitious glance at Magnus from out of the corner of her eye, surprised that he would have mentioned it but not surprised he would have made it seem of youthful unimportance. No longer shifting, he sat as still as one of the druids' mystical standing stones. "Aye," she said cautiously. "Though we were not children. Magnus was ten and nine when we met."

"Hmm," the king said. "I can't imagine your brothers were very happy when they found out about your, uh . . . friendship."

This time she didn't dare look at Magnus, fearing the accusation she would see in his gaze. She recalled exactly how her brother had reacted. And how she had as well: by rejecting his offer of marriage.

She shook her head, a pained pinch in her chest. "Nay, Sire. The feud was still too fresh in their minds."

Magnus said nothing, his silence feeling like a condemnation of its own.

I would do differently today! she wanted to shout. *Just give me a chance.*

But he wouldn't look at her.

Perhaps sensing her discomfort, Bruce switched the subject. "Aye, well, feuds and old alliances are all in the past." He smiled. "Since I've been confined to my chambers, I've spent some time at the window, watching the training. Your brother Kenneth is a skilled knight."

She felt Magnus tense at her side. She knew he and Kenneth had been locked in one competition after another the past few weeks, but the king's observation pleased her nonetheless. She was proud of her brothers and her clan. She nodded. "Aye, he is. At Barra Hill, Kenneth held off a thousand rebels with two hundred men by positioning his archers at . . ." All of a sudden her voice dropped off, as she realized what she was saying. She'd been so eager to sing Kenneth's praises, she'd forgotten the "rebels" were Bruce's men.

The king saw her expression and laughed, giving her hand a fond pat. "That's all right. I take no offense. Your loyalty to your brother does you proud. I remember that battle well, though I did not realize it was your brother in command. If all of Buchan's men had used such tactics we would not have fared as well that day."

Helen's shoulders sagged with relief.

"He fostered with Ross?" the king asked.

She wondered at the king's sudden interest in her brother. "Aye, both my brothers did, as is the tradition in our clan."

"And that's how you came to know William Gordon?"

She stilled, glancing anxiously at Magnus. But he gave no sign that the question affected him. "Aye. Kenneth and William were foster brothers. I never knew him—only of him. Kenneth would come with tales to tell of their mischief." She smiled unwittingly at the memories. "Although I'm sure I heard only a small portion of it. They were like brothers from the start. Our grandfathers had fought in the last crusade together, and the bond carried on through the following generations. Though I don't think that connection was always appreciated. The Earl of Ross was furious when they started a fire in his stable after concocting some recipe from one of my grandfather's journals—he considered himself something of an alchemist."

Both men stilled as if she'd said something important. "Recipe?" the king asked carefully.

She shrugged. "The Saracen's powder, but nothing ever

came of it. The journal was lost in the fire and Ross made them promise never to tinker with 'sorcery' again." She winked. "But I don't think they listened."

The king exchanged a glance with Magnus, and Helen realized the time was getting late. The midday meal had already started, and she still needed to change her dress. Will was going to be angry with her again, this time with cause.

She stood. "I should be going."

The king stopped her. "What about tomorrow?"

Her mouth twitched.

"You didn't think I'd forget."

"Hardly," she said dryly. He'd been asking her every day for nearly a week. "Tomorrow you may take a turn outside. For an hour—no longer."

Bruce laughed. "I think I should prefer to have that old priest back. He was much less of a tyrant."

Helen smiled sweetly. "He's eager to bleed you again, if you'd like me to—"

"Nay! An hour, no more, I promise. Your enforcer will see to it." He shot Magnus a glare. "Although I seem to remember you giving your oath to *me*."

Magnus didn't blink. "Seeing that Lady Helen's instructions are followed ensures I have an oath to keep."

The king shook his head. "You are quite a pair." Her chest twisted. They were. Why wouldn't he see it? "I know when I'm outnumbered." The king gave her a look. "But I won't give up. I feel better than I have in years and intend to be rid of this bed by the end of the week. We've delayed our journey and intruded on your hospitality long enough."

The stab in her chest intensified. They couldn't leave. Not until she'd convinced Magnus to give her another chance.

But maybe he would never be convinced. Maybe she'd been deluding herself. Maybe the passion she sensed behind the impassive facade was only wishful thinking.

Maybe she'd been right all those years ago. Maybe he didn't feel that way about her at all.

Her chest squeezed. Was that it? Did he not care for her anymore?

Nay. Magnus was the most steadfast man she knew—as well as the most stubborn. It was her family and her marriage to William that were holding him back. How could she show him that loving her was not a betrayal of the man she'd barely known?

Discouraged nonetheless, Helen murmured her farewells and left the room. She'd closed the door behind her and taken a few steps down the stairs when she heard it open again. "Helen, wait."

Her heart stopped just hearing his voice.

She turned. Magnus's big form loomed on the stair above her, blocking the light, the air suddenly heavy and warm. He seemed to take up the entire stairwell. She was deeply conscious of the tight space. If she leaned forward a few inches her breasts would graze his . . .

She blushed.

Almost as if he could read her thoughts, he took a step back and pulled her back into the small corridor. "Thank you," he said. "For all you've done for the king. The medicines, the meals, the ale," he said, lifting a goblet that she hadn't noticed.

Her senses had been otherwise occupied. Her nose with the warm masculine spice. Her eyes with the rough stubble along his jaw and the broad, muscular wall of chest that faced her. Her taste with the memory of his kiss. And her ears with the sharpness of her breath.

"You've nothing to thank me for," she said unevenly. "The king is under our roof; it is my duty to care for him."

"We both know you've gone well beyond your duty. I've noticed how you've personally seen to his meals. You didn't need to do that."

He trusted her. Helen felt a pang of conscience that she

told herself was unwarranted. The change in diet was help-ing. There was no reason to suspect anything else.

"Bruce looks healthier than he has in years," he added.

A wry smile turned her mouth. "I'm not sure the king shares your gratitude. He isn't very fond of greenery."

Magnus grinned, and it went straight to her heart. God, he was so handsome. She felt herself pulled by an invisible rope. They were alone, and she wanted him so desperately. She leaned toward him, her breasts brushing against the leather of his *cotun*.

He was so warm. She remembered how it felt to have his arms around her and willed them to close around her again. "Magnus, I . . ."

He flinched; his muscles turned as rigid and cold as stone. Instinctively, she pulled away. The visceral rejection stung. *He doesn't want me.*

"I'm sorry," she said, toneless, unable to look at him. "I need to go. They will be waiting for me."

She spun away, knocking his arm. At least she thought she knocked it. For the next minute she cried out in sur-prise as ale doused her gown.

"Oh, no!" Her hands flew to the front of her bodice, the left side of which was now soaked with the lemony brew. "My dress!"

"Ah, hell."

Something in his voice made her eyes fly to his face. He looked away quickly, but she'd seen it. Hunger. Raw hunger.

He'd been looking at her breast. She glanced down. Whatever had been hidden by her gown was hidden no longer. The water molded the fabric to her like a second skin. She might have been naked after all. She sucked in her breath, the primal awareness of his attraction washing over her in a hot wave.

"It's ruined," she said.

He'd gotten his reaction under control. "Is it?" He didn't

seem overly concerned. Actually he seemed pleased. "What a shame."

Her eyes narrowed. It was almost as if . . . he'd done it on purpose. "It's a *new* dress."

He didn't say anything.

She stuck out her chest and held the skirts wide. "Don't you like it?"

He gave her a swift once-over, assiduously avoiding her chest. "It's stained."

"I shall have to go change."

"I won't keep you."

He *was* pleased. But why would he do such a thing? Only one explanation made sense.

"Here," he said, taking the plaid from around his shoulders and wrapping it around her, covering her up. "You don't want to catch a chill."

For one flight of stairs? Her room was located directly under the king's. He'd bundled her up as if it were the middle of winter in Norway. Very interesting. Very interesting indeed. It seemed her brother had been wrong after all. Not only had he noticed, he didn't want her wearing the gown.

Magnus looked so pleased with himself, she couldn't resist taking him down a notch. "It's fortunate I ordered a number of new gowns along with this one."

He stilled, and Helen felt a deep wave of satisfaction surge through her. Good God, she hadn't thought him capable! He actually looked scared.

"You did?" he choked out.

She smiled with wide-eyed innocence. "Aye, though I've been a bit nervous to wear them."

"Why's that?" This time it was more of a squeak.

She grinned devilishly. "They aren't nearly as modest as this one."

She was rewarded with white lines around his mouth and the faint hint of a tic below his jaw.

When Helen left him standing there, he was clenching his fists, and she . . .

She had a decided skip in her step. The doubts of a few moments ago were gone. He did want her, and if his reaction was any indication, badly. Things were going to work out all right in the end—she just knew it.

A little more prodding and she'd have him.

Magnus watched her prance away and knew he'd just been deftly outmaneuvered. Worse, it was his own damned fault.

He'd been half-crazed with lust watching her serve the king his meal. It had taken every scrap of discipline he had not to let her see it. He'd done a good job of it, too—except for the shifting. Piles, Jesus! He shook his head with disgust. He'd been swollen all right. His cock had been as hard as an iron spike.

And Bruce—the blasted cur—had enjoyed every minute of his discomfort. A little too much. Magnus had seen the way the king's eyes had lingered appreciatively on the swell of flesh rising above her bodice.

Magnus knew that he had better do something if he didn't want to be fighting the urge to slam his fist into jaws all day. He thought he'd been so clever, coming up with the idea of the ale.

But he'd miscalculated. Badly. He hadn't anticipated the effect of wet fabric.

Jesus, his mouth went dry just thinking about it. The heaviness. The roundness. The faint, wrinkly edge around the perfect bud of a nipple. He ached to slide his finger over the soft ridges. To lower his head, put his lips around the taut tip, and suck every last bit of ale from her skin.

His cock swelled, throbbing at the memory.

Hell, he'd go to bed with every inch of that incredible breast emblazoned on his mind. And he knew that as he'd done many nights before, he'd take himself in hand and try to take the edge off.

But the edginess only got worse over the next few days. His hand didn't help. Working himself senseless on the practice field didn't help. Nothing helped.

Helen had found his weakness and took every opportunity she could find to test him. Brushing up against him. Dropping things at his feet so she could bend over and pick them up. Reaching for anything she could on high shelves.

He'd never known her to take an interest in needlework, but it seemed as if every gown she wore had been taken down two inches in the neck and taken in two inches everywhere else. He was surprised she could breathe, they were so bloody tight.

But it wasn't just the clothing—or lack thereof—that was driving him into a frenzy. Far more dangerous was the open, honest desire he saw in her eyes.

Bloody hell, couldn't she at least try to hide it? Show some proper decorum for once? But artifice wasn't Helen's way. It never had been. She wanted him, and he could see it in her eyes every time she looked at him. Resisting that had stretched him to the limit.

Thank God, the end was in sight. The king had recovered, Magnus had kept his word to Gordon, and Helen wasn't in any danger. He could leave with a clear conscience.

But his conscience wasn't clear. Something nagged at him. A vague uneasiness that he attributed to being so long under his enemy's roof.

He was hardly objective when it came to the Sutherlands, but he didn't trust them. Bruce might think them loyal subjects, but Magnus wasn't so easily convinced. Swallowing pride wasn't part of the Highland creed. Vengeance. Retribution. An eye for an eye. Those were the mother's milk of Highland warriors.

But suspicion and lifelong enmity weren't enough to

jeopardize the tentative alliance with the Sutherlands that Bruce had fought so hard to win. The betrothal between the king's sister and the earl was all but agreed upon.

Magnus had survived the past few years by instinct, and pushing it aside didn't sit well.

So as he did every day, he took his frustrations out on the practice field on a series of opponents, including Munro. Unable to properly quiet his taunts by beating him into the ground, Magnus was in a foul temper by the time the king called the day's "exercises" complete. Holding back— whether on the lists or every time Helen looked up at him with those take-me-in-your-arms-and-ravish-me eyes—left him feeling like a lion in a very small cage.

The last thing he needed was Kenneth Sutherland tossing oil on the flames of his discontent. If it weren't so danger-ous, Magnus might actually admire the bastard's tenacity.

Magnus was returning his arsenal of weaponry to the armory for storage when Helen's brother cornered him. "Munro gave you an opening, why didn't you take it?"

Magnus turned around slowly. "I would have, if I'd seen it in time."

Sutherland shook his head. "You pulled back. I saw you."

Magnus shrugged. "It's nice to know I have such an ad-mirer in the Sutherland ranks. I'm flattered by your appre-ciation of my skill. Perhaps I can give you a few pointers tomorrow?"

A rewarding flush of anger crept up the other man's face. "You can give me a fair fight."

"Haven't you heard?" Magnus said with a lift of his brow. "We're friends now."

"You and I will never be friends."

He held his gaze. "Something we agree on."

What Gordon had seen in the arrogant, hot-tempered arse he didn't know. Magnus had hated the Sutherlands for as long as he could remember, and proximity sure as hell hadn't changed his mind any.

Sutherland stepped forward, effectively—due to his size and the small building—blocking Magnus's way to the door. Magnus, his back to the wall, gave no indication that he recognized the threat. But his muscles tensed with readiness.

"I want the damned truth about what happened to Gordon."

Magnus tried to rein in his impatience, but he felt the horses pulling away. "You've had it. We were attacked. He took an arrow in the chest and fell overboard before anyone could catch him. His armor dragged him down."

Sutherland wouldn't have believed him, even if it had been the truth. "It's merely a coincidence, then, that I heard of a battle in Galloway at the very time you were gone. A battle where Bruce's phantom warriors fought off thousands of English soldiers to rescue Edward Bruce from Threave Castle?"

Magnus laughed, though it was the last thing he felt like doing. "Do you believe in ghosts and goblins, too? If these phantoms did half the feats attributed to them, I'd be skeptical. But believe what you want; it doesn't change the truth. Did your reports also tell you Forfar Castle fell at the same time?"

"Aye, but the attack to free the king's brother involved something unusual—an explosion." Magnus felt the other man's scrutiny and knew he wasn't going to like what he said next. "Is it a coincidence that Gordon used to tinker with black powder when we were lads?"

The danger posed by those carelessly uttered words caused him to snap. Before Sutherland could react, Magnus had his hand wrapped around his throat and his back against the wall.

But rather than show fear, Sutherland smiled as if this was what he'd wanted.

"Believe in peasants' tales if you want—I don't give a shite," Magnus seethed. "But your wild speculations are putting your sister in danger." The other man's smile fell. "Aye, did you ever think what would happen to her if someone were to actually listen to your ravings? Keep your bloody fantasies to yourself or Helen will pay."

"Let me worry about my sister. You stay away from her. I know what you are thinking, even if she does not. You're sick—depraved—God damn it, she was your friend's wife! I would think even a MacKay would have some honor—"

Magnus squeezed his hand around his throat, wanting to shut him up. But his enemy's words were merely echoes of his own thoughts.

He might have kept squeezing had the door not opened. Magnus released him as MacGregor and a few of the other men strode inside.

Sutherland looked surprisingly pleased, despite the fact that Magnus had been seconds away from squeezing the life from him. "You're hiding something," he murmured, as he passed by. "And I intend to find out what it is."

Magnus let him go, but the threat lingered in his wake. He jammed the last weapon on the shelf and turned to leave.

"Have care, Saint, before you do something you'll regret."

Magnus scanned the area, realizing he and MacGregor were alone. He supposed it wasn't surprising, given his mood of late, that the other men had been avoiding him.

When Magnus didn't respond, MacGregor added, "You're letting him get to you. He's waiting for you to make a slip. And if what I just saw is any indication, you are close to doing so. He's been asking a lot of questions about you."

Ah hell. Apparently, Sutherland had broadened his scope. He was too close to the damned truth as it was. "What kind of questions?"

"He's interested in your movements the past few years, especially in recent months."

"Let him ask all he wants—only a handful of people know the answer to that question and none of them will answer it."

"Aye, but that isn't all. I heard him mention to one of Fraser's men that he was surprised Bruce had so many Highlanders in his personal guard, including so many past champions from the Highland Games."

Bruce's phantom warriors' reputation as the best of the best had led to much speculation, but no one had made the connection to the Games until now. MacLeod, MacGregor, and Boyd were most at risk—their reputation as champions well known—but Magnus would not be immune from scrutiny as well.

Magnus's mouth fell in a grim line. "Sutherland is a pain in the arse."

"A *dangerous* pain in the arse. And a perceptive one. You have to admire him." Magnus shot him a traitorous look. It was bad enough that the king had taken notice of Sutherland; now MacGregor, too? "Both he and Munro are watching you closely—you need to get them off the scent." The famed archer gave him a hard look. "I'd tell you to lose, if I thought you would do it."

His jaw locked. He'd rather have a bounty on his head, as was sure to happen were his identity discovered.

"Well, you'd better do something," MacGregor said. "You've been pulled as tight as one of my bowstrings—by all the Sutherlands," he added.

Magnus knew that MacGregor suspected the truth: he lusted after their dead friend's widow. The fact that he'd loved her first didn't stop his shame.

"Did he know?" MacGregor asked.

Magnus stilled, knowing who MacGregor meant. Eventually, he shook his head. "Not until after the wedding."

Unlike MacRuairi, MacGregor didn't voice his disapproval, but Magnus could see it on his face.

He should have told Gordon sooner. But he was too damned stubborn. Too damned sure he could control his feelings. And now it was too late. Damn, he missed him. They all did. Gordon's death had left a hole in the Guard that would never be filled.

MacGregor gave him a long look. Though Magnus had never told any of the Highland Guard what happened the day Gordon died, he wondered whether some suspected the truth.

The famed archer didn't waste time with questions; he cut right to the quick. "Either find yourself a woman or stop punishing yourself and take the one you want—I don't give a shite which, but do *something*."

Punishing himself with Helen? Perhaps he was. But some guilts were impossible to absolve.

Even if he could forget, he wouldn't put her in danger. Her brother was doing that enough on his own. Sutherland had reminded him of how much was at risk. He wouldn't add to that risk by linking her to another member of the Highland Guard.

For more reasons than one, Helen was lost to him forever.

"I'll take care of it," he said.

Thirteen

❧

What is he doing?

Helen sat at the dais with her heart squeezed in a vise of hurt and jealousy, unable to believe what she was seeing. The little tugs in her chest that had started at the beginning of the evening meal when she'd seen Magnus smile at the serving maid—Joanna, the daughter of the alewife, who had a reputation for being free with her favors—had sharpened as the meal drew on, and the signs of what he was doing became more blatant.

He was flirting. Showing Joanna that he wanted her in ways of which Helen had only dreamed.

Unable to turn away, Helen saw Joanna bend over— bend *way* over—to refill his goblet. She started to back away, but he stopped her, capturing her wrist in his hand and spinning her back toward him. She almost ended up in his lap. Then, he whispered something in her ear that caused her to giggle like a lass of six and ten rather than a woman at least twice that old.

Well, maybe not twice, Helen conceded. But she was definitely far too old to be giggling.

Helen had never noticed how beautiful the other woman was, with her long, dark hair and bold features. Muriel had never liked her, though Helen wondered now whether it might have had something to do with her brother. Joanna had been linked to Will a number of years ago.

She was even more convinced that there was something between her brother and Muriel after Donald had returned with the news that he'd found Muriel, but upon hearing that the king was no longer in danger, she'd declined to return; if Will needed her he could come and ask himself. Will had flown into a rage, cursing her and calling her ungrateful, his anger far too disproportionate to the offense.

But her brother's problem was not what concerned her now. Watching Magnus, Helen felt as if acid were eating her up inside. She reached for her goblet, lifted it to her mouth, and drained the contents in a desperate attempt to maintain the illusion of control. She needed something to shore up her crumbling defenses. Something to heat the blood in her icy veins. Something to stop her from running over there and demanding to know why he was doing this. It was just like the wedding . . .

It's nothing, she told herself. *A little harmless flirting.*

But it wasn't harmless at all. It hurt.

Helen gasped, her body buckling as if she'd just taken a fist to the gut, when Magnus slid his hand from the woman's wrist to her waist, and then to her bottom. His fingers spread wide to cup her curvaceous backside. He let it sit there. Possessively. Intimately. The soft caress a promise, a hint of what was to come.

Helen might have rushed over there right then had the king not stopped her.

" 'Tis a fine feast, Lady Helen. I fear my men and I will be leaving your larder bare."

Helen forced herself to attend the king, realizing she'd been neglecting her hostess duties for most of the meal.

Had he noticed?

If he had, he was good enough not to show it.

She tried to smile, but the reminder that the king's party was leaving in a matter of days sent another surge of panic through her chest. "You are welcome to stay as long as you like, Sire. Our larder is well stocked and ready for many more feasts. Are you sure it is wise to leave so soon?"

The Bruce waved at the wine attendant to refill his goblet, and then motioned to hers to do the same. After handing her the wine, he leaned back in his chair. "We've been here nearly a month. I've many stops to make before the Games next month." He smiled. "I thought you pronounced me healed?"

She frowned. "I said you appeared in good health. But that does not mean—"

He stopped her with a wave of his hand and a laugh. "I heard your instructions the first time or two."

Helen quirked a brow and glanced to his plate. "Yet I do not see any of the kale I asked the cook to prepare on your trencher."

The king made a face. "There are certain things I will not eat even for the sake of health. I did have your beets."

Helen lifted her brow again.

He laughed. "Well, a bite of them anyway. They taste like dirt no matter how much sauce you put on them."

Helen shook her head. The king could be as obstinate as a five-year-old when it came to eating something he didn't like.

"What am I going to do when you are not there to watch over me?" he said with an exaggerated sigh.

"I suspect eat far fewer vegetables," Helen replied dryly.

The king was still laughing when her brother Will drew him back into conversation.

Helen took another fortifying gulp of wine—savoring the feeling of warmth from the flush it induced—before chancing another glance at Magnus.

To her relief, the serving woman had moved off, and he was laughing with MacGregor and some of the other men. He looked relaxed, she realized. Happier and more at ease than she'd seen him in years. What had wrought this

change in him? Was it the drink? The ale was certainly
flowing freely at that corner of the table.

Too freely. The ever-efficient Joanna was making her
rounds again with the jug and headed in his direction. The
smile of anticipation on her face turned Helen's chest inside
out. She felt exposed—vulnerable—knowing that whatever
happened next, it would hurt.

It did.

Joanna brushed against him as she leaned over to fill his
cup. Her generous breasts dangled before him like two ripe
melons, waiting to be picked. The invitation couldn't be
much clearer.

Helen held her breath. *Tell her no. Please, tell her no.*

Magnus leaned over to whisper something in her ear.
Something that caused Joanna to nod excitedly.

A knife twisted in Helen's chest. His answer was
clear, and it wasn't no.

Don't do this.

But her silent pleas had no effect. A few moments later,
Magnus took another long drink of ale, slammed his cup
down, and pushed back from the table. He stood, said
something to his companions that caused them to laugh,
and then made his way out of the Hall, his destination—or
assignation—clear.

Every step he took landed on her heart, a heavy footfall
that ground her hope into the dirt.

Why was he doing this? Was he trying to prove to her
how little she meant to him? Was he trying to discourage
her? Had she pushed him too hard?

Helen didn't know. She just knew that she couldn't let
him do this. She wasn't naive enough to think there hadn't
been other women in his past. But this wasn't the past, this
was now. She had to stop him before he did something . . .

Something that would break her heart for good.

She waited as long as she dared. But when she saw Joanna
leave the Hall, she knew she couldn't wait any longer.

* * *

A short while later, Helen had the information she needed and headed to the alehouse—more precisely, to the small storage room inside it. Like many of the larger and more modern castles, Dunrobin had an alehouse within its gates. The small wooden building adjoined the kitchens, and both buildings had vaulted floors with storage below.

In one of those rooms, Magnus was waiting.

Helen pursed her mouth, steeling herself for what was sure to be her second unpleasant conversation of the evening.

Joanna had not given up the information willingly. Helen bit her lip, feeling a tad guilty for the lies she'd told. But a "strange rash on his groin" could be completely harmless—just as she'd told her.

Her mouth twitched. Being the castle healer was not without its benefits. In any event, she didn't think Magnus would be making any more assignations, at least not while he was at Dunrobin.

The pungent, yeasty smell of the ale hit her as soon as she entered the alehouse. A fire crackled in the brazier, and a candle flickered on a large table, but with everyone at the Hall, the room was empty. Unfamiliar with the building, it took her a moment to find the storeroom.

But no sooner had she pushed the door open than an arm reached out to snake around her waist and pull her inside. She gasped in surprise. In one smooth move, he spun her around so her back was to his chest and pushed her up against the door, closing it.

The room was nearly pitch black—only the barest hint of light from the candle outside flitted through the wooden planks of the door. The heady scent of yeast filled her nose, drowning out everything else.

For a moment her senses were cut off, blind to everything but the sheer masculine force of the body at her back. He was hot and hard. She could feel the proof of his profession in every inch of steely, ripped muscle. The years of war and training had honed him to the peak of physical strength.

His arm tightened, pulling her a little snugger, as his lips brushed against her ear and sent a shiver whispering down her spine.

"I've been waiting for you," he said huskily, drink heavy in his voice.

Helen's eyes widened. *He doesn't know it's me—the wretch!*

She opened her mouth to identify herself, but suddenly forgot how to talk when he ground his hips against her bottom. She sucked in her breath; she could feel him grow big and hard against her.

Goodness! Her eyes widened with amazement. Knowing she could do that to him made her feel somehow stronger— empowered.

He moved the thick column lower, positioning himself between her legs. The blunt tip nudged intimately at her entry.

Dear God.

She shuddered. Awareness spread over her in a hot wave, the proof of his arousal triggering her body's response to the primitive call. She started to tingle; a flush of fevered heat spread over her skin in a shimmering wave. She felt alive in a way that she never had before.

I should tell him . . .

But all thoughts of telling him anything slid from her mind when his lips found her neck and his hand covered her breast. He groaned, cupping and squeezing while his mouth ravished her neck. She'd never imagined him like this. Rough. Demanding. Unabashedly sensual.

He was devouring her as if he couldn't get enough of her, his lips and tongue trailing hot wet kisses down to the nape of her neck. The scrape of his jaw along the sensitive skin burned like a brand.

Her knees felt weak, her entire body boneless with the

wonder of it. The passion she'd always dreamed of was in her grasp.

She didn't want to let go.

His body was moving against hers in a wicked dance that demanded a response. But she didn't know the steps. When his hips moved against her she had to press back, increasing the friction. The harder he kissed her neck, the more he squeezed her breast, the faster his movements became, the more bold were her responses. She arched her back, circled her hips, and let the gasps of her pleasure fall more freely from between her lips.

Her body was not her own. It was his. It had always been his.

Magnus should have done this a long time ago. What the hell had he been waiting for? Blood pounded through his veins in anticipation. His heart hammered. He couldn't wait to be inside her.

He felt as if a weight were being lifted off his shoulders. Despite what his brethren thought, he hadn't lived like a saint in the years since Helen had refused him. But always before, he'd been burdened by guilt—unwarranted or not.

Tonight he would be free; he could feel it.

He was more than a little drunk, but he didn't care. He couldn't believe how turned on the gel was getting him with those little breathy sounds she was making. He loved the way her tight little bottom moved against his hardness, teasing him, driving him mad with the urge to thrust inside her. He loved her smooth, silky skin that tasted like honey, and the full, ripe breasts that could almost make him forget the full, ripe breasts that had been tormenting him for days. Those damned gowns!

Don't think about her.

He distracted himself with her chest—Joanna, he reminded himself—squeezing the soft flesh a little more insistently, savoring the heavy weight of it, and then burying his nose in her hair with a groan as the force of his desire pounded through him. If the soft silkiness and faint scent of lavender stirred a familiar memory, he shook it off. Then, to prove the memory false, he slipped his hand below the fabric of her dress and cupped her bare breast in his hand.

He liked the way she gasped. Liked it so much, in fact, that he set about eliciting some more. He ran his thumb over the taut little tip, caressing it to a firm peak. When it was nice and hard, he rolled it between his fingers and gave it a gentle pinch. He was rewarded with another gasp.

Liked that, did she?

For a moment, he fought the urge to flip the little wanton around and cover that gasp with his mouth. But he shied from the intimacy. He didn't want to kiss her, he wanted to swive her. So badly that he didn't know how much longer he could wait.

Helen was awash in sensation. The shock she'd felt when his big, callused hand had made contact with her naked breast had turned to wonder as he began to caress her, and then to urgent moans as his stroking intensified.

Her breasts felt so heavy in his hands. Her nipples were so hard and tight they throbbed. And when he began to pinch them between his fingers, tiny needles of pleasure shot through her straight to her toes.

She felt so strange. So hot and restless. She'd never imagined this kind of passion from him. There was nothing chaste and reverent about his touch. He wanted her, and he was showing her exactly how much.

"God, it's been so long," he groaned, his breath coming hard and fast in her ear.

How long? she wanted to ask, but dared not speak for fear he would realize it was her and stop. She didn't want him to stop. Her body was clamoring for something she didn't understand. She was hot everywhere he touched her and needy everywhere he hadn't.

"I can't wait much longer, I need to be inside you. I hope

you like it from behind." He moved against her again, slower and more sensually—like his voice—showing her what he meant. The sheer naughtiness of it sent a wicked thrill running through her.

Why has he never talked to me like this? It was a side of him she'd never seen before. A little base. A little crude. And more than a little exciting. A passionate, fiercely carnal side that he'd kept hidden from her. It sent a flood of desire pooling between her legs. Damp. Warm. Needy. But it was nothing compared to what happened when his hand covered that warm and achy place. He gripped her firmly, holding her to him.

"Do you?" he teased with that smooth, velvety voice, rocking against her in silent question.

Helen couldn't seem to breathe. Glad that he couldn't see her shocked, wide eyes, she nodded furiously, not really knowing what she was agreeing to except that she wanted whatever he wanted to do to her.

"Naughty lass." He chuckled and flipped her skirts up. A blast of cool air swept over her backside. He paused to give her bottom a swift caress before his hand slipped around the front of her thigh to reach between her legs.

Oh God . . .

Her heart jumped; her knees buckled at the contact. She hadn't known what she wanted until he touched her. Until she felt the pressure of his hand on her mound. Until she felt his big, strong finger delve inside her. Stroking, plunging in and out, making the pool of desire low in her belly start to tighten and coil. And pulse. Frantically. She pushed back against his hand, wanting him to go faster. Deeper. Harder. She cried out, feeling the pleasure build.

It was everything she'd always dreamed of. And so much more.

"God, you're so wet and tight. You've got me so hard, I feel like I'm going to explode. I can't wait to come inside you, Joanna."

Joanna.

Helen stilled, the sound of the other woman's name in his voice a cold shock of reality. All this passion wasn't for her, it was for Joanna. Suddenly, the fact that he thought he was doing this with someone else wasn't enough. She needed him to know it was her.

"Magnus, I—"

The suddenness of his movement stopped her. His hand was gone and he pushed away from her as if she'd burned him.

Perhaps she had.

Jerking her away from the door, he swung it open. A beam of soft candlelight flooded the room.

He swore, the look of disgust on his face cutting her to the quick.

She staggered, her legs unsteady from the loss of his support and from the harshness of his expression.

"You!" The accusation of that one word pierced her heart.

Helen took a step toward him, her body still pulsing with desire. "Aye, me." She reached out to put her hand on his arm, but he flinched from her touch.

"Don't," he bit out through clenched teeth.

"Why not? I want to touch you. A moment ago you said you couldn't wait—"

He grabbed her arm and hauled her up against him, his cheeks stained red. "I know what I said, damn it. I know exactly what I said. But that wasn't meant for you. None of it was meant for you!"

Helen flinched at the brutal cruelty. Heat tightened her throat. But she refused to let his words hurt her. "But it *was* me. It is me you want." She looked up into that handsome face fierce with anger and embarrassment, and dared him to deny her. "I can still feel your hands on my body. In my body," she said softly. "I still ache for you." She lowered her eyes, letting her gaze rest on the big bulge between his legs. "And I think you still ache for me."

The drink had made her bold. Now was not the time for maidenly reserve. *Seize the day.* Before he guessed what she meant to do, she reached down and covered him with her hand.

She'd never touched a man before and the feel of him beating beneath her palm, hard and thick, only heightened her curiosity. She knew what was supposed to happen, but he felt much too big to go inside her.

A sound almost like a hiss seeped out from between his tightly clenched lips. But it was the only crack in his otherwise implacable facade. If her touch affected him, he wasn't going to do anything about it. His control angered her when her own body was still weeping for his touch.

"Do you deny that you want me?" She leaned against him, letting her breasts brush against his chest.

She was rewarded with the flex of a muscle beneath his jaw. He did want her, but he was determined to deny them both. Throwing caution completely into the fire, she lifted up on her tiptoes and pressed her lips against that spot. His skin was warm and scratchy, with the faint taste of soap and salt. She'd placed her hand on his chest to balance herself and felt his heart stop for a beat. But then it began to beat again, hard and angry.

Furious, he set her aside, every muscle straining with anger. "I know what you are doing and it won't work. I'm not going to change my mind."

Helen stared at him, not understanding why he was choosing to hold on to the past and his memories of a friend over her. The hot prick of frustration gathered behind her eyes. How easy it was for him to pull himself back from a precipice when she was still falling! "Would it be so horrible if you did?"

For one moment his expression cracked, and she could see the longing that mirrored her own.

"There are things you don't know," he said hoarsely.

"Then tell me."

He held her gaze, a strange look crossing his face. Guilt? Shame? But then the mask fell back into place, and he turned away. "It makes no difference. It will not change anything. I can't do this."

A steel curtain had come down around him, and she knew it was useless to argue, but she couldn't help trying. "Can't, or won't?" He didn't say anything, but the look of pity in his gaze made it seem so much worse. She wanted to bang on his chest and force him to let her inside. She wasn't alone in this. She wasn't. "Yet you had no problem when you thought it was someone else?"

He turned from the accusation in her gaze. "I owe you no explanations, Helen. I can bed whomever I wish."

She sucked in her breath at the cold strike of pain. She held his gaze, the crushing truth of that statement hitting her with finality. He owed her nothing. The only bond between them existed in her heart.

She stood squarely in front of him, forcing him to look at her one more time. "Except me."

His eyes met hers. "Except you."

And with that, he turned on his heel and left.

Helen let him go, resisting the urge to go after him. She knew he wouldn't change his mind right now. He was too angry. Too determined.

He wanted her, but he was intent on resisting her. Why was he being so stubborn? Why was he trying to hard so make her give up?

Her eyes widened. Was that it? Did he want her to give up? Was this some kind of test to see if she was as feckless and inconstant as before?

Helen straightened her spine, shaking off the discouragement of moments before. She wouldn't give up. She would fight for him for as long as it took. If seducing him didn't work, she would wear him down in other ways. She could be stubborn, too.

But how to prove it when he was leaving, and she would remain at—

She stopped, remembering something the king had said earlier. A smile crept up her features. "What am I going to do without you?"

Perhaps they didn't need to find out.

Fourteen

❧

"Absolutely not."

The king lifted a brow at Magnus's bold pronouncement.

Magnus gritted his teeth and amended, "I mean, I do not believe that is a good idea, Sire. Our delay at Dunrobin means we will have much ground to cover and many places to visit. It will not be a pace for ladies." Especially *that* lady. "Besides, you do not appear to be in any need of a healer. I thought you declared yourself healthier than you've felt in years?"

The king smiled. "All due to Lady Helen. That peasant diet of hers is unpalatable, but it is not without effect. She has graciously offered to continue serving as my healer on our progress."

Graciously I'll bet—the devious little termagant. Magnus could kill her. When the king had asked him to come to his chamber after breaking his fast to discuss their journey, he hadn't anticipated having to fend off another one of Helen's ploys. He was still in a rage after the trick she'd pulled last night. When he thought of some of the things he'd said to her . . .

A sickly heat crawled up his face. He would never have talked that way if he'd known it was Helen. Hell, he would never have done any of it, if he'd known it was Helen.

When he thought of how he'd touched her . . .

Damn it, he couldn't *stop* thinking about how he'd touched her. He could still feel the lush weight of her breast in his hand, still taste her honey-sweet skin on his lips, and still hear the echo of those frantic little pants in his ear as he'd stroked her. She'd been so soft and wet, her body warm and ready for him. All he could think about was slipping inside that tight little glove and . . .

Devil take the little temptress, he'd been seconds away from taking her from behind like a rabid dog!

Pulling back when his body had been primed to the point of pain had taken every ounce of his strength. Then she'd pushed harder when she'd covered him with her hand. The feel of her dainty fingers wrapped around his cock had set off every primal instinct in his body. He'd been a hair's breadth from giving in to his body's demands. From giving in to her.

Jesus.

Shame bit at him. How could he not have known it was her? The room had been dark and heavy with the scent of ale. He'd been drunk. But he hadn't been *that* drunk. He should have known. Perhaps he had. Perhaps on some unconscious level he'd known it all along.

The ramifications of that were too wretched to contemplate. He'd thought he was free of her, but what if he could never be free?

And now that he'd touched her, felt her body respond to him, it was even worse. She was in his blood. He'd unleashed his passion and there was no pulling it back.

Damn her, this was all her fault. And now she was trying to insinuate herself further into this living hell of his consciousness by attaching herself to their progress. A fresh wave of anger hit. "If you would like someone to accompany us, your grace, I can send for the royal physician in Edinburgh."

The king's gaze hardened. "I don't want the royal physician, I want Lady Helen. None of the concoctions that Lord Oliver forced down my throat did a tenth of the good that Lady Helen has done."

Magnus could hear the king's heels digging in and knew he'd better switch tactics. Perhaps an appeal to his chivalrous nature? "I will ensure that Lady Helen's instructions are seen to. It is not necessary to put her in danger. We might be at peace, but the roads are still no place for a lady."

But Bruce waved off his concern. "Women are usually part of a royal progress. Indeed, were my wife and daughter not in England, I would have them here with me. The lady will be safe enough with you and her brother to protect her."

Magnus stilled. He clenched his fists, trying to hold back his anger. But this battle he was losing. "Sutherland?" he spit out. "You can't be serious!"

The first spark of anger flashed in the king's dark eyes. He allowed Magnus more leeway than he gave most, but he would not have his judgment questioned. "Quite serious," he said stonily. "I've been impressed with Sutherland. We can use more men like him."

Magnus bit back the caustic retort but could feel the blood pounding in his temples. "Sutherland is dangerous. I don't trust him." Any of them, for that matter.

The king's eyes narrowed. "Do you have cause for this concern?"

"A lifetime of experience." Knowing that would not be enough, he added, "As I told you, he's guessed Gordon's place in the Guard and suspects mine. I've tried to impart the danger those kinds of suspicions could have to his family, but he's never known when to keep his mouth shut."

Bruce frowned and seemed to consider his response. "There is an old Saracen adage: keep your friends close and your enemies even closer. If it is as you say, it is better to have him close where we can keep an eye on him and ensure that he is not tempted to repeat his suspicions to others."

Magnus attempted to argue, but the king forestalled him. "What is this really about? Is there another reason you do not wish Lady Helen to accompany us that you are not telling me? I thought you and the lass were longtime friends? Childhood companions, isn't that how you put it?"

Magnus's mouth fell into a hard line. "I might have understated the nature of our relationship."

"I thought you might have. I've noticed the lass's efforts to catch your eye the past few weeks. I take it you are not eager to rekindle this relationship?"

Magnus shook his head.

"Because of Templar?" the king asked softly. Bruce was one of the few men who knew the truth.

Magnus nodded. "Aye."

The king studied him a moment longer. That he didn't choose to question him further indicated he understood the nature of Magnus's struggle and perhaps even agreed with it. "Very well. I shall do without Lady Helen's eagle-eyed scrutiny of my meals on our journey. I will not say I won't miss her personal attendance, but perhaps it is best that she is not drawn back into danger. We are fortunate that Gordon's identity as a member of my 'phantom' guard has not been discovered. I do not wish to see the lass endangered."

The king's words proved ironically prophetic. Barely had Magnus enjoyed the relief of knowing that Helen would not be tormenting him for weeks on end, when disaster struck in the form of a messenger with news that changed everything.

The sun was high in the sky when the rider came thundering through the gate. Magnus was training with the men at the time and didn't pay him much attention. Messengers were always arriving for the king. He suspected something was wrong, however, when the king immediately summoned him and MacGregor to the laird's solar.

They were still thick with dirt and sweat when they entered the small chamber off the Great Hall. The earl had relinquished the room for the king's use during his stay, and it was usually filled with Bruce's large retinue. The room was empty, however, but for Bruce and Sir Neil Campbell.

He could tell by their grim expressions that the news was not good.

"I've news from England," the king said.

At first Magnus thought it must have something to do with the king's family, who were still being held by King Edward. But then he realized that given the current occupants of the room, it must have something to do with the Guard.

It did.

"A body was retrieved from beneath the rubble at Threave."

Magnus tensed. "He won't be identified."

The king gave him a sorrowful look. "I'm afraid he already has been."

Magnus shook his head. "That's impossible."

"Sir Adam Gordon was sent to Roxburgh to make sure of it."

Magnus sat, his legs suddenly unable to support his weight. "How?" he said tonelessly. "I made sure . . ." He let his voice fall off, unable to say the words. The horror of thinking about them was enough. He cleared his throat, but his voice still sounded strained. "None of us carry anything on missions that could identify us. Gordon was careful. He wouldn't have made that kind of mistake."

"He didn't," Sir Neil responded. "But were either of you aware that he had a mark on his skin from birth?"

Ah hell. He felt ill.

"Aye," MacGregor said grimly. "It was on his ankle."

Sir Neil nodded. "Aye, well apparently it was a common mark in his family. His grandfather had one as well—as did his uncle Sir Adam."

The nausea grew worse. Magnus didn't want to believe that it could all have been for nothing. The nightmares of his dreams had just found daylight. "If they know the truth, then why haven't we heard anything about it?"

Bruce held up the missive. "My source says they are keeping it quiet for now until they can figure out how best to make use of the information. We were fortunate to learn of it at all."

"How did you learn of it?"

Bruce shrugged. "It isn't important, but I have no doubt as to its truth."

It wasn't the first time the king had received a message from a secret source. The spy must be trusted and important for the king not to share his identity with the members of the Guard. Magnus and some of the other guardsmen speculated that it might be De Monthermer, who'd helped the king before in the early days of his kingship. But in the end, the identity of the spy didn't matter. All that mattered was that the king trusted the information.

God, it was true! Gordon had been unmasked.

If the English knew about Gordon, it wouldn't take long for the information to lead them to Helen. The potential threat looming since Gordon's death had just become real. Everything Magnus had done to protect her hadn't been enough. She was in danger anyway.

The king's gaze was not without sympathy. "It's probably nothing to worry about. But in light of this new information, we must take precautions."

Magnus hardened his resolve, but he knew he had no choice. It probably wasn't good enough. "Lady Helen must accompany us on the progress as your healer."

There was nothing else he could do. Everything had just

changed. He wasn't going to be able to walk away. He'd made a promise to protect her.

He wished to hell that was all there was to it. But Magnus knew his promise to Gordon had very little to do with the fierce emotion driving him right now. The urge to protect, the fear from the thought of her being in danger—those emotions stemmed from a vicinity much nearer his heart.

The realization that Helen was in danger stripped him of all his carefully constructed walls of delusion and forced him to admit the truth. His feelings weren't as dead as he wanted them to be. His feelings weren't dead at all.

He might not want to love her, and God knew it was wrong of him to do so, but heaven help him, he still did.

It was late when Helen returned to the castle. Though the midsummer days were long, the last breath of daylight was flickering over the horizon.

She'd stayed longer than she had expected. But after she'd tended the arm of the fletcher's son, who'd broken it when he fell out of a tree he'd been climbing, the family had been so grateful, they insisted she stay to eat something with them.

In addition to the five-year-old tree-climber Tommy, the fletcher had seven more children, ranging in age from sixteen months to four and ten. Once their awe at having "the lady" in their home had worn off, they'd bombarded her with questions and enchanted her with their songs; she'd lost track of time. If only she'd thought to ask for a torch before she left.

She hurried through the forest, wondering whether the king had made his decision yet. Helen had approached the king first thing in the morning with the possibility of her accompanying them on the royal progress as his healer. She'd been encouraged by his initial response—he'd seemed quite amenable to the idea—but she knew there would be resistance from at least one of his men.

She bit her lip, acknowledging that avoiding that particular Highlander might have something to do with her lingering at the fletcher's hearth.

But she'd lingered too long. The darker it grew, the faster her pulse raced. The forest wasn't her favorite place at night.

She blinked, as if that would make her be able to see better. There were so many shadows.

She jumped at a rustling toss of leaves behind her. And so many noises.

She was being silly. There was nothing to be scared of—

She yelped when something darted across the path in front of her. A squirrel. At least she hoped it was a squirrel and not a rat. *Oh God.* She ran her hands over her arms; her flesh had started to crawl.

She hurried her step, stumbling forward when her foot landed awkwardly on a rock. She went down hard, crying out when her hands made harsh contact with the forest floor. Her chin followed a moment later.

Stunned, the breath jarred from her lungs, it took her a moment to realize she was all right. After brushing herself off as best she could, she stood. Her ankle was tender, but fortunately, she was able to walk.

Feeling more than a little foolish, she proceeded at a far more cautious pace and did her best to ignore her scary surroundings.

Her heart didn't stop beating at a frantic pace, however, until the first glimpse of the castle gates came into view. She frowned, noticing the unusual number of torches, and, from the number of voices coming from within, an unusual amount of activity.

It wasn't until the cry went out when she came into view, however, that she felt the first prickle of trepidation. A prickle that turned to a full-fledged stab when a handful of men came rushing out of the gate.

She wasn't surprised to see her brothers; she was, however, surprised to see Magnus in the lead. For once the life-long enemies appeared to be presenting a unified front. If she weren't the cause of that unity, she might have savored the moment she'd despaired of ever seeing.

She bit her lip, catching a glimpse of Magnus's expression in the flickering torchlight. She suspected it was only the presence of her brothers that prevented him from grabbing her by the shoulders and . . .

She couldn't tell. He looked angry enough to shake her and worried enough to haul her into his arms.

"Where the hell have you been?" he demanded.

The fact that none of her brothers objected to the blasphemy wasn't a good sign. Indeed, Will appeared to take no issue with it at all. "Damn it, Helen, we were just about to send a search party out for you."

"A search party? Surely that's rather extreme. This is not the first time I've been gone for hours tending to one of the clansmen."

Will's mouth thinned. "Aye, but you were always with Muriel."

She gave him a look as if to say, *and whose fault is it that I am not?*

"MacKay insisted. He thought you might be in danger," Kenneth added.

Helen glanced back at Magnus, perversely pleased to hear the overreaction had been his. Had he been worried about her? He must have guessed her thoughts, because his eyes narrowed dangerously. The smile playing about her lips fell.

"I was only at the fletcher's. His son fell from a tree and broke his arm," she explained, Magnus's impatient glare—reminiscent of the "wayward lamb" look her brothers had perfected—making her feel more than a little defensive.

"The fletcher?" Donald interjected, aghast. "He lives at least five miles away!" He turned to Will. "I warned you this was not a good idea."

Will's gaze narrowed on his henchman. Donald had overstepped his bounds. An earl did not take criticism from one of his men. "Return to the castle, Munro. Inform the king that Lady Helen has been found. We will attend him in the Hall in a few moments."

After his initial question, Magnus had remained suspiciously silent during the exchange with her brother. "The king wishes to see you. When you could not be found, we became concerned. The countryside is not a place for women alone. Did you tell no one where you were going?"

Helen thought back, ashamed to realize she hadn't. She'd been in the garden when the fletcher arrived and had simply gone to her room to retrieve a few items before leaving. She hadn't thought . . .

"I'm sorry. I was in a hurry. I didn't think—"

"You're hurt!" Magnus cut her off. "Damn it, what happened to your chin?" This time her brothers' presence wasn't enough to stop him from touching her. The back of his finger grazed her jaw, tilting her head back to the light.

"It's nothing." She shied from his scrutiny, embarrassed. "A little stumble, that's all."

She hoped it was the torchlight making his face look red, but his clenched jaw rather suggested he was angry again. Had she really wanted to see more emotion from him? She was beginning to miss the even-tempered Magnus.

She took care to hide her hands in her skirts, but his narrowed glance toward her fists told her he suspected there was more.

Anxious to escape his scrutiny, she turned to her brothers. "I shall need a moment to freshen up. Please tell the king I shall attend him in a few moments."

She spun away before they could respond. But she'd forgotten about her ankle. The swift movement sent a knife of pain up her leg, making her cry out. She would have stumbled again had Magnus not caught her.

She gasped at the contact. Their eyes held. For a moment, the memories of the night before flooded her. A slight tightening of his hold told her he remembered, too.

"Damn it, Helen."

It wasn't the most romantic declaration she'd ever heard, but the look in his eyes and gruffness of his tone more than made up for it. He was concerned. He did care about her. It was another chink in the armor of his resistance. Emotion swelled in her chest.

She was prevented from savoring the moment, however, by her brother. Kenneth nearly twisted her other ankle in his eagerness to tear her from Magnus's gasp. "Get your hands off her!"

Apparently, the moment of unity was over.

Helen had had more than enough of her brothers' constant interfering. She spun on Kenneth and snapped, "He was only helping me. I would have fallen had he not caught me. If it hasn't escaped your notice, I seem to have twisted my ankle. Now, if you are done treating me like a bone to fight over, I'm going to my chamber."

If she weren't so angry, the men's unanimous look of shock might have made her laugh.

Her ankle prevented her from stomping off, but it was definitely implied.

In less than half an hour, Helen had washed her face and hands free of dirt and debris, bound her ankle in a cloth, changed her gown, and made her way back down to the Great Hall.

She felt a flutter of nerves, anxious to hear what the king had decided. The circumstances of her return had prevented her from gauging Magnus's reaction.

The tables in the Hall had been cleared for the men to

sleep, so Helen wasn't surprised to be ushered into her brother's solar. She was, however, surprised to see who was waiting for her.

He stood guard at the door. Something about the way he was leaning with his arms folded across his chest made her pulse stutter. The deceptively lazy stance didn't fool her. He was furious. But what for: last night, joining their progress, or her late return?

He appeared not to notice her until she tried to pass him, and he moved to block her. Normally, she would very much like the sensations that came with having that broad chest so near, but the fury emanating from him was setting off rather loud warning bells.

She ventured a glance up at him from under her lashes and bit her lip. Not good. Not good at all.

"Excuse me," she said chirpily, trying to hide her nervousness. "The king is waiting for me."

He wasn't fooled. He leaned closer, trying to intimidate her with his size. It was appallingly effective. He towered over her, and outweighed her at least two times over. It was clear she wasn't going anywhere until he wanted her to.

"Aye, but we haven't finished talking about your wee excursion today."

The late return. At least she knew which of her many transgressions had angered him this time.

She lifted her chin, refusing to be bullied by yet another overprotective male. "I apologize if I caused you any trouble, but I assure you there was nothing to worry about. Besides, I hardly see what concern it could be of yours."

His mouth thinned. "Don't press me, Helen. I'm not in the mood for games. You will not go anywhere from now on without a proper escort. Do you understand? I'll not have you in danger."

She definitely didn't like his tone. "Danger? Don't you think you are overreacting just a bit? And you are not my brother or my *husband;* you have no right to order me about."

She would have flounced past him, but he caught her arm. She could feel the warm imprint of his fingers seeping through her gown.

He acted as if she hadn't spoken. "I'll have your promise, Helen. You will not go anywhere alone."

One look at his face and she knew he would not be denied. She gazed into the impenetrable mask, wondering what this was truly about. Had she worried him that much? "This is that important to you?"

"It is."

The fight seeped out of her. She might not like the way he'd gone about issuing his edicts, but she warmed to the sentiment behind it. "Very well. I promise."

He nodded and let her go, standing back so she could go inside. He waited for her to pass by him before he whispered, "And Helen, there is still the matter of a certain rash to discuss."

Her step faltered. She winced, a guilty flush staining her cheeks. He'd found out about that, had he? She was not deceived by his light tone. She knew there would be the devil to pay for that later.

The talking stopped when she entered the room, but she could see from the men's expressions that she'd entered in the midst of a heated discussion.

Will, in particular, looked furious, though he was doing his best not to show it.

"Ah, Lady Helen." The king rose to greet her, ever the knight. "I heard you had a bit of a mishap—I hope you are all right?"

Magnus closed the door behind her and moved around to take his position beside the king.

"Perfectly fine, Sire. I would not be much of a healer if I could not tend to a few scrapes and a twisted ankle."

She'd given him the opening, hoping he'd take it, and he

did so with a broad smile. "It is your healing skills that we were just discussing. I've expressed to your brother my desire to have you join our progress across the Highlands. I fear I've come to depend on you quite shamefully."

"I'm honored, Your Grace." Helen beamed. It had worked! Her plan had worked!

She chanced a glance at Magnus, but his stony countenance gave no hint of his thoughts on the subject. Yet she couldn't believe he'd gone along with this willingly. He'd made no secret of his eagerness to be rid of her.

Will's thoughts as he addressed her, however, were far more obvious. "We are indeed honored, but as your brother and laird, I am of course concerned about your safety." He turned to the king. "Helen is not a healer; she is a gently reared lady who has been gracious enough to help our clan until another healer can be found."

The king smiled. "Your sister's position is not in doubt. She will be my guest, not my servant. I understand your concern, but I assure you she will be well looked after and protected as if she were my own sister, which I hope she will be soon enough."

Will's gaze slid to Magnus and his mouth tightened, as if he suspected exactly who would be protecting her.

"Of course," the king conceded, "I can understand if you would like to send some of your men along as guardsmen. Perhaps your brother would care to join our party as well?"

Helen's gaze flew to Magnus, but his lack of reaction told her he probably knew of the king's suggestion to include Kenneth ahead of time. She scrunched her nose, not pleased by the new wrinkle in her plan. Having Kenneth along was certainly less than ideal, but she supposed the fact that she was going at all was what mattered. Besides, she couldn't help but feel proud for her brother, who was obviously pleased to have caught the king's attention.

But Will was being backed into a corner and didn't like it. It was clear he didn't want her to go, but also didn't want to outright refuse the king to whom he'd just pledged his loyalty. He had to tread very carefully. "Additional men would relieve some of my concern."

"I would be honored to protect Lady Helen," Donald volunteered.

This time Magnus couldn't completely hide his reaction. His jaw clenched as if he were grinding his teeth hard—very hard. Helen felt much the same. Kenneth *and* Donald, saints preserve her!

Will shook his head. Helen knew that look. She could see her chance slipping away. Her stubborn brother was going to ruin everything and jeopardize his standing with the king. "I'm afraid I can't—"

"Perhaps I might speak to my brother, Sire?" Helen said, cutting him off before he could finish.

"Of course," the king said, standing from his chair. "It's getting late. I believe I shall retire for the evening and hear your answer in the morning," he added to Will. "But I would consider it a personal favor, Sir William, were you to agree to my request."

With that less-than-subtle admonition, the king left the solar, his men following behind him. Helen held her breath as Magnus walked by and caught her eye. A nervous flush rose to her cheeks. From the look on his face, she knew there was still a reckoning to come.

Kenneth hadn't missed the exchange. He turned to Will. "You have to find an excuse. You can't let her go. Not with him—"

Helen interrupted. "I have every intention of going with him, Kenneth. Your concern about Magnus is misplaced. He wants nothing to do with me."

"And I intend to see it stays that way," he said.

"If you could look beyond the feud for one blessed moment, you would see that you have nothing to worry about." She turned to Will. "I hope I shall have your blessing, Will."

"But you will go without it?"

She didn't want to challenge his authority if she didn't have to. She had no power. They both knew that. Just as they also both knew that if he reminded her of that, it would never be the same between them. "You cannot refuse the king, Will. Surely you can see that?"

"The lass is right," Donald said. "Bruce has left you little choice in the matter. If you refuse, he will consider it a personal slight. It is in the best interest of the clan to let her go. You can use it as an opportunity to improve the clan's standing in his new government."

Helen was surprised—and grateful—to have Donald come to her defense.

Will had the belligerent look in his eye of a man who knew he'd been beaten but didn't want to admit it. "If you go, you will leave us without a healer."

"You have a healer if you want one, Will. Muriel will come back if you ask her."

A strange look crossed his face. Longing? Regret? Anger? Helen didn't know, but she was certain she'd guessed correctly: there was something between Will and Muriel.

Or, at least, there had been.

His mouth thinned. "She puts too high a price on her return."

Helen smiled sadly. She suspected the source of conflict for her brother, and perhaps more than anyone, understood his struggle. Love and duty rarely twined together. "Then I suppose you must decide how badly you need her."

Fifteen

Muriel pulled the cloak over her head and hurried across the narrow streets and wynds of Inverness. As the sun fell over the horizon, a damp mist had descended over the royal burgh, blanketing the hills and rooftops in a murky haze.

Normally the short walk from the guild to the small room the Earl of Ross had rented for her above the cobbler's shop was a pleasant way to stretch her legs after a long day's work. But on a ghostly night like tonight, she wished she'd accepted Lord Henry's offer to escort her.

Lord Henry was a new master physician, and she was grateful for his friendship, of which she'd had precious little since arriving in Inverness. To say that the physicians of the guild did not welcome her was an understatement.

But friendship was not all Lord Henry wanted, and she knew it would be wrong to encourage him. Right now her focus was on knocking down whatever obstacles the venerable physicians put in her path, and not making any mistakes while she completed her apprenticeship. She couldn't give them any excuse to get rid of her. And so far, to her surprise as much as she suspected to theirs, she was doing just that—and perhaps even winning a few supporters along the way.

But focus on her work was not the only reason she did not wish to encourage Lord Henry. Her chest pinched. Someday she would put the Earl of Sutherland behind her. But that day had not yet come. It would, though. By all that was holy, it would.

When she'd first realized Will was looking for her, she'd foolishly thought he'd wanted her back. Not trusting herself to be strong enough to refuse, she'd avoided his messengers. It wasn't until Donald cornered her as she left the guild that she'd learned the truth: Will hadn't wanted her back at all. It was the king who'd needed her.

Stung, she'd sent her reply, knowing well that in issuing the petty challenge she was ensuring he would never come for her. William Sutherland of Moray, the proud Earl of Sutherland, would not lower himself to chase after anyone. Even the woman he professed to love. Not when she'd spurned that love—or rather, his "offer."

As she turned the corner onto the high street, her step slowed. The street was well lit, a hubbub of activity, filled with merchants, alehouses, and even an inn. The noise was oddly reassuring.

Her room was just up the road ahead. She could make out the torch that the cobbler had left for her as she walked past the alehouse. The sounds of shouts and breaking glass weren't all that unusual. But a moment later, a man stumbled out—or more accurately, was shoved out—right into her path. Unable to avoid a collision, she bumped into him and barely caught herself from falling.

"Pardon," she murmured, instinctively trying to move away. But he caught her around the waist and spun her back to him.

"What do we have here?" he slurred, the stench of ale heavy on his breath. He was a big man, heavy and blunt-featured. *A soldier.* Ice ran down her spine. His arm tightened around her waist and he drew his heavily bearded face closer. "Ye're a pretty littl' piece, aren't ye?"

Helen recoiled from the look in his eyes. Panic rose to wrap around her throat. *No, no, no! Not again!* She couldn't go through it again.

"Let go of me!" she choked, trying to pull away.

He laughed. "What's the hurry, pretty? We're just getting to know one other."

He wiggled her against his body. The feel of his hardened member sent a fresh burst of panic surging through her. She went half-crazed, hitting him, pushing against him with everything she had, knowing she had to get away.

"What the—?" His voice was cut off.

A black shadow crossed in front of her, and suddenly she was free. She heard the crush of bone as a fist slammed into the jaw of the brute who'd accosted her. He flew backward, landing on the stone ground in front of her. She could see the flash of steel in the torchlight from the blade at his throat.

"Give me one reason I shouldn't kill you," her rescuer said.

Muriel gasped. "Will!"

The dark, shadowy figure turned toward her. Their eyes caught, and she staggered.

He swore, lurching forward to catch her before she fell. He tucked her to his chest with one arm, the other still holding the sword, and she collapsed against him. "It's all right," he said softly, holding her up. "You're safe."

Will. He was really here! The soothing sound of his voice was like a dream come true.

The man on the ground took the opportunity to escape. Will started after him, but Muriel clung to him like a lifeline. "Just let him go," she sobbed, the fear that had gripped her releasing in a flood of tears. "Don't leave me."

He held her close as he led her down the street to her room at the cobbler's. He must have been waiting for her when he'd seen the man accost her.

He'd been waiting for her. Could it mean . . . ?

Treacherous hope kindled in her chest.

He opened the door and led her into the shop. After lighting a candle, he sat her in a chair, while he went to the back of the shop and rummaged around for something. A moment later, he was back at her side, holding out a cup. "Here, it's all I could find."

Her nose wrinkled at the smell, but she drank the foul-tasting, fiery brew without protest. The whisky burned a path down her throat, warming the chill from her blood.

When some of the shock had worn off, she stared at him in disbelief. "You came."

His handsome face hardened. "It's a good thing I did. Damn it, Muriel, what were you thinking? You should know better than to walk alone at night. Don't you know—"

He stopped, a look of shame washing over him.

She flinched. "Aye, I know what could have happened."

"I didn't mean . . ."

She laughed at his discomfort. "To remind me? God, Will, do you think I could ever forget? Do you think I didn't see the men who raped me in his eyes? Do you think I wasn't remembering every moment of that day in my head?" He reached for her, but she turned away. Pity wasn't what she wanted from him. "Do you think I could forget what those men cost me?"

She'd been fourteen. The war had reached Berwick-upon-Tweed, and King Edward's men had flooded the city. Her father had been at the hospital caring for the wounded when the soldiers came. Eight of them. Each one taking a turn raping her before they tossed her in the street like garbage. One of her neighbors had found her battered and bleeding to death in the street. Someone had sent for her father. He'd managed to save her life, but not all of her could be healed.

Because of what those men did to her, she would never be able to give Will a son and heir. Nothing she could do would change that.

They never should have fallen in love, the earl's heir and the physician's daughter. The first couple of years after she arrived at Dunrobin he'd barely seemed to acknowledge her. But perhaps she'd just been too wrapped up in her own pain to notice. Their friendship started out slowly at first, she'd thought, by accident. He'd be walking along the beach at the same time she was, or she'd run into him on the way back from tending one of the clansmen.

She'd been nervous around him at first—scared, really— the handsome young heir to the earldom. But after a while the wariness lessened. She began to trust him. She began to like him. He was kinder than she'd realized. Funnier, too. Single-handedly, he'd wooed her back into the realm of the living.

She'd begun to dream.

And miraculously, it seemed her dreams were answered. When she finally shared the truth of her past with him, he'd held her in his arms and comforted her. And then he'd kissed her—so tenderly—and told her that he loved her. She'd never forget the hope of that moment. It was beyond her wildest dreams. She thought it surprised even him. They reveled in their newfound feelings—in her slowly awakening passion—for months.

Until he asked her to marry him. He would have ignored his duty to marry for the benefit of the clan and taken a woman with only a few pounds to her name as his wife. But then she told him she would never be able to give him a son. That was the one duty he could not ignore.

They'd existed in a state of perdition for nearly two years, the hopelessness of the situation making them both miserable. But it wasn't until he'd made his "offer" that she'd broken it off. He'd refused to accept it, in anger reverting to the cold, imperious earl he appeared to everyone else.

But now he was here. Thank God, he'd come just in time. She cleared the emotion from her throat with a hard swallow and lifted her gaze back to his. "I let my guard down. It's a short walk from the guild, and I've grown accustomed to walking by myself. I shall take precaution next time."

"There won't be a next time."

The imperialistic tone in his voice should have alerted her, but she couldn't tamp the pang of hope. Had he reconsidered? Had he decided to put aside his duty to marry her?

She didn't believe it. Not really. But the ache of hope in her chest proclaimed her a liar.

"Why are you here, Will?" she asked quietly.

He bristled. "I've come to fetch you back myself as you commanded."

"But why?" She held his gaze, but he turned away.

"You are needed." *Not "I need you." Not "I can't live without you." Not "I love you."* "Helen decided to accompany the king on his progress."

How was it possible that she still could feel disappointment? She took a deep breath. "So you came to bring me back as your healer?"

He flinched at the hollowness in her voice. Had she pricked his elusive conscience? "Aye."

I'm a fool. Nothing had changed. She couldn't blame him for not marrying her. She understood his duty. But she did blame him for not letting her go.

She shook her head. "I'm sorry, I can't leave right now. I'm in the middle of—"

"I shall speak to them. You will be allowed to return when you wish."

His disregard for her work, as well as his certainty that the men would bow to the great Earl of Sutherland, infuriated her. "No, Will. I said no!"

His eyes sparked dangerously. God, how he hated to be denied! "Damn it, Muriel." Before she realized what he intended to do, he grabbed her arm, hauled her up against him, and covered her mouth with his.

Her traitorous heart shattered at the contact. The first familiar taste of him drenched her with heat and happiness. Emotions she'd been trying to suppress broke free in an instant.

His kiss was bruising, punishing, his lips plundering with every demanding stroke. His passion for her had always been her weakness. He'd never kissed her like a damaged piece of china, he'd kissed her like a woman who could feel passion.

And God help her for a fool, she did. She slid her tongue against his and kissed him back every bit as ravenously, every bit as desperately. She loved him so much and wanted every inch of him. She clutched the steely muscles of his back, pressing herself more firmly against him. She loved the way he felt against her. Hard and strong. Warm and safe.

He groaned into her mouth, digging his fingers through her hair to bring her mouth more firmly against him. He opened her mouth wider, slid his tongue in deeper, stroking her harder and harder.

He was losing control. She could feel the stiff facade of the earl start to break apart and the warm, passionate man she'd fallen in love with begin to shine through.

But then he remembered himself.

With a fierce groan, he tore away. In profile, she watched the heaviness of his breath start to slow as he composed himself. "I'm sorry. I didn't mean . . ." His eyes locked on hers. "I shouldn't have done that. It's not why I came."

Muriel thought her heart was done breaking, but she was crumbling inside. He'd remembered his duty. The stiff, formidable earl had returned. The man who wouldn't be denied. The man whose love would make her a whore.

"It will only be for a short while. Until a suitable replacement can be found."

Her chest burned. *A wife. The woman who would take her place. Oh God.* She couldn't bear it.

She would have refused him again, but he knew her weakness.

"You owe me, Muriel. You owe my family."

She staggered at the blow. The expertly wielded dagger that pierced her heart. He was right. She did owe him. His family had taken her in and given her a place to heal. When her father died, Will had not forced her to take a husband like anyone else would have done. It didn't matter that his motivation was selfish. But she hated him for using her gratitude against her. He'd given her freedom; now he was taking it away.

She forced her gaze to his, though the burning in her chest made it feel as if the air had been squeezed from her lungs. "I will come for one month. But after that, any debt I have to you will be paid in full."

Cool, arrogant eyes met hers. He nodded. "Very well. A month."

He thought he could change her mind. But he couldn't. He'd done what she'd thought impossible: he'd made her hate him.

Sixteen

❦

Motte of Dingwall, Cromarty

They'd been at the Earl of Ross's fortress of Dingwall for
a few days before Magnus had the opportunity to speak to
Helen alone. His duties on the road, and their natural sepa-
ration when they arrived, not to mention her brother and
Munro's hovering, had forced Magnus to keep a watch on
her from a distance. He was almost—almost—glad for the
other men's presence. Sutherland and Munro's vigilance
was added protection against something happening to her.
Of course, they thought *he* was the threat.

He hoped to hell they were right. But he wouldn't relax
his guard until . . .

He didn't know when he'd ever be able to relax his
guard. The danger would be there as long as there was
anyone who sought to uncover the identities of Bruce's
phantom warriors. Helen was connected to the Guard,
whether she wanted to be or not.

Magnus felt an unexpected flare of anger at his dead
friend. Had Gordon even thought of the danger he was
exposing her to when he'd married her?

The potential danger was all Magnus could think about.
If their enemies thought Helen knew something . . .

Hell, he didn't want to think about what they would do to her to extract it. He'd already thought about it plenty the night she'd been late in returning to the castle.

He never panicked. Never. No matter how dire the situation, he always knew what to do. Even among the cool, unflappable members of the Highland Guard, Magnus was known for his steely nerves and levelheaded thinking in the heat of battle. But for one horrible moment, he'd felt the icy grip of fear close around him to lock him in a mind-numbing state of helplessness. If anything happened to her . . .

He'd become completely unhinged.

In retrospect he'd overreacted, but at the time all he could think about was Helen in the grasp of some sadistic bastard bent on extracting information from her.

The king was right. There was probably nothing to worry about. But he wouldn't be able to relax until he was damned sure of it.

Of course, in addition to watching Helen he also had his duty to the king. Like the Sutherlands', Ross's fealty had been recently and reluctantly given. Though Bruce had accepted Ross back into the fold for the good of the realm, never far from any of their minds was that Ross had been the man responsible for violating church sanctuary to turn Bruce's queen, his sisters, his daughter, and the Countess of Buchan over to the English.

The tension in the Hall was understandably thick and the possibility of further treachery never far from their minds. But like the Sutherlands, Bruce had sought to solidify Ross's pledge with an alliance, this one between Ross's heir, Sir Hugh, and the king's sister Maud. It was the agreement to the betrothal that they were celebrating in the Great Hall when Magnus saw Helen slip away.

Since they'd arrived at Dingwall she'd been acting strangely. Especially around the other ladies, she seemed unusually quiet and subdued. It reminded him of when he'd first seen her at Dunstaffnage—as if there were something missing. He could not fault her appearance. He'd never seen her hair so artfully arranged, and she'd returned to a more modest gown selection—thank God!—but he wondered if something was wrong.

After a quick glance to MacGregor to keep an eye on the king, Magnus slipped outside after her. It was his duty. It wasn't because he was worried about her.

Though the sky was clear, it was windy, and this close to the sea, cold for a midsummer day. Dingwall, an old Viking fortress garrisoned by the English and recently given to Ross to keep, was situated on a large motte fortified by a stone rampart and a hundred feet below by a wide ditch. The circular tower had been added to over the years, and now the castle was said to be the largest north of Stirling.

Magnus looked around but didn't see her right away. There were a number of people about: servants rushing back and forth from the kitchens to the Hall, as well as soldiers patrolling the wall and guarding the gates.

He forced his heart to beat and clenched his jaw—he wasn't going to panic, damn it—and methodically looked around again. He almost missed her. She was half-hidden behind a wall overlooking the ramparts; only a banner of long auburn hair blowing in the wind gave away her location.

With a deeper sigh of relief than he wanted to admit, he headed toward her. When he caught how quickly he was walking, however, he frowned. At Dunrobin he'd been doing his damnedest—without success—to avoid her. But after nearly a week of watching her from afar and speaking only when surrounded by others, if he didn't know better he'd think he was anxious to see her. That he missed her.

Ah hell. He knew he was slipping, and there wasn't a damned thing he could do about it. They were together, whether he liked it or not. He might as well make the best of it.

Captivated by the seaside view of the Firth below her, she didn't hear him approach.

"I thought you liked dancing?"

She jumped at the sound of his voice and spun around with a start. But when she realized who it was, a bright smile turned her lips. Her delight at seeing him shouldn't make him so happy—but it did. That smile settled right between his ribs and radiated through him. He felt as if he'd inhaled a ray of sunlight.

"Magnus, you surprised me!"

He smiled wryly. "I can see that. You appeared to be lost in thought." Their eyes met. "Thinking up new cures for rashes, by chance?"

A delicate pink flush bloomed over her sun-kissed cheeks. She glanced up at him uncertainly from under long, dark lashes. "Are you very angry?"

Their gazes held for a long pause, the memories of what had happened hanging thick and hot in the air between them. A primal kick of awareness that hit right in the groin. Angry? He should be. But he wasn't. He'd touched her. Had his hands in places he'd only dreamed of. Felt her body move against his. Tasted passion unlike anything he'd ever imagined. She'd tricked him into doing what honor would never have allowed him to do. Given him excuse. He wasn't hypocritical enough to regret it.

But he didn't want to encourage her. He wasn't sure he would be strong enough to pull back again. "I was."

"But you aren't any longer?"

She looked up at him with such wide-eyed hopefulness, he had to force a stern expression. "I might be persuaded to forgive you, *if* you give me your word you will never do something like that again."

She pursed her mouth distastefully. "I was provoked. And it isn't my fault she jumped to the wrong conclusion. 'Strange rash' could have meant anything."

The defiant little minx. "Helen . . ."

From the way she tossed up her chin, he assumed she didn't like his tone.

"Very well, as long as you promise not to do something like that again as well." Her face fell, and she lost some of her bravado. "It was wrong of you to do that in front of me."

"You weren't the only one feeling provoked." He glanced down at her dress. "I noticed you aren't wearing any more of those 'modest' gowns."

She blushed and turned away.

Content to simply stand beside her, he followed the direction of her gaze and watched the fishing boats going in and out of the port of Dingwall below.

Finally, she broke the silence. "Does the king have need of me?"

He frowned. "Nay, why do you ask?"

She lifted a brow wryly. "I figured you must have a reason to seek me out."

The wryness of her tone bothered him. He felt a twinge of guilt. But he could no longer avoid her—even if he wanted to, which he realized he didn't. "I thought there might be something wrong. You didn't appear to be enjoying yourself at the meal, and you left before the dancing started. Munro didn't look very pleased to see you go."

He frowned, thinking how possessively the other man had been watching her. Had Sutherland not prevented him, Magnus suspected Munro would have followed her out of the Hall. It shouldn't bother him so damned much.

She tilted her head, studying him with a contemplative look on her face. "I didn't realize you were watching me so closely." When he didn't react, she gave him a rueful smile. "I just felt like I needed a breath of fresh air."

"I saw you with Ross's sisters. It must be nice to have ladies near your own age to talk to."

"It is."

He frowned again, realizing he was missing something. "But . . . ?"

She shrugged. "I just don't always know what to say."

"You? I've never known you to be at a loss for words."

She laughed. "You say it as if you wished otherwise."

His mouth twitched. "I used to sit there listening to you, wondering how a young lass could have so much to talk about. I fell asleep in the sun more than once listening to you."

She gave him a playful shove. "You were supposed to be fishing."

"How could I, when your chattering was chasing all the fish away?"

"I never chattered," she said indignantly.

With her hands on her hips, her hair blowing around her head in a blaze of sunlight, big blue eyes staring up at him from out of that elfin face, it was so reminiscent of one of those days that a fierce wave of longing hit him square in the chest. He wanted to go back. He wanted to catch her against him and never let her go.

How could he have thought he could forget her? She was a part of him. It was his own bloody tragedy.

"Magnus?" Her brows furrowed.

He shook off the memories and gave her a sheepish smile. "Aye, you did, but I didn't mind. I liked listening to you. So why now have you run out of things to say?"

She shrugged. "You were always different. You never made me feel like I was saying the wrong thing. I was always comfortable around you. Well, not always, but that was later."

He wasn't following her, but he knew there was something important in what she was saying.

She saw his confused expression and tried to explain. "I haven't run out of things to say, I just say the wrong thing." When he looked at her disbelievingly, she gave him a wry smile. "Earlier today I was in the solar with the other women and they were discussing the pig they were roasting for the feast, and before I knew it I was going on about the first time I'd seen a piglet born and how incredible it was—needless to say, not something they wanted to think about before our meal." She pointed down to a large rock on the edge of the water. "I'm like that baby gannet down there—see the black one in the midst of all the yellow-headed ones?—a little odd."

He frowned. "Nonsense."

But as he thought back on it, he realized he had noticed that she'd rarely interacted with the other young girls when they were at the Games. "What about Muriel?"

"Muriel's different. We have things in common."

"Don't you have things in common with the others?"

"Some things." She shrugged. "I don't know, it's hard to explain. I want things that they don't."

"Like what?"

She thought about it a minute and said simply, "More."

Helen could see from his expression that he didn't understand, which wasn't surprising, as she didn't know how to put words to the "wayward" part of her that wanted to follow her heart, and to the vague sense of guilt and unease that came over her when she listened to the other ladies who were content to do what was expected of them.

"It's nothing," she said, suddenly embarrassed. "I'm just being silly."

He took her arm and turned her to face him. "Nay. Tell me. I want to understand."

That's what had always made him so different: the willingness to try. "I want to live a life beyond a castle gate. I want to have what you have."

"What's that?"

"Freedom. Choice. The ability to travel beyond a gate without someone sending out a search party."

He gave her a sharp look, but then smiled ruefully, seeming to understand what she meant. "We are all bound by convention, Helen. I have my duty to the king—and to my clan."

"But you like what you do and must take satisfaction out of being good at it. You wouldn't wish to be a scholar or a prelate rather than a warrior?"

"Good God, no!"

His expression made her laugh. "What if there was but one path before you? One road that you had to take? Sometimes when I listen to the other women talk, I start to feel this weight coming down on me, and I get so antsy I have to move, I have to *do* something."

He studied her, perhaps seeing her more clearly than she did herself. "I should think being healer to a king is doing something."

She smiled. "Making sure he eats his vegetables hardly qualifies. You and I both know I'm here as more of a precaution. I don't know what I want, but it's more than living behind a ten-foot-thick wall like this one." One corner of her mouth lifted wryly. "And definitely more than a woman in my position should want." She felt a prickle of shame for her selfishness. "I've a good lot in life; I should be content with it."

"Is that why you refused me?" he asked quietly.

She startled, surprised not only that he'd raised the subject, but also that he'd made a connection she never had before. "Perhaps that was part of it," she admitted. "Your mother . . . I worried that I could never be like that and didn't want to disappoint you. I-I wasn't sure I was ready."

She felt his eyes on her. "Perhaps you will feel differently when you do marry and have children."

It was what she was supposed to want. And she did. But . . .

What if it wasn't enough?

She looked up at him sadly. "That is what my brothers

said. But it didn't turn out very well the first time. It was a mistake to marry a man I didn't love."

Their eyes held for a long heartbeat before he looked away. She would have given anything at that moment to know what he was thinking. But he'd shut her out, and she could feel him pulling away from her.

She regretted the mention of her marriage to William, but how could they move past the past if he refused to talk about it? If the ghost of his friend was still between them?

He pushed back from the wall. "We should get back. Your army will be looking for you soon."

She made a face. That army was one of the reasons she felt like she was suffocating and needed air. "I suppose you're right."

"Don't tell me you've finally seen the light?"

She gave him a sharp glance. "You are just as bad as they are. If you weren't so busy hating each other, I think you and Kenneth could be friends. You have *much* in common."

She was glad he wasn't eating something, for he might have choked to death. She heard him mutter something about snow in Hades before he said, "So I assume it's Munro you wish to avoid?" A dangerous glint appeared in his eyes. "Has he done something—"

"He wants to dance with me," she said glumly.

He looked confused. "As much as I dislike the bast—" he stopped himself—"him, dancing is hardly a reason to avoid a man."

"He doesn't just want to dance. I suspect he's going to ask me to marry him." She paused. "It's everything I could want, isn't it?"

He stilled at her subtle taunt. But it was the tightness of his mouth and the barest hint of a flex beneath his jaw that made her pulse quicken.

"And it's your response that you are hesitating over?" He was tense. Too tense for a man who didn't care.

"Nay, I know my response. It's his reaction that I'm not looking forward to."

He didn't bother to hide his relief. It was foolish to read so much into a sigh, but it was what he said next that made hope soar in her chest. "I know a way to distract him."

"How?"

"Dance with me."

Her heart swelled. She'd dreamed of having him swing her around a crowded Hall, holding her, touching her, for all the world to see.

And a short while later, when he led her in a reel across the crowded stone floor of the Great Hall of Dingwall Castle before her scowling brother, an amused king, and a furious Donald, it was a dream come true.

For the first time in years, the happiness she sought, the elusive "more" she wanted, seemed a little closer.

The euphoria of the dance sustained Helen through the rest of the day and into the following morning. It was working!

In the days since they'd left Dunrobin, she'd felt a subtle shift in Magnus's attitude toward her. Rather than avoiding her as he'd done before, he seemed to be seeking ways of being closer to her. She'd felt him watching her. And now, after the conversation yesterday and the dance, she was sure that he was softening toward her.

Their conversation had done something else. It made her realize that part of what had held her back from accepting his proposal all those years ago was fear that she would let him down. Fear that she would never be the kind of lady of the keep that his mother was. That she would never fit into the life that was demanded of her.

So, after breaking her fast, Helen made a concerted effort to spend more time with the other women. But after three hours of sitting around a tapestry in the Countess of Ross's small solar, sewing and discussing every nuance and angle of the betrothal while trying not to say the wrong thing (she'd barely caught herself from remarking that the only time she enjoyed sewing was when it was necessary to close a wound), the thick stone walls of the small room seemed to be closing in on her again.

The midday meal was a welcome escape, although she was disappointed not to see Magnus in the Hall.

Unfortunately, she was seated on the dais beside the Countess of Ross. The austere Englishwoman was said to have been a beauty thirty years ago when she'd captured the heart of the Scottish earl, but any signs of that beauty had faded into the gray, colorless woman who looked at her with sharp-eyed condescension, as if she could see every one of Helen's faults. Even without her penchant for saying the wrong thing, Helen doubted she could ever say the right thing around the formidable countess. She hated to so much as open her mouth.

She felt the countess's gaze on her. "Will you be joining my daughters' falconing this afternoon, Lady Helen?"

She blanched. In yet another oddity, Helen did not enjoy the popular pursuit of noblemen and women alike. She liked watching the predatory birds dip and soar from afar, but up close . . .

She shivered. The birds terrified her.

She tried to cover her reaction, but feared the other woman could see through it. "I'm afraid not."

Before she could add an excuse, the countess said, "Good. Then I shall look forward to more of your help with the tapestry after the meal. You're obviously out of practice, but your stitches are competent when you concentrate." Helen supposed that was high praise coming from her. "You can tell me how it is that a daughter of Sutherland came to be a loyal attendant of King Hoo—" She stopped herself, realizing the man she'd been about to call King Hood was seated five feet away. "King Robert," she smiled thinly, unable to fully conceal her aversion.

Some thought the Earl of Ross's ongoing resistance to Robert Bruce had stemmed from his English wife's sympathies. There was undoubtedly some truth to the rumor.

Helen swallowed hard. The sharp-eyed birds or hours alone with the sharp-eyed countess—she didn't know which was more terrifying.

She opened her mouth, trying to think of an excuse to get out of this predicament, but slammed it shut again when she realized she was stammering.

Suddenly, she felt someone behind her. She turned, surprised to see Magnus. Their eyes caught, and from the flicker of sympathy she realized he must have heard enough to understand the nature of her predicament.

"Lady Helen, I'm sorry to interrupt your meal, but your assistance is required in the barracks."

The Countess of Ross's eyes narrowed. "What's the matter? Why is Lady Helen—"

"I'm afraid the matter is of some delicacy, my lady," he said, implying that it was a matter for the king. "Lady Helen?"

He held out his hand, which she readily slipped hers into. Big and warm, his strong, callused palm swallowed her tiny fingers in a protective hold as he helped her from the table and led her out of the boisterous Hall.

She looked behind her, half-expecting her brother or Donald to come racing after them demanding an explanation, but realized that Gregor MacGregor had both men locked in conversation with their gazes drawn away from the door.

"Your doing?" she said with a glance in their direction.

He grinned and shrugged, a devilish look in his eye. "Might be."

She laughed with a sense of joy and freedom that she hadn't experienced in a long time, feeling so much like the naughty girl who'd snuck away at the Highland Games to meet her secret love.

She slowed her step as soon as they exited the Hall into the bright and sunny courtyard. Drawing a deep breath, she said, "Thank you for rescuing me. I fear I was not relishing the thought of a long afternoon with Lady Euphemia."

He made a face. "I don't blame you. The woman terrifies me. But come, we need to hurry."

He steered her across the courtyard toward the barracks. Surprised, Helen immediately became alarmed. "You were serious? I thought it was a ruse. What's the matter?"

"You are needed," he said simply.

The words filled her with an unexpected warmth.

Rather than opening the door to the barracks, a large wooden structure that had been built against a section of the wall, Magnus drew her around to the side of the building in the narrow space that separated it from the stables.

She was about to ask him why they were there, when she saw a child kneeling at the back edge of the wall.

The little girl, who appeared to be about seven or eight, turned as they approached. Even from a distance, Helen could see that she'd been crying. Fearing the child had been hurt, she rushed forward and knelt down beside her.

She did a quick scan, but could see no obvious signs of injury. "Where are you hurt, little one?"

She little girl shook her head mutely, staring at Helen as if she were an apparition. She was a funny-looking little thing with a mop of bedraggled brown hair that hung in her eyes and a dirt-streaked face on which the tears had cleared paths of freckled skin.

Magnus had knelt beside her, his big body blocking the narrow passageway. "Lady Helen," he said. "I would like you to meet Mistress Elizabeth, the cook's youngest daughter."

The girl sniffled wetly. "My da calls me Beth."

"It's lovely to meet you, Beth. What seems to be the—"

A soft meow coming from under the back corner of the

building forestalled her question. There was a small gap between the ground and the wooden foundation where the cat had obviously taken refuge.

"It's a kitten," Magnus explained. "It wandered away from the rest of the litter in the kitchens and got underfoot. One of the servants stepped on its leg."

The little girl started to cry again. Her small face scrunched up. "My d-da said n-nothing done and l-let it die," she sobbed uncontrollably. Helen tried to soothe her, looking to Magnus.

"I ran into Mistress Beth on my way to the Hall and told her I knew someone who might be able to help."

Their eyes locked. The echoes of the day that had bound them together long ago passed between them.

She held her breath as he reached out and tucked a lock of hair behind her ear. Her heart tugged at the contact. She savored the gentle touch that lasted only an instant before he seemed to remember himself.

His hand fell. "What do you need?"

"Help me get him—"

"It's a her," the little girl wailed.

"Help me get *her* out," Helen amended, "and we shall see."

For the next two hours, Helen worked diligently on the tiny ball of fur with the mangled leg. Magnus was by her side the entire time. He helped when needed and whittled some tiny splints for the kitten's leg, while Beth fetched the things that Helen needed for a cast and a draught that would put the poor little thing to sleep. Helen made sure to not tell her all the items at once, knowing that fetching things kept the little girl too busy to cry.

It was delicate work, and Helen feared accidentally giving the tiny creature too much medicine, but when she finished, the kitten's leg was held with tiny wooden splints, bound with thin swatches of egg-and-flour-coated linen, and *she* was sleeping peacefully in a wooden crate that Beth carried carefully back to the kitchens.

Helen couldn't help smiling as she watched them go. Magnus helped her to her feet. Her legs wobbled in protest after kneeling for so long, and he slid his hand around her waist to steady her.

He smiled. "You've earned someone else's undying gratitude today."

"I'm glad you thought to come find me. Thank you."

She looked into his eyes. For a moment neither one of them said anything.

"We should get back."

She nodded, disappointed but not wanting to push him. They walked back in silence to the tower. Her skirts were dirty and dusty from kneeling beside the barracks; she would need to change for the evening meal.

"I will leave you here," he said.

He started to walk away, but she stopped him. "Magnus." He turned. "I won't give up."

She spoke softly, but he'd heard her. With a tip of his head, he left her.

Seventeen

❧

Dunraith Castle, Wester Ross

"Have you seen the lady, my lord?"

Magnus glanced up from the shaft of yew he was working on to see a lad of about four and ten standing before
him. One of Macraith's foster sons, he guessed from
the boy's clothing. He wore the heavily padded *cotun*
and steel helm of a warrior-in-training. Macraith, one of
MacKenzie's chieftains, was one of the Highlanders who'd
given shelter to Bruce on his escape across the Highlands.

Magnus didn't need to ask to which lady the boy referred. Since the day Helen performed her latest miracle on
the kitten, word of her skills had spread, and "the lady"
had been in almost constant demand for the rest of their
stay at Dingwall and continuing on their next stop, a few
miles west at Macraith's castle, on what had been an ancient Norse fort.

Magnus knew he was somewhat responsible, having
pointed more than one person in her direction. But watching her that day, he'd been struck, as he had been when he
aided MacGregor and the king, with how alive she seemed.

Nay, "alive" wasn't exactly right. Perhaps "thriving"
was the better word. It was the same way Hawk looked

when he was holding the ropes of his sail: at home and in control. As if this was exactly where she was supposed to be. Clearly it made her happy, and just as clearly he liked seeing her happy.

Magnus didn't need to turn his head and look through the postern gate down the ravine to the river to catch a glimpse of auburn blazing in the sunlight to answer the lad's question. He'd seated himself on this bale of hay by the practice yard for a reason. For the better part of the three weeks since word of Gordon's body being discovered had arrived at Dunrobin (and the day after he'd nearly taken her in the alehouse), he was painfully aware of exactly where "the lady" was.

The role of vigilant protector had taken its toll, eroding the barrier he'd erected between them like waves on a wall of sand. Every time her eyes lit up when she saw him, every time her hand fell on his arm as if it belonged there, every time she asked him for help added to his torment. He knew his feelings were wrong, but he couldn't stop them.

He should be glad that they would be beginning the final stage of their journey through the mountains tomorrow. In a handful of days they would be at MacAulay's castle of Dun Lagaidh on the northern banks of Loch Broom. From there they would board a *birlinn* for the quick sail to the final stop of Dunstaffnage for the Highland Games. His guard duty to the king on his royal progress would be over.

But what about Helen? When would his duty to her end? *Damn you, Gordon. Do you know what you've done to me?*

He shook off the memory. "She's down by the river, teaching some of the lasses how to fish."

The lad looked as if Magnus had just told him the world was round. "Lasses can't fish! They talk too much."

Magnus bit back a laugh. Helen had always been a horrible fisherman, but he didn't think she'd ever noticed. And it hadn't stopped her from offering to cure a few of the younger girls' boredom on a hot, sunny summer day. From what he'd seen earlier, Macraith's daughter was faring much better. Not coincidentally, she was as shy as a mouse and hardly said a word.

"What's wrong?" he asked.

The lad stopped frowning, remembering why he was there. "Malcolm's hand slipped while he was sharpening the laird's blade and he's bleedin' real bad."

Malcolm had to be one of Macraith's other foster sons. "You'd better hurry then, lad. The lady will see to it."

A few minutes later, he saw Helen come rushing through the gate alongside the boy. She had her battle face on and was so focused on the task ahead, she passed right by without noticing him before disappearing into the armory.

Over the hour or so it took to treat the boy, a succession of people ran in and out of the small building, fetching cloth, water, various jars of her different ointments and medicines, and the special bag he'd had the tanner make for her to hold the various tools she'd collected (more than half of which had been "borrowed" from him).

The look on her face when he'd presented it to her . . .

Damn it, don't think about it. But his chest squeezed nonetheless.

He'd just finished the final touches on his latest project when he heard the door open. A few moments later, a shadow crossed in front of him.

"Have you been sitting here the whole time?"

He steeled himself and looked up. It didn't help. He was hit with a wave of longing so hard it stole his breath.

Would it be so wrong? He knew the answer, but by all that was holy, he was tempted.

"Aye. How's young Malcolm?"

Her brows drew together, concerned. "I'm not sure. 'Twas a deep cut, which nearly took off his right thumb and didn't seem to want to stop bleeding."

"He's a tough lad. I didn't hear him cry out when you set the hot iron upon it."

She squeezed down on the bale to sit beside him. The feel of her pressed up against him sent every nerve-ending on edge. His heart hammered. He tried not to breathe, but her soft, feminine scent permeated his skin, infusing him with the intoxicating aroma that he thought was lavender.

She bit her lip, and he had to turn away. But the sharp tug in his groin lingered. He ached for her. Touching her had been a mistake. He'd tasted her passion, felt her body move against his, heard her moan, and now it was all he could think of.

"I didn't burn the wound closed."

"Why not?" It was the preferred method of sealing a wound.

"He asked me if the scar would interfere with his ability to hold a sword, and I said it might. Sewing the wound leaves a thinner scar."

"But is more likely to lead to infection."

She nodded. "Aye. He chose to chance the greater risk."

Magnus understood. Malcolm was training to be a warrior. Not being able to hold his sword properly would be like a death knell to a young lad.

He gave her a sidelong look. "So I take it you have enough to keep you busy?"

Their eyes met. A flicker of understanding passed between them. She smiled almost shyly at the reminder of their conversation. "Aye, thank you."

At first the conversation on the ramparts at Dingwall had unsettled him. It was strange to realize he didn't know her as well as he'd thought. She'd always been so naturally at ease with him, he'd never realized it wasn't that way with everyone. Nor had he realized how anxious she'd been about assuming her role as lady of the keep. But the more he thought about it, the more he understood. She had a skill, and she wanted to put it to use. She liked the challenge and excitement just as much as he did.

Helen glanced down at the wooden implement in his hand. "Is that an arrow spoon?"

One corner of his mouth lifted. "It was supposed to be a surprise."

Her eyes lit up, looking at it as if he held a jeweled scepter in his hand. "It's for me?"

He chuckled and handed it to her. "Aye, you mentioned it once, and after one of Fraser's men was nearly hit with an arrow hunting last week, I realized you might have need of it."

Helen held it to the light, examining it from all sides. "It's wonderful. I never realized how talented you were with your hands." He felt another tug in his groin. This one more a heavy swell. His body didn't care that her words were spoken innocently. "You are a man of surprising talents, Magnus MacKay. Gregor told me that you've also forged some interesting weapons."

MacGregor should keep his bloody mouth shut, and why was she talking to MacGregor? He bit back the prickle of what he suspected was jealousy and shrugged. "It's a hobby. I'm no armorer." It was more that he liked to experiment and modify tools to better serve their purpose—even killing.

"I've a few things I was thinking about . . ."

For the next twenty minutes, Helen didn't seem to take a breath as she spoke excitedly about ways to modify some of the tools he'd given her to improve their efficiency. He found himself caught up in her enthusiasm and didn't realize how late it was until the shadows started to fall across her face, and he heard the thunder of hooves coming through the gates.

"I'll see what I can do about your tools, but it won't be until we reach Loch Broom." Reluctantly, he stood and held out his hand to help her up. "The men are back."

Helen wrinkled her nose. "I assume that means you have to go."

"The king will want a report."

She gave him a sly look. "My brother and Donald seem to be spending a lot of time scouting and hunting since we departed Dingwall."

His jaw tightened. Though he welcomed the absence of the other men, it hadn't been at his command. Sutherland seemed almost as eager as he was to keep Munro away from his sister. He could almost feel grateful to him. Almost. Had she reconsidered? "Is that a complaint?"

She looked at him as if he were addled—which was exactly how she made him feel. "Of course not. I'm able to breathe without their constant hovering. I just wonder the reason why."

He pretended not to see the speculative gleam in her eye. "We're heading into the mountains tomorrow—the most difficult part of our journey."

"But also the most exciting!"

He hated to dampen her spirits, but he couldn't help cautioning, "Don't let the beauty fool you, these mountains can be treacherous—deadly, even. You need to be careful not to wander away from camp or veer too far off the road. It will be slow traveling with the carts and horses. The road is a rough one as it is, and there was a lot of snow last year and many of the burns flooded. Your brother volunteered to scout with MacGregor."

She didn't hide her disappointment. "So you didn't send them?"

"I'm afraid not."

Their eyes held.

"*I won't give up.*" He could hear the gauntlet she'd thrown down ringing in his ears. Was it true, or would she falter again? He didn't know which answer scared him more.

"Ah well," she said, not letting the disappointment that

he'd had nothing to do with removing her suitor get her down for too long. "Perhaps he's reconsidered."

But one look over her shoulder at the men who'd just come into view in the courtyard told him otherwise. Seeing Magnus and Helen together, Munro's face grew as dark as a thundercloud.

Magnus looked back to Helen with a wry grin. "I wouldn't count on it, *m'aingeal*."

Helen couldn't remember ever feeling this happy. She didn't know whether it was her growing closeness to Magnus (he couldn't seem to let her out of his sight!), the growing pride she felt in her healing skills (which were getting plenty of practice), or the majesty of their surroundings and the freedom she felt with each mile of their journey into the forests and hills of Wester Ross, but she wanted it to never end.

They'd left the Macraiths' castle after prayers and breaking their fast, and traveled along the rocky banks of the Blackwater River into the forests and gently rolling hills of Strathgrave. With the horse, carts, and long procession of knights, men-at-arms, and attendants, the pace was every bit as slow as Magnus had predicted this morning.

"Four days, perhaps five," he'd said, as he'd helped her on her small hobby. The sturdy, short-legged horses had originally come from Ireland and were well suited to the mountainous terrain of the Scottish Highlands.

"Is that all?" She was unable to hide her disappointment.

He and Gregor MacGregor, who'd been standing nearby, looked at her as if she were crazed.

"'Is that all?' It's only forty miles, my lady," Gregor said. "It should take no more than two."

"I've run longer distances in a day," Magnus added. "I could be there by nightfall."

Helen laughed at the boast.

Gregor arched a brow. "Nightfall?"

Magnus shrugged. "It's uphill."

Helen looked back and forth between them. They were joking, weren't they?

She didn't know, but it was clear as the day drew on that as much as she was enjoying and savoring every minute of the beautiful scenery, Magnus was finding the pace agonizing. A pace made slower when they found the bridge at Garve unpassable, forcing them to cross the Blackwater farther upstream.

By the time they camped for the night along the banks of the river, with the pine forest surrounding them, and the mountain of Ben Wyvis looming in the distance, Helen was content to laze near the river, eating her meal with the two attendants her brother had insisted she bring, and watch the magnificent sunset.

She sighed contentedly and stood from the table that had been set up in their tent. Although by no means luxurious, the royal progress was not without basic comforts. Unlike Bruce's journey across the Highlands three years ago, when he'd been fleeing with little more than the clothes on his back and the sword in his hand, the king's carts were laden with household plate and furniture. Large canvas tents were fitted with finely woven floor coverings brought back from the crusades, along with tables, chairs, and pallets. They drank from silver goblets, ate from pewter trenchers, and lit the rooms with oil lamps and candles in fine candelabra.

Her attendants rose after her, but she waved them back down. "Sit. I shall only be a moment." She grabbed the ewer that had been set out on small table with a wide bowl. "I'm just going to fetch some water with which to clean."

Ellen, a woman who'd been attending her from birth, looked appalled—though really after two and twenty years she should know better.

"Let me do that, my lady."

"Nonsense," Helen said, sliding through the tied-back flap of the tent. "It will feel good to stretch my legs."

And if Magnus just happened to be nearby, it would be merely happenstance. She smiled, knowing it would be anything but. She'd grown quite accustomed to—maybe even dependent on—Magnus watching over her. Her heart raced a little in anticipation.

But surprisingly, to her disappointment, he didn't appear.

She made her way over to the large granite slabs of rock that formed the bank of the river to the dark water that had given the river its name. After washing her hands and filling the ewer, she retreated a few feet to find a dry patch of rock to sit upon as she watched the sun slip behind the mountains and fade over the horizon. She inhaled deeply. Heavenly! How she loved the fresh scent of pine.

Everything about this journey had been heavenly thus far. Magnus's attentiveness had to mean something. *M'aingeal*. My angel. Did he realize he'd used the endearment he'd once called her? If he hadn't forgiven her, she was confident he would soon. And although content with his friendship for now, she couldn't erase from her mind what had happened between them. Every time she looked at his hands she remembered.

She blushed, a warm glow coming over her. It was all going to turn out perfectly, she knew it.

Suddenly aware of someone behind her, she turned excitedly. But it wasn't Magnus—it was Donald.

Her disappointment must have shown on her face. His eyes narrowed. "Were you expecting someone?"

Helen shook her head and stood, reaching for the ewer. "I was just fetching some water."

He blocked her with his body. "I was hoping you might have a moment. I've been trying to speak with you alone for over a week. If I didn't know better, I'd think you were avoiding me."

She hoped the fading daylight hid her guilty flush. It

wasn't Donald she wished to avoid really, but the unpleasantness of the conversation that she feared was coming.

"I really should go," she said, unable to stop her gaze from scanning the camp behind him, hoping someone would come to her rescue. Nay, not someone: Magnus.

"He's not here. MacKay and some of the other men have gone to scout the road ahead." His mouth had hardened. He anticipated her next thought. "Your brother is with the king."

He sneered the last, but she didn't attempt to chide him. At least he was saying "king" now and not "hood" or "usurper." Resolved to having it done, she took a deep breath and faced him. "Very well. What is it you would like to speak to me about?"

"I think that should be obvious. I'm a patient man, lass, but I've been patient long enough. I'll have your answer."

Helen lifted her brows, annoyed by his high-handedness. "I wasn't aware I owed you one."

He grabbed her arm and pulled her against him. Harder and more roughly than she liked. Water sloshed from the pitcher onto the sleeve of her gown.

"Don't play games with me, lass. I want you to be my wife. Now will you or won't you marry me?"

Helen felt her own temper rise, anger overriding her concern for his feelings. She jerked her arm free. "Our long-standing *friendship* may excuse your presumption, but it does not give you a right to touch or speak to me like this. I've done nothing to warrant your anger. I've never encouraged your suit or given you any reason to expect that it would be welcome."

The look of cold fury on his face sent a chill across the back of her neck. Belatedly, she realized her mistake. Her anger had struck in the most dangerous place: his pride.

"I meant no offense, *my lady.*"

His jaw was clamped shut, but his eyes burned into her with such intensity, she felt an immediate twinge of regret.

"I'm sorry, Donald. I don't wish to hurt you." She put her hand on his arm, but he flinched away. "It has nothing to do with you. I've no wish to marry anyone right now."

Though kindly meant, it wasn't true, and he wouldn't let it stand. "I may be a fool, but I'm not a blind one. Do you think I don't see the way you're throwing yourself at MacKay? I don't know why he's suddenly decided to dance attendance on you, but if you think he will marry you, you are a bigger fool than I."

"Is something wrong here?"

Magnus! Saints preserve her, she was glad to see him.

The two men squared off in the shadowy twilight. For a moment, she feared they might come to blows. Equally stubborn and proud, neither of them was the type to back down from a challenge.

But to her surprise, Donald took a step back. "Nay, we are finished, aren't we, my lady?"

Helen was so grateful there wouldn't be a fight, she nodded furiously. "Aye. Thank you, Donald. I'm sorry—"

She stopped, not knowing what to say. She didn't want to embarrass him further. She could already see his eyes darkening.

He smiled thinly. "I'll bid you good night." With a curt nod, he stomped back to camp.

Magnus put his hand on her arm. She was surprised how unsettled she was by what had happened, and the solid comfort of his touch proved immediately steadying.

"Are you all right?"

She took a deep breath. "I'm fine."

He slid his finger under her chin to tip her head back, forcing her to meet his gaze. "Helen . . . ?"

She melted at the concern in his warm brown eyes. A wry smile curved her mouth. "Really, I'm fine."

Now that you are here. And she was. He'd always made her feel that way. God, how much she loved him!

"Was it as unpleasant as you feared?"

"It's over," she said firmly.

He appeared undecided as to whether to pursue the matter further, but after a moment he dropped his hand. "It's late. You should get to bed. We have a long day ahead of us."

He said the latter with such dread, she couldn't resist teasing him. "I hope we won't be traveling at such a fast pace tomorrow?"

He gave a sharp laugh. "Minx." He swatted her on the backside and pushed her back up the bank.

Despite Helen's assurances, Magnus was still worried the next day. Munro had upset her. God knew what she saw in the arse, but she obviously considered Munro a friend and refusing him had caused her distress—undue, to his mind.

If her exuberance as they painstakingly—and he did mean painstakingly—made their way through the boggy hills and forests seemed more muted than the previous day, Magnus knew exactly whom to blame.

And the bastard wasn't exactly helping matters with his barely concealed fury.

When Magnus wasn't riding ahead, helping pull a cart out of the bogs (he hoped they would move faster once they hit the rocky terrain of Shgurr Mor and Beinn Dearg) or doing his best to ensure they were moving as fast as they could, he tried to distract her by identifying the names of the forests and mountains they passed: Ben Wyvis, Garbat, Carn Mor, Bein nan Eun, and Strath Rannoch on their right, and Corriemoillie, Carn na Dubh Choille, and Inchbae on their left.

But it wasn't until they stopped on the banks of Loch Glascarnoch for the night that the pixie smile that seemed to light up her whole face returned. She came up to him, just after he'd finished overseeing the erecting of the king's tent, holding one hand behind her back. "Guess what my brother found?"

"Another retinue to travel with?"

She rolled her eyes and held out her hand, opening her fist slowly. "Averins!"

Magnus smiled. The English called them cloudberries, but by whatever name, the rare red and orange brambles were delicious. Before she could pull her hand away, he plucked one from her palm and popped it in his mouth. The bright flavors of orange, apple, and honey were a burst of sweetness.

"Hey!" she protested, yanking her hand back.

"Thanks for sharing," he said with a wink. "I used to make myself ill eating them as a lad when I could find them. They only flower every so often around here."

She ate the last one before he could try to snatch it away—which he'd been contemplating.

"Will you take me to find some more? I should like to surprise the king. I think he should prefer them to the peas the cook has prepared for the evening meal."

He made a face. "I should think so. Where did your brother find them?"

"A few miles back—I wish he'd thought to mention it earlier. But as the patch was close to the road, he said most were already gone. Is there someplace else we might look?"

He thought for a minute. "They grow in the bogs and forests around Ben Wyvis, but there might be a place we could try that's not too far away. But I'm afraid your surprise for the king—if we can find them—will have to wait until after the evening meal. I cannot sneak away right now."

She frowned, noticing her brother watching them from the other side of the king's tent. "Sneak away is right. Perhaps you could send my brother and Donald on a long scouting mission? To Ireland perhaps?"

He chuckled. "I'll see what I can do. But as I recall, you were always fairly good at eluding them."

Her mouth twitched mischievously. "I think I feel the beginnings of a horrible headache."

Fortunately, the headache wasn't necessary. Sutherland and Munro volunteered for scouting duties, and after attending his duties and leaving MacGregor to watch the king, Magnus found Helen with her tiring women by the loch. She muttered a hasty excuse that the king must have need of her and raced away before the poor women could stop her.

"I feel a bit sorry for them with you for a charge."

She grinned unrepentantly. "Don't worry, they're used to it. You did notice all the gray hair beneath the veils?"

He shook his head. She'd given him one or two that he could remember as well. Some of the places she used to hide . . .

He shuddered, glad those days were past.

With the long days of summer, there was still an hour or two left of daylight as Magnus led her away from the camp into the forests along the lower slopes of Beinn Liath Mhor. They fell into a familiar banter of her talking and him listening. It was so reminiscent of the way things used to be, he had to force himself not to reach for her hand, reminding himself that it wasn't the same—and never would be again.

But if his hand lingered on hers as he helped her over boggy patches and uneven ground, he told himself he had a duty to ensure she didn't stumble.

They had to walk about a mile before a telltale patch of orange appeared low on a hillside ahead of them.

Her cry of delight went right to his chest. His heart tugged so hard, he had a hard time reining it in. He was in trouble and knew it. He'd let his guard down. The forced proximity had drawn him in. But like Icarus from the sun, he could not pull himself back.

After they gorged themselves silly, and she filled her veil (as a makeshift basket) with dozens of the plump and juicy berries, he reluctantly told her it was time to go back. It would be dark soon; already the forest was filled with shadows.

"Do we have to?"

"If you'd rather, we can wait here for your brother to come looking for you."

She looked up at him with those big blue eyes, a hint of a challenge in the tilt of her chin. "I don't mind."

"Aye, well, as much as I'm tempted to put another crook in your brother's nose, I'd prefer to end the day on a pleasant note."

She bit her lip, eyes twinkling. "It has been nice, hasn't it?"

"Aye." The temptation was getting harder to resist. The hopefulness in her gaze . . .

Forcibly, he tore his eyes away and started back through the forest.

Not yours . . .

But she had been, damn it. The past few days—weeks—had brought it all back to him. She could be again.

His mouth tightened. That was, if her family disappeared and he could forget . . .

Not bloody likely.

"Does this remind you of anything?" she asked from behind him. The path had narrowed and he had taken the lead.

There was an amused edge to her voice that should have alerted him.

He glanced over his shoulder. "I'd say it looks like most forests around here."

She knew he was being purposefully obtuse. She was remembering all those times before, just as he was—how easily they slipped back into their old camaraderie. If he turned back around, he wouldn't be surprised to see her lips slam shut, hiding the tongue that he suspected was aimed at his back.

But it wasn't just camaraderie, it had always been more than that. And stirring up memories best forgotten was dangerous. He'd touched her, damn it. In a way he'd never forget. He'd die with the memory of that silky, wet flesh, the tightness, how her hips had moved against him, and hearing the little breathing sounds she'd made as he stroked her.

Christ, he got hard just thinking about it.

"It reminds me of when I used to sneak away to meet you," she said, refusing to be put off.

This time he didn't turn around. He feared if he saw that look of expectation and hope in her eyes again, he'd do something foolish. Like pull her into his arms and kiss her in a way he'd never dared to do all those years ago.

After a few moments of silence, he knew something was wrong. She was too quiet.

He turned his head and stopped dead in his tracks. His heart thudded to a skittering halt, his pulse leaping right out of his chest.

His eyes scanned the area behind him, but he already knew: Helen was gone.

Eighteen

❧

Helen didn't want the day to end. Her long siege was toppling the wall Magnus had erected between them, and he was close to surrender.

The memories were drawing them back together. So when they passed the stack of boulders, and she saw the small opening, she entered it. Her hiding and him finding her was a game they used to play. It had started after she'd boasted that she'd always been able to hide from her brother, and Magnus told her she would never be able to hide from him. She'd set out to prove him wrong, only *he'd* proved to have an uncanny ability to ferret her out—the blighter!

To her surprise, the boulders she'd noticed were actually the entrance to a small cave. The darkness and dank smell gave her second thoughts, but she sniffed and, not detecting any musky scents that might harken a beast who wouldn't like being disturbed, cautiously stepped inside. Magnus's shout a few moments later propelled her forward another few steps.

She blinked rapidly, trying to get her eyes to adjust, but the darkness in front of her was impenetrable—a black hole of nothingness. The cave must be deep. She shivered, deciding to go no farther. Magnus finding her was the best part of the game anyway.

The cave didn't just swallow the light, it also swallowed sound. Magnus's shouts were growing fainter. Her heart pounded. Or maybe he'd started to look in the other direction?

Suddenly, she had an uneasy feeling about this. His warnings about the mountains came back to her. And belatedly, she remembered her promise not to go anywhere alone. Perhaps this hadn't been the most well-thought-through idea . . .

Crack.

Her pulse shot through her throat at the soft sound from near the entrance. "M-Magnus?"

Why wasn't he calling her name?

If he was trying to scare her it was working. Quelling the urge to retreat into the cave, she took a few tentative steps forward. "This isn't funny." She shouted a little louder, "Magnus!"

Her heart stopped. Fear washed over her in an icy rush. Someone was there. Right by the entrance. She could feel the heaviness in the air. "Ma . . ." Her voice strangled in her throat.

But then the air shifted and the sensation was gone. It must have been her imagination.

"Helen!"

Relief crashed over her; Magnus was close.

"I'm here!" she shouted, slipping out from behind the rocks.

He was about ten feet away, but the moment he saw her, he seemed to close the distance between them in one stride. He took her by the shoulders, gave her one long look as if checking to make sure she was in one piece, and then hugged her so tightly against his chest she could barely breathe. "Thank God," he murmured against her head.

Pressed up so snugly against the hard wall of his chest,

she could feel the frantic pounding of his heart begin to slow. He was usually so calm and steady, it took her a moment to realize what it was. She nuzzled her cheek against the soft, fuzzy wool of the plaid he wore around his shoulders, letting the warmth of his body ease the chill from her bones.

Just as suddenly as he'd taken her in his arms, however, he held her away from him, grasping her by the shoulders. "Damn it, Helen, what the hell were you thinking?"

The fierceness of his expression took her aback. She blinked up at him uncertainly. "I saw the gap behind the rocks and thought it would be fun to have you try to find me, like we used—"

He shook her—actually *shook* her. And if eyes could flash, his were a veritable lightning storm. "Damn it, this is not a game. I warned you it could be dangerous."

Perhaps it hadn't been her best idea, but neither did she think it warranted this kind of reaction. Conveniently forgetting how scared she'd been, she bristled defensively. "I don't see the danger in hiding a few feet away from the road—" She stopped when his face started to darken. Something about this wasn't right. His reaction was too extreme. Helen wasn't the most perceptive person, but even she could see he was hiding something. "What's the matter? What are you not telling me? I've never seen you so jittery."

His mouth clamped shut, and he released her.

But she didn't want him to let her go. She stepped toward him and put her hand on his chest. She could see the tension along the hard line of his jaw, darkened by two days of very attractive stubble. The shadow of his beard only enhanced the rugged masculinity.

She knew him so well, sometimes she forgot how handsome he was. But the boyish good looks of his youth had aged seamlessly into the rough and rugged handsomeness of manhood.

Awareness sharpened the air between them. But he stood perfectly still—unrelenting. She loved him so much, and wanted him so badly. Why did he have to be so stubborn?

"We used to do this all the time and you never seemed to mind."

His jaw tightened. "It's not the same, Helen. It can never be the same. Stop pretending that it can."

His cool rejection stung. She'd thought . . .

She'd thought the past few weeks had meant something. She'd thought he'd begun to forgive her. But he was the one still living in the past.

She pushed away from him, having reached her breaking point. For weeks she'd been trying to prove her love, prove that she'd changed, but he wasn't going to let her.

"I'm not the one who is stubbornly holding to the past. Do you intend to punish me forever for the mistakes I made in my youth? I'm sorry for what happened. I'm sorry I didn't take the five minutes you gave me to decide the rest of my life, cut myself off from my family forever, abandon my home, and run away with you by accepting your offer of marriage. But I'm tired of taking the blame for everything. It wasn't all my fault. Had you given me a chance to think . . ." She looked up into his shocked face accusingly. "Had you given me any indication that you felt something for me beyond fondness, five minutes might have been enough."

"What are you talking about? You knew how I felt."

"Did I? How could I when you never said anything? You never told me you loved me. Was I to guess your feelings?"

He looked utterly thunderstruck. "How could you not have known? I *kissed* you."

She made a sharp sound. "You touched your lips to mine and then pulled back so quickly I feared I had the plague."

Her sarcasm pricked his temper. He stiffened. "I was showing you honor and respect."

"I didn't want honor and respect, I wanted passion. I

was a young girl dreaming of romance, not a convent. I wanted to think you loved me. But when you didn't come for me, didn't give me another chance, I feared I was wrong. I waited for you, Magnus. Every night I looked out my window, peering into the shadows, and wondered if you were there. For months I made up excuses to walk in the forest." Her heart squeezed, and tears burned behind her eyes. "But you never came. Your pride was stronger than any feelings you had for me."

Magnus was reeling from her accusations. God, was it possible she hadn't known how he felt? He thought back on it, looking at what had happened through her eyes, and realized that it wasn't only possible, it was likely. He'd never said he loved her. Never even told her how much he cared about her. He'd assumed that his actions would be enough. But even these she'd misinterpreted. Not feel passion for her? She had no bloody idea.

He dragged his fingers through his hair. Christ, what a mess! "I'm sorry, I thought you knew how I felt. You weren't the only one who was young." He'd hated that her brother—his enemy—had witnessed her refusal. "My pride stopped me from coming back. By the time I realized my mistake it was too late. You were betrothed to my friend—and then you married him."

"You could have stopped me. But you lied to me. You were too stubborn to admit you still cared for me."

His mouth tightened, unable to deny the bitterness that still rose inside him. "I never thought you'd go through with it."

"I was hurt, Magnus—confused. If I wasn't certain of your feelings before, should I have been certain of them three years later? I tried, but you told me you no longer cared for me. I only knew the truth at the wedding feast when I saw your face. I knew then I'd made a mistake. William realized it, too—"

She started to say something but he cut her off. Gordon was the last thing he wanted to talk about with her. Even the mention of his name served as a brutal reminder. The hopelessness of the situation bored down on him. "It doesn't matter. We both made mistakes. But I'm not trying to punish you. I don't blame you for what happened, and haven't for a long time."

"Then why are you still doing this? I know you care about me."

He didn't bother to deny it. But love wasn't always enough. "Have you forgotten about your family?"

"Of course not. I told you that I will not let them stand in the way again." She came closer. "I'll prove it to you. Just give me the chance."

Did she know what kind of temptation she presented? *Prove it to you.* God, she was killing him. He wanted her with every fiber of his being. Wanted to take those sinfully red lips under his and show her all the passion he'd kept in check for far too long.

But she was offering him the one thing he didn't deserve: happiness.

He turned away. "There are things you don't know."

She drew closer, putting her small hand on his chest again. His body shook at the contact. "Then tell me."

"I can't." The Guard. Gordon. He could speak of neither.

Her mouth tightened. "It has something to do with William, doesn't it? You think your feelings for me are a betrayal. But I never belonged to William. I barely knew him. You are choosing the memory of your friend—a ghost— over the flesh-and-blood woman who loves you."

To prove her point, she slid her arms around his neck, lifted on her tiptoes, and pressed her soft body against his.

Jesus. His body jerked at the contact. He felt as if he were jumping out of his own damned skin.

Instinctively, his arm circled around her waist, holding

her to him. Her soft, feminine curves fit in all the right places.

"You are the most stubborn man I know. But you know something, I can be stubborn, too. I want you, Magnus, and I intend to fight for you."

Their eyes met in the semidarkness. It was a mistake. He felt the pull. The irresistible temptation. His head lowered. Just one kiss. One little taste. Was that too much to ask?

He let his lips fall on hers for only a moment. But even the fleeting contact was enough to harken danger. His senses exploded. Her lips were so soft and sweet. She tasted of passion and desire held in check for too long. His body hammered, ached to deepen the kiss. But he knew that if he didn't pull back soon, he wouldn't be able to.

Still, he couldn't force himself to break the contact, needing to absorb just a little more of her sweetness . . .

Suddenly, he felt her tiny fist pound on his chest. She tore her mouth away with a cry. "Stop! Damn you, stop!"

What in Hades? Magnus gazed down into fierce blue eyes glistening with unshed tears. "What's wrong? I thought you wanted me to kiss you."

"I do, damn you. But did you hear nothing I said? Why are you holding back? I want you to kiss me like you started to in the forest. I want you to kiss me like you did the woman at the wedding. I want you to touch me. Talk to me. Tell me everything you want to do to me like you did when you thought I was Joanna. I want you to stop treating me like a—"

"Virgin?"

Magnus snapped. He captured her fist from his chest and pinned it behind her back, dragging her against him. He knew it was wrong to begrudge his dead friend what was rightfully his, but he did. *She should have been mine.* There, he'd put it to words. Damn his soul to hell for it.

Her eyes widened. "Nun, that's what I was going to say." Nun. Virgin. What difference did it make? "Just once," she pleaded. "Just once can't you kiss me—touch me—like you did them? Or do you not feel the same for me?"

Her gaze met his, challenging, but also uncertain. It was the uncertainty that did him in.

Damn her. He was past caring. All the desire, all the lust he'd held in check came bursting forward in a hot rush. He was a man, not a saint. If she wanted raw and base, he was going to give it to her. Even if he had to go to hell afterward.

He slid his hand down to cup her bottom, hauling her against him.

She gasped at the forcefulness of the contact.

"Do you feel my passion for you, Helen? It's nothing like I felt for them. God, do you have any idea how badly I want you?" Her eyes widened, but he didn't care. She'd put this game in motion; she'd see it through to the end. He took her hand and guided it to him, wrapping her fingers around his thickness. Despite his anger, he groaned at the sensation, pulsing harder. "One little pump in that dainty little hand of yours and I would explode. But as fine as that sounds, that's not what I really want."

He pushed her back against the rocks that had hidden her a few moments ago, pinning her with his weight.

He didn't kiss her. Not yet. Instead, his lips and tongue found the velvety-soft skin of her neck and throat. He devoured—ravished, the hard flutter of her heartbeat urging him on.

Her breath started to hitch as his hand moved over her body, claiming every inch of her. He cupped her breast, his mouth right by her ear. "You know what I really want?"

He took her nipple between his fingertips, twisting it gently to a tight bud.

She shook her head, her breath coming fast.

He was hot and aroused, and past the point of restraint. There was no rein on his passion now. Nothing to hold him back.

His mouth dipped lower, to the edge of her bodice. He pushed the fabric aside just enough to let his tongue flick out and lick the hard bead of her nipple.

She startled, but her gasp of surprise turned to a moan of pleasure when he took her between this teeth and sucked. She was arching and pressing against him so hard he almost forgot his question. Her breasts were incredible. Plump and soft, with just the right amount of weight. Her nipples were tight and berry pink. He swirled his tongue around the delectable little tip one more time before releasing her.

"I want to come inside you. I want to feel that tight little glove between your legs gripping me. I want you wet and hot, and quivering. I want you to scream my name as I'm deep inside you."

She seemed to be holding her breath as she waited for what he would do next. Maybe she even anticipated it. He slid his hand down her hip, down her leg, and under the edge of her gown. He groaned when his hand met the soft bare skin of her leg.

Her lips parted. Her eyes lost focus. Her breath hitched. Desire. She was flush with it. He wanted to draw it out. Tease her a little more. Have her begging for him to touch her. But he couldn't wait. Blood pounded through his veins, the soft scent of her feminine need an irresistible aphrodisiac.

She wanted talking? He'd talk until she begged for him to stop.

"Are you wet for me, Helen?" he drawled huskily.

The blush that rose to her cheeks made him chuckle.

"I take it that's a yes?"

She nodded.

His hand skimmed the delicate skin of her inner thigh, achingly close to that dampness. "Tell me what you want."

He kissed her throat again, dragging a trail of kisses up

to the corner of her mouth. He could feel her restlessness, feel her body shaking with need for his touch.

"Touch me," she breathed. "I want you to touch me."

He gave her what she wanted, sweeping his finger over the silky flesh. A deep shudder ran through him at the contact. She was so warm and wet, he couldn't wait to be inside her. But not yet.

"Is that all you want?"

Frustrated with desire, Helen shot him a glare and shook her head.

He laughed and slipped his finger inside the tight, wet heat.

The gasp she made went right to his already swollen groin.

He closed his eyes and let the rush of sensations crash over him. Savoring the moment. He dipped inside her again. Deeper. Stretching her gently with his fingers. "You're so tight," he managed from between clenched teeth. "But you feel so good."

He plunged again, and she gave a soft moan of pleasure. Her eyes fluttered at half-mast. Her cheeks were pink with pleasure and her lips . . .

God, he couldn't wait another minute to taste those too-red lips.

The next time he stroked her, he smothered her moan with his mouth.

Helen's heart slammed into her chest when his mouth finally covered hers. He did not hold back. His lips claimed hers possessively. Fiercely. Urgently. Demanding her response. Just like his hand. His fingers were stroking her even as his tongue slid into her mouth, plunging deep and purposefully, claiming every corner of it.

She felt her heart soar. This was the promise of passion she'd felt in the forest brought to fruition. The passion of which she'd always dreamed. He kissed her as if he couldn't get enough of her. As if he'd die if he couldn't have her.

She wrapped her tongue around his and opened her mouth wider, responding to the carnal invitation.

The stoking between her legs intensified, his finger plunging faster, harder, deeper. Oh God . . .

Pressure that she didn't understand was building low in her belly. She clutched at his arms. At his shoulders. Feeling the hard, rigid muscles flare under her fingertips. Wanting to get closer. To rub herself against the hard wall of muscle.

She wanted skin. Wanted to feel his strength and heat under her palms.

She tugged the shirt from his chausses and slid her hands underneath the linen and leather of his *cotun*.

He hissed when her hands made contact with the smooth spans of hot skin.

She clutched him harder as her body started to climb.

He broke the kiss, his breath coming heavy in her ear. "I want to see you come, love."

Love. He called her love.

Her heart burst with pleasure even as her hips started to circle, unconsciously seeking the pressure of his hand.

"That's it," he urged softly. "Does that feel good? I can feel you starting to shudder. God, you're so sweet. Next time I'm going to taste you. I'm going to put my tongue right here."

She was too far gone to be shocked. Instead, she shuddered with wicked anticipation.

He moved his finger to a place . . .

To a place that made her womb contract. She cried out, her fingers digging into the steely muscles of his back, as the pulsing spasms overtook her. As pleasure so intense washed over her in a shattering embrace.

"That's it, love," he whispered. "Come for me. God, you're beautiful!"

Magnus couldn't wait another minute. Seeing her come had pushed him past the point of all restraint.

He'd never felt so aroused in his life.

All he could think about was making her his. He was so hard, so throbbing, so close to exploding, he knew it was going to be quick.

He fumbled with the ties of his braies and pushed aside his chausses enough to release himself, the rush of cold air on the hot skin stretched painfully thin a welcome relief.

Helen was still weak from her release, her body lax against the rocks. But she roused when he flipped up her gown and she realized what he was doing.

Her eyes feasted on the part of him that he didn't think could get any harder. But her curiosity proved him wrong. He gritted his teeth, and his stomach clenched as she reached out and touched him.

"You're so . . ." She gazed up at him hesitantly, wrapping her fingers around him as he'd shown her earlier. "Big."

And much to his pain, getting bigger by the moment.

"And so soft and hard at the same time."

Jesus. Maybe talking hadn't been such a great idea. But neither was looking. When he glanced down and saw those dainty, milky-white fingers wrapped around him, he almost came in her hand. He'd dreamed of his moment since he'd been a lad; he couldn't believe it was actually happening.

He pulsed, and her eyes widened. "Am I doing that?"

Blood was pounding so hard through him, he couldn't speak for a moment. His eyes blazed fiercely. "Aye."

A dangerous little smile turned her mouth. It was the smile of a woman who'd just discovered a source of power.

"What did you mean by pump?"

The naughty little minx. He let out a deep groan when her hand moved up and down.

"Like this?" She dragged him hard from base to tip, her grip firm and tight.

He couldn't even nod, it felt so good. Every muscle strained.

"I like touching you," she whispered. "Feeling you beat in my hand."

Talking definitely not a good idea. He clenched, trying to hold back the surge that threatened to break free. But a milky-white bead escaped. "Tell me what you want, Magnus." She squeezed tighter, milking him harder.

He'd be angry at the little temptress for turning his words on him later, but right now it felt too good. He wanted to come. In her hand. In her mouth. But most of all deep inside her.

He clenched. Felt his stomach muscles tighten as pressure built and raced down to the base of his spine. As the throbbing intensified.

She stopped. "Tell me."

"I want to—"

Suddenly he stilled. An icy shiver of awareness ran across the back of his neck. He'd heard something.

Helen's hand dropped, sensing the change that had come over him. "What's wrong?"

He was already shoving himself back in his clothes, which, as he'd been only moments from release, wasn't easy. No doubt his bollocks were a bright shade of blue right now, but he pushed past the pain. The battle instinct had taken over. "Someone's out there."

Nineteen

❧

He almost had her in the cave. A few more moments, a few more steps, and Donald would have had her in his hold.

But he couldn't afford to make a mistake, not when he was this close to ridding Scotland of the false king. He was just waiting for the right opportunity.

Taking Helen would have been perfect. Not only would he be able to discover what she knew about Bruce's army, it would also get MacKay away from the king.

But no matter how tempting, he couldn't act precipitously. He couldn't risk MacKay discovering him—or the killing team—before they were ready to attack. Like Bruce's warriors, surprise was an important part of their strategy.

So he let her slip through his fingers. But God, he'd wanted her. Even though she'd rejected him. Perhaps more so. He liked a challenge. It made victory all the more rewarding. And he never doubted that he would defeat them both: the woman who'd rejected him and the man who'd made a fool of him on the battlefield.

Donald moved away from the cave when MacKay drew too close and watched from a distance. Watched every minute. At first he was pleased by what he saw. They seemed to be arguing. The foolish chit kept throwing herself at

MacKay and for whatever reason, he kept rejecting her. But when MacKay kissed her, everything changed.

He couldn't believe what he was seeing. Anger ate like acid through his chest. His blood started to burn as his body filled with rage. How could she? How could she whore herself like this?

She was giving herself to him. MacKay had his mouth on her perfect breast, his hand between her legs. He was touching her. The woman Donald had honored to make his wife was panting like a bitch in heat. The body he'd dreamed of was undulating and arching for another man's touch. He could almost feel her pleasure wrapping around him, taunting him, humiliating him, squeezing the love from his heart.

And when he heard her cries a few moments later he wanted to kill them both. A dirk to the back of MacKay's neck, and then into Helen's treacherous heart.

MacKay was lifting her skirts. He would never be more vulnerable than when he was fucking her.

Fucking my woman. Damn her, she'd had her chance.

He slid the dirk from his waist, but in his eagerness the blade accidentally tinged the metal of his belt.

He swore. He saw MacKay stiffen and knew that he'd heard the small sound. Donald knew he'd made a mistake. He had to warn the others.

The haze of pleasure evaporated in a wave of panic. The heat on Helen's skin turned to a sheet of ice. She looked around the shadowy darkness that had seemed so romantic only moments ago, but now seemed menacing and impenetrable.

If it weren't for Magnus's presence she would be terrified. But his presence calmed her. He wouldn't let anything happen to them. He drew his sword, using his body to shield her, as he scanned the area.

"Where?" she whispered.

"The copse of trees on the other side of the road. But I think they've gone." He steered her back into the entry of the cave and thrust a dirk in her hand. "Stay here."

Her eyes widened to what she was sure were enormous proportions. "You're leaving me?"

His hand cupped her cheek, and he gave her a tender smile. "Only for a moment. I need to make sure they're gone."

He was good to his word, never letting her out of his sight and returning only a few frantic heartbeats later, his expression grim.

"Did you find something?" she asked.

He shook his head. "Nay, but I'm certain someone was there."

Helen shivered. "I thought I heard someone earlier."

"What?" he roared, turning on her in not very happy-looking surprise. "When?"

She bit her lip. "When I was in the cave, I thought I heard someone by the entry. I thought it was you, trying to scare me."

His teeth clenched as if he were fighting for patience—and losing. "Why didn't you tell me?"

Heat burned her cheeks. "I thought I'd imagined it."

His face darkened. "Damn it, Helen. I told you not to run off. It's dangerous. You need to be careful."

He was furious, but she didn't understand why. "What is out there? What are you not telling me? Why would someone be watching us?"

His jaw clenched until his mouth turned white. He held her gaze, seeming to be warring with himself about something. Not telling her must have won. "Come on," he said, taking her by the arm. "I need to get you back to camp. I should never have brought you here. This was a mistake."

"What do you mean 'a mistake'? Magnus, what's wrong?" He wasn't regretting what had happened between them, was he?

It was clear he wasn't going to share his thoughts right now. He raced them back to camp as if the devil were nipping at their heels. Realizing the pace was due to his concern for her, she waited until she could see the torches and firelight of camp before forcing him to stop. "I want to know what this is all about."

"I intend to find out, once I get you back to camp."

Her eyes widened. "You're going after them?" She put her hand on his arm. "Are you sure that's wise? I thought you said it might be dangerous."

A flicker of a amusement crossed his face. "I can take care of myself, Helen. It's your safety that worries me."

"Mine? But why would I be—?"

"Helen!"

She groaned, hearing the sound of her brother's voice, coming not from the camp ahead of them but out of the darkness to the right. Good gracious, not now!

"Where have you been?" Kenneth demanded.

"Perhaps we should ask you the same thing," Magnus interjected. "Why are you alone and away from camp?"

It was clear what he was thinking, and Helen didn't like it. Her brother hadn't been following them . . . had he?

No. If he'd been spying on them, he wouldn't have stayed quiet. She cringed at the thought.

"Looking for my sister. When I returned from scouting and couldn't find you, I became worried. I should have guessed MacKay would take advantage of my absence." His eyes pinned hers. "Where were you? And why do I find you with him alone? What were you doing?"

"I asked Magnus to go with me to pick some averins for the king."

Her brother looked down at her empty hands, and she chewed on her lower lip, dismayed to realize she'd left the berries in the cave.

But it wasn't the missing berries that had caught his attention. He took in her hair, her face, her mouth, and then her rumpled clothing.

Helen looked down. *Oh no!* The guilty flush drained from her face in horror. The ties of her chemise were hanging outside her gown.

Kenneth's eyes flashed wildly toward Magnus. "You bastard! By God, I'll kill you."

He reached for his sword.

Helen didn't think. She recognized that look on her brother's face—the fierce temper that would see no reason—and knew what he was going to do. She heard the whoosh of steel sliding from its scabbard and reacted.

"Don't!" she cried, lunging in front of Magnus, trying to cut off her brother. But she misjudged Kenneth's speed; he was much quicker than she remembered.

Magnus shouted a warning in a voice she'd never heard before. "God, Helen, no!"

It happened so fast, yet it seemed to pass in slow motion. She could see the razor-sharp edge of steel coming toward her. See her brother's tortured expression as he realized what was about to happen and tried to stop the arc of the sword already on it's downward path. She heard Magnus's cry of fury as he fought to get his sword, and then his body around in time to protect her. Her eyes widened in horror, as she realized none of it would be in time.

She waited for the pain that she hoped wouldn't last too long.

But at the last second, Magnus wrapped his ankle around hers, tripping her, and twisted her underneath him as they hit the ground, protecting her with the shield of his body.

She'd never forget the sound the blade made as it whizzed by her ear and landed in the dirt with a thud a few inches from her head.

It was deathly quiet for a long heartbeat. Eventually, her brother's anguished voice broke the silence. "Oh God, Helen. I'm sorry." He knelt beside her. "Are you all right?"

But Magnus had pinned her with his gaze, a deadly calm surrounding him. His heart was beating unnaturally slowly—ominously slowly. "Are you all right?"

She was shaking inside but forced herself to answer firmly, "I'm fine."

He rolled off her and calmly helped her to her feet, but she was not fooled—she could sense the fury emanating from him like the fiery blast of a blacksmith's bellows. Sailors talked of the eerie calm right before the gates of hell opened wide. This was what it must feel like to be in the eye of the storm, harkening disaster. Her brother didn't know what was about to hit him.

"Thank God," Kenneth said.

He started to get to his feet, but Magnus grabbed him by the neck and thrust him up against the closest tree. "You rash, bloody fool! You almost killed her!" He gripped him tighter, cutting off his breath. "I should kill you."

He seemed intent on doing just that. Kenneth was pulling at his hands, trying to get him to let go. But some kind of supernatural strength had come over Magnus. His arm was like a steel rod; her big, muscular brother couldn't budge him an inch.

She grabbed at Magnus's arm, trying to pull it away. "Magnus, please let him go. You're hurting him."

His eyes were flat, black with cold rage. For a moment, she didn't think he heard her. "He almost killed you."

"He didn't mean to," she said softly, as if trying to soothe an angry beast. "It was an accident."

"Accident? He can't control his damned temper. He's undisciplined, rash, and a danger to everyone around him. How can you defend him?"

Tears filled her eyes. "I'm not. But he's my brother, and I love him. Magnus, please . . ."

Their eyes held, and slowly she could see the fiery rage begin to dim. He loosened his grip, but gave her brother one last hard shake before releasing him. "If you ever draw your blade around her again, I'll kill you."

To her surprise, her brother didn't threaten him back. For once, Kenneth's fierce temper seemed chastened.

The two men faced off silently in the darkness, exchanging silent accusations. There was something more going on between them that Helen didn't understand.

"Did you dishonor her?" Kenneth managed, his breath still ragged and hoarse.

Magnus stiffened, but before he could answer, Helen turned on her brother. "That's enough, Kenneth! You are my brother, not my father. I've had enough of your interference, and I won't have any more. I did what you asked of me once, but I won't do it again. I love him. Nothing Magnus could do would dishonor me."

Her brother ignored her. His eyes burned into Magnus's. "Did you?" he seethed. "I'm her guardian for this journey; I have a right to know."

Magnus's mouth thinned. It was clear he wanted to tell her brother to go to Hades, but equally clear that he recognized Kenneth's authority even if she did not. "Nay."

"But I should like him to," Helen insisted.

They both turned to her at the same time and said, "Helen, shut up!"

Or maybe Kenneth had said it, and Magnus had only looked it, but the shock to her was the same. Perhaps she should be glad that they were always at one another's throats; if they ever decided to join forces against her she might be in trouble.

"Stay away from her," Kenneth said in a low voice. "Would you bring more danger down upon her?"

That did it. Helen's irritation exploded. "Good God, you, too? What is this supposed danger that I know nothing about?"

Magnus's mouth was white as he and her brother shot silent daggers at one another.

"Aye, why don't you tell her, MacKay?" Kenneth taunted.

Magnus looked like he was seriously regretting removing his hand from her brother's throat. "I warned you before, Sutherland. Shut. The. Hell. Up."

"Not if you won't keep your hands off her. She deserves to know what she's getting herself into." Kenneth turned to her. "Go ahead, ask him. Ask him about the secrets he's been hiding. Ask him about Gordon. Ask him about the rumors of Bruce's phantom warriors attacking Threave Castle a few days after your wedding."

Helen's eyes widened. Everyone had heard the stories of the impossible feats performed by a small band of seemingly invincible warriors who slipped in and out of the shadows like phantoms. 'Twas said no one could defeat them. She'd enjoyed the stories as much as anyone else, but had never put much thought into the men behind them. Real or imagined, no one knew their identities. But she felt an eerie prickle of premonition whisper behind her neck. "Bruce's phantoms? What does that have to do with William?"

Magnus took a step toward Kenneth, but Helen blocked him. "Tell me, Magnus. What is he talking about?"

Magnus's gaze fell to hers. She could tell he was furious but watching his words carefully. "He's talking about things he doesn't know a damned thing about."

But her brother wouldn't back down. "Ask him about the strange explosion that took down part of the wall at Threave, Helen. Does it remind you of any stories I used to tell you about?"

She gasped, and her gaze shot to Magnus's. Knowledge of the Saracen black powder was rare enough to be remarkable. "Is it true? Is what my brother says true? Was William part of this phantom army?"

But she didn't need to ask. His eyes burned into hers, hot and full of torment.

She stepped back, covering her mouth in shock. "Dear God!"

It seemed incredible that William could have been part of something that seemed almost mythical or apocryphal. How little she'd known him!

To her surprise, her brother looked just as stunned as she was. "Damn," Kenneth muttered. "It's true."

"If you care anything about your sister's safety you will never mention it again."

Kenneth's mouth fell in a grim line.

She looked back and forth between them. "What does it have to do with my safety?"

The men exchanged looks; clearly neither was eager to explain. After a long pause, Magnus broke the silence. "There are many people who would be willing to pay a price to learn the identities of the alleged 'phantom army.' Anyone known to be connected to any of them is in danger."

"But I don't know anything about it."

"Aye, but no one knows that," her brother pointed out.

God, he was right. Helen stared at Magnus. "Am I in danger?"

"I don't know."

"But you have a reason to believe I might be."

He nodded.

"That's why you were so worried in the forest."

"What happened in the forest?" her brother demanded.

Magnus looked as if he wished Kenneth far away, but eventually he said, "I thought someone was watching us."

Kenneth swore. "Why didn't you go after them?"

His mouth thinned at the criticism. "Because I wanted to get your sister to safety, that's why. I couldn't very well take her along. I was about to organize a scouting party when you got in my way."

"I'm going with you." Before Magnus could object, he added, "She's my sister. If she's in danger I'll protect her."

He turned to her. "Come, Helen. I'll take you back to camp."

She shook her head. "Magnus will do it." She watched Kenneth's expression darken. "It shall only take a few minutes and you can see me from camp. There is something I must say to him."

"If you need help finding the right words, I have a few suggestions."

Helen ignored him, not needing much of an imagination to guess what those words might be.

"Get MacGregor and Fraser," Magnus said to him. "I don't want to take any more men from camp than that. We will leave as soon as I am done."

Kenneth didn't like it, but he left them alone.

The ramifications of William's involvement with the mysterious warriors were staggering, but one possibility loomed above the others. She thought of the changes in Magnus. His closeness to William. The tight bond he seemed to have with the king. "And what about you, Magnus? What does Bruce's phantom army have to do with you?"

"The king acknowledges no such army."

"So because it's not official, it doesn't exist? You're part of it, aren't you?"

He held her gaze, his expression perfectly unreadable. "Don't ask me a question I cannot answer."

But she didn't need to ask. She knew. He was part of the group, too. Her brother suspected the truth as well. That was one of the reasons he wanted him to stay away from her.

Was it also one of the things that was keeping Magnus from admitting his love for her? Was he trying to protect her? Her heart swelled.

She stepped closer to him, until their bodies were almost brushing. "I don't want your protection, Magnus. I want your love."

His expression was fierce in the moonlight, almost as if she had him on the rack. He was waging some kind of horrible war inside himself that she didn't understand. He shook her off. "Nay. I promised to protect you, damn it, and I will."

Her heart caught mid-beat. She stilled. Promised? A horrible premonition crept up inside her. "To whom did you make this promise?"

He seemed to realize he'd made a mistake and wished the words back, but it was too late. She could see the apology in his gaze. "To Gordon. I vowed to him that I would protect you."

Helen let out a very slow breath through the hot vise fitted tightly around her chest. "Is that why I am on this trip? Is it so that you could watch over me?"

He tried to avoid her eyes, but she stared at him until he met them. "Aye."

She nodded. "I see." And she did. Clearly. Without the blindness of illusions. It was duty that had forced his nearness, not that he'd softened toward her.

Stung, hurt, and not a little angry, she started to walk away, but he caught her arm, preventing her. "Helen, wait. It's not like that."

Her eyes blurred. Hot tears pressed against the back of her throat. "Oh really, then how is it? Are you here—am I here—because you love me, or because you want to protect me?"

His silence was all the answer she needed.

It was a long night. Magnus, MacGregor, Sutherland, and Fraser rode for hours patrolling the forests, mountains, and countryside near their camp at the eastern end of Loch Glascarnoch, trying to find any sign of the interloper. But whoever it was had vanished without a sign.

There were few inhabitants in the area—only a handful of stalker huts and bothies—and so far no one they questioned reported seeing or hearing anything since the king's party had traveled through. No suspicious men, no riders, no armed warriors, no brigands, nothing. Of course, it would be a hell of a lot easier if they knew exactly what they were looking for.

They were just returning to their horses after wresting an unhappy cottager and his wife from their beds when Sutherland fell into step beside Magnus.

Magnus tensed, the muscles at his neck and shoulders bunched in anticipation.

"Are you sure someone was there?" Sutherland asked. "Perhaps it was an animal."

He gritted his teeth. Coming from anyone other than Sutherland, the question wouldn't have riled him so much. But he couldn't look at the bastard without seeing that damned sword and feeling the blood-chilling moment of uncertainty when he hadn't known whether he was going to be able to get Helen out of its way.

Sutherland's hot-tempered recklessness had been inches away from costing his sister her life. Only the knowledge that the bastard had cause for his anger—and Magnus's own guilt for what had nearly happened with Helen— prevented him from fully regretting his decision to let him go. But he was waiting for an excuse to shed some of that too-hot blood and didn't doubt Sutherland would give him one.

"It wasn't an animal. Someone was there. I heard the ting of metal on metal."

"It could have been someone from camp."

Fraser had overheard Sutherland's question. "But why wouldn't they make themselves known?"

Magnus and Sutherland exchanged angry glares in the darkness, both thinking the same thing: perhaps the person had been too embarrassed to interrupt what was happening.

"It wasn't someone from camp," Magnus said flatly. He

didn't know how to describe it, except that he'd felt the weight of malevolence in the air and it had been aimed at him—or them, he didn't know which. It was that extra sense. The primitive instinct that detected danger and set every nerve-ending on edge. His gut told him someone was there and that person was a threat. And his instincts had helped him survive too many times for him to ignore them.

"We can't take any chances," MacGregor said, sidestepping Fraser's question.

"But you aren't certain my sister is in danger?"

Magnus's mouth fell in a flat line. He knew Sutherland wasn't satisfied with the little he'd told him of the King's message—simply that there was a vague rumor of Gordon being connected to the secret army—but that was all he needed to know. Hell, he already knew too much. With MacRuairi and Gordon's unmasking, and Sutherland and Helen's suspicions about him and MacGregor, the identities of the Highland Guard were fast becoming one of the worst-kept secrets in Scotland. "I'm certain of nothing."

"There is also the king's safety to consider," MacGregor pointed out.

Sutherland shook his head. "So we have an unspecified target from an unspecified threat?"

Magnus clenched his fists, which were itching to connect with the other man's jaw. He was sure as hell earning his war name in having to put up with Sutherland right now. "You wanted to come along tonight. If you don't want to be here, you're free to return at any time. Join your friend Munro on the watch. But I intend to make damned sure your sister, the king, and everyone in that traveling party is safe."

"Your duty is to the king; I'll worry about my sister."

Magnus met Sutherland's glare, hearing the unspoken challenge: was he going to make a claim on Helen?

God, he wanted to. With every fiber of his being he wanted to. No matter how wrong. He'd been moments away from having no choice. He thought of what had happened. How she'd fallen apart in his arms. How ready she'd been for him. Her responses had been so honest. So sweet and innocent—nay, inexperienced. She wasn't innocent, damn it.

His promise to Gordon to keep her safe sure as hell didn't extend to what had happened, nor did his fear for Helen relieve him of his duty to the king. Her arse of a brother had reminded him of that and saved him from making a big mistake.

But he wished she hadn't learned the truth. He could still see her face when he'd accidentally let slip his promise to Gordon. She looked like a little girl who'd just learned that her favorite faerie tale wasn't real. And then when she'd tried to force a declaration from him . . .

He wanted to tell her both—it was love *and* his promise—but knew it was better if he let her walk away.

His mouth tightened, letting his anger at himself—at the bloody situation—find a worthy target: Sutherland. "I don't need you to remind me of my duty."

"Glad to hear it."

Magnus wanted to tell him to go to Hades, but it would only provoke the fight that was being held back by threads, and right now his focus needed to be on finding the source of the threat.

After returning to camp to check with the sentries he'd posted that nothing was amiss, they followed the stalker paths up along the strath—the wide river valley—north to Loch Vaich. The forest in Stratvaich was known for its deer, and stalker paths crossed all over these hills.

They'd ridden no more than a few miles from camp when they came upon a fisherman readying his boat at the jetty. After exchanging greetings, Magnus said, "An early start to the day, is it?"

"Aye," the man replied. He was young and cheerful, if

humbly attired. "The darker the night, the bigger the trout."

Magnus smiled at the familiar fisherman's adage and explained their purpose.

The man's cheerful expression changed. "I'm not sure if they are the men you're looking for, but I was fishing with my laddie at the other end of the loch the day before last and saw a group of warriors in the trees along the western bank."

A buzz ran over his skin. "How many?"

The man shrugged. "Eight, maybe nine. I didn't stay long to find out."

"Why not?" MacGregor asked.

The man shivered. "As soon as they saw us, they donned their helms and picked up their swords. I thought they were going to jump in the water and come after us. I rowed as fast as I could in the other direction. But they frightened my laddie something fierce." He laughed, uncomfortably. "With the blackened helms covering their faces and the black clothing, in the darkness he thought they looked like phantoms. Bruce's phantoms, he said." Knowing Sutherland was watching him, Magnus didn't chance a glance at MacGregor. "But to me they just looked like brigands."

After pinning down exactly where the fisherman had seen the warriors, Magnus thanked him, and they rode hard to the location the man had given them, not a mile up the western side of the loch.

It wasn't difficult to find where the men had made camp.

"Whoever it was, they didn't leave that long ago," MacGregor said, kneeling over a pile of wood covered by dirt. "The fires are still warm."

They searched the area, but although the brigands had made no effort to hide their presence, they hadn't been generous enough to leave anything behind that would identify them.

"Do you think it was the same men?" Fraser asked.

Magnus nodded grimly. "The timing is too close to be coincidence."

"Whoever it was, it looks like you ran them off," Sutherland said, pointing to the hoof marks in the ground that led north through the forest.

He hoped so, but he didn't like it. If they were brigands or a roaming war band, it would seem more logical for them to be camped nearer the road. And if they weren't brigands, then who the hell were they?

Magnus and the others followed the tracks around the loch west until they met the main road to Dingwall, before finally returning to camp. Whoever the warriors were, they seemed to be long gone.

The first tentative rays of dawn were breaking through the mist on the loch and the camp already had begun to stir. They'd have maybe an hour or two to sleep before the carts would need to be packed for the day's journey.

But sleep didn't come to Magnus. He couldn't shake the unease, the sense that something wasn't right.

Hours later, as the royal party neared the far end of Loch Glascarnoch, Magnus had confirmation.

From his position scouting high on the hilltop of Beinn Liath Mhor, he caught sight of a flash of metal in the sunlight. Skillfully and stealthily, at a distance safe enough to avoid detection, they were being hunted.

Twenty

William Sutherland of Moray was one of the most powerful men in Scotland. For as long as he could remember, people had jumped to do his bidding. He was the chief, damn it. An earl. The head of one of the most ancient Mormaerdoms. A feared and formidable warrior. But he was being defied at every turn by a woman who should be insignificant to him.

He should never have noticed the physician's pretty daughter. He hadn't at first. Muriel had been like a ghost when she'd come to Dunrobin, and at one and twenty he was too young and proud to notice a chit six years his junior. But she'd avoided him, and that had pricked his pride and his curiosity. He'd looked closer, seeing not a ghost but a wounded, haunted lass who'd stolen his heart and never let it go.

She'd been so damned vulnerable. He didn't know what he'd wanted at first. To help her, maybe? To make her not so sad? But he'd never forget the moment she'd trusted him enough to tell him her secret. Hearing the horror of her rape . . .

It had unleashed something inside him. Emotions that could never be reined back. He would have given anything to take that pain away from her. He'd wanted to comfort her, to protect her, and kill for her. But most of all he'd wanted to never let her go.

Earls didn't fall in love, damn it. He had a duty.

He paced around the small solar, straining against invisible chains. He knocked aside the wine that had been brought for him by one of his bevy of servants, and reached instead for the *uisge beatha*. After emptying a good portion of the jug into his flagon, he stood before the fire, staring into the flames and refusing to allow himself to go to the window to see if she would answer his summons—this time.

He tossed back the cup, downing the fiery amber brew as if it were watered-down ale. He was too angry, too frustrated, too pushed to the edge of his tether to notice. What the hell did she want from him?

He didn't understand her. Since her return a few weeks ago, he'd tried everything he could think of to convince her to stay with him. He'd showered her with gifts—jewels, silks for gowns, fine household plate—a king's ransom of riches that could keep her in luxury for the rest of her life. But she'd refused every one of them.

He thought if he brought her back to Dunrobin, she would see how much he missed her—and how much she missed him. How being together was all that mattered. But she avoided him, refused to come near the castle, and stayed in that damned hovel of hers. He should have burnt it to the ground. Then she would have to come to him.

Not even when he'd been forced to submit to Bruce had his pride taken such a beating. He'd gone to Inverness after her, damn it. He wouldn't go after her again.

So he'd ordered her to come to the Hall a few days ago for a feast. She obeyed, but she'd barely glanced in his direction. When he'd forced her to speak to him, she answered politely, "my lording" him to death, and generally treating him as if he meant nothing to her.

Infuriated, he'd tried to make her jealous by flirting with

Joanna, a servant he'd made the mistake of bedding years ago. But Muriel's indifference to his actions made him panic. He sent for her later that night—claiming he had a headache—and she'd sent a posset . . . with *Joanna*.

It would have served Muriel right if he'd bedded the lass. She was eager enough. But he wouldn't hurt Muriel like that, no matter how much she deserved it for defying him like this.

Will refused to consider that she no longer cared for him. That forcing her to come here might have been a mistake. She was just being stubborn, that was all. But with one week left, he was running out of time and ideas.

He stilled at a knock on the door.

"Come in," he said, bracing himself.

The door opened and he almost let out a sigh of relief. He'd half-expected her to send Joanna again, but it was Muriel who entered the room.

God, she was lovely. So fragile-looking, but with the un-mistakable air of strength that had always drawn him. Long, wavy blond hair, porcelain skin, pale blue eyes, and refined features set in perfect repose and . . . *indifference*.

He felt a strange hitch in his chest—not just of longing, but of fear. It twisted like a rope, getting tighter and tighter until the tension reached the snapping point. She couldn't be this indifferent to him; he wouldn't allow it.

She glanced at the jug in his hand—what the hell had happened to his flagon? There was nothing disapproving in her gaze, but he felt it all the same.

Suddenly, he felt naked and exposed. As though she'd stripped down the venerable earl and saw the uncertainty and desperation he was trying to drown in drink. He pushed the flagon aside, disgusted with his weakness. He was stronger than she, damn it. It was she who needed him.

"You wished to see me, my lord?"

"Damn it, Muriel, stop calling me 'my lord.'"

She looked at him blankly. "What should you like me to call you?"

He crossed the room and slammed the door shut behind her, his fists clenched at his sides in fury. "What you've called me for years. Will. William . . ." *Love.*

He was flailing like a ship in a storm, but she simply shrugged as if nothing about him made any difference to her. "Very well. Why did you send for me, William?"

The cool, impersonal tone sent a fresh surge of panic raging through his blood. He grabbed her arm and forced her to look at him, fighting the urge to shake some sense back into her. "Stop it, Muriel. Why are you doing this? Why are you being so stubborn?"

A small, mocking smile turned her lips. "What did you think, that bringing me back here would change my mind? That you could bend me to your will? Crush me in your iron fist like you do anyone else who refuses you?"

"No, damn it." But that's exactly what he'd thought. He released her, raking his fingers through his hair. "I want you with me. I love you, Muriel. If I could marry you I would. I'm just trying to make the best of a horrible situation. You will never want for anything. I will treat you like a queen. I will care for you as if you were my wife."

"Except that I shan't be your wife," she said matter-of-factly, ignoring the emotion he couldn't seem to contain. "If you truly loved me, William, you wouldn't ask this of me. I can forgive you for what you must do; won't you show me the same respect?" He didn't say anything. Couldn't say anything. "How do you think I should feel, when you marry and bring your wife here to stay?"

He felt a flicker of hope. "Is that what's bothering you? I would never do that to you. You will never have to see her. I will send her to a different castle."

"I see." She pretended to consider his words. "You are very accommodating. How well you have it all planned out! You seem to have thought of everything. It is a very good offer, and one I'm sure I should regret refusing. But I intend to return to Inverness in one week's time, and nothing you can say and no amount of gold is going to tempt me to change my mind."

He believed her. Damn her to Hades, he believed her. Rage roared through his blood, making him mad with it.

Look at her! A willowy, delicate woman. He could crush her in one hand. She wasn't stronger than he was, damn it, she wasn't.

His mouth pulled into a cruel semblance of a smile. "What if you have nothing in Inverness to go back to? What then, Muriel? One word from me and Ross will remove his patronage. How long do you think the gentleman physicians of Inverness will let you apprentice in their guild without it?"

But his cruel threat didn't even elicit the bat of a damned eyelash. Long, thick, doe-like eyelashes that were so feathery soft, like the wings of a butterfly. He thought of how they curved against her cheek when he held her in his arms.

"I don't suppose very long," she said quietly. "But it will not change my mind. There will be someplace that needs a healer, someplace that the mighty Earl of Sutherland cannot reach. Even if I have to go to England, I will find a place to make a new life."

She'd despised England ever since the soldiers had raped her. When he'd found out what had happened to her, he'd made it his personal mission to hunt every one of them down. He'd been cheated only once—one of the men had fallen in battle before he'd found him. That she would rather to go England than be with him . . .

"You don't mean it." But he feared she did. He felt himself lose control, as if the world—his world—were spinning away from him and he was helpless to stop it. He backed her up against the door. "I won't let you go."

Their eyes met. He couldn't think about the way she was

looking at him. He didn't want to put a name to it because he feared it would mean he'd lost her. But how could blue eyes turn so black?

He hated himself for what he was doing—cornering her, using his physical size to intimidate her—but he was too far gone to stop. This was a battle he would not—*could* not—lose.

She saw it, too. With one long look that shook him more than any blow from a sword, he saw the moment of recognition and acceptance in her eyes.

He'd won . . . my God, he'd won.

But then a strange look crossed her face. A look that made him feel the first flicker of unease.

"Very well, Will. I will give you what you want."

He moved back slowly, warily, as if he were watching a snake that was coiled and only pretending to sleep. "You will stay?"

She smiled pityingly. "Is that what you want? I was under the impression you wanted something else from me."

She unbuckled the plaid that she wore around her shoulders and let it fall to the ground. She began to untie the laces of her gown.

He was so stunned, it wasn't until the kirtle, too, fell in a heap by the plaid that he realized what she meant. His heart pounded. His mouth suddenly went dry, seeing her standing there in nothing more than a thin shift, her hose, and her soft leather slippers. Oh God . . .

"Muriel . . ." His voice was raw as she lifted the hem of her shift to lower her hose and remove her shoes, revealing a seductive hint of long, creamy-smooth, shapely legs.

She arched a brow, a wry look of challenge in an otherwise impassive face. "Is this not what you want, Will? Is this not the offer you have made? I will give you my body and you will give me everything I could want, isn't that right? Well, let's start now. Show me. Perhaps you can convince me that the wonder of your lovemaking will be enough?"

He felt the world rocking the way he did when he stepped off a boat after being at sea for too long. Unsteady. Odd. Like something wasn't right. Something *wasn't* right, but he was too damned blind to see it. All he could see was the woman he loved standing before him half-naked, giving herself to him.

His blood burned hot through his veins. He'd wanted this for so long.

She moved toward him. Sliding her hands around his neck and letting her breasts brush against his chest. "You'll have to forgive me. It's been some time since I've done this."

His chest knifed. The brutal reminder of what had happened to her burned. He shouldn't do this. It was wrong.

"Don't, Muriel." His hands went around her waist to push her away. It was so tiny he could almost span it with two hands.

But she wouldn't let him stop. "Why not?" She swept her hand down his chest, over the taut bands of his stomach muscles to the bulge that swelled between his legs. He let out a slow hiss when he felt the weight of her hand covering him.

He wanted to weep with pleasure, it felt so good.

She slid up next to him again, rubbing her delicately curved body against his. Heat flared inside him and his skin tightened, suddenly feeling too small.

"You want me. You can have me. I'm giving myself to you. No obligations, no conditions, just the way you want."

The soft, seductive offer proved too much to resist. He crushed her in his embrace, covering her mouth with his, drinking in every sweet inch of her. He felt the slide of her tongue against his and told himself it was all right.

But a vague sense of unease penetrated the haze of desire. She was responding to him, but it wasn't with the intensity and urgency of before. She'd always kissed him as though she couldn't get enough of him. But this felt—this felt different.

His hand slid through her hair, cupping her head to bring her more fully to him, intensifying the kiss. Determined to make her want him as much as he wanted her.

It would be all right. He knew he would bring her pleasure.

His hands skimmed her back, her hips, her bottom. But even the thin piece of fabric that separated them was too much. He wanted to touch her. Feel her skin against his. Make her moan for him.

But she wasn't moaning. Wasn't making those soft, little gasps at the back of her throat. She wasn't melting into him, clutching the muscles of his arms and digging her fingers into him as if she were holding on for dear life.

In frustration, he cupped her bottom, bringing her more fully against him, and started to rock. Slowly at first, then quickening the pace as desire built inside him and he felt her body start to respond. Her hips circled against his, finding the perfect rhythm.

He knew through experience that he could make her want him. He thought of all the times in the past that he'd made her come just by rubbing against her. And how she'd take him in her hand and give him release. But they'd always stopped. They'd never taken it to the final step.

He'd lived like a damned monk for years, damn it.

Finally, he heard the moans he'd been aching to hear. He kissed her harder, feeling her surrender to the maelstrom surging between them. He cupped her breast, felt the nipple tighten between his fingers, and let out a deep guttural groan of masculine satisfaction when she arched into his hand.

His body pounded. His cock swelled harder, knowing she was almost ready for him. Knowing in a few minutes he was going to be inside her.

He broke away, looking into her eyes, as he gently leaned her back against the table and started to lift the edge of her chemise. She wasn't going to stop him this time.

She looked exactly the way he'd dreamed she would look at this moment. Cheeks flushed, lips swollen and gently parted, her hair gently mussed. But something was wrong. Her eyes . . . Her eyes . . .

Oh, Jesus.

She was surrendering to him, but she didn't want him. She didn't even *like* him. What she was feeling wasn't love, it was lust.

The realization broke through the haze of passion with a fist of clarity. Making love to her wasn't going to change a damned thing. It wasn't going to prove they were meant to be together. And it wasn't going to change her mind. It would only make her hate him more.

She was right. He was trying to force her—bend her to his will. But she was stronger than he. This woman who'd survived so much.

He pushed her away, keeling over as if he'd taken a blow to the gut. In that moment when she was giving him exactly what he wanted—what he thought he wanted—he knew it wasn't what he wanted at all. And what he'd wanted, he'd lost.

He wanted her back. The girl who'd looked at him with love in her eyes. Who'd made him feel as if he were the most important person in the world to her. Who'd trusted him enough to give him her heart and a body that should never have wanted a man's touch again.

How could he have done this to her? He *loved* her.

It was time to start acting like it.

"Go," he said hoarsely, disgust at what he'd done making his throat thick. "Go back to Inverness. I never should have brought you here. I'm . . . God, I'm sorry."

She didn't look at him again. She picked her clothes up from off the floor, donned them quickly, and left without a backward glance.

He loved her enough to let her go.

Twenty-one

Helen had plenty of time to think about all that had transpired. During the long, mostly sleepless night while she waited for Magnus and Kenneth to return safely (even though neither of them deserved her worry), and the even longer and far more arduous day of travel, she could think of little else. Having one's heart crushed tended to have that effect.

She'd thought she and Magnus might have a chance. That he'd softened toward her—toward them—but it had only been a promise to William.

Or was it?

Once the initial stab of hurt dulled, she began to wonder if that was truly all it was about. Perhaps it had started out that way, but what about what had happened in the forest? Magnus might like to *think* it was only about protecting her, but his promise to William didn't have anything to do with the passion that had exploded between them.

And the look in his eyes when her brother's sword had nearly cut her in two . . .

He cared for her. She was sure of it. But something was preventing him from acting on it. Whether it was due to his involvement with Bruce's phantom army (she still couldn't believe the lad who'd once chased her through the forest was one of the most feared warriors in Christendom), her family and the feud, her marriage to William and his feelings of loyalty to his friend, or a combination of them all, she didn't know. But she intended to find out.

Nothing was insurmountable. Not if they truly loved one another. She just needed the stubborn ox to realize it.

Which was easier said than done. He wasn't exactly avoiding her, but as the day progressed it was clear that something beyond the torturously slow place was bothering him. There was an intensity—a watchfulness—to him that she'd never seen before. For the first time, she was seeing him in full warrior mode: fierce, hard, emotionless, and utterly focused on his duties. It was strange to see a side of him of which she'd never been a part.

It was late in the afternoon when he and Gregor MacGregor came racing to the place where the royal party had stopped for a short break along Loch Glascarnoch. Right away she knew something was wrong. The two men immediately pulled the king and some of the higher-ranking members of his retinue, including her brother and Donald, aside for what appeared to be an intense conversation.

She could tell by the way the king's face darkened that whatever news they brought, it wasn't good. And when her brother's gaze flicked over to her where she sat on the banks of the loch eating a small piece of bread and cheese, she feared it had to do with her.

She wished she could hear what was being said. It was clear there was some kind of disagreement, not surprisingly with Donald and her brother on one side and Magnus on the other.

Waiting patiently wasn't one of her virtues. She was just about to start ever-so-subtly creeping toward the men when the group disbanded, and Magnus came striding toward her.

Their eyes met, and though she knew he was trying to hide it, she could see that he was worried.

Her heart tugged. Whatever the hurt of last night—no matter how much she wanted to talk about what had happened—it was clear that it would have to wait.

She came forward to meet him, putting her hand on his arm as if she could somehow ease his burden. Touching him, seeking that instinctive connection, seemed the most natural thing in the world. It always had.

"What is it?" she asked.

"We're being followed."

She stilled. "By whom?"

He shook his head, his expression grim. "I don't know, but I intend to find out."

She feared she wasn't going to like the answer to the question, but she asked it anyway. "What are you going to do?"

A slow smile curved his mouth. "Wait for them."

"What do you mean, wait for them? And why do you look like you are looking forward to it?"

His expression turned as hard as stone. "I *am* looking forward to it. I don't like when people threaten someone I—" He stopped himself, and then added, "Someone I'm responsible for."

She swallowed. Had he been about to say "love"? "Is it me they are after, then?"

"I don't know. It could just be a war band of malcontents, but I'm not taking any chances with you or anyone else. We're going to set a trap for them tonight. There's a perfect place at the far end of the loch. A natural gully where the path narrows, with the mountains and forest on one side and the loch on the other. As soon as they enter it, we'll have them surrounded."

It sounded dangerous, no matter how easy he was trying to make it seem. "But how many of them are there? How many men will you have? What if something goes wrong?"

"You don't need to worry about it. You and the king will be perfectly safe—"

"Me? I'm not worried about me, it's you I'm worried about."

He shook his head, clearly amused. "I know what I'm doing, Helen. I've done this many times before."

"Wouldn't it be better to go for help?"

"Take a look around—there isn't help for miles." His face hardened again. "I'll say this for them. Whoever it is, they've chosen their place well. We are still too far from Loch Broom to go for help, and too far from Dunraith to try to return. Either they have some knowledge of these mountains or they're damned lucky."

"Doesn't that concern you?"

"Aye, which is why I'm being cautious."

"Setting a trap where you intend to spring a surprise attack on an unknown number of warriors is being cautious?"

He grinned. "Normally, I'd take a handful of men and go after them right now, which is what your brother and Munro were advocating, so aye, I am being cautious."

Helen blanched. "Perhaps it's better if I don't know what 'normal' is."

His expression changed. "Maybe it was a bad idea to bring you along. If I'd known . . ." His voice dropped off. "I thought you'd be safer with me then you would be at Dunrobin."

"I am," she said unequivocally. "If it is me they are after, I'd rather be here with you than at home. My brother couldn't have kept me locked up forever."

"Why not?"

Good God, he was being serious. "Being confined isn't living, Magnus, even if it keeps me safe."

Their eyes held. After a moment, he nodded. "Your brother and Munro will stay back with a few of the other men to protect you and the rest of the party."

Of the roughly three score of people who made up their traveling party, there were perhaps a dozen knights and

three times that many men-at-arms, the rest being attendants and household servants. They were fortunate. Normally, a king's party would include far more of the latter,
but they were traveling with a large percentage of fighting
men.

"And what of the king?" she said.

"He's staying with you."

Helen glanced over to the Bruce, seeing an expression
very similar to the one on Magnus's face only moments
before. "Does he know that?"

Magnus made a face. "Not yet." He looked at her hopefully. "Perhaps you can think of a reason?"

"Ha!" she laughed sharply. "I'm afraid you're on your
own."

"I'll remember that," he said, folding his arms across his
chest. She sucked in her breath, unable to look away from
the impressive display of muscle.

The air suddenly grew charged with awareness. There
were so many things left unsaid. So many things left undone.

"Be careful," she said softly.

He wanted to kiss her. She could see that he did. Perhaps
he would have had they not been standing in the middle of
the camp. But all he could do was unfold his arms and nod.
"I will."

He started to walk away, but then turned back to her.
"Be ready, Helen. We may have need of you."

She bit her lip, understanding. Men might be hurt. She
nodded and repeated just as he had, "I will."

She would let him do his job, and when the time came,
she would do hers. *But please, please keep him safe.*

"I don't like this," MacGregor said softly.

"Neither do I," Magnus replied.

The two men had crept on their bellies as far forward as
they could on the darkened hillside from which they would

launch their attack. Below them lay the forested gully where the hillside met the far edge of the loch before opening up into the Dirrie More pass, where the rest of the royal party waited.

Magnus had chosen the place to launch their attack well, using his knowledge of the terrain to put the ten men he'd brought with him at an advantage even should they be outnumbered. But if Fraser's scouting was correct, they'd be evenly matched. The road here was narrow; once their enemies entered, they would be easily surrounded by Magnus's men on the hillside with nowhere to run but the loch. But where were they?

"They should have been here by now. Fraser said they were only a few miles back."

"I can't see a damned thing," MacGregor said. "The mist is as thick as pitch. I'd feel a hell of a lot better if Ranger were here."

Arthur "Ranger" Campbell was prized not only for his scouting abilities, but also for his uncanny, eerie senses, which had helped them avoid more than one dire situation. And this sure as hell qualified.

Magnus had downplayed the situation to Helen, but if there was one place on their journey that he wouldn't want to be caught with over fifty people to protect from an attack, this part of the road was it. Miles from help, deep in the heart of the mountainous countryside, they could be pinned down as easily as he hoped to pin down the men following them.

"I'd feel a hell of a lot better if the entire team were here," Magnus agreed.

Though he'd chosen the men he'd brought with him well, they weren't the Highland Guard. They weren't even the ten best men he had. He couldn't risk leaving Helen and the rest of the party inadequately protected. It was how he'd finally convinced the king—one of the best knights in Christendom—to stay behind with Sutherland and Munro.

Normally, Magnus would welcome the Bruce's sword. But Bruce was king now and needed to be protected. His role had changed, but Bruce had held the sword in his hand for too long to relish putting it aside—even for the sake of the realm. And with his queen and his only heir currently in an English prison, he had to exercise caution.

Magnus hated to divide their forces, even by a short distance, but he had no choice. This was the best chance to defuse the threat with as little damage as possible. Ironically, the very thing that had given the Highland Guard an advantage over the English was being used against him: the size and inability of the royal party to maneuver quickly. He had no doubt they would win if they came under attack, but it would be far more difficult to protect Helen and the king. This way he could ensure their safety.

"Something's wrong," he said, peering into the nearly impenetrable darkness and mist. "We need to check—"

A fierce war cry shattered the silent night.

Magnus swore. Leaping to his feet, he reached for his war hammer. MacGregor echoed a similar sentiment and reached for his sword—his bow would be of little use in close combat—realizing as Magnus did that their surprise attack had just gone to hell.

They were the ones under attack—from behind.

He and MacGregor raced back to the place where the other men he'd brought with him were waiting. The battle was already in full force.

On first glance Magnus wasn't overly concerned, counting only a handful of men. But that was before he noticed four of the men-at-arms he'd brought with him on the ground. Whatever advantage they'd had in numbers had all but disappeared in the opening strokes of the attack. Still, the numbers didn't worry him. He and MacGregor would make short work of them. They'd taken down twice—four times—this many before.

But when another of his men—this one a knight—fell, Magnus knew this might not be so easy.

"What in Hades?" MacGregor said, not wasting time to look in his direction but jumping right into the battle.

The words echoed Magnus's thoughts exactly. Even before his sword locked on his first opponents, he knew there was something different about these warriors—brigands—whoever they were.

The men were dressed all in black. Although they wore shirts of mail and not *cotuns* as the Highland Guard did, the mail was blackened, as were the helms that completely hid their faces. Like the Highland Guard, they employed a variety of weapons, from swords to battle-axes, war hammers, and pikes. Magnus would like to say that was where the similarities ended, but he couldn't. He could tell from the first swing of his opponent's sword that he was no common swordsman. The man knew how to fight. Well.

Locked in a surprisingly difficult contest, the din of battle all around, it took Magnus a moment to realize that the noise wasn't just coming from around him. It was also coming from the west below, where the rest of the party was waiting.

The king. Helen. Bloody hell, they were under attack! He needed to get to them. But the attackers were positioned to block his path.

Perfectly positioned. Almost as if they'd known exactly where they would be.

His blood spiked, heat surging through his veins in a sharp rush. He forced his opponent back with crushing blows of the hammer. Using a curved spike that he'd forged on the other end, he hooked the edge of the opponent's targe, ripping it from his hand. Without the shield to protect the man, Magnus took the advantage. He waited for the defensive swing of the sword, twisted out of the way, and brought down his hammer with full force on his skull. The man staggered and then fell. Though the blow would probably kill him, Magnus plunged a blade through the mail coif under his helm just to make sure.

One down, four to go. MacGregor, Fraser, and De la Hay were holding their own, but the remaining man-at-arms—one of Fraser's men—was clearly overmatched. Magnus was surprised he'd lasted this long.

Magnus went to his aid, but before he could reach Fraser's man, the attacker's blade cleared the man's head from his shoulders. Magnus swung the hammer at the attacker's head a moment after, but he blocked it with his sword, pushing him back.

Damn, the man was nearly as big as Robbie Boyd and from what he could see, wielded a two-handed great sword with enough skill to give MacLeod a contest. Magnus couldn't find an opening. It was all he could do to keep the long blade from lopping off his own head.

It wasn't often Magnus found himself at a disadvantage, but the shorter length of his hammer was proving a detriment against the long blade. He couldn't get close enough to do damage.

Where had this man come from?

In between blows, he could see out of the corner of his eye as MacGregor finally dispatched his man and went to the aid of Fraser, who seemed to be having difficulty. Magnus heaved a sigh of relief, not wanting to explain to MacLeod how they'd managed to get his young brother-in-law killed on a nice, "peaceful" journey across the Highlands.

Magnus preferred to fight with the hammer, but right now he needed the sword at his back. When the third of the attackers fell under Fraser's blade and Magnus's opponent glanced toward him, Magnus had his chance. He pulled the blade from the scabbard at his back, but before he could bring it down toward his opponent's head, the man let out a sharp whistle. The next instant he and his remaining companion were fleeing back into the darkness of the forest.

Fraser started to go after them, but Magnus stopped him. "Let them go—we have to get to the king." They'd been delayed too long already.

"Don't you hear it, lad?" De la Hay said to Fraser. "The king and the others are under attack."

It was less than a half-mile to where they'd left the royal party, but the two minutes it took them to get there felt like forever.

"How the hell did they know?" MacGregor asked, racing through the forest beside him.

Magnus gave him a quick glance, wondering the same thing. "Either they're damned lucky or—"

"Or we've been betrayed," MacGregor finished.

Aye, but by whom?

Magnus didn't have time to think about it. His only concern was reaching the king and Helen before . . .

He didn't let himself finish. But ice was shooting through his veins.

The scene that met them was one of utter pandemonium. Carts were overturned. Men were scattered, some hidden, a few locked in battle, at least a dozen littered across the grassy floor.

He scanned the darkness, not seeing either Helen or the king right away. He hoped to hell they'd both had the good sense to get back. But he knew the king. Robert the Bruce would be leading the charge.

So where is he?

Magnus helped one of his men fight off an attacker before he finally caught sight of Sutherland. "Where are they?" he shouted, not needing to specify who.

Sutherland didn't get a chance to reply. One of the attackers came out of his blind side with a battle-axe. Sutherland barely had the chance to block it with his targe, and the blow caused him to let down his guard. The attacker lifted the axe high above his head.

Magnus didn't hesitate. He pulled his dirk from his waist and threw it with all his strength at the man's upraised arm. It landed with a dull thud, penetrating the mail and causing the attacker to drop his hand and howl in pain. The brigand let out an oath in Gaelic—*Irish* Gaelic. Sutherland took full advantage and stuck his sword deep into the man's padded but unmailed leg.

From the amount of blood that spurted out, Magnus knew even before the Irishman toppled to the ground that it was a death blow.

"How many?" Magnus asked.

"Only a handful. But they're skilled."

He'd noticed. Something to ponder after he helped the other men fight off the remaining attackers. But as the first group of attackers had done, with a whistle the remaining brigands retreated into the forest.

Magnus met MacGregor's gaze and nodded. MacGregor quickly organized a handful of men to go after them, including Fraser, De la Hay, Sutherland, and Munro.

Magnus was already looking for Bruce and Helen. But the minutes passed, each second in increasing agony.

Where the hell are they? He searched frantically, like a man possessed.

Panic nipped at his heels. He tried to kick it back. They were here. Somewhere in the chaos and misty darkness, they had to be here.

He ordered the torches lit, then searched the bodies that littered the forest floor and anywhere else he could find. But it wasn't until he saw Sir Neil Campbell staggering through the trees, blood streaming down his face, that ice penetrated his bones. The vaunted knight would never have willingly left the king's side.

"Where are they?" Magnus asked, dreading the answer.

Sir Neil shook his head dazedly. "I don't know. God's bones, I don't know."

It all happened so fast, Helen didn't have time to be scared. One minute she was waiting—praying—for Magnus and the others to return safely, and the next they were under attack.

"Get back!" Bruce shouted to her. "Take them and get back."

But the king's command wasn't necessary. Once the initial moment of shock—when the first brigand had stepped out of the trees and with one swipe of his sword brought down two unfortunate guardsmen—had worn off, Helen had leapt into action. She gathered her two terrified tiring women and the servants who wouldn't know what to do with a weapon if one were put in their hands, and whispered for them to follow her. She didn't know where they were going, just that she had to get them out of the way so the warriors could do their job.

A safe refuge was too much to ask for, but the mist and darkness provided some shroud. In the desolate landscape of the Dirrie More, there were few natural hiding places. The patch of pine trees would have to do.

From behind the trees, Helen and the others watched the battle unfold. At first Helen was relieved. She counted only a handful of attackers, while the king had perhaps four times that many at his command.

The surprise of the attack had caught the king's men unaware, but not unprepared. It took them only seconds to take the weapons that had been readied in hand and begin to repel the attack.

But to her growing horror, she saw the king's men falling. She lost sight of her brother and Donald, but the king and Sir Neil Campbell had taken a defensive position in front of her and the others.

One of the attackers was pushing toward them, cutting

down all the men in his path. Sir Neil moved forward to engage him just as another attacker came into view.

She lost Sir Neil in the hazy darkness, but could still make out the king's mail-clad form and the steel helm laden with a golden crown as his sword clashed with the brigand's.

Helen's heart jumped with every horrible clash of steel. Though she knew the king was one of the greatest knights in Christendom, it didn't take her long to realize that the man who faced him was no common brigand. He wielded his sword with a strength equal to that of the king—if not more.

The battle between the two men seemed to go on forever. But where were the others? Why had no one come to his aid?

To her horror, she realized that the brigand was purposefully moving the king toward the pine trees where they were hidden, away from the main battle.

The closer they drew, the more the tension in the small group began to mount. She motioned for the others to stay quiet, but from the wide, horror-filled eyes of her ladies, she feared they weren't going to last much longer.

They could hear the heavy breathing of the men as they exchanged blow after blow, until finally, the king's blade met the other man's with such force, the sword slipped from his hands.

Helen nearly gasped with relief. The king lifted his sword to deliver the death blow. But the other man was not going to surrender to death without a fight. Somehow he managed to extricate a battle-axe from his body. Even as the blade of Bruce's sword was slicing through the air, the brigand landed a one-handed blow of the axe to the king's head.

Momentum finished the king's job for him—the brigand's neck was nearly severed in two—but Bruce staggered, the blade of the axe still stuck in his helm.

He lowered to his knees, and then stopped himself from keeling forward by extending his hands.

Helen didn't think. With the bag that Magnus had made for her looped over her shoulder across her body, she ordered the rest of the group to stay there and raced forward to help the king.

When she reached him, she fell to her knees at his side. It was dark, but there was enough moonlight shining through the mist to see the blood gushing down his face.

It was like some macabre farce. The blade of the axe was stuck into his helm and had penetrated the steel into his brow.

Dear God, let it not be deep.

"Sire," she said gently. "Let me help."

He was rocking side-to-side, obviously in a daze. "My head," he mumbled.

She soothed him as best she could, easing him back until he was seated on the ground.

Every instinct recoiled from removing the helm and its hideous appendage—fearing what she would find—but she had to see the extent of the damage and stop the bleeding.

"I need to take off your helm," she said gently. "Can you help me?"

He tried to nod, but winced with pain.

Helen held her breath and slowly started to pull the helm from his head. There was one horrible moment when it seemed the helm would not come off—that the axe was embedded too deep in his forehead—but with one hard tug she pulled it free.

Helm and axe fell to the ground as Helen did her best to staunch the blood gushing from the king's brow with one of the swatches of linen she kept in the bag. But the small pad of fabric was soon drenched.

If only it weren't so dark. It was hard to see the extent of the injury. But aside from the ringing to his head the king was sure to be feeling from the blow, it looked as if the vertical gash bisecting his left eyebrow and forehead was deep but not necessarily deadly. *If* she could stop the bleeding.

The king's shock had seemed to fade with the removal of the helm and axe.

"You shouldn't be here, Lady Helen. I told you to hide."

"I will. Just as soon as I tend your wound. Does it hurt badly?"

A silly question to ask a warrior. In her experience, nothing ever hurt.

"Nay," the king said, true to form. "Where's my sword?"

Helen gazed toward the body of the fallen man where the sword had landed when the blow had struck.

The king lunged for it, but Helen had to keep him upright when he nearly fell over, dizzy. "You're losing a lot of blood. I need to get something to bind the wound."

He was able to hold the pad as she used the scissors in her bag to cut a section of linen from her shift to make a larger pad, and a second thinner piece to secure it with. She knew it wouldn't last long, but she needed something until she could get some salve—

Suddenly, she heard men moving toward them. The king heard them, too.

"Hood," she heard a man say.

The king stiffened, detecting the same thing she had: English.

Then, a moment later, another muffled voice said, "Find the lass."

The king was already getting to his feet and reaching for his sword. By sheer force of will, he seemed to be fighting against the urge to sway.

"Go," he said. "I'll keep them back."

Helen's heart stopped, realizing he intended to try to fight them off himself. But he was far too weak. Thinking quickly, she said, "Please, Sire. You can't mean to leave me. What if one of them comes after me?"

Chivalrous to a fault, he saw her point. "Aye, I need to get you somewhere safe."

She almost headed back toward the trees where the others were hidden before realizing the danger she would be putting them in.

The king seemed to have a different idea anyway. He took her hand and started pulling her away from the battle into the mist and darkness.

When they heard a shout behind them, they started to run.

Twenty-two

❧

Helen ran until the ground began to climb, and the king started to slow. Her own lungs were close to bursting. With the amount of blood he'd lost, the king had to be struggling.

"Did they see us?" she asked.

He listened for a moment. "I don't know."

They stood side-by-side in the darkness, sucking in deep breaths of air. Although she could see little around her, the hulking shadows of the mountains loomed all around them. Beautiful by day, at night they took on a sinister cast.

"Do you know where we are?"

The king shook his head. "A few miles to the north of the loch. But I don't know these mountains like—" He stopped.

"Like Magnus," she finished.

He nodded. Neither of them wanted to voice what they both were thinking: where was he? If they'd been attacked, did that mean the attackers had made it past Magnus?

She shuddered, her mind instinctively shrinking from the possibility.

The king gave her a compassionate smile. "Don't give up, Lady Helen. MacKay is one of my best men. It would take more than a few brigands to bring him down."

She nodded, but they both knew those weren't normal brigands. "Who were they, do you think?"

Bruce shook his head and when he swayed a little, Helen urged him to sit down on a large rock. "I don't know. But at least one of them was English, and they knew it was the royal party they attacked."

"They also knew about me," she said quietly.

Bruce nodded. "Aye, it seems so."

Helen frowned, noticing the blood seeping through the bandage around the king's head. She moved forward to examine it. She needed something better with which to bind it . . . but what?

"It's still bleeding?"

She nodded. "Aye. I don't suppose we can light a fire?" It would be the surest way of sealing it closed.

"Not until we're sure they're gone."

"I wish I'd thought to grab my sewing basket. The embroidery thread would do in a bind."

"Perhaps if you tie the cloth tighter?"

She was just about to unknot the piece of linen when she heard a sound in the distance.

A voice? A footstep?

The king had heard it, too. Without another word, they ran, having no choice but to flee higher into the impenetrable mountains. Magnus's warning came back to her. She knew how dangerous it was to attempt to navigate the treacherous terrain, especially in the darkness.

But it soon became clear that they would not make it very far up the steep mountains. Nor were they going to be able to outrun their attackers. The king was losing strength. He started to stumble, obviously fighting the dizziness from the prodigious amounts of blood he was losing from his head.

The blood! she realized. That must be how they were being followed.

"Wait," she said, forcing the king to come to a stop. "I have an idea."

Not bothering with the scissors this time, she tore another large section of linen from her chemise. The wool of her skirts was now touching her thighs. She quickly made a pad and carefully exchanged it for the sodden one.

They were fortunate that the heather and boggy grasses of the ground near the loch had given way gradually to a rockier terrain as they climbed the hill. But what she wouldn't give for a forest or a . . .

She peered down into the darkness, hearing the unmistakable flow of water over rocks. A burn!

Explaining what she intended to do, the king waited while she very carefully climbed higher on the hill, squeezing drops of blood from the cloth as she went. She went as far she dared—hopefully near enough to the summit—and then turned back, taking care not to leave any footprints, though she doubted it was possible to see them in the darkness.

After she collected the king, they headed in the opposite direction toward the water, using rocks whenever they could to step upon. It was slow going, but eventually they hit the river. From there they moved faster, following the rocky bank until she found what she was looking for: a large gap between the rocks. It wasn't big enough to fully hide in, but at least they would have some shelter, while she tended the weakened king and they waited for daylight and—she prayed—help.

Magnus lost the trail just before dawn.

After sorting through the varying accounts of what had happened from Helen's attendants and the others who'd hidden in the forest, he hadn't wasted any time and had set out after them.

According to the women, only one of the attackers had followed Helen and the king. Knowing he would be faster on his own, and with few men to spare (MacGregor had most of their best men hunting down the other attackers), Magnus left Sir Neil to attend to the survivors, sent one of the remaining knights west, another east, and took to the north in the direction the tracks seemed to lead.

What a mess! At least a score of men dead, the rest scattered; the king was badly—perhaps gravely—injured, and Helen . . .

Somewhere out there in the dark, dangerous countryside, Helen was trying to keep them both alive. But how long would she be able to elude their pursuers? And just who in the hell were they? Brigands? Mercenaries? If they were, they were some of the best he'd ever come across.

The attack had been well planned, well executed, and very nearly disastrous. His heart twisted. He just hoped to hell he could find them in time.

He wouldn't consider the alternative. He was supposed to keep them safe, damn it.

He forced himself to focus on the task at hand, knowing he'd lose his mind if he thought of all the things that could go wrong. Not just if their pursuer caught up with them, but also what might happen in the merciless, unforgiving terrain of these hills and mountains. One misstep . . .

Don't think about it. He couldn't lose her. Not again.

He kept his gaze fixed on the ground, but with little moonlight piercing the mist it was difficult to follow the tracks. He wished Hunter were here. Ewen Lamont could follow a ghost in a snowstorm. A torch would have helped, but Magnus couldn't risk giving away his position.

About a half-mile from camp, he saw the first drop of blood. If the women's accounts of what had happened were correct, he suspected it was Bruce's. An axe in the head? *Bloody hell.*

Magnus quickened his pace, the trail becoming much easier to follow. *Too* easy. Dread twisted in his gut as the sporadic drops became long streaks. Whatever Helen had done to tend the wound, it hadn't held. Worse, he knew that if he could follow the path, so could someone else.

The first gasp of dawn appeared over the eastern horizon when the trail of blood came to an abrupt end near the ridge of Meall Leacachain.

His heart dropped like a stone. The hill fell off steeply on the far side, and in the dark it would be easy to slide off the rocky ridge . . .

He held his breath as he glanced over the ridge. He scanned the ground below still cast in the shadowy darkness of early morning, and slowly exhaled when he didn't see anything other than rocks littering the corrie below.

But his relief was short-lived. Where the hell were they?

He looked around, willing them to materialize from out of the vast wilderness around him. He was surrounded by mountains, the largest of which, Beinn Dearg, loomed forbiddingly to the north ahead of him. Below, a river cut through the narrow gorge, and to his right behind him he could just make out the forest and the loch where he'd left the rest of the royal party.

Damn it, where could they have gone?

Suddenly a harrowing sound pierced the morning air. His blood went cold, recognizing the clash of steel. It was coming from the corrie below.

Knowing he would never make it in time if he followed the path, which wound back down the hill, he took one look over the steep, rocky ridge and realized it was the only way.

Without a moment's hesitation, he dropped over the edge and drew on every one of his climbing skills. He was going to need them. One slip and they'd all be dead.

Helen knew they couldn't stay here. As the black of the midnight sky began to lighten on the slow creep toward dawn, it became apparent that the gap in the rocks would not hide them for long. Situated as they were in the gorge between the mountains, in the daylight they would be visible from above.

She needed to find a better shelter, a place where she could do something to tend to the king's wound. It seemed to have stopped bleeding for now, but he'd lost too much blood, and each time he woke it was for shorter periods. His skin was pale and cool to the touch, which could be attributed to the cold night air, but she feared differently. Head injuries were always dangerous, but it was the unseen damage that was often the most deadly.

About an hour before dawn, she knew she couldn't wait any longer. Cramped as they were between the rocks, she didn't know whether to be relieved or worried when her movement did not wake the king.

Carefully, she climbed out from between the rocks and peered over the edge of the riverbank. The foggy mist had not completely cleared but had thinned enough for her to make out her general surroundings.

Mountains. Lots of them. With plenty of heather, crags, and intimidating rocky cliffsides, but unfortunately bereft of trees or other obvious hiding places. The river stretched as far as she could see in both directions, with no bridge or natural crossing point. But to the southeast, back in the direction from which they'd come, she could see the river widen into what looked like a small lochan. With any luck, they might find a nice thick copse of trees nearby to take cover in.

It was the only option she had. She wasn't fool enough to attempt to climb those mountains in the hopes of finding a cave, not with the ailing king and not with Magnus's warning ringing in her ears.

Magnus. Dear God, where is he?

She was cold and scared, more than intimidated by their bleak, unfriendly surroundings, and overwhelmed by the responsibility of keeping them both alive. What she wouldn't do for his rocklike, solid presence right now.

But it was up to her. She'd gotten them this far. All she had to do was find them someplace safe, and Magnus would find them. He had to.

With the cover of night quickly slipping away, Helen woke the king. "Sire." She shook him gently, and then harder when he stirred groggily. "Sire."

He opened his eyes, but it took him a few moments to focus. "Lady Helen." He brought his hand to his head. "By the rood, my head hurts!"

She smiled encouragingly. "Aye, I suspect it does. I'm sorry, but we can't stay here. If someone is looking for us, they will see us as soon as the sun comes up."

He started to nod but stopped with a pained wince. It took some effort to help extricate him from the rocks. His movements were sluggish and unsteady. But Robert the Bruce was a fighter, and once again he proved his mettle. By sheer force of will and determination, he stood and readied his sword in his hand.

She was glad of the dark plaids they both wore around their shoulders, not simply for warmth on the cold, damp morning—the higher they walked the more it felt like December rather than late July—but also to hide the king's mail.

But they'd gone no more than a few hundred feet when the king stopped her.

"What is it?" she whispered.

He motioned toward the mountains, instinctively herding her behind his back. "I saw something move. There. On the hillside behind the rocks."

The next moment Helen saw it, too, when two men stood from a crouched position behind a pile of stones.

Her breath caught. She looked frantically around for someplace to run, but it was too late. They'd been seen.

The two warriors with their ghastly helm-covered visages started toward them. They looked like two fearsome war machines ready to cut down anything in their path.

But Robert Bruce hadn't become king by sitting on a throne; he'd won the position with his sword. He had no intention of giving up without a fight, and neither did she.

As the king lifted his sword to meet the onslaught of the two warriors who attacked, Helen slid her eating knife from her waist, keeping it hidden in the folds of her skirt.

The two men were so focused on the king that they didn't pay any attention to her. The sounds were terrifying. Their blades were moving so fast. She didn't know how the king was fending them off.

"Who are you?" Bruce asked in between blows, his breath heaving from the exertion.

The men exchanged glances from behind the slits of their helms and laughed. "The reapers," one said, in a thick Irish accent.

They weren't all English, she realized. As did the king.

"What do you want?" Bruce asked between another furious series of blows.

"Death," the same man said. "What else?"

The king was weakening. Both men knew it, as did Helen. She knew she couldn't wait much longer. But with the mail, there were few places her small knife could penetrate.

Finally, the man who remained silent gave her his back. She didn't hesitate. Rushing forward with one target in mind, she plunged her blade deep into the leather of his chausses.

He yelped in surprised pain as the blade cut through the back of his thigh. The king took advantage of his surprise and plunged the heavy blade of his sword right through his belly.

The other man roared in fury. He came at the king with a vengeance, making Helen realize that the two men had been toying with them, dragging out the battle. No longer. This man intended to kill.

The attacker forced Bruce back to the river. Helen

shouted a warning, but it was too late. The king stumbled on a rock and fell backward. Helen lurched forward with a cry as he landed with a thud. He wasn't moving.

The warrior lifted his sword with both hands high above his head.

"No!" she shouted. "Don't!"

She raced forward, barreling into him with all her strength. But it wasn't enough. It was as if she'd run headlong into a stone wall; he barely moved.

He turned his head in her direction. "You'll get your turn—"

He stopped, his attention caught by something behind her.

She turned instinctively, recognizing him even before the sound of his battle cry roared in her ears. *"Airson an Leòmhann!"* For the lion.

Magnus! She nearly wept with relief. And she might have, if the king weren't in need of her.

She scrambled to his side, trying to revive him while keeping one eye on the battle taking place not a few feet away.

If it weren't Magnus fighting, and if her heart weren't lodged in her throat, she might be impressed. As skilled and invincible as the attackers had seemed to her, it was clear Magnus was even more so. But she was too worried about him to notice how fast he moved. How powerfully his sword crashed into the other. How his broad chest and powerful arms seemed built to wield the steel.

She would admire him later. Right now she just wanted it to end.

He granted her wish. One powerful blow brought the man to his knees. She turned her head, not needing to see the one that would bring his death.

She closed her eyes, fighting the wave of emotion that threatened to overwhelm her. But when she opened them again, Magnus was standing before her.

Their eyes met.

Her heart lurched.

There was no holding back this emotion.

When he opened his arms, she ran into them.

Magnus held her as if he would never let her go. When he thought of what he'd seen, how close he'd come to losing her again, he doubted he'd be able to ever again.

He cupped her chin, turned her face to his, and with one long look that spoke of the truth in his heart, he kissed her. The soft sweetness of her mouth made his heart clench. God, he loved her. He could no longer fight it.

He swept his tongue against hers, crushing her against him, and for one blistering moment gave in to the fierce emotion ripping through him and tearing him to shreds.

She kissed him back, every bit as passionately. Every bit as desperately.

But a moan brought him back to reality. A moan not from Helen, but from the king.

Reluctantly, he released her. Their eyes held for one long heartbeat. In that one look, they said everything that mattered. Tears of happiness welled in her eyes. And God, no matter how wrong, he felt it, too.

Another moan, however, dropped her to her knees at the king's side. "Careful," she said softly as Bruce started to rise. "You hit your head when you fell."

The king groaned. "Again? What happened . . . ?"

He turned, for the first time noticing Magnus. "Saint, took you long enough to find us."

"Saint?" Helen looked at him in surprise. "You?"

Magnus bit back a smile, helping the king to his feet. He'd explain later. "I apologize for the delay, Sire. Someone did a good job of leading me on a false trail."

The king grinned and turned to Helen. "It seems your plan worked. That was quick thinking on your part, my lady. As was the knife in the leg."

She blushed under the praise.

Magnus had lost a few years of his life when he'd seen her plunge the blade into the warrior. But he wanted to know all of it. "What happened?"

The king quickly explained how they'd been forced to flee deeper into the mountains, how his injury had weakened him, and how Helen had set the false path, and then led them down the hill to hide in the rocks.

When he finished his tale, it wasn't only the king who was impressed. He'd always thought of Helen as fragile—something to be cherished and protected. But she was tougher than he realized. And had far more grit and determination than he'd given her credit for. "How did you navigate the hill in the darkness?"

When Helen appeared confused, he gestured to the hill behind him. She blanched when she saw what she had done. Even though they hadn't descended from the summit as he had, it was a treacherous "path" all the same.

"It didn't seem that steep in the darkness. We walked slowly."

Magnus held her gaze. He tried not to let himself think of what could have happened, but it didn't work. He was tempted to take her in his arms again, but that would have to wait.

"We need to get back to the others. There might be more of them around. Can you walk, Sire?"

Despite his pale, blood-streaked face, Bruce looked affronted. "Of course I can walk." He straightened, and in the process swayed. He would have fallen had Magnus not caught him. "Ah hell."

Helen rushed to his side and inspected the bandage on his forehead. "It's started to bleed again. The bind isn't strong enough. I need to seal it closed."

Magnus noticed she carried the bag he'd made for her across her shoulder. "But you didn't have a fire?"

She nodded.

"We'll do it as soon as we get back to camp. I'll help the king. I don't want to stay here . . ."

His voice dropped off. He swore.

"What is it?" Helen asked.

But Bruce had seen what he had. "Horsemen." He nodded to the ridge above them from which they'd all descended. "Three of them."

Helen's eyes widened. "And they're not . . . ?" her voice dropped off.

"Nay," Magnus said. "They're not ours."

Helen's gaze met his. "What are we going to do?"

His mouth fell in a grim line. If it were just him or if the king wasn't about to fall at his feet, he would stay and fight. But as he'd learned from Bruce, sometimes you had to know when to pick your battles. This wasn't one of those times. His first duty was to protect Helen and the king.

But they'd never make it back to camp.

He looked at the looming cliff on the other side of the river. They'd lose them in the mountains—his mountains. "We're going to take the high road to Loch Broom."

When Helen realized what he meant, she paled but gave him a look of such trust it made his chest tighten. "I hope you aren't planning on running?"

He grinned. "Not this time."

Twenty-three

❦

Helen's lungs were bursting and her legs burning when Magnus finally stopped to let them rest, while he filled the skins with water from the lochan in the center of the wide corrie.

She tried to catch her breath, taking in great gulps of air, but her lungs were too busy heaving. Good God, they'd been climbing for only a short while, and she felt as if she'd just run for miles! She looked at Magnus in disbelief. He wasn't breathing hard at all. What was wrong with him?

But as exhausted as she was, the king looked far worse—despite the fact that Magnus had borne much of his weight, half-carrying him against his side over the rough, rocky terrain.

It was no more than an hour since they'd crossed the river and journeyed into the forbidding mountains. It had taken Magnus only minutes to pick out a virtually invisible path of rocks through the rushing waters.

Beinn Dearg, Gaelic for red mountain (if the color of the rock was the basis of the name, she thought pink was more accurate), was the highest of a series of four peaks around an impressive array of corries, gorges, and lochans. Or so she would take Magnus's word for it. Right now, the beauty of the scenery was bathed in fear and danger—not to mention an ever-darkening layer of clouds and winds. The higher they climbed, the darker and colder it seemed to become. Magnus said it wasn't unusual to see patches of snow up here in midsummer. She didn't doubt him. She was grateful for the extra plaid, but the wind cut through the layers of wool as if it were the sheerest silk.

After he finished filling the skins, he handed one to the king and the other to her. "Drink."

She shook her head, ignoring the loose strands of hair that blew across her face like shredded red ribbons. She'd given up attempting to contain them. The wind was blowing too hard. The moment she tucked them back, they just came loose again. "I'm not thirsty."

"That's why you need to drink. One of the biggest dangers in these mountains is not drinking enough."

Realizing she was well beyond her area of expertise, she took his advice. Fortunately, Magnus also had some beef and oatcakes with him. She hadn't eaten anything since last night, and she attacked those with more enthusiasm than the bland food deserved. The king took a few bites and pushed it away. Her brow furrowed with concern. The lack of appetite was not a good sign.

She could see Magnus scanning the countryside behind them and felt her pulse give an anxious start. "Have we lost them?"

He shrugged noncommittally. "If not, we've slowed them down. It will take some time to cross the river, and their horses won't be much use in the mountains. They'll have to leave them behind."

"Don't worry, Lady Helen," the king interjected wearily from his seat on a boulder where Magnus had set him. "We've the best guide around. No one knows these mountains like MacKay. They'll not catch him."

Helen did not doubt Magnus's abilities; it was hers and the king's she was worried about. They were slowing him down. She'd loved scampering across the countryside in her youth, but these mountains were a different beast altogether.

She frowned, seeing fresh blood trickling down the king's face. "Why didn't you tell me it started bleeding again?"

Bruce reached up, feeling around his forehead. "Did it? I didn't realize."

Helen looked at Magnus. "We need to do something."

She didn't need to say the rest. The king was already weak from the loss of blood. The fact that he'd managed this far—even with Magnus's help—without passing out was quite a feat.

"We can't light a fire until I'm sure they're not following us." He stopped. "Damn, I should have thought of it before."

"What?"

He reached into his sporran and pulled out a cloth. Unwrapping it, he revealed twigs with leaves wrapped around the ends. "Pine sap," he said, unwrapping some of the leaves from around the twigs to reveal the yellowish, viscous material. "This is still fresh, but when it hardens I use it to help a fire catch in the damp. It makes a good glue if you mix it with ash and can also be used to seal wounds."

"It's perfect," she said, taking the clean ends of one of the twigs. "I've had this on my hands enough times to know how sticky it can be."

He quirked a brow, and she dimpled mischievously, knowing he was remembering all those trees in which she'd hid.

Their eyes held and emotion swelled in her chest. She felt it again. The same certainty she'd felt when she'd looked into his eyes this morning after he'd dispensed with the second attacker. *He loves me.*

She'd done it. Somehow she'd broken through his resistance.

If every bone in her body didn't ache with exhaustion, if there weren't three murderous scourges chasing after them, if the King of Scotland wasn't about to keel over from an axe wound to his head, she could have enjoyed being with him like this.

There was no man she would rather have by her side in these circumstances. Not just because of her feelings for him, but because he always seemed to know what to do. Helen knew how precarious their situation was, but with Magnus by her side it didn't feel that way. He seemed to have been built for these surroundings. Rugged, tough, resourceful, and honed to the peak of physical endurance, he was made to survive whatever nature threw at him. He would get them through this.

Carefully, she unbound the strips of linen from the king's head. With as many wounds as she'd seen, she'd thought her stomach had become impervious. But it rolled when she saw the deep gash in the daylight for the first time. She caught a glimpse of white at his brow that she knew was bone. No wonder it was still oozing blood.

While Magnus held the two edges of the cut together, she rolled the sap end of the twig down the gaping wound. Before unwrapping the leaves, he warmed the next one in his hands for a few minutes, and it went on even easier. She was about to bind it with another piece of cloth, but he stopped her.

"You won't be able to get it off. The sap should do the trick on its own."

He was right. After a few minutes, it became clear that the blood could not permeate the thick sap. It looked a sight, but it was working.

The king, however, looked as if he'd reached the end of his rope.

He couldn't go much farther. Helen caught Magnus's gaze and saw that he realized it as well. "There's a place a little higher up that should be safe to rest for a while."

Up? Helen glanced up the steep slope of the mountain on her left and bit back a groan. He didn't intend to . . .

Aye, he did.

When the king didn't argue or object to Magnus's support, she realized just how horrible he must be feeling.

Helen trudged up the scree-covered slope behind the two men. With every foot of elevation, the wind seemed to grow stronger. She had to clutch the edges of her plaid together to keep it from blowing off. Once or twice, a powerful gust nearly unbalanced her on the rocky ground.

Magnus was right. This was no place for the inexperienced. One wrong step and she could end up . . .

She felt her stomach sway and quickly turned her gaze back to the path. *Don't look down.*

With the sun lost behind the clouds, it was hard to say what time it was. But she suspected it must be close to midday by the time they'd reached Magnus's place a "little" higher up.

"You can rest here for a while," he said, helping the king to sit on a natural shelf in the cliffside.

It was somewhat inset and, she suspected, hidden from sight in most directions.

Magnus handed her one of the skins and a few more small pieces of the oatcakes and beef. He also handed her a dirk.

She looked up at him in surprise.

"If you should need it. It will be more effective than your eating knife."

Heat rose to her cheeks, and then drained when she realized what he meant. "Where are you going?"

"To make sure they aren't following us."

"But . . ." She didn't want him to leave. Surely, he must be tired? He'd practically carried the king halfway up the mountain. "But don't you need to rest first?"

He reached down and swept a piece of hair from her face with the back of his finger. "I'm fine, Helen. I'll rest when we reach Loch Broom."

She thought the king was too exhausted to speak, but he

laughed. "MacKay has the endurance of an ox. MacLeod said he could run for miles in armor without getting winded."

Helen didn't doubt it. He was stubborn as an ox, too. But in this case, she didn't mind it. That stubbornness and determination would see them through this. "MacLeod?" she asked. "The West Highland chief?"

Magnus shot the king a look, but Bruce already had his head turned back to the ground as if he was fighting nausea.

"It's nothing," Magnus said.

But she knew it must have something to do with the secret army.

"How long will you be gone?"

He dropped a kiss atop her head. The tenderness of the gesture sent a rush of warmth over her icy skin. "You won't even have a chance to miss me."

But he was wrong. She missed him the moment he left. The rocky perch on the mountainside suddenly felt much colder and windier, and the day a little darker.

Helen was glad when the king closed his eyes, wishing she could do the same. But she needed to stay alert—at least until Magnus returned.

She clutched the hilt of the dirk in her hand and kept watch over their bleak surroundings. The minutes stretched with increasing anxiousness. It seemed he'd been gone forever, but it was probably only three-quarters of an hour before a form appeared on the hillside above her.

She sighed with relief, recognizing Magnus right away. But one look at his face stopped her heart cold. Cool. Calm. Perfectly under control. She knew what that meant.

His words confirmed it. "We have to move. They're right behind us."

How the hell had they found them so quickly? Magnus knew these mountains better than just about anyone. But whoever was tracking them was keeping pace—hell, doing better than keeping pace.

When he'd seen the two black-clad figures hurrying up the slope, he'd been tempted to surprise them. Despite the skill of the men who'd attacked them, he was confident he could defeat them. Two of them. It was the whereabouts of the third man that held him back. He hoped he'd gone, but couldn't count on it. Had he only himself to worry about, he wouldn't have a second thought.

Caution didn't come easily to Magnus, but his duty to the king and Helen came first. As much as he'd like to kill those two men, he wanted to see Helen and the Bruce safely to Loch Broom even more. He was confident that he would be able to lose the pursuers in the mountains.

Helen had done an admirable job of keeping them alive to this point, but she would not be able to carry the king out of these mountains if Magnus was injured. At nearly six feet tall, thick with muscle, and covered in chain mail, Robert Bruce was not an insubstantial load. Magnus was more tired than he let on. But he'd carry the king to hell and back if that's what it took.

And it appeared as if it just might come to that. After helping Helen to her feet, he attempted to rouse the king. But it was as if Bruce had drunk a barrel of whisky. He was slow to wake, slurring his speech, and barely able to stand. Magnus held him upright by wrapping the king's arm around his shoulder and sliding his own arm around the king's waist.

After telling Helen to stay close and watch her step, he led them up the mountain. He had no choice. There was only one path through these cliffs, and—

That was it.

The markers.

He walked faster now, practically dragging the king up the steep ascent beside him. Even with his training, it didn't take long for his breath to start coming hard.

"Sorry, Saint," Bruce said with a wobbly smile. " 'Fraid I'm not much help."

The slip of his war name concerned him far less than the gray cast to the king's skin and his glassy eyes. He didn't need Helen to tell him how bad it was.

"You're doing fine, Sire."

"Feels like someone split my head open with an axe," he mumbled, and then more lucidly, "Hell, someone did."

Magnus laughed.

Helen must have overheard because she joined in from behind. Being able to laugh in trying circumstances was an asset for a warrior. It shouldn't surprise him that Helen shared this quality.

Finally, he saw what he was looking for: a pile of white stones. He stopped, and once Bruce had his balance, went to work.

"What are you doing?" Helen said, watching him lift the heavy pieces of marble in his arms.

The white stones were an oddity on Beinn Dearg amongst the red rock, and served as markers on the path. Using piles of rocks to serve as guideposts was common in the Highlands, as were the cairns that marked the peaks.

"The stones are markers. I'm going to try to throw them off the trail." And if they were lucky, off the mountain. "There's a fork in the road. I'm going to move the rocks to the other path."

"Where does that way lead?"

Magnus gave her a look. "It's the fast way down."

Her eyes widened a little, understanding his meaning. "But what if someone else—"

"I'll put them back as soon as I can."

It took him no more than a few minutes to move the small cairn. If it didn't send their pursuers over the edge of the cliff, at least it should slow them down. Especially in the thickening clouds. It was easy to get turned around and lose your bearings.

A storm was brewing, but he decided to keep that information to himself.

Helen was holding up surprisingly well, but he was aware of every line of exhaustion on her face—no matter how hard she was trying to hide it. Both she and the king needed to rest. He hated to push her like this, but rest would have to wait until he knew whether his ploy had worked. For now, they had to put as much distance between them and the men pursuing them as possible.

Once they reached the summit, the path would take them down the west side of the mountain into a narrow gorge. From there, they could follow the gorge to the wide glen, and then the forest that would lead them straight to Loch Broom. But Magnus intended to take a more circuitous route over another of the peaks, taking shelter in a cave he knew of on the mountain before taking a more northerly path to Loch Broom.

The first route was more direct and far less strenuous, but it would also leave them extremely vulnerable to attack. There was no place to hide.

His knowledge of the hills was their greatest asset and he intended to take advantage of it. If they were attacked, it would be on his choice of terrain.

But first he had to get them there.

Over the next few hours, Magnus navigated them through some of the most treacherous terrain in the Highlands. The king grew weaker with every passing minute. By the time they reached the summit, he collapsed. Magnus was surprised he'd made it this far.

He maneuvered the king across his shoulders, which enabled him to distribute his weight more evenly.

Helen came up beside him and realized what he intended. "You can't mean to carry him like that?"

"It's downhill from here," he said lightly. *For a while.*

"But—"

"He can't go on, and we can't stop."

She bit her lip. He could see the worry in her eyes as she scanned his face. He would love nothing more than to ease that worry, but it would have to wait. "What about your shoulder?"

It was going to hurt like the devil when this was all over. "My shoulder will be fine." He grinned and teased, "Perhaps I'll let you rub some ointment on it?"

He knew his attempt to distract her had worked when she blushed. But then it was he who felt the heat when she replied huskily, "I'm going to hold you to that."

The promise in her eyes was difficult to turn away from, even with a good two hundred pounds laden across his shoulders.

The path down wasn't as physically strenuous, but it was even more treacherous. The rocks made for difficult footing, and by time they reached the bottom his knees were on fire. But he pushed through the pain, crossing the gorge and finding the path that led up to the next peak.

Every so often he glanced behind him, not only to check on Helen but also to make sure no one was following them.

He gave her an encouraging smile, though the entire time she hadn't uttered one word of complaint. *Every day was May Day.* Even under these hideous circumstances she made the best of them. "Not much farther now."

Her cheeks were flushed from the wind as well as exertion. "I think you've said that before," she said with a wry lift of her mouth.

"I'm sorry, Helen. I know you're tired."

She shook him off with a determined clench of her jaw. "If you can do it with the king across your shoulders, I can do it without."

He smiled. "That's my lass."

Their eyes met. "I'll hold you to that, too."

"Helen . . ."

What could he tell her? That it was true? That she would always be his? That he would try?

But why did part of him want to warn her?

Perhaps she sensed his struggle. "Are you going to dally all day? I thought we had a hill to climb."

He smiled, grateful for the reprieve, and gave a playful groan. "Remind me to introduce you to MacLeod. You have a lot in common."

"Is he your leader?"

He'd forgotten how much she knew. He started up the path, not answering her right away. "The less you know, the better."

He thought she'd dropped the subject, but a few moments later she said, "Well, it isn't hard to guess why the king wanted you for his secret army."

He glanced over to her in between grunts of exertion and lifted a brow.

"You maneuver over this terrain better than anyone."

His mouth quirked. "Is that the only reason you can think of?"

She took a deep breath and wiped a long strand of silky red hair out of her face. "You're far too stubborn to lose." He let out a bark of laughter, but she wasn't finished. "And you fight well."

His gaze narrowed. Definitely like MacLeod. They both conceded compliments with the same ease.

"Just well?" He could count on one hand the men who could defeat him on the battlefield. He was probably the best overall warrior in the Highland Guard across all disciplines of warfare, from the sword to the hammer, axe, pike, and hand-to-hand combat. "You're a hard woman to impress."

Despite her weariness, an impish glint appeared in her eyes. "If I'd known you were trying to impress me, I would have paid more attention. Now Gregor MacGregor, he's an excellent—"

"Helen . . ." His eyes darkened forbiddingly. He knew

she was teasing him, but damn it, he didn't want to hear her praising MacGregor.

She laughed, and the sound was so sweet it was almost worth the irritation.

She shook her head. "For someone so tough, you sure are sensitive."

"Sensitive!" He straightened so quickly he almost dropped the king. "I'm not bloody sensitive!"

When she burst into laughter, he knew she'd done it again.

"Did I mention proud?" she said with a broad smile.

His mouth twitched. "I don't think you did."

Their eyes held, and something impossibly sweet passed between them.

"And I forgot the most important thing."

He almost hesitated to ask. "What's that?"

All the teasing was gone from her voice. "You don't give up," she said softly.

Her words stunned him. She had no idea what she said. *Bàs roimh Gèill.* Death before surrender. It was the creed of the Highland Guard. The one thing that bound them together.

"Aye, you're right about that, lass. We'll get through this."

She nodded, tears shimmering in her eyes. "I know."

Her unwavering confidence filled him with warmth. They walked in silence for a while, even the sounds of their hard breathing lost in the swirling wind.

"It looks like it might rain," she observed.

Aye, they were in for a vicious downpour. "The cave will be dry enough. I suspect you must be getting hungry?"

She groaned. "Don't mention food. I think if I ever see another dried piece of beef or oatcake after this, it will be too soon."

He chuckled, adjusting the king to take more of the weight off his bad shoulder. Ignoring the pain had become impossible; now it was simply enduring. The brief stops he took to rest were becoming more frequent.

"Although the deer are plentiful, I do not think you would like your meat raw?"

She made a face.

"Then I'm afraid our feast will have to wait until we reach Dun Lagaidh Castle."

"When do you think that will be?"

"We'll rest the night in the cave. If they haven't followed us, tomorrow by midday."

"And if they have?"

His mouth fell in a grim line. Then he would have to chance an attack. But he would better the odds by choosing the perfect spot. "We'll worry about that if it happens."

By the time they reached the cave, Helen was in a state of sheer exhaustion. She didn't know how Magnus did it. The climb was strenuous enough without the added weight of the king. *Stubborn and tough.*

Bruce had stirred a few times on the journey, but it wasn't until Magnus set him down in the cave and gave her a chance to examine him that she could assure herself that his condition had not worsened. His collapse had been from exhaustion and loss of blood. Now that the wound had been sealed, and with some rest, she hoped he would improve. He managed to drink some water and nibble on a few bites of oatcake before he drifted back into the healing balm of oblivion.

"How is he?" Magnus asked.

The rain had started not long after they reached the cave, and she could hear it splattering against the rocky ground. "Weak," she said. "But his wound doesn't look any worse and there is no sign of a fever." She tucked the plaid more firmly around the sleeping king. "If we weren't in a cave on a mountain in a rainstorm, I should think he would be resting quite comfortably."

"Thank you," he said.

She tilted her head.

"For keeping him alive. Your women told me how you left your hiding place to help him."

She blushed. "I had to."

He gave her a look as if he thought that was debatable.

After ensuring that she and the king were as comfortable as they could be, he handed her the dirk again. "You are going to look for them?"

He nodded. "Aye. I won't return until daybreak."

Her heart squeezed with fear. She longed to cling to him and beg him not to go, but she knew there was no choice. After all he'd done to keep them safe, she could be brave for him. "Be careful."

The boyish grin tugged at her heart with aching familiarity. "Always. Besides, I have something to protect me." He withdrew a small piece of glass from his sporran and held it out in his palm. "I didn't know how else to preserve it."

She sucked in her breath. Greenish-tinged in color, it was the size and shape of a coin, and suspended in the middle were the dried petals of a purple flower. Her flower. The one she'd given him all those years ago.

Emotion strangled her throat. She looked up at him with tears in her eyes. He really had loved her. All this time. This big, strong warrior—proud, noble, and stubborn to a fault—had given her his heart and never taken it back. *Steadfast.*

"I'm so sorry," she whispered.

Their eyes held, and the ghost of all that had been lost passed between them. He reached out and stroked the side of her face, regret poignant in his gaze. "I am, too, *m'aingeal.*"

Helen watched him stride away, feeling as if her heart were going along with him. He would come back to her. *Please, come back to me.*

Twenty-four

꧁

Magnus climbed higher on the ridge, moving with extra care. His shoulder was on fire and every muscle in his body felt shredded with fatigue. Of course the storm only complicated matters, making his footing and handholds slippery.

It took him twice as long as it should have to reach the ledge where he could keep watch overnight. There were still a few hours of light in the long summer days, but the clouds made it feel like midnight.

On a clear day, this vantage on the cliff would give him a view for miles—to Loch Broom in the west, the hills of Assynt in the north, An Teallach and Sgurr Mor in the south, and Loch Glascarnoch, from where they'd come, in the east. In the storm, however, he couldn't see more than a hundred yards. But those hundred yards would be all he needed if someone approached. The narrowest part of the path was just beneath him and fell off sharply on the opposite side. It was the perfect place for a surprise attack.

He settled in for the long night. He ate a small ration of food and drank his fill of the water he'd replenished in the burn before they'd started up the hill. Leaning back against the rock, he stretched his legs out before him and rested his very weary limbs.

The hours passed slowly. Somewhere in the middle of the night it stopped raining, not that it mattered—since the ledge was only partially protected, he was soaked through.

No longer focused on the threat against getting them to safety, his thoughts slid to Helen. He was determined to put the past behind them and give them a chance. He could forget, damn it.

Was it so wrong of him to want a little happiness?

But in the long hours of the night, Helen's face wasn't the only one he saw. The nightmares returned.

Would he ever forget?

It seemed like eternity before dawn broke and chased away the ghosts.

He focused on the road, waiting for any signs that they'd been followed. He'd begun to think that perhaps they were in the clear when suddenly he caught a movement.

Damn. Two men. Although one, it appeared, was limping and had something wrapped around his leg. A satisfied smile curved his mouth. He hadn't fallen to his death, but he suspected the man had come close.

The tenacity of the two men surprised him. They were going to a lot of trouble for one woman who *might* know something about the Highland Guard. It seemed more likely that this was about the king. But he couldn't be sure. Bruce had told him the men had specifically mentioned "the lass."

Had they been betrayed by one of their own? It seemed likely. But who? He trusted everyone except . . .

The Sutherlands. But they wouldn't put Helen at risk, would they? "*Lass.*" Could they have been trying to protect her?

He scanned the area, seeing no sign of the other man. Where had he gone? His absence bothered him. As did the fact that the men had managed to find them. It was as if someone were guessing his every move.

Well, they weren't going to guess this one.

Magnus readied himself, moving across the rocky ledge to the place where he would wait. He felt the rush of battle surge through his veins. Caution hadn't worked. It was time to end this his way.

He keened his senses toward the ground below him, waiting for the first sound. They would only be able to traverse this path one man at a time. If all went well, he'd catch the first man unaware and get rid of him before the second realized what was happening.

Unfortunately, it didn't go as well as he'd planned. The first man made the turn around the hill. It was the injured man. Magnus would have preferred to use the element of surprise against the other. But as it was, he jumped down in front of the injured warrior, with a fierce battle cry that nearly shocked him off the hillside. Magnus helped him along with one crushing blow of his sword on his shoulder and a hard kick to his gut. The man's scream was punctuated with a hard thud a moment later.

The second man, however, reacted more quickly than he'd anticipated.

He came at Magnus hard, his blade crashing toward his head.

Magnus just managed to block the blow with his own. Infuriated by the narrow escape, he attacked with a vengeance, driving the other man back with blows so powerful they should have crushed him. But the other man fended them off with skill almost equal to his own. Almost.

But Magnus wore him down. Through the slits of his helm, Magnus could see the man knew it, too. His reactions slowed. His blocks started to shake as the muscles in his arms weakened. He breathed hard through the steel punctures of his helm.

In between blows he looked around, almost as if he were

waiting for someone. A shiver of premonition ran through Magnus. Was the third man out there?

If he was, he wasn't coming to this man's rescue. Magnus let his opponent come at him and met the blow while turning to the left. Locking his foot around the other man's, he brought him to the ground in a move that would have made Robbie Boyd proud. With both hands he brought his sword down hard into the man's gut, piercing the mail and sinking into his entrails. A hard kick sent him flying after his compatriot.

Magnus kept his sword ready, waiting, watching. He turned, scanning the area all around and listening for any sound of movement.

Someone was out there and Magnus was challenging him to meet him. But whoever it was must have thought better of it.

The feeling of being watched dissipated like the mist in sunshine. By the time he'd caught his breath, it was gone.

Helen waited anxiously for Magnus to return. The king had slept restfully through the night, waking at dawn with an "axe-splitting" headache, but stronger and far more alert than he'd been since the injury. The pine sap had worked better than she'd imagined. While the wound was still an ugly, bloody mess, there were no signs of infection or fever.

But unlike the king, Helen had enjoyed precious few moments of sleep. She was too worried about Magnus.

The storm and dreary skies of the day before seemed a distant memory as the new day dawned bright and sunny.

Where is he?

Finally, about an hour after daybreak, she caught sight of him. The rush of relief turned to horror as he drew closer, and she saw the dirt and splattered blood on his *cotun*. He'd been fighting.

Without thinking, she raced toward him and catapulted

herself into his arms. He caught her to him, holding her wordlessly until she steadied.

She didn't realize she was crying until he took her chin and tilted her face to his. "What's wrong, *m'aingeal*? Why are you crying?"

"I was worried." She sniffled. "And rightly so—you were in a fight!"

He grinned. "Aye, but I'm here, aren't I?" Suddenly, his brow furrowed. "Did you think I would not win?"

How could she want to throw her arms around his neck one moment and strangle it the next? It was just like all those years ago, when he'd shown up bruised and battered after beating Donald at the Highland Games.

"Of course I don't doubt you. But you are not invulnerable. No matter how good you are."

His eyes darkened with pain. "Aye, you never know what can happen." Helen winced, realizing he was thinking of William. "But it wasn't my time. Not today."

Sensing the dark emotions swirling inside him and knowing that William still stood between them, she knew they would need to talk about him at some time. But not now.

Wishing she'd never brought up the subject in the first place, she wiped her tears and asked, "What happened?"

The king had come out of the cave to greet him as well—how much of the conversation he'd overheard she didn't know—and Magnus explained how he'd rid them of their pursuers. Two of them at least.

"And you never saw the third man?" the king asked.

"Not since yesterday morning at the river, but I know he was there."

The king accepted his word without question. "Let's hope he's given up. If MacGregor and the others have been successful in hunting them down, he won't have much support." The king stroked his dark beard to a point. "Do you have any ideas on who is responsible?"

"Nay."

"But you have some thoughts."

"Perhaps it's best we speak of this once we've reached Loch Broom." Magnus didn't need to look in Helen's direction to explain. Obviously, he didn't want to discuss it in front of her. "Are you feeling strong enough?"

"Nay," Bruce admitted in a rare moment of warriorly candor. "But I'll manage. We've enjoyed the hospitality of these mountains long enough. Living in the wild lost its appeal for me after Methven. I'm afraid I've become quite accustomed to the luxuries afforded by a crown. Like well-cooked food, a mattress, and a hot bath."

That sounded so good, Helen had to hold back a groan of longing.

But Magnus seemed to have heard it anyway. He laughed. "Come. We'll be there before you know it."

Well, perhaps not before she knew it, but after the travails of the day before, the long hike out of the mountains through the glen and up the southern bank of Loch Broom to the MacAulay chief's castle of Dun Lagaidh seemed pleasant by comparison. With no sign of any pursuers, they were able to slow their pace to a more manageable speed. They arrived in the early evening before vespers, dirty and exhausted, but safe.

Thanks to Magnus.

She wanted to thank him but lost him in the mob of people who flooded the yard and hall on their arrival. Alerted of what had transpired by a rider from the royal party, the castle was in an uproar. The rest of the royal party had yet to arrive, but should be there soon. Helen was relieved to hear that her brother was the man who'd ridden ahead with the news. Magnus didn't look as pleased as she was to hear that Kenneth was safe.

Helen, Magnus, and the king were immediately given bedchambers (the king in the laird's room, Magnus in a small guardroom, and Helen in what she suspected was the laird's children's room), food, and plenty of hot water. After she'd bathed, Helen went in search of the king. Happy to find him resting peacefully, she left instructions for a tonic to be prepared by MacAulay's lady, then collapsed on her own bed, falling into a deep sleep.

When she woke it was dark and quiet. She tiptoed past the serving girl who must have been sent to look after her but had fallen asleep in the chair by the brazier while she waited, out of her chamber and up the stairs to the king's chamber.

The guard standing outside his door quickly stepped aside, allowing her to enter. Helen was surprised to see the lady herself sitting beside the king's bed. In hushed whispers, she assured Helen that the king had woken for long enough to eat a large meal—without vegetables—and drink the "vile brew" Helen had ordered prepared for him. Promising her that she would send for Helen if he needed her, the formidable chief's wife shooed her out of the room like a child underfoot and told her to get some rest.

Helen intended to do just that. *After* she saw Magnus.

Though she'd been relieved to reach safety, from the moment of their arrival they'd been treated like heroes risen from the dead and torn in different directions. She needed to see him. To assure herself that what had happened on the road wasn't her imagination. She sensed he was waging some kind of war with himself and didn't want to give him time to change his mind.

Suddenly, she had an idea.

Perhaps it was time to take her brother's advice.

Coming to a stop before his door, she looked around to make sure no one was about and slipped quietly inside the darkened chamber. Gently closing the door behind her, she stilled, letting her eyes adjust to the darkness and listening to the even sounds of his breathing.

Slowly, she began to undress, letting her night robe and

chemise fall to a pile at her feet. Slipping off her shoes, she padded barefoot and naked over the cool wooden planks. When she reached the edge of the bed, she drew a deep breath. Before she could reconsider, she lifted the bedsheet and slipped into bed beside him.

Twenty-five

❧

Magnus was dreaming. Something soft and warm was pressed against his backside—

He stopped, coming awake with a hard start.

It was dark, his sight robbed but his senses infused with the scent of soap, flowers, and warm, pliant female.

He was aware of two things at once. It was Helen, and she was naked. Completely naked. Every inch of her silky, soft skin was plastered against his. One tiny hand was slipped around his waist to hold her firmly to him, her groin was cupping his arse, and two hard, little points were poking into this back.

Her nipples.

His body reacted instantaneously, flushing with heat and hardening with arousal. Nay, not arousal. Hunger. Need. The primal desire of a man who wants to claim his mate.

Lust surged through him in a fiery blast nearly impossible to contain. He couldn't breathe. All he could do was want—nay, crave—with every fiber of his being.

Absently, her feathery-soft fingers slid over the bands of muscle across his stomach.

He clenched, his body rigid. Blood pounded in his ears. The urge to turn over, flip her on her back, and plunge deep inside her took hold. He wanted to wrap her legs around his waist and sink into her so deep and hard they could never be torn apart. He wanted to hear her gasp as he slammed into her over and over. Hear the hitch of her breath quicken into cries as he pleasured her. He wanted to hear her cry out his name as she came all around him. And then he wanted to come. Deep and hot and hard. To feel the satisfaction that had always eluded him.

"Magnus." She leaned up to whisper in his ear. "Are you awake?"

What the hell did she think? Every muscle in his body was awake. His cock was straining to his ribs. And her fingers . . .

God, her fingers were dancing achingly close to the throbbing tip of him. *Touch me. Taste me. Take me in your mouth and suck me.* She brought out every base thought in his mind.

He struggled to find his voice. "Aye," he said in a harsh whisper. "What are you doing here, Helen?"

She laughed with the knowledge of a siren. "I should think that was fairly obvious. I'm seducing you."

Her hand dipped, and—oh Jesus!—circled him. He couldn't fight the urge to thrust in her hand. It felt too good. Those small, velvety fingers wrapped around him, pressing, squeezing, stroking.

It set off a cacophony of sensation that fired inside him like thousands of successive explosions. He closed his eyes, groaning. The innocent touch was killing him.

"Why?" he managed hoarsely.

She stilled. Her hand released him. "I thought . . ." The siren's assurance was gone. "I thought you might want to finish what we started in the forest. I thought you wanted me."

The uncertainty in her voice broke him. He did want her. For longer than it was probably proper he'd wanted her. And damn it, he was going to have her.

Mine. The knowledge rose inside him with a certainty

that could not be denied. He was done resisting. She'd always belonged to him, as he'd always belonged to her.

How could this be wrong?

He turned and rolled on top of her.

She gasped at the contact. He could just make out the shadow of her face below his in the darkness. Her lips were parted in invitation too sweet to resist. He covered them with his, sliding his tongue deep in her mouth with a hard, carnal kiss of possession. It was a soul-searing, ravishing kiss that left no doubt of his intentions.

When he finally released her, they were both hot and breathing hard. "Does that answer your question? Aye, I want you. I've wanted you every minute, every day, since—" He stopped, smiling. "Since you were sixteen years old and too damned young to do anything about it."

She smiled, and her hand reached up to cup his face. Tears of happiness glistening in the darkness. "Oh, Magnus. That's sweet."

"Sweet?" *Bloody hell!* He lowered his hips, letting her feel him, fitting himself against her. His erection was wedged intimately against her. One swift move and he'd be sheathed inside her. Sweat beaded on his forehead with restraint. "I'm not sweet, and I assure you nothing I'm thinking about doing to you right now is either."

He could hear her sharp intake of breath and swear he saw her eyes sparkle with anticipation. "Like what?"

He laughed and kissed her again. "I could tell you, but I think it will be much more fun if I show you."

Or maybe he'd do both.

He rolled off her and slid off the bed.

"Where are you going?"

She sounded so disappointed he chuckled. "I've waited too long for this not to see it." He reached for the candle by the bed, took it over to the brazier, and lit it from the embers.

Returning to the bed, he stopped mid-step and almost

stumbled. Actually, his heart did. She was sitting up in the bed with the bedsheets tucked around her chest, and she looked so damned beautiful it nearly brought him to his knees. Her glorious hair tumbled around her shoulders in wild disarray, her lips were red and bruised from his kiss, and her eyes were wide with . . . maidenly modesty.

He grinned. "You can't be shy. You just climbed into my bed naked."

She scowled. "And why can't I? What if you don't . . ." She bit her lip. "What if you don't like what you see?"

He laughed. He couldn't help it, he laughed. He placed the candle back down on the bedside table and slid under the covers, taking her in his arms.

She bristled. "I don't think it's funny."

He skimmed his hands over her naked body, caressing every inch of velvety skin until it was warm and pliable. "If you only knew how beautiful you are to me, you'd think it was funny, too." He shook his head. "Men love seeing women naked. And you . . ."

He slid his hands down the slim curve of her waist, over her shapely bottom, and up her smooth stomach to cup her breasts in his hands. "Your body is a fantasy."

He kissed her again, but he could still sense her nervousness. He shook his head in mock disappointment. "I thought you were seducing me."

"Aye, well I've never done this before."

He frowned, the vague outline of a question forming in his mind. Seduction, that's what she must mean. She was inexperienced but not innocent. He forced his mind away. He couldn't let himself think about it.

Put it in the past.

So he kissed her, kissed her until he couldn't think about anything other than the sweet taste of her mouth and the incredible sensation of her body moving under his. Skin to skin.

He broke the kiss, rolled onto his knees before her, and slowly inched the sheet from her body.

He kneeled before her, taking in every inch of creamy skin.

Jesus. His mouth went dry. He'd imagined this—hell, even tried to put together pieces of glimpses he'd caught before—but nothing, nothing prepared him for the vision splayed out before him.

Her breasts were high and round, tipped by small, raspberry-pink nipples. He took one between his fingertips because they were too tempting not to touch. He rolled the hard tip between his fingers, gently caressing her to an even harder peak.

He liked the way her breath started to hitch.

He let his gaze drop to her stomach. To her slim waist and gently curved hips. To the woman's place between her legs. To the long, shapely legs and high-arched feet.

"God, you're beautiful," he rasped, his throat too tight with longing.

His gaze locked on hers, and he could see her relax. See the breath that she'd been holding exhale.

"So are you," she said, her eyes exploring the wide spans of his chest, his arms, his legs, and then—God, have mercy!—his manhood.

Heat flooded her cheeks and she lifted her gaze back to his, aware that she'd been staring.

"I like it when you look at me, love," he said huskily.

Her eyes widened a little. "You do?"

He nodded, because he couldn't speak.

Boldly, her gaze took him in again, and then as he'd done to her, she touched him. Sculpting her hands over the muscles of his shoulders and arms, testing his strength with soft little squeezes. He flexed hard under her fingertips.

"Your arms are as yielding as stone. You're much more muscular than you were before."

He laughed. "I should hope so. I've four years of battle behind me."

"What's this?"

Her fingers trailed over the mark on his arm. The same mark borne by all the members of the Highland Guard. The Lion Rampant, the symbol of Scotland's kingship, with a torque-like band of a spiderweb around his arm. The spider in the cave that had reminded the king at his lowest point to not give up.

"It's nothing." He took her hands from his body, gripping her by the wrist, and slammed them back against the mattress on either side of her head.

She gasped, startled.

He loomed over her, locking his gaze on hers. "Do you want to ask questions, Helen, or do you want me to make love to you?"

He didn't wait for an answer; the eager glint in her eyes told him everything he needed to know.

Helen gazed up at the man leaning over her. This rough, physical side of him was a surprise. He was always so courteous and gentle, so noble and reserved. But there was nothing noble and reserved about him now. He looked fierce and dangerous, his handsome face cast to wickedness in the shadows.

With her hands pinned on either side of her head, he held her completely at his mercy. She couldn't move if she wanted to. But she had no intention of going anywhere.

She liked him like this. Physical. Dominating. A little rough. She liked the weight of his body on top of hers, liked to see the way the muscles of his broad chest and big arms rippled and flexed in the candlelight above her, liked to feel his strength.

Instead of threatening, it made her feel safe and protected. She knew he would never hurt her. She bit her lip. At least she hoped. She had to admit being a little nervous about the first time. He was a big man, and she . . . she wasn't quite sure how well they would fit together. But she assured herself that if women could give birth to babies, her body could adjust.

Now was probably not the best time to remember all the screams that accompanied those babies.

Fortunately, Magnus distracted her with far more pleasant thoughts.

He kissed her mouth, her neck, her throat. Dragging his tongue and lips on a shivery trail to her breasts.

Oh yes. She felt a quiver of anticipation between her legs.

He cupped them in his big hands, rubbing the hard calluses of his thumbs over each tip. The gentle touch sent off flickers of sensation darting through her.

"Your breasts are beautiful." He tore his gaze away long enough to look into her eyes. "So soft and round." He demonstrated his point with a gentle squeeze that made her hips press up against his. "Flawless ivory skin topped with two ripe little berries." His eyes hooded as he gazed on them hungrily. A rush of dampness flooded between her legs. "I can't wait to taste them."

Suddenly, she was glad he'd lit the candle. Glad she could see his desire for her. Just looking at him made her feel hot and restless. The air felt so thick and alive, heavy with anticipation.

Instinctively, she arched her back. A soft cry escaped her lips.

He smiled like a fox. "Aye, first I'm going to kiss your breasts." He lowered his mouth and took one turgid peak between his teeth. The warm, wet suction of his lips lasted only an instant before he released her. One hand trailed down her stomach. "Then I'm going to kiss you right here." She sucked in her breath when his finger swept over the warm, damp cavern of her womanhood. How could she ever have thought he wasn't passionate? He was raw passion. Sensual and virile to the bone. "And then, after I make you come against my mouth, I'm going to slide my cock inside you and make you come again."

Oh God. The naughty words made her shudder with anticipation. The wicked promise of his voice sent off wave after wave of heated sensation.

His mouth was on her breast, his tongue sucking and swirling until sharp needles of pleasure shot to her womb. But her mind was already on the next of his promises.

The place between her legs was twitching, dampening, waiting. She couldn't think about anything else. His mouth *there.*

No. Yes. *Now.*

Magnus could feel her body shake with pleasure. Feel the rush of desire surging through her blood. Those soft, eager little moans were driving him on. And every press of her hips told him exactly where to go.

Her raw sensuality, her trust, both humbled and aroused him.

He slid down her body, kissing a trail from her breasts, over the soft curve of her stomach to her hips, and finally to the baby-soft skin of her inner thigh. Cupping her bottom, he settled himself intimately between her legs and looked up her naked body to catch her gaze.

She was watching him with a wanton mixture of uncertainty and eagerness. As if she thought she should issue some maidenly form of protest but didn't want to. He was glad when she didn't. He loved the honesty of her passion. Loved that she liked it just as much as he did. "I've dreamed of doing this to you," he said huskily.

"You have?"

He nodded. "I can't wait to taste you."

The last vestiges of her uncertainty faded as he placed a feathery-soft kiss on the silky pink flesh. "Mmm," he said, with a gentle lap of his tongue. "Sweet as honey."

The feel of his mouth—his tongue—on her was unlike anything Helen had ever imagined. Heat drenched through her in a wicked wave of need. She felt so hot. So wet. So wildly sensual.

It was the most erotic moment of her life. Seeing him like this. Having him do *this* to her. Her body began to shake. She moaned. Lifted her hips and silently begged him for more.

He gave it to her. He kissed her harder, deeper, the pressure of his mouth against her, his tongue flicking inside her, the scrape of his jaw against her thighs . . . It was too much. She writhed with the memory of what was to come. She felt the building pleasure, the tightening sensation, and the delicious coiling low in her belly.

This time she knew what she wanted. She gave over to the sensations and let them take her to the highest peak . . .

Her body stilled. The quivering between her legs paused for one heart-stopping moment. Then everything broke apart in one hot, long, spasming wave. She cried out her release as pleasure crashed over her.

Magnus couldn't wait any longer. The sound of her cries sent him over the edge. With one last drag of his mouth, he positioned himself between her legs.

She was still shuddering with pleasure. Her eyes were closed, her lips parted, her cheeks flushed. She was warm and soft and wet—deliciously wet for him.

Mine. She'd always been his.

God, he loved her. He closed his eyes, threw his head back, and drove inside her in one hard thrust.

Tight! Christ, *tight.* And . . .

Resistance?

Shock opened his eyes even as she cried out. Not in pleasure this time, but in pain.

What the hell?

As if she sensed what he was about to do, she twined her legs around his and lifted her hips against his, preventing him from pulling back. "Don't stop," she whispered. "Please, don't stop. I'm fine."

Their eyes held. He didn't understand. He had so many questions in his mind, but the cravings of his body wouldn't be denied. He was so close to coming, he couldn't have stopped if he'd wanted to. Not when he was inside her. Deep inside her. His throbbing cock surrounded by tight wet heat.

He levered his chest over her and thrust. Gently, this time, with a soft circle of his hips.

She gasped, her eyes widening. Aye, it felt good. Very good. Her body clung to him like a fist. A hot, wet fist. Milking him to mindless oblivion.

Sensation fired through his body, threatening to overtake him. His body strained against it, wanting to drag it out. Squeeze every last moment of this that he could.

He pumped again, circling, nudging deeper and deeper with each long stroke.

"You feel so good," he moaned. She did. It was unlike anything he'd ever felt before. The passion he felt for her wasn't just from his body but also from his heart. It consumed him. He felt it every time he looked at her. Eyes connected. Bodies connected. One. "I love you so much."

"I love you, too. I've always loved you."

For a moment, as he held her to him and looked into her eyes, he felt true happiness.

The pressure was building at the base of his spine, and he knew he wasn't going to be able to hold it off much longer. Her words of love echoed in his ears. He clenched his jaw, fighting against the urge to let go. His stomach muscles tightened. His thrusts quickened. But he needed her to come with him.

She started to move against him and he knew he was about to get what what he wanted. She was close.

Love. He'd said he'd loved her! Helen felt the surge of pleasure rise again inside her as the force of his body slammed into hers. Feeling him inside her, filling her, loving her—it was possession in its most primitive form. A claim. A connection. Intimacy that she'd never imagined.

And it felt so good. The sharp shock of pain had faded into a distant memory as her body warmed and softened to accommodate him.

With each thrust, he brought her closer to the edge of the precipice. She could feel her pulse quicken. Feel anticipation course through her.

Their eyes locked. He looked so fierce and intense, every muscle in his body drawn tight as he fought for something.

For her, she realized. He was waiting for her.

Their eyes met. She felt the love from the bottom of her heart.

The swell of emotion pushed her over. She loved him so much. And this—what she was feeling—was the culmination of that love. It was the moment she'd been awaiting for so long. She cried out as pleasure engulfed her one more time.

It was all he needed. She could feel the violent roar surge through him. Feel the overwhelming force of his love slam into her. Feel the blast of heat explode inside her as their passion collided in a heavenly torrent.

For a moment she felt transposed. It felt as if she'd touched a piece of heaven. A star. The sun. A place not of this world.

His release wracked through him in slow, strained thrusts. He surged into her with one last push and, as if it had sapped every ounce of his energy, collapsed on top of her.

His heat, his crushing weight, barely had a chance to penetrate before he rolled off her.

Helen was still too flush with pleasure, moved by what had just happened, and exhausted to realize there was something wrong.

But when the heat on her skin prickled from the cool air, when her breathing has slowed, and when the last ebb of sensation had faded, she became painfully aware of the quiet.

She cast him a surreptitious glance from under her lashes. He was lying on his back, staring at the ceiling. His stony expression matched his silence.

A whisper of trepidation skittered across her naked skin with a prickle.

He should be saying something, shouldn't he? Holding her in his arms and telling her how wonderful it had been. How much he loved her.

So why wasn't he?

Magnus tried to tell himself it didn't matter, but it did. She'd been innocent. A virgin.

"Why didn't you tell me?"

Helen leaned up on her elbow to look at him, a small frown gathered between her brows. "I tried to a couple of times. But you made it clear that you didn't want to speak about Wi—" She stopped. "About my marriage."

He knew she was right, but it didn't stop him from saying bitterly, "You sure as hell didn't try very hard."

She flinched. "Perhaps not. But what was I supposed to do, blurt out at dinner, 'And by the way I'm a virgin'?" She studied his face. "I didn't realize it was so important to you."

"Not important?" He made a harsh scoffing sound. Could she be that naive? Apparently, yes, if the guileless look in her eyes was any indication. "You didn't think I might care that you and Gordon hadn't consummated your vows?"

Her cheeks flushed hot. "I thought I was what was important to you, not the state of my maidenhead. I've not asked you about the women you've taken to your bed."

If he were thinking rationally, he would realize she was right. But he wasn't. In the back of his mind, Magnus knew he was being unfair, but he couldn't stop himself. "It's not the same."

She quirked her brow. "It isn't? If anything, I would have thought this would have pleased you."

His mouth hardened. Part of him—the primitive male in him—*was* pleased. All that passion had been for him, her innocent responses a natural and instinctive reflection of her feelings for him. But it was also a harsh reminder of all that he'd taken from his friend. His life, and now his wife.

Perhaps sensing his guilt, she tried to explain. "When William came to my room that night, he'd guessed the truth of my feelings for you. He gave me a choice to go to his bed without thinking of another man or to seek an annulment—or if one could not be obtained, a divorce."

Ah hell. Magnus felt a sharp stab in his gut. In trying to ease his guilt, she was only making it worse. Knowing that his friend had been prepared to give up his wife for him . . . God.

Magnus had been so angry that day. Had the anger made him sloppy? Had he been at fault for what happened? Buried in the darkest corner of his consciousness—something he'd never voiced even to himself—was the deep-seeded fear that MacLeod's warning had been prophetic, and that somehow he could have done something to prevent it.

"I knew it would anger my family, I knew it would probably make no difference to you, but I also knew it was not fair to William—I would never have been able to love him as he deserved. So I decided to seek the annulment. But before I could give him my answer, he left. And after . . ." Her voice dropped off sadly. "And after, it didn't seem to matter. Perhaps it was wrong of me to pretend, but what point was there in making a scandal?"

None. But she still should have told him.

"Would it have made any difference to you, Magnus? Would you have seen your feelings for me as any less of a betrayal whether my marriage was consummated or not?"

He clamped his jaw down angrily, knowing she was right. It wasn't her marriage to Gordon that haunted him, but what he'd done to end it.

A twinge of guilt crept up her cheeks. "And I must admit I liked the freedom afforded being a widow. You know my brothers."

He gritted his teeth. Unfortunately, he did.

He stared at her, trying to control the cacophony of divergent emotions firing inside him. Perhaps he understood her reasoning but it didn't stop his anger, the feeling that she'd kept something from him. Her face merged with that of another.

"Watch over her . . ."

He couldn't breathe. He needed to get out of here. Before he said something he regretted. Before he lashed out at her in anger for something she didn't understand. Of course she didn't understand, how could she? He couldn't tell her the truth. Seeing the horror and disgust in her eyes, he couldn't bear it.

He thought he could do this. But maybe he'd been a fool to try. He could never put the past behind him. Not with what he'd done.

Yet he loved her so much.

God, he couldn't think straight!

The grate of the gate in the bailey below felt like a reprieve.

He moved his legs over the edge of the bed and began to toss on his clothes.

"Where are you going?"

The note of panic in her voice only added to his guilt. He should be holding her in his arms right now, reveling in the joys of conjugal bliss. Not feeling the overwhelming urge to escape.

"That's the gate and unless I'm mistaken, the rest of our party."

Her eyes widened. "My brother?"

He nodded and crossed the room to pick up her clothes. Handing them to her, he said, "You'd better get dressed and return to your room."

The last thing he needed with Sutherland was to complicate matters. They were already complicated enough.

Twenty-six

꘎

It took a week for William Sutherland to accept the truth but only a few days for him to decide what to do about it.

Muriel could be happy without him, but he could never be happy without her. Happiness wasn't supposed to matter to him, and it might not have if he'd never met her. But he had. So now he knew both happiness and the unfortunate corollary, unhappiness.

He might have existed without the former, but he could not go on in a perpetual state of the latter.

The realization that she was the most important thing in the world to him and that he'd made her hate him shamed him—and terrified him. He'd been so blind with the thought of losing her, he hadn't realized what he was doing. Forcing her, *Jesus!*

He'd thought that as long as they were together, that was all that mattered. That a little bit of love was better than none. But he was wrong. She deserved more than half a life, than the piece of himself he'd been willing to give her.

She was right. Love without respect was not love. Being his leman would make her think she was not good enough. As if the damage those men had done had made her lacking somehow. How could he not have seen it?

He'd loved her enough to let her go, but did he love her

enough to bring her back? In the dark depths of his despair, he searched for an answer. How could he do his duty and have the woman he loved?

But maybe that had been the wrong question all along. Maybe the question he should have been asking was how could he do his duty and not have her by his side?

But would she still want him?

The wind is sharp tonight, Muriel thought as she walked through the narrow wynds of Inverness. Night had fallen about an hour ago and a ghostly veil of mist that had descended over the city along with it was already starting to thicken.

It was a night to send chills up even the bravest of spines. A dangerous night for a woman alone. But she wasn't alone. Since she'd returned to Inverness well over a week ago, Lord Henry's solid presence at her side had been a nightly fixture on her walks home. Nay, not home. The small room above the cobbler's would never be home. She pushed aside the wave of sadness and came to a stop beside her companion.

"We're here," he said cheerily. "Safe and sound."

Muriel gazed up into his kind face, illuminated in the soft glow of torchlight the cobbler had left for her. Lord Henry was a kind man. Smart, pleasant to look upon, and a highly skilled physician, he had a bright future ahead of him. He was the type of man who would spend the rest of his life trying to make her happy. She was a fool not to let him try.

"Thank you," she said. "I know it's out of your way."

He waved her off. "An extra few minutes, nothing more. And it makes me feel better to know that you are safe." Their eyes held, and Muriel could see his questions. His care for her. His hurt. His smile fell. "Are you sure you won't reconsider? They might be old, cantankerous, and set in their ways, but you are making headway here. It won't be any easier in France."

It would be much easier in France. In France she would not have to stop herself from going back to him. In France there would be no hope. In France she would protect herself from herself. In France she would disappear.

She shook her head. "I've longed to see the continent since I was a little girl." The lie fell easily from her tongue; she almost believed it herself. "But if you have reconsidered your offer to write a letter to your friend at the guild in Paris, I should understand."

"Of course not. They will be lucky to have you." He reached down and cupped her chin, tilting her face to his. His hands were warm and strong, but his touch elicited not a flicker of . . . anything.

"I've not given up, Muriel. I intend to spend the next few days until you leave trying to persuade you to change your mind."

She recognized the look in his eyes and for a moment she thought he was going to kiss her. But apparently he thought better of it, and she was saved from having to pull away.

He dropped her chin. "*Bonne nuit,* Muriel."

"Good night," she said, opening the door and slipping inside. She leaned her back against the closed door, relieved—grateful to be alone again.

But she wasn't alone.

Out of the corner of her eye she caught the flicker of a shadow in the candlelight. She startled—gasped—until she recognized him.

Panic was smothered by joy. A traitorous joy. Her heart actually leapt until she yanked it down again and forced it back in its cold, hard shell.

"What are you doing here, Will? Who let you—"

She stopped. Of course, the cobbler had let him in. Who would refuse the Earl of Sutherland anything he asked? Except for her. And even she wanted to accept his devil's bargain. Every night she tortured herself with memories. Would it really be so bad? They would be together, and—

She stopped herself. It would be horrible. She would end up hating herself as much as she hated him.

"Who was that man?" He stepped out of the shadows. Her heart twanged. He looked terrible. As if he hadn't slept or eaten in days. As if the past weeks had ravaged him as much as they had her. "What is he to you?" he demanded.

She bristled at his tone. It reminded her of what he was. The imperious earl. The man who would not be denied.

She expected anger. She expected him to grab her, force her to answer him. She didn't expect him to slump, rake his fingers through his disheveled hair, and look at her as if she'd just told him his best friend had died. "God, tell me I'm not too late."

What was he talking about? "Too late for what?"

"Too late to convince you to come back with me."

She stiffened, her body taking fierce umbrage at his words.

Seeing her reaction, he swore. "God's blood, I'm doing a horrible job of this." He dragged his fingers through his hair again. She felt a twinge of concern, never having seen him look so unsure of himself, before she forced it back. "You're making me nervous standing." *Will, nervous?* Muriel's eyes widened. Dear Lord, what was wrong with him? He motioned to a chair beside the unlighted brazier. "Would you please sit down?"

As she was feeling a little unsteady herself, she didn't hesitate to comply. She watched in confusion as he paced the room a few times before stopping to face her again. "I can't lose you, Muriel. You are the best thing that's ever happened to me. You are the most important person in the world to me. I love you."

Was he trying to torture her? No matter how beautiful his words, she could not let herself listen to them. But the ice around her heart wanted to crack.

"What is it that you want, Will?" She looked into his eyes, but it was a mistake. She felt the pull and shifted her head sharply away. She knew what he wanted. In a cool voice, she added, "Please say what you have to say and go."

She startled again when he dropped down to his knees before her. Taking her hand in his, he forced her to look at him. "I can do my duty or marry you." He paused. "Or I can do both."

She stilled, not daring to breathe. Clamping down her heart to prevent it from lurching. "What are you talking about, Will?"

"I don't need an heir, I already have one."

What did he mean? Did he have a bastard—?

"My brother," he said, perhaps guessing the direction of her thoughts. "Kenneth is my heir and there is no reason he cannot be a permanent one. He will have children. And if he doesn't, Helen will." He made a face. "Though I sure as hell hope Munro can persuade her to marry him. It'll be a cold day in Hades before I see a MacKay—" He stopped, giving her a rueful smile. "We can discuss that later. What I'm trying to say is that I want you to come home with me. I want you to be my wife."

No clamp could prevent her heart from lurching this time. She stared at him wordlessly. Was this some kind of cruel trick? Could he really mean it?

He squeezed her hand, reading her uncertainty. "Please, Muriel, I know you have every reason to hate me. What I did was unconscionable. More so because I love you. I should never have forced you to come back, never have forced you to—" He stopped, shame washing over him.

Was this really happening? Was the great Earl of Sutherland kneeling before her, asking her to marry him?

"Lust is not what I want from you—well, not all I want. If I ever made it seem like that, I'm sorry. I love you. I want you by my side, not just in the bedchamber but in my life. I know I don't deserve it, but I'm asking you anyway."

He drew a deep breath. "Please forgive me and do me the great honor of becoming my wife."

Muriel had been fighting fierce waves of emotion for the duration of his impassioned speech. He'd said no more than a few tender words to her for as long as she'd known him; to have so many at once was rather overwhelming. As much as she wanted to latch on to his words, the pain he'd caused her the past months had made her cautious. "What of the king? I thought you were to marry his sister."

"I never formally agreed to the alliance."

"Does the king know that?"

He winced. "I'm not sure. But it doesn't matter. I will do whatever I must to make it right with the king—except marry his sister. Perhaps my brother can be persuaded to stand in my stead."

Muriel gave him a look that told him she believed that just as little as he did. If there was anyone who was less in want of a wife than Kenneth Sutherland, she couldn't imagine him.

"What of my work?" she said softly. "I won't give it up."

"I'm not asking you to." He swallowed hard, and she knew whatever what he was about to say was difficult for him. "If you wish to stay here and finish your apprenticeship, I will wait for you. I will come visit you as often as I can. And after." He paused. "We will cross that road when we come to it."

She stared at him in wonder. He meant it. My God, he actually meant it! That he would do that for her told her more than anything else how much he loved her.

"I never wanted this, Will. I only came here because I couldn't stay at Dunrobin and watch . . ." Her voice strangled. "I couldn't watch you marry someone else." The tears she'd been holding back blurred her vision. "I'm good at what I do; I don't need a guild to tell me that. I was leaving at the end of the week anyway."

He made a sharp sound of surprise. "Leaving?"

She nodded. "For France."

He stared at her in growing horror. "God, Muriel, I'm sorry."

She shook her head, tears streaming down her cheeks. "I didn't know if I'd be strong enough."

His expression hardened. "You are more than strong enough. You were strong enough for both of us. I don't know why it took me so long to see the truth." He brushed a tear from her cheek with the soft sweep of his thumb. The tender touch made her heart squeeze. "You haven't given me your answer."

She nodded. "Yes, Will. Yes, I'll marry you."

He stood, pulling her along with him, and took her in his arms. "Thank God. Thank God."

The emotion in his voice matched her own. For a moment they just stood there together, both knowing how close they'd come to losing one another forever.

But then the closeness of their bodies started to elicit other reactions. She could feel him harden against her. Feel the spike of his heartbeat against hers. Feel the heat building between them.

He kissed her. Tenderly at first. A soft brush of his lips over hers. She could taste the faint salt of her tears when he kissed her again. This time with a groan, his mouth covering hers in a hard claim of possession.

She opened against him, letting him in. Letting his tongue slide against hers. Letting him sate his hunger, quench his thirst, with her complete surrender.

Deeper. Wetter. Faster. His mouth moved over hers in tender plunder.

She grasped his shoulders, steadying herself, pulling herself closer, needing to be as close to him as she could be. Every inch of his hard, muscular body was melded to hers. She could feel him leaning into her deeper, fitting the curve of her hips to his, her breasts to his chest.

She wanted him. She showed him just how much by rubbing against him, moaning as their tongues waged a desperate battle.

"No!" He tore his mouth away and set her determinedly away from him. "Not until after we are married. I've waited this long."

Still breathing hard, Muriel lifted a brow. He sounded like he was trying to convince himself. "What if I don't want to wait?"

Memories of what had happened to her would always be there, but with Will she would make a new start. He would never hurt her.

He gave her a look that suggested he wasn't very pleased with her comment. "You aren't making this any easier, looking at me like that. But you won't change my mind."

She lifted her brow again, challenging that statement. She'd see about that. But right now, she was content to let him think what he would. The poor man's pride could take only so many blows in one day. Poor man. She smiled. The Earl of Sutherland. Who would ever have thought?

His eyes narrowed. "What are you smiling about?"

Her mouth twitched. Not wanting to tell him the truth, she improvised. "I should like to see your brother's face when you tell him the news."

He smiled. God, he was handsome when he smiled. "Perhaps you shall."

She looked at him in question.

"I came by ship. I would like to tell the king of the, uh . . . change of plans as soon as possible." His expression darkened. "And I've heard some rumors recently about my sister's husband that Kenneth will want to hear."

"I'm surprised that you allowed Helen to go with . . ."

His eyes hardened. "MacKay? Aye, well, I didn't have much choice. The king insisted. At least Munro is going along. Hopefully, he'll have been able to persuade her to marry him."

She frowned before she could stop herself.

"What's wrong?"

Muriel knew how irrational he was—all the Sutherlands were—about MacKay, but she didn't like Donald Munro. "Are you sure Munro is the best man for your sister?"

He watched her carefully. "Kenneth expressed something similar before he left. You don't like him?"

She shrugged. "He's a hard man." Too proud, but that wouldn't impress William. "If it were up to him, you'd be in Ireland with his friend John MacDougall."

Will nodded. "He was against submitting to Bruce. But that's not reason alone not to like him."

"Helen doesn't love him."

They both knew whom she loved. Will's eyes met hers. Would he deny his sister what they had found? After a moment, he sighed. "I've never understood my sister. She never could do what was expected of her." He shook his head. "We never could figure out where that red hair came from."

"I have no idea." Muriel hid her smile, as the candlelight caught the occasional burnished auburn strands of his dark brown hair. Not do what was expected? Brother and sister were more alike than he wanted to acknowledge.

Twenty-seven

❧

Magnus had put this off for long enough. He would have done it sooner, but in the three days since MacGregor and the others had descended on Dun Lagaidh he'd been tending his duties or locked away in private meetings with the king and MacGregor, trying to uncover the source of their betrayal. It had to be a betrayal. The attackers couldn't have been that lucky.

But the king refused to act without proof. Magnus was convinced the treachery had sprung from the Sutherland camp. The attackers' knowledge of the terrain had to come from someone with a connection to the area. But whether it was from Sutherland himself, Munro, or one of their men, he didn't know. They were all being watched.

MacGregor had hunted down the remaining attackers, accounting for all ten men Fraser had initially counted. Magnus had taken a party of scouts to replace the rocks he'd moved and to scour the mountainous countryside. But the mysterious third warrior had disappeared. The similarities between the band of warriors who'd attacked them and the Highland Guard could not be ignored. It seemed they had imitators.

The king bore an ugly scar but had otherwise almost fully recovered from his ordeal. Indeed, he'd just taken his first meal in the Great Hall and had granted a private audience with the Earl of Sutherland, who'd unexpectedly arrived at the castle a short while before, accompanied by Lady Muriel.

Leaving Fraser and MacGregor to guard the king, Magnus took the opportunity to do what he should have done days before. He'd taken Helen's innocence; honor demanded he marry her.

What the hell was he saying? Putting it that way might ease his guilt, but the truth was it was just a damned excuse. He *wanted* to marry her. Demons or nay.

He might not deserve happiness, but he would take it.

He left the hall and went to search for her. She'd left after the meal so quickly he hadn't had a chance to pull her aside.

He frowned. He knew he'd been unfair the other night. He'd overreacted and felt bad for the way he'd behaved. If the look on her face the few times their paths had crossed was any indication, he'd hurt her.

He felt a pang of conscience. He'd make it up to her. He smiled. He'd have a lifetime to make it up to her.

Now that he'd made his decision, not once did it cross his mind that she would refuse.

Helen sat by the water's edge, her bare feet tucked underneath her skirts. Squeezing the rocky sand between her toes, she tossed stones into the water.

"You never did know how to make them skip."

The voice of the very man she'd been thinking about startled her.

She turned to see Magnus standing behind her. He gave her a wry smile and sat down beside her, effortlessly tossing a rock across the water. It skipped one, two, three, four times before finally sinking beneath the gently lapping waves.

She made no comment. No jest about how she'd always

hated that he could do that. No mention of the countless times he'd tried to teach her how to do it. For once, memories weren't enough. She didn't want to live in the past any longer.

She was confused and more than anything, hurt. She didn't understand why he'd acted the way he did the other night, and then avoided her for the better part of three days. Thank God she had her work to keep her mind if not off what had happened, at least occupied. Word had spread quickly of her healing skills, and when she wasn't attending the king, Helen had found herself in high demand.

She didn't understand his reaction—or rather his over-reaction—to the discovery of her virginity. It didn't make any sense. If anything, she thought it would make it easier for him to move past thinking of her as another man's wife.

But it had become more and more clear that something beyond her family and her marriage to William was preventing him from committing to her.

There was something tormenting him that she didn't understand but sensed lurking just under the surface. A dark, simmering anger that at times seemed directed toward her.

"I'm sorry," he said. "My actions the other night were unforgivable, but I hope you will be able to do so."

"Which actions, Magnus? Making love to me, or lashing out at me for 'deceiving' you about my innocence and then spending three days acting as if I didn't exist?" She laughed sharply. "Isn't it supposed to be the other way around? Aren't you supposed to be angry to find I'm *not* a virgin?"

The tightening of his mouth was the only sign that he didn't find her sarcasm amusing. He turned his gaze to hers. "I'm not sorry for making love to you."

Their eyes held, the memories flush between them. But she wouldn't let her desire for him intrude—not this time. "Are you sure about that? It certainly felt like you regretted it the other night."

"I acted like an arse the other night, Helen. I'm trying to apologize, if you'll let me."

"It's not an apology I want but an explanation. Why did it matter to you so much, Magnus? And why did it upset you to learn that I intended to dissolve my marriage?"

A steel curtain fell down behind his gaze. He turned away harshly. His jaw locked. "I do not wish to discuss this, Helen. I *never* want to discuss this again. If we are going to have any chance—"

"But don't you see? If we are ever going to have a chance we *have* to discuss this. Unless you tell me what it is that haunts you, it will always be between us—*he* will always be between us."

For one moment the curtain lifted, and she could see the depth of the anguish churning inside him. But then he shook his head. "I can't."

Helen stood up, dusting the sand off her skirts, trying to smother the wave of hurt and disappointment knotting her throat. For three days she'd fought off tears, but they threatened to storm at any moment.

"Wait," he said, reaching out to catch her hand. "Where are you going? I haven't finished."

Helen looked at him, blinking back tears. How could he be so obtuse? Did he not realize how much his refusal hurt her? "What is there left to say?"

He stood up to face her. "Plenty. I'm trying to make this right, Helen. I took your innocence." He drew a deep breath. "I want to marry you, Helen. I want you to be my wife."

Her heart stilled. Part of her wanted to cry with joy to finally hear the words she'd so longed for. The other part of her, however, wanted to weep, knowing what had driven them. She knew him too well. "Of course, it's the only honorable thing to do in the circumstances."

He frowned, looking at her uncertainly—as if this were

some kind of trick question. Perhaps it was. After all these years she finally had what she wanted, but it wasn't enough.

She wanted more.

But maybe he understood more than she realized. He grabbed her by the shoulders and forced her to look at him. "Aye, it's the only honorable thing to do, but it's not the only reason I ask. I love you, Helen. I've always loved you. You're the only woman I've ever wanted to marry."

Helen looked in his eyes and saw the truth. Her heart swelled. Some of her uncertainty began to fade. They would get past this. They would—

Suddenly, they both turned at the sound of what could only be described as a roar of complete rage. "You murderous bastard, don't touch her!"

Helen's heart sank as her brother Kenneth came storming toward them.

Seeing his fist pulled back, instinctively, she moved in front of Magnus. "Stop, Kenneth, you don't understand. He's asked me to marry him."

But Magnus was having none of her "protection." He easily lifted her aside and blocked her as her brother squared off in front of him.

"Marry him?" Kenneth scoffed. "Over my dead body."

He launched his fist toward Magnus's face. Magnus blocked the punch. But when Helen lurched forward to try to put herself between them, she distracted Magnus and Kenneth's second blow found its mark. Magnus pushed her forcibly back. "Stay out of this, Helen."

The two men exchanged a few more blows. She'd never seen her brother like this. He was known for his hot temper, but this was something more. This was rage and hatred unlike anything she'd ever seen. He looked like he wanted to kill Magnus. This wasn't just the enmity between their clans at work. "Stop!" she yelled at her brother. "Stop. Why are you doing this?"

Magnus connected with Kenneth's gut, bending him in

two. Or at least Kenneth pretended to be bent in two, because in the next instant he'd brought his fist up under Magnus's jaw, snapping his head back. "Tell her," Kenneth sneered, challenging Magnus with his gaze. "Tell her how you killed her husband."

Helen was so shocked by her brother's pronouncement, it took her a moment to realize that Magnus had turned a ghastly shade of gray. He'd also stopped defending himself against her brother's blows. Kenneth's fists pounded into his jaw and face like a hammer. He was beating him to a pulp and Magnus was letting him. "Fight me back, you bastard!" Kenneth shouted, pummeling him to the ground.

But Magnus wouldn't. Helen lurched forward again, reaching this time for her brother's arm. "Stop, Kenneth! You're going to kill him."

Kenneth was seething and huffing like an angry dragon. "It's no more than he deserves." Behind the rage she could see the anguish in her brother's gaze. "They found him, Helen. They found Gordon. In the bottom of the tower at Threave, pinned in by rocks, with his throat cut and his face disfigured. One of his own men had killed him."

Helen felt horror rise at the back of her throat. "There must be some misunderstanding." She looked at Magnus. He'd managed to get to his feet, but he wouldn't meet her gaze. "Tell him, Magnus. Tell him it isn't true."

"I can't do that," he said stonily.

Helen gasped in horror, realizing the truth. This was the dark secret. This was what he'd been hiding from her.

Kenneth let out an expletive and would have gone at Magnus again, but she held him back by hanging on his arm.

"Stop!" she yelled. "I won't let you kill him no matter what he's done." She looked at Magnus again, knowing there was more. "Why? Why would you do such a thing?"

William was his friend. There had to be a reason.

"Because he wanted you," Kenneth said. "He's always wanted you."

Helen spun on Kenneth in anger. "You know that's not true. William was just as much his friend as he was yours. I want you to leave, Kenneth. You've done enough damage for the day."

"I haven't done nearly enough damage. He's still standing. I won't leave until I hear an explanation."

"Go to hell, Sutherland. I don't owe you a goddamned thing."

Kenneth lunged, prepared to go at Magnus again, but she stopped him. "Please. Please just go. Let me talk to him."

Her brother met her gaze. His mouth fell in a hard line, but he heeded her plea. "If you marry him, Helen, you are dead to me." He threw Magus one more angry glare. "This isn't over, MacKay. I told my brother this would never work. I'll not spend one more day under the same roof with you."

With one more warning look at Helen, Kenneth stormed off the beach.

She looked at Magnus's bruised and battered face and said, "Come. I'd better tend to your face."

His expression was terrifyingly blank. "Helen—"

She cut him off. "Your face first, then we talk."

She needed to give herself a moment to calm down. But part of her feared that if they talked now, fixing the cuts on his face would be the last thing either of them wanted to do.

He followed her to the kitchens. A small storage room at the back housed the castle's apothecary. She washed the blood from his face with a cloth she dipped in a bucket of water one of the kitchen maids had fetched from the well, and then began to spread a salve over the cuts and abrasions. He didn't flinch or move a muscle the entire time, even when she touched the worst, a wide gash on his cheek, but he had deep cuts and bruises along his jaw as well. It was as if he were numb.

"If it doesn't stop bleeding I will need to stitch it closed."

He nodded indifferently.

Finally, Helen wiped her hands on the linen apron she'd donned and turned to face him. She could put it off no longer.

"Why, Magnus? You must have had a reason."

Her unwavering faith in him, however, only seemed to make him angrier. Guilt, she realized, was twisting inside him. That was the darkness.

"I had no choice." In a cold, emotionless voice, he explained what had happened. How William had been pinned by the rocks. How the English were swarming them. How he'd tried to get him free but couldn't. How William had been dying, but he'd been forced to take his life to prevent him from being captured or identified, and how it hadn't mattered in the end because of the birthmark.

It wasn't what Magnus said that filled her with horror, but what he didn't say. He'd done it to protect the identity of William's brethren, but he'd also done it to protect her.

She staggered, finally understanding the gravity of what stood between them. It wasn't just her family. It wasn't just that she'd married William and his loyalty to his friend. It was so much worse. He'd been forced to do the unthinkable in part to protect her. And part of him blamed her for it.

She'd thought love was all that mattered. In her naïveté, she thought nothing was insurmountable if they loved each other. But she was wrong. Even if he loved her, guilt, blame, and the ghost of William would always be between them. He would never forgive himself, and he would never forgive her.

But even as her heart was breaking, she sought to ease the burden that he'd obviously been carrying for a long time. "You had no choice," she said, putting her hand on his arm. "You did what you had to do. Blood in the lungs like that . . ." She shook her head. "There was nothing anyone could have done. He was as good as dead."

He jerked away from her touch. "I know that, Helen. I don't need absolution from you."

She knew he was only lashing out in pain, but the words stung nonetheless. "What is it that you need from me then, Magnus? Because it seems whatever I do, it will never be enough."

Their eyes met, and for a moment she thought her words might have penetrated through the guilt and anger, and that maybe they had a chance.

But she was only seeing what she wanted to see. In the cold echo of his silence, she knew what he'd known all those months ago, but which she'd refused to understand. William Gordon's death would always be between them. Magnus might love her, but the guilt would prevent them from ever finding true happiness. Could she marry him knowing that?

Her chest squeezed with the answer.

But she was saved from telling him so when a deafening clap of thunder followed by a loud boom tore through the air. Without thinking, she hurled herself against his chest, trying to block out the terrifying sound.

Thunder? It couldn't be thunder, she realized. The sun had been shining outside.

"What was that?" she said, gazing up at Magnus. It was a sound unlike anything she'd ever heard before.

But Magnus obviously had. His mouth tightened. "Black powder." The boom had barely stopped when he started pulling her back through the kitchens outside, into the *barmkin*.

People were rushing all over the place in panic. An unfamiliar acrid smoke filled the air and, seconds later, her lungs. They looked up and saw the newer of the castle's two donjons on fire.

Not just the donjon, she realized with growing horror.

"The king!" she exclaimed.

Twenty-eight

꧁

If it signaled anything but the king in danger, Magnus might have actually been grateful for the interruption. His proposal hadn't gone as he'd planned, and now that she'd learned his secret . . .

Blast Sutherland and his damned interfering! He'd never wanted her to know. He'd never wanted to see that look of horror and disgust on her face as she realized what he'd done.

But she hadn't looked at him like that at all. Hell, maybe compassion and understanding was worse.

He shook off the thought as he raced toward the burning tower. Sensing Helen behind him, he turned around and shouted for her to stay back.

A lot of good it did him.

She shook her head. "You may have need of me."

His mouth hardened. Damn it, she was right. But he wasn't happy about it. She should be running away from danger, not toward it. Their eyes held for a long pause. "You aren't going in that tower, you will wait outside—where I tell you."

Not giving her a chance to argue, he pulled her through the crowd across the courtyard toward the burning donjon.

As it always did in a time of crisis—except if that crisis had to do with a certain lass—an odd calmness descended over him. His mind cleared of all but the tasks before him, which came to him in a series of simple successive acts: find the king, control and assess the damage, decide how to rectify it. He wouldn't fill his mind with worst-case scenarios and hypothetical disasters; he focused on what he needed to do. If the king was in that tower, he was going to find him and bring him out.

MacGregor had planned to return the king to his chamber after the audience with the Earl of Sutherland. As that had been some time ago, Magnus knew there was every reason to suspect they were in there.

Except they weren't. He and Helen were almost at the tower when he caught sight of the king, MacGregor, and the cadre of knights Magnus had left to protect him standing near the postern gate. The Earl of Sutherland and MacAulay were rushing out of the Great Hall, which sat between the two donjons, and saw the king about the same time Magnus did. They all converged on the royal party at once.

But no one was getting near Bruce; MacGregor had ordered a protective circle around the king.

With the king safe, Magnus's cold calm turned to fury. "What the hell happened?"

MacGregor met his angry gaze with one of his own. The members of the Highland Guard didn't like surprises, and another attack on the king under their watch sure as hell qualified.

"We should have been in there, that's what happened," MacGregor said. "We were almost at the king's solar when he insisted on going to the barracks to check on some of the men who'd been injured. We'd just come out of the stairwell on the first floor when the first blast sounded."

The king pushed his way through the protective wall of

men in front of him. "My ears are still ringing," he said angrily. "By the rood, that was too bloody close!"

"Did you see anything?" Magnus asked.

MacGregor shook his head. "My only thought was to get the king somewhere safe. It was like an inferno. If anyone was in there, I doubt they could have survived that."

Magnus thought so, too. Whoever had done this was either gone or dead. But he intended to make sure.

For the next few hours, he set about making order out of chaos. The king's security was first. Another chamber was found for Bruce in the old tower. Magnus had the entire building searched and cleared before installing a guard of soldiers at the only entry to control access.

MacGregor took charge of organizing the attempt to put out the flames in the castle. But it was an exercise in futility. The wooden floors of the upper chambers and wooden roof had lit up like tinder. Only the smoking shell of the tower remained. Fortunately, as it was the middle of the day, the tower appeared to have been empty but for the king's party, who'd barely escaped disaster.

The placement of the powder left no doubt as to the target. MacGregor was certain the sound had come from the chamber under the king's.

Once Magnus had assured the king's safety, his focus turned to one thing: who could have been responsible. It didn't take him long to realize who was missing. A party of knights had ridden out right before the explosion; among them were Sutherland and Munro. But only one of them had familiarity with black powder.

He and MacGregor were standing in the courtyard, which—despite their efforts—was still mildly chaotic. In addition to the castle patrol, which had been increased, MacGregor had a team of men keeping watch on the tower shell to ensure the smoldering embers did not once again catch flame. Then, of course, there were the folks who couldn't stay away.

"Where did they go?" Magnus asked about the scouting party.

"We had a report of brigands attacking a group of pilgrims making their way home from Iona just north of here. They went to investigate." MacGregor's mouth hardened. "Sutherland wasn't supposed to go; he joined at the last minute."

Magnus swore. "Get the horses. I don't care how much of a head start he has, we're going after him."

MacGregor didn't argue. Magnus went to inform the king, who for once was in agreement about Sutherland. The use of the black powder all but pointed to him.

Magnus closed the door to the king's room behind him and nearly ran into Helen in the corridor. Though he was glad to see her—she'd gone off with MacAulay's wife to help calm the fears of the clansmen who thought the explosion had been a sign of God's wrath—he wished it wasn't at this moment.

She looked up at him, eyes wide. "You're wrong. My brother had nothing to do with this."

Damn. "Listening at doors, Helen?"

"I was about to knock when I heard you. You weren't exactly whispering."

"I can't talk about this right now." He started to walk down the stairs, not surprised to hear footsteps behind him.

He walked faster, but she had no intention of letting him go.

"Wait!" She caught up with him, grabbing his arm as he stepped into the courtyard.

He could see MacGregor waiting for him with the horses near the gate. He turned impatiently. "We'll speak when I return."

"Kenneth didn't do what you are thinking."

He fought to control his temper, but he was damned tired of her family coming between them. "Then who did? You said it yourself: your brother had knowledge of black powder just like Gordon. It isn't exactly common knowledge."

Denial reverberated from every inch of her. "But why? Why would he do such a thing?"

"He wasn't exactly eager to submit to the king."

She pursed her mouth and shook her head adamantly. "Perhaps not initially, but my brothers have come to believe in the king as much as you do. Kenneth wouldn't do something like this. He wouldn't be so rash."

"Hell, everything your brother does is rash. You saw how angry he was earlier."

Her cheeks heated. "At *you*, not the king."

"Are you sure about that? Perhaps this was his intent all along."

"You're not suggesting he had anything to do with the men in the forest or—"

Suddenly she stopped.

"What is it?"

She shook her head. "Nothing."

But he'd caught something in her eyes: the flash of guilt. He took her arm and forced her to look at him. "Tell me."

She bit her lip nervously, but he wasn't going to let it distract him.

"If you know something . . ."

"I wasn't sure. I'm still not sure. But I thought—I thought there was a possibility that the king's illness might not have been the sailor's malady."

He dropped her arm, stepping back as if scalded. "Poison? My God, you thought the king had been poisoned, and you said nothing to me?"

She bristled at the accusation in his voice. "Because I know you would react exactly the way you are now. I knew you would blame my family."

He made a harsh scoffing sound. "Why the hell would I do that? Maybe because they were guilty?"

He couldn't believe he'd trusted her. He hadn't questioned her conclusion about the king's illness at all, but had accepted what she'd said without thought. If he'd known, he would have been on his guard. What had happened in the mountains could have been avoided.

"I'm sorry," she said. "I should have said something, but—"

"But you didn't trust me."

"You aren't exactly rational when it comes to my brothers. And I wasn't the only one who was keeping secrets."

He ignored the quip about the Highland Guard—warranted or not. "By God, you are still defending them?"

Their eyes met. He stood there, blood pounding through his veins, trying to keep a rein on his temper and not saying something he would regret.

But it wasn't necessary. She could see it.

He saw her sharp intake of breath. "You still haven't forgiven me. Not for any of it. For choosing them over you. For marrying William. For doing what you had to do to protect me."

"Not now, Helen." He seethed between clenched teeth. He was trying, damn it. "I don't want to talk about this right now."

"That's the problem. You never want to talk about this. And never will."

His eyes narrowed at the finality in her voice. "What do you mean? We have plenty of time to talk. For God's sake, I asked you to marry me, what more do you want?"

She held his gaze for one moment before looking away.

Oh God. His chest squeezed with disbelief—with memory. *"I'm sorry, I can't."*

He knew what she was going to say before she spoke. "I love you, Magnus, but I won't marry you. Not like this."

He couldn't help himself. He was so angry, he grabbed her. How could she do this? How could she refuse him *again,* after all that they'd been through? His heart hammered. "What do you mean, 'not like this'?"

"I won't spend the rest of my life putting myself between you and my brothers." Tears streamed from her eyes. "Nor will I spend it with a ghost."

Whether he'd let her go or she'd wrenched away, he didn't know, but the next moment she was walking away. And as before, he didn't go after her. He stood there with acid pouring down his chest, leaving him with an emptiness he'd never thought he would feel again.

She didn't love him enough. Not then. Not now.

Helen knew she was doing the right thing, but it didn't stop her heart from feeling as if it were being ripped in two. Slowly. Twisting and squeezing along the way.

Refusing Magnus had been the hardest thing she'd ever done. She'd loved him for so long, she'd thought nothing would make her happier than to marry him. For months it had seemed an impossible dream, with winning him back her only goal. It was strange to realize that now that she had what she wanted, it wasn't enough.

She loved him with all her heart. But she would not live in constant fear of saying the wrong thing or evoking the wrong memory. She would not live with a ghost of guilt and blame between them.

Until he forgave himself, he would not be able to forgive her. She hoped it didn't take him too long, but she wasn't going to keep banging her head on a stone wall waiting for something that might never happen.

It was time for her to take control of her own happiness. To follow her own path. *Carpe diem.* The past few months had given her an inkling of how to do that.

With her future in her own hands, she went to find the king.

Magnus didn't say a word as he strode across the courtyard and joined MacGregor. His friend was wise enough not to speak until they were well beyond the castle, heading north in the direction in which the castle guards had seen the scouting party ride off.

His chest felt as if it were on fire. His heart pounded in his ears. His throat felt dry and parched, as though he hadn't had anything to drink in weeks.

He couldn't believe it.

She'd refused him again, and the sting hadn't lessened any the second time around. Part of him told himself not to believe it. She was angry; she would change her mind. But the other part of him knew she'd meant every word. She'd learned the truth about Gordon and understood. Far more than he wanted her to.

How could he have let this happen again? How could he let himself believe that they had a chance? He was a fool. How could he have thought to find happiness at the cost of his friend's life?

They'd ridden about half an hour before MacGregor broke the silence. "I take it the lass was not happy to hear you were going after her brother."

Magnus gave him a blank look. "You could say that."

"You have to admire her loyalty."

Magnus didn't say anything, but his mouth tightened. Just once, he wished that loyalty was for him.

"She loves you." The famous archer smiled. "I've seen enough women in love to recognize the look."

Normally, that might have elicited a laugh or jest about it hardly being a surprise with that "pretty" face, but Magnus was in no mood for prodding. "Aye, well, it doesn't matter."

He'd tried, but it wasn't enough. She'd refused him, damn it. The lash of pain in his chest tightened. *Don't think about it. Focus.* Forcing it from his mind, he scanned the road ahead of him. "I think I see something."

He kicked his heels and the horse sped off ahead.

"It's them!" he shouted back, a moment later.

Magnus wasn't surprised to see some of the scouting

party riding toward them—he'd assumed Sutherland would have used it as a ruse to effect his escape. He was, however, surprised to see that one of the two men was the man he sought. The other was MacLeod's young brother-in-law.

Magnus felt the first prickle of uncertainty.

He and MacGregor drew their horses in, coming to a stop on the road in front of them.

Sutherland's eyes narrowed. "So eager to finish what we started?"

He was too cool, Magnus realized. Sutherland wasn't acting like someone who'd just tried to kill the king. He and MacGregor exchanged glances, and Magnus could see that he was thinking the same thing.

Magnus ignored the offer—though it was bloody tempting. "Where are the rest of the men?"

"We separated a few miles back. What's wrong?" he said with more concern. "Did something happen to Helen?"

"Your sister is fine," MacGregor answered. "But someone tried to kill the king."

Both men greeted the news with too much astonishment to be feigned.

"Again?" Sutherland said.

"How?" Fraser asked at the same time.

"You've heard of the Saracen powder?" Magnus said, and the young knight nodded.

Sutherland's gaze shot to Magnus's. His mouth hardened. "So naturally, you assumed it was me?"

"Do you know anyone else with familiarity with black powder?"

"Aye, but you killed him."

Magnus flinched, as he knew was Sutherland's intention. But suddenly the hatred cleared from Sutherland's expression, replaced by something else. Dread. "Ah hell," he said.

"What is it?" Magnus asked.

"Munro," Sutherland said. "We have to go back."

"He's not with you?" Magnus said.

Sutherland shook his head. "He rode out with us, but turned around a few minutes later with some excuse. I warned my brother he could do something like this. He was furious when Will agreed to submit to Bruce. But Will has a blind spot for his old foster brother."

"How would he know how to use the powder?"

"I don't know," Sutherland said. "I sure as hell never showed him what I knew—and I never knew half as much as Gordon did. Look, I don't care whether you believe me or not. But if it is Munro and he's alive, you can sure as hell bet he hasn't given up."

Magnus didn't wait to hear any more. In what was becoming an alarming frequency, he and Sutherland were in agreement. Hell-bent for leather, they rode back to the castle.

Twenty-nine

❧

It hadn't worked.

When Donald saw the king and MacGregor race out of the burning tower just before he'd jumped down the garde-robe into the sea to escape the fiery inferno, he'd had to bite back the cry of pure rage. He was in agony, not only from another failure, but also from the burning beam that had nearly taken his life.

He'd miscalculated how long it would take to light the bags. The first had exploded as he was trying to light the fourth, causing a burning beam from the ceiling to land on his head. The helm hadn't completely protected him from the melting heat.

The pain had been excruciating. It still was excruciating. But he harnessed it, using it to motivate him for the task before him.

Donald knew this was his last chance.

He'd been so certain the explosion would work. That the four sacks he'd stolen all those months ago would end this.

The night of the wedding at Dunstaffnage, he'd thought it the luckiest piss he'd ever taken. He'd spied Gordon moving across the courtyard and followed him—not to the bridal chamber where he should have been, but to the armory. When he'd seen Gordon remove a number of linen bags from a large storage box and slip them into his sporran, it had piqued his curiosity. He'd waited until Gordon left, and then had gone in to investigate. Though at the time he wasn't sure it was actual black powder, he'd been smart enough to take a few bags for later.

When he'd heard about the explosion, his suspicions about what he had were confirmed.

He'd thought the bags would be his salvation. His means of restoring glory and honor to his clan. All he did, he did for the Sutherlands.

Will would come around, he reasoned. When the false king was dead and the rebel cause put down for good.

He still couldn't believe the attack in the forest hadn't worked. Damn, MacKay and Helen both! How they'd managed to fend off some of the best warriors in Christendom . . .

Fury shot through his veins in a hot rush. But not him. They wouldn't defeat him.

But ten men lost. After all that training. All that money. MacDougall had been furious. And worse, he was losing faith. Two men had been all he'd sent to aid Donald in this final attempt.

MacKay was already suspicious enough to have him watched. Time was running out.

He looked at the two men as they stood near the edge of the loch. "Are you ready?"

He couldn't see their expressions beneath the dark helms, but they nodded. "Aye, my lord."

Munro gazed toward the old tower. Was Bruce in there? He hoped he'd guessed right.

Helen knelt before the king, taking his hand in hers. "Thank you, Sire. You won't regret this."

"I already do." The king laughed. "I have the feeling a certain Highlander isn't going to be very happy with our plans."

Helen didn't argue. Magnus was going to be furious. But she was going to do it anyway. She shrugged. "He'll come around eventually."

The king was too much a knight to argue with her. "You're sure you want to leave so soon?"

"My brother and Muriel are sailing to Dunstaffnage tomorrow. I am anxious to get started."

The king held her gaze a moment longer. She feared he was about to reconsider, but instead, after a long pause, he nodded. "Very well. Safe travels. You will have my letter before you go. You know whom to give it to?" She nodded. "Then take care."

"I will." Helen made her way from the king's solar before he could change his mind. She bit her lip, feeling a prickle of apprehension. What she contemplated was not only dangerous but "unconventional"—to put it mildly. But it was also exciting, and, more than anything, important. She would be putting her healing skills to use. To the very best use.

She had just entered the stairwell when she heard a series of muffled sounds followed by a loud clank coming from a room just off the the landing. The garderobe, she realized.

Although her first instinct was to blush and move away quickly, she realized the sounds were not the normal sounds someone might make while relieving himself.

And what was someone doing up here anyway? There wasn't supposed to be anyone in this tower except the king and the guards who were stationed at the entry below.

The next sound stopped her cold. Whispering, and at least *two* voices.

Grateful for the darkness that had descended over the castle and the sky in the last hour, she hugged the wall and slowly inched closer toward the small room. The door was closed, but there was just enough of a gap between two wooden slats to make out the dark, shadowy figures of men bent over the hole in the rock and looking down.

Helen sucked in her breath, realizing what they were doing. The garderobe was positioned on the outside wall of the tower to empty directly into the water of the loch. Somehow, these men had figured out a way to climb up it.

Although her first instinct was to cry out and attempt to warn the guards below, she wasn't sure they would hear her from here. But the men in the garderobe certainly would. They would have time to kill her and the king before the guards could reach them.

No, her best chance was to warn the king and try to get past them before—

Too late. The door started to open.

She sank back into the shadows and retreated up the stairs and down the dark corridor to the king's chamber. The men's footsteps were just behind her.

Heart hammering in her chest, she opened the door, slid inside the narrow opening, and quickly closed it behind her.

"Lady Helen!" the king exclaimed, surprised to see her again. "What is it?"

Helen was looking around the room, praying for a miracle, at the same time she answered, "Men, Sire. At least three of them, coming this way. Blow out the candles. We don't have much time—it won't take them long to search the rooms for yours."

It was a small donjon with only a few solars on each of the three levels. And they would guess the king would be placed up high.

Bruce had already grabbed his sword, but they both knew they were doomed if it came to that. Three men were too many for the still weakened king. And there was always the fear that there could be more.

"You try to summon help," Bruce said. "I'll hold them off."

But Helen had another idea.

* * *

Magnus and the others stormed through the gate just as the first cry was raised. They raced to the tower where the king had been moved after the fire.

The wall of guardsmen he'd left to keep watch on the tower was in disarray. Without stopping to ask questions, he pushed through the guardsmen and raced up the stairwell, MacGregor, Sutherland, and Fraser right on his heels.

He heard the clash of swords above him and then the unmistakable thud of a body hitting the wooden floor. Reaching the third level, he exited the stairwell into the outer area of the three chambers on this floor—the largest at the end serving as the king's temporary solar.

The body of one of his men was on the floor, a man in black standing over him. The horrible stench that filled the air told him how they'd gotten in. Magnus let out a roar, pulled the mail-piercing dirk from his waist—the area was too small to use a sword or hammer effectively—and attacked.

But he feared they were already too late when he noticed two more men had come out into the corridor from the king's chamber.

The space wasn't large enough to accommodate so many. But it didn't take him long to rectify that by one.

After the first man fell, Magnus went for the man on the left, whom he recognized despite the helm, and MacGregor took the one on the right.

They squared off, blades drawn. "You wanted your rematch, Munro," Magnus said. "You have it."

"You figured it out, did you?" Munro laughed and jerked off his helm, which would be a detriment in such close combat.

Magnus recoiled from the sight of blistering skin on the left side of his face. Most of his hair on that side had been singed off as well. "Get caught in the blast? Looks painful."

"Bastard." Munro came at him. There was little room to

move about, and both men knew it would come down to the first few blows. Munro's missed. Magnus's didn't.

Munro's weakness was his arrogance and aggressiveness. As Magnus anticipated, the other man went on the immediate attack. He was waiting. As the blade came toward him, he sidestepped at the last minute. Turning, he jabbed his elbow into Munro's nose. If Munro had space to retreat it would not have been as deadly a mistake. But he had nowhere to go. Magnus used the moment of distraction to insert his blade right through the mail and into his gut.

Munro slumped against him in shock. Magnus held him there until his body went limp. Tossing him to the side, he saw MacGregor do the same with his man, and then followed Sutherland, who was ahead of them, into the king's chamber.

It was dark.

Fearing the worst, he tore open the shutters, allowing moonlight to spill into the chamber.

His gaze scanned the chamber. No body. Nothing. *What the hell?*

"Where is he?" MacGregor asked, voicing Magnus's question.

Suddenly they heard a loud thump as someone dropped from the fireplace. "Right here," Bruce said. He turned around to help someone down.

Magnus's stomach dropped as he recognized the light blue of a gown. The light blue of the gown Helen had been wearing earlier.

Oh, Jesus. "Helen?" His voice was filled with the same sick disbelief churning in his stomach.

"Helen?" Sutherland echoed at his side.

"Damn it, what are you doing here?" Magnus said.

The king gave him a sharp look. "Coming to my rescue. Again," he added to Helen with a wink.

She blushed.

Magnus listened with blood pounding in his ears as the

king explained—with a few clarifications from Helen—how Helen had been returning to her chamber when she'd heard the men coming up the garderobe. She'd come back to warn the king, but not wanting to alert the attackers to their location, she'd had the idea of throwing items out of the king's window to alert the guards. Then, to give them more time, they'd blown out all the candles, tried to clear the room of all traces of the king, and she'd found a hiding place in the fireplace. It didn't look large enough to hold one person, let alone two.

"Clever of her, wasn't it?" the king said with another smile. "I would never have thought of it."

Magnus might have appreciated the irony of their game coming to such good use, might have been impressed, and might have been proud of her, if he could see anything but the red haze in front of his eyes. When he thought of the danger . . . how close she'd been . . .

Helplessness. Rage. Panic. He felt like killing someone all over again. He tried to rein in his temper, but patience eluded him. For the second—third?—time in the space of a week, he'd nearly lost her.

His instinct was to sweep her into his arms and never let her go. He took a step toward her, but then stopped, remembering. Wait. He *had* lost her. She'd refused him.

Their eyes caught. A fierce surge of emotion passed between them, but it was too tangled and confused for him to decipher. All it did was make the hole in his chest deepen and burn hotter.

She turned back to the king. "I believe I shall retire. I've much to do before tomorrow."

She was hiding it well, but Magnus knew she wasn't as calm as she appeared. Her hand trembled at her side before she caught it with a clench of her skirts.

"Wait, I will escort you," he offered.

"That won't be necessary."

His mouth hardened. "There are men outside." He paused. "One of them is Munro."

Her eyes widened. "Oh," she said. "I see."

"I'll take you," Sutherland said.

Helen seemed to take notice of him for the first time. Her too-red lips drew in a thin line and her blue eyes flashed in anger. "I'm dead to you, remember?"

Sutherland shot Magnus a black glare. "Does that mean you've decided to marry him?"

Magnus stilled. But she didn't even glance in his direction. "No," she said in a soft voice.

Sutherland immediately brightened and started to say something, but she stopped him.

"I intend to take you up on your threat in any event. I'm tired of your interference." She glanced back and forth between the two of them. "You two can kill one another if you want. I'm done trying to stop you."

"I'll take you to your room, my lady," MacGregor said.

Helen gave him a grateful look. "Thank you. There is something I should like to speak with you about."

What did she mean by that? Magnus watched them go, wanting to go after her, but . . .

But what? She'd refused him.

He steeled himself for some kind of taunt from Sutherland, but the immediate concerns of the situation took over when MacAulay, Sir Neil, and some of the other high-ranking members of the king's retinue burst into the chamber.

Magnus spent the next couple of hours again trying to make order out of chaos. The men were apprised of what had happened, the bodies removed, the shocked Earl of Sutherland questioned about Munro, and finally, the king put safely to bed. So much for his "peacetime" mission.

His duties done for the night, Magnus poured himself a tall flagon of whisky and sat down, for the first time in what seemed like days, on a bench near the fireplace in the

Great Hall. The trestle tables had been removed, and some of the men—the higher-ranking members of the king's party enjoyed the Great Hall, while the rest of the men slept in the barracks—were already abed.

But he was wound too tightly right now to think about sleep. He couldn't believe it. He heard her words all over again. *"I love you, Magnus, but I won't marry you. Not like this."* He'd been too stung by the refusal to understand what she meant, but he did now. But how could he do what she wanted? God knows, he'd tried to put it behind him. But how could he forgive himself? Yet it was that or lose her.

Sutherland entered the hall. He scanned the large room, and seeing Magnus, headed toward him. Magnus's fingers tightened around the cup.

"Not now, Sutherland," he warned. "We'll end this, but not right now."

Ignoring him, Sutherland plopped down on the bench beside him.

Magnus stiffened.

"I thought you might want to apologize," Sutherland said.

"What the hell for?"

"I don't know, maybe accusing me of trying to blow up the king?"

Magnus's mouth tightened. "It wasn't without cause."

Sutherland just stared at him, a contemplative look on his face. "You're more like Munro than you want to admit."

Magnus muttered an expletive and then told him what he could do with it.

"He was too stubborn and proud to see what was right in front of him."

"Your sister refused me, or didn't you hear that part?"

"I heard it. But if I cared for someone as much as you

appear to care for my sister, I would do whatever the hell I needed to do to change her mind."

"Coming from you, that's ironic. From what I hear, you've never cared about a woman in your life." Magnus looked at him suspiciously. "Why are you doing this? You've been doing everything you can to prevent this for years."

"Aye, but the difference between you and me is that I can admit when I've made a mistake. I thought you were lying about Gordon."

"I was."

"But not for the reasons I thought. Helen told me—well, actually she told Will, as she's not talking to me—what happened. I'm only going to say this once, so make sure you're listening. You did what no one hopes they are ever called upon to do, but something that could happen to any one of us. It's part of war—an ugly part, but a part none-theless. I would have done the same thing in your place, as would Gordon."

Magnus didn't say anything. The burning in his chest had crawled up his throat.

"He wouldn't have wanted you to carry this burden. Nor would he have demanded a lifetime of penance."

Magnus sat there not knowing what do say. Sutherland was the last person he would have expected to say this to him.

"She's better off without me," he finally said. "Have you forgotten the risk she could be in?"

"The way I see it, she's at risk already with Gordon's name circulating. You can keep her safe." He gave a decid-edly evil laugh. "You can look after her for a while."

But Magnus had known Sutherland too long. "Why are you really doing this? I can't believe it's just to see your sister happy."

Sutherland's mouth tightened. "You're a suspicious bas-tard. Whatever else you might think of me, I do care about my sister. But all right. There is something. The way I see it, I'm standing in the way of something you want, and you're standing in the way of something I want. I suggest we both swallow our pride and step aside."

Magnus's eyes narrowed, suspecting the answer to the question he was about to ask. "And what do you want?"

Sutherland gave him a hard look. "To be part of the secret army."

It was proof of his prodigious control that Magnus didn't explode in anger the way he wanted to. "Over my dead body."

"Aye, well I hope it doesn't come to that, but I intend to make my case whether you agree to step aside or not. Though I admit it will be easier if you do."

"You'll have to defeat me on the battlefield first. You're supposed to be the best at something—and being the best at losing your temper doesn't count."

"Aye, well, I'm working on that, too. I could have killed her."

Magnus's fingers bit into the metal engravings on the flagon, remembering how close the blade had come to Helen. "Have you talked to the king about this?"

Sutherland shrugged. Perhaps sensing that he'd pushed Magnus as far as he could this night, he stood to leave. "Just think about what I've said. But you might not want to take too long."

"Why's that?"

"Helen's packing. She's leaving with Will and Muriel in the morning."

Magnus went cold. *Leaving?* Stunned, he barely even noticed when Sutherland walked away.

How could she leave him like this? It was just like last time, when he'd watched her ride out the next morning with her family. Pride had prevented him from going after her then.

Sutherland's words came back to him. But damn it, he was nothing like Munro . . .

Too stubborn. Too proud. Blind to what was in front of him.

Munro's stubborn refusal to accept Bruce as king had cost him everything. And Magnus's stubborn refusal to forgive himself was about to cost him the same.

Ah hell.

Thirty

Helen had just slid the chemise over her damp head when the door opened. The blast of cool air sent the warm, sultry air from her bath right out the door.

Her heart startled in panic, before coming to a jerking stop upon seeing Magnus standing in the doorway. He entered the room and closed the door behind him. His eyes moved to the tub of steamy water, and then to her damp hair and barely covered body. He lifted his brow. "Looks like I'm a few minutes too late."

Her cheeks warmed from the suggestiveness of his tone, but she refused to let her desire for him weaken her resolve. "What are you doing here, Magnus?"

His gaze flickered to the small pile of belongings she'd stacked on the bed to place in Muriel's trunk in the morning. Most of the items were hers, anyway.

"I heard you were leaving me again, but I didn't want to believe you would give up so easily."

"Easily?" she sputtered. How dare he! She'd been fighting for months to change his stubborn mind.

"You aren't taking much," he pointed out, ignoring her outraged glare.

"My trunks were in the other tower. The one that

burned," she reminded him. Her eyes narrowed. "Why are you smiling?"

"I was just thinking what a misfortune it was to lose all those fashionable new gowns of yours."

The wretch! Helen crossed her arms. "I'll just have to order some more."

He didn't say anything, but the look he gave her was a definite "We'll see about that."

Why was he acting like he had some kind of hold on her? As if he had a say over anything she did. Had he not heard her refusal?

Apparently not.

Helen's eyes widened in shock when he started to remove his *cotun.* He tossed it on the chair and then lifted off the linen shirt underneath. The next minute she was staring at his naked chest. Her mouth started to water and her legs started to quiver. Tanned, broad, chiseled with layers of well-defined muscle gleaming in the candlelight, it really was magnificent.

And the churl knew it. He knew exactly what the sight of his bare chest was doing to her. He was fighting dirty now. Her eyes narrowed. "What are you doing?"

"The bath looks good. I hate to waste all that warm water."

"I thought you liked cold lochs."

He laughed. "Aye, well, I suspect I won't be needing those quite as often."

She didn't understand. "Didn't you hear what I said earlier? I *refused* your offer of marriage."

He shot her an annoyed glare. "Oh, I heard you."

Whatever she might have said was lost when he loosened the ties of his chausses, and then his braies. Both dropped to the floor with a wicked, blood-rushing thud. Completely, perfectly, and mouthwateringly naked, he stepped into the bath, sinking into the warm water with a groan that sent a shiver of desire right to her toes. "God, this feels good."

He sank under the water, popping back up a moment later with his hair slicked back from his face. He rested his arms on the rim of the wooden tub and sat back to watch her. Helen had the distinct Lord of the Castle impression, with her playing the role of bidding lady. He'd probably ask her to wash him next!

"You can't do this." She eyed the door. "You shouldn't be here."

"If you're waiting for your brother to come bursting through the door and interrupt us again, you've nothing to worry about. He's the one who told me you were leaving."

She gaped at him in astonishment, as if he'd suddenly sprouted two heads. "Was he breathing when you left him?"

Magnus smiled. "For now. I can't promise how long it will last, but we've reached something of an understanding."

Her already weakened legs gave out completely, and she sank on the bed behind her. "An understanding?"

"Well, don't get your hopes up. We aren't friends—more like reluctant allies."

"Allies in what?"

"You." His smile fell, his expression becoming serious. Their eyes met. "I figure if my worst enemy can forgive me, I can forgive myself."

She sucked in her breath, realizing what he meant. "William?"

He nodded. "Who the hell thought your brother would say something worthwhile, let alone find some wisdom to impart?" He looked into her eyes intently, his expression turning grave. "I wish to God it had never happened, but it did. I did what I had to do and would do it again if necessary. Just as Gordon would have done for me."

She stared at him. This man who'd held her heart for so long. She probed every corner of his eyes and face, searching for a sign of guilt or anger. She knew how good he was at hiding his emotions—at projecting the cool, calm confidence. But there was no sign of anything but relief, as if a weight had been lifted from his shoulders.

"Ask me anything, Helen. If you want to talk about him I will."

Helen shook her head, emotion welling in her eyes and throat. It had never been about William, but about his ghost. The dark sadness that had hovered around Magnus that she'd never understood. But now she did. And miraculously, some of that sadness had dissipated.

His eyes met hers. "Are we going to keep making the same mistakes? Marry me, Helen. However many times you refuse me, I'm going to keep asking until you give me the right answer."

Helen's chest swelled with joy. She'd longed for this moment for so many years, it didn't seem possible that everything she wanted was finally within her grasp.

Well, not quite everything she wanted. There was one more thing they had to discuss before she agreed. She bit her lip, anticipating his reaction. "I wasn't going to give up, you know."

He frowned. "You weren't leaving?"

Instead of answering, she reached for the note that sat atop the pile of belongings and handed it to him.

"This has the king's seal," he said, examining it.

"Read it. If necessary I will ask him to reseal it."

Breaking the glob of hardened wax with a snap, Magnus unfolded the parchment and scanned the missive. As a chief's heir, he'd had some learning. Enough to read the short note in Gaelic addressed to Tor MacLeod.

Magnus's face darkened as he read. By the time he'd finished, he looked up at her with such a fierce expression, it might have caused a less determined woman to have second thoughts.

In a cold, final voice that brokered no argument, he said (or rather shouted), "Absolutely not!"

* * *

Magnus stood from the bath, grabbing the damp drying cloth she'd used to brush the water from his skin. Wrapping it around his waist, he stepped out of the tub and took her by the arm, lifting her from the bed to face him.

Was she out of her mind? Had the king gone completely mad?

"I won't allow it."

She tilted that pixieish face to his. If he'd been any less furious, her pursed mouth and flashing eyes might have made him exercise a bit more diplomacy. "As you have no say in the matter, I'm afraid what you will or will not allow is immaterial."

He growled—actually growled. "If you think I'm going to let you become a part of this you are out of your bloody mind. I don't want you anywhere near our missions. Don't you know how dangerous—"

"Of course I know how dangerous it is! That's why I've decided to be the healer for your secret army. What did the king call it, 'The Highland Guard'? Aye, that's it. And it's not as if I'm planning on picking up a weapon and rushing into battle with you. I'll just be nearby if you or any of the others need me."

"Ah well, that's a relief," he bit out with heavy sarcasm.

Her eyes narrowed at him angrily. "It is hardly unusual to have a healer waiting nearby to tend the wounded after battle. Plenty of women follow their men into battle."

Her dismissiveness only fueled the angry fires licking through his blood. "Not *my* woman."

"I'm not your woman," she reminded him calmly. "I haven't said I will marry you."

He dragged her against him. Molded her body to his, the thin fabric a paltry barrier to the heat that combusted between them. "You'll marry me, all right. If I have to drag you kicking and screaming to the church, you'll marry me."

And then to prove it, he kissed her. Hard. With a fierce possessiveness that left no doubt of his words. She was his.

His tongue lashed against hers, probing the sweet, warm depths of her mouth. He sucked in her gasp, sucking in her breath, feeding the wild frenzy of emotion lashing inside him.

Her body melted against his. Breasts. Hips. Legs and arms entwined. Her fingers clutched at him, drawing him closer.

He groaned when her tongue wrapped around his, meeting the frenzied desperation with some of her own.

Suddenly, she tore her mouth away with a harsh gasp. She was breathing hard, her lips swollen and eyes hazy with passion. "It won't work, Magnus. You're not going to change my mind like this. You aren't the only one who can be stubborn."

The determination in her voice only increased his own. His eyes blazed into hers with fiery challenge. "We'll see about that."

In one smooth motion, he grabbed the gap at the neck of her chemise and pulled it apart, ripping the thin linen fabric from nape to seam.

She gasped in outrage, trying to clasp the torn edges together, but he was having none of it. Tearing the towel from around his waist, he pushed her back on the bed. In a naked tangle of limbs and shredded fabric, he pinned her with his body.

He looked down into her eyes. Looked at the face that had haunted him since he was barely a man. He loved her so much it hurt. "You're mine, Helen. Mine," his voice broke, not with possessiveness but with love.

She reached up and cupped his face in her tiny hand. "I know."

Her eyes glistened with tears of happiness. He kissed her again. Far gentler this time, with all the love and tenderness erupting in his chest.

She opened to him. Her mouth. Her body.

Holding her tight, he slid inside her. Slowly. Wanting to feel every inch of her body taking him in, every inch of connection, every inch of his love for her. And when he'd reached the deepest part he stilled, holding her to him with his gaze. Then, he nudged a little deeper.

It was the sweetest gasp he'd ever heard. A gasp to hold his heart forever.

"I love you, *m'aingeal*," he said softly.

The smile that lit her face was unlike any he'd ever seen. "I love you, too."

He held her gaze and started to move his hips. Slowly at first, in small grinding circles.

Her legs tightened around his. Her breath started to quicken. Her eyes lost focus and her cheeks started to flush.

"Oh God . . ." She moaned.

His hips circled faster. Harder. Increasing the pressure. She started to gasp. Her naked breasts arching against his chest, her legs wrapping tighter around his buttocks, pulling him deeper.

It felt too good.

Pleasure crashed over him in a heated rush, gathering in his groin, coiling at the base of his spine. His heart hammered in his ears.

He clenched. His muscles hardened as he fought to hold on for the last few moments.

She cried out and he let go. With a groan torn from the depths of his soul, he came in hot spasming waves, giving her everything he had to give.

Even when the last wave of pleasure had ebbed, he held her to him, not wanting to let her go.

He should have been content to stay like that forever, but he feared he would crush her to death. Rolling to the side, he wrapped his arm around her and tucked her firmly against his side.

She rested her cheek against his chest, drawing tiny shapes with her fingertips on his chest.

He knew why she was so quiet. The anger had dissipated, but the far more important emotion—fear—was still there.

"You're serious about this, aren't you?"

She rested her palm flat on his chest, perching her chin on the back of her hand to look up at him. "I am. I need to do this, Magnus. And you need me. Your friends need me. If there's a chance I could save you or one of them, I have to take it. This is what I'm supposed to do, I know it. It's where I belong. By your side in all things." She smiled. "Besides, you need someone to protect you."

He groaned, feeling as if he were fighting against the inevitable. "Aye, but who's going to protect *you*?"

Her eyes sparkled with mischief. "Remember how MacGregor told me if there was anything he could do to repay me I only had to ask? Well, he's promised to watch out for me."

"MacGregor?" he choked.

She wrinkled her nose. "I know how sensitive you are about him. He is rather distracting to be around—with that face and all—but perhaps there is someone not quite so attractive who could protect me? Although from what I've seen of the men in this army, I fear one is just as distracting as the other. I suppose there's always my brother."

He knew she was teasing him, but it didn't quite stop the dark flare from sparking inside him. "I'm not sensitive about MacGregor, damn it. I'm sensitive about *you*. And if you think I'd let that hothead of a brother watch over you—the only person who's going to protect you is me."

He couldn't believe he was agreeing to this. It went against every bone in his body. But Helen's uniqueness—that wildness of spirit—was the very thing that had drawn him to her. He knew that if he tried to quash it, tried to keep her locked up in a castle somewhere to keep her safe, it would kill the very heart of her.

The smile on her face stole his heart. "Does that mean you'll agree?"

"With some conditions."

She looked at him with marked—and well-founded—suspicion. "What kind of conditions?"

"A long list of them." He tipped her chin from his chest, drawing her up closer to him. "But the first one is the most important. If I'm to have a new 'partner,' it's going to be as my wife. Marry me, Helen."

And at long last, she gave him the answer he'd been waiting for: "Yes. Yes, I'll marry you."

It wasn't until much later that she heard the rest of his conditions. By then, she was too well sated to put up much of an argument.

Epilogue

❦

Six months later

Helen turned to her husband, who was riding beside her with a deepening scowl on his face. Not coincidentally, Dunrobin Castle had just appeared on the horizon ahead of them.

She laughed. "It won't be that bad. It's only for a few days."

He mumbled something that sounded like "a few days underwater."

She shook her head. "I haven't seen Muriel and Will since we were married."

He grumbled something else.

"I don't see what the problem is—you never disliked Will as much as you did Kenneth, and you and Kenneth are practically brothers now," she managed to say without bursting into laughter.

He shot her a deadly glare. "Your brother is an arse."

"So you've said a few times," she said with a grin.

In some matters he was still as stubborn as he'd always been. In others . . .

She thought of the past six months of acting as a healer for the secret army known as the Highland Guard. As he'd seen how it could work, gradually Magnus had loosened up on some of his more ridiculous "conditions"—as if she could promise to never scare him or get so much as "one bruise"! Others, well, she was working on them. She knew perfectly well how to follow a command—in the right circumstances.

She smiled. The Saint and the Angel. MacSorley had overheard Magnus call her *m'aingeal* one day and couldn't resist teasing the "holy" pair. Not surprisingly, the other Guardsmen had taken to calling her Angel. But recalling how he'd put her to bed last night and woken her this morning . . . perhaps sinner and harlot were more appropriate?

So far the danger had been minimal. But King Edward was moving on Scotland again. War would find them soon enough. But first the king had given them a few days to visit her family, and she intended to enjoy every minute of the time, grumpy husband or not.

Muriel and Will were in the *barmkin,* waiting to greet them as they rode in. After hugging her brother and new sister-in-law, she glanced down at the curious set of eyes peering from behind Muriel's skirts.

Helen's heart constricted. At her wedding, Muriel had shared with her the tragedy of her past. She knew how much this child who'd come into their life so unexpectedly must mean to them both.

She bent down. "And who is this?"

Gently, Muriel eased the little redheaded child out from behind her. "This is Meggie. Meggie, say hello to your aunt and uncle."

Her brother made a choking sound at the reminder of Magnus's place in the family, and Helen glared up at him sharply before turning her attention back to the shy child.

The lass was three years old and had been left an orphan after both her parents were stricken by a fever. The little girl had nearly died as well, but Muriel had nursed her back to health. With no relatives willing to take the child in, Muriel and Will had welcomed her into their home and into their hearts. Her austere, formidable brother . . . who would have thought?

"You have hair just like mine," the little girl said, reaching out to clasp a handful between her chubby fingers.

Will groaned again, and Magnus laughed with far too much pleasure at his expense.

Ignoring them both, Helen smiled at the little girl and gave her a conspiratorial wink. "Only the luckiest little girls have red hair, you know. It means the faeries have blessed you."

"Have they blessed you, m'lady?"

Helen gazed up at her husband, meeting his gaze. "Aye, very much."

She had everything she wanted. She'd found her more.

AUTHOR'S NOTE

The earliest record of the great, long-running feud between the MacKays and Sutherlands was in the late fourteenth century, when a Sutherland chieftain was said to have murdered two MacKay chieftains at Dingwall Castle. But given the two clans' neighboring lands—and the conflict *that* seems to always cause—it doesn't seem unreasonable to suspect that it began earlier.

Magnus, the Chief of MacKay, who was said to have fought alongside Bruce at Bannockburn in 1314, was the son of Martin, who was killed at Keanloch-Eylk in Lochaber. But by whose hand, and on what date he fell, it is not recorded. One of the MacKay clan sites (www.mackaycountry.com) referred to the MacKays as "a mountain race of people," which made his skill in my Highland Guard easy. The real Bruce must have had a number of scouts and guides by his side to help him navigate the difficult and treacherous terrain of the Scottish "high lands." I loved the idea of the proud, tough "quintessential" Highlander.

Magnus had two sons, Morgan and Farquhar, but the name of his wife is not recorded. Helen is a fictional daughter of William, the second Earl of Sutherland. Her brothers William and Kenneth, however, are based on the third and fourth earls, respectively. Kenneth became chief on the death of his brother William in 1333, who died without an heir—the inspiration for William and Muriel's fictional relationship. Kenneth's son, also (shockingly!) named William, married Bruce's daughter Margaret. Their son John was briefly designated heir to his uncle King David II of Scotland, but unfortunately, he died of the plague.

A recurring theme in my author's note is the problem with names—repeat names, choice of names, et cetera. Given that surnames and clan names were not firmly established in this period, it is often difficult to decide what to call a character. For ease, I typically use modern clan names rather than the patronymic byname (Magnus "mac"—son of—Martin) or locative byname (William of Moray/de Moravia). There is some evidence that Sutherland ("south land") might have been used as a surname at this time. It appears that when the two branches of the Sutherland lines broke off in the mid-thirteenth century, the northern (senior) branch took Sutherland and the other line became Murrays (from de Moravia/Moray, which to my surprise is pronounced "Murray"). At some point, the Earls of Sutherland dropped the "of Moray," "de Moravia" designation, probably with William and Kenneth's grandfather, but it's unclear exactly when this happened. I went back and forth, and ultimately decided to use Kenneth Sutherland of Moray and Helen Sutherland of Moray to make it less confusing.

The Sutherlands came over to Bruce's side sometime in 1309. Given their ties to the Earl of Ross—they were allies at the time and William Sutherland was said to have been his ward—it made sense to me to tie the timing to Ross's submission.

William Gordon is the fictional nephew of Sir Adam Gordon, who did have an uncle William who fought in the Eighth Crusade (1270)—the inspiration for "Templar's" black powder. Sir Adam was loyal to the exiled King John Balliol, and thus sided against Bruce with the English until the relatively late date of 1313.

The battle where my William dies combines a few events. Edward Bruce actually deserves credit (along with James

Douglas, Robert Boyd, and Angus MacDonald's Hebridean forces) for the cover-of-mist attack. With a force of about fifty men, Edward Bruce planned to use the mist to hide his surprise attack of a force of fifteen hundred English soldiers under the command of Aymer St. John. When the mist suddenly rose, Edward found his small force exposed. Instead of retreating, he boldly attacked the flank of the English cavalry and created such surprise and confusion that the English forces broke. It's one of those great David and Goliath apocryphal stories that seem to permeate the cult of the Bruce. Whether true or not, you can decide.

There were actually two battles fought in the area around this time by Edward Bruce against the English. The first was along the banks of the River Dee, where the English fled and took refuge in Threave Castle, which Edward eventually took and destroyed (at the time it was probably a wooden castle, not a stone one as I suggested). The second battle was along the River Cree when the English fled to Buittle Castle, which Edward was unable to take at that time.

The place of Robert the Bruce's first parliament is generally believed to have been St. Andrews on March 6, 1309. However, some sources claim that Bruce had an earlier council or meeting at Ardchattan Priory, which is said to have been the last Scottish parliament in Gaelic.

Bruce did indeed make a royal progress to thank the Highland chiefs who had come to his aid during those dark days after Methven. It made sense to me that he might have also used the progress to check up on some of his new allies. The progress probably occurred the following spring (March 1310), but as Bruce was in Loch Broom around August 1309, it could have been earlier.

Duncan MacAulay held the oft-photographed castle of Eileen Donan for the MacKenzie chief. His castle on Loch Broom, however, is not named. I thought Dun Lagaidh, located on a key defensive position overlooking the sea loch, a possibility. The ancient dun was thought to have been converted to use as a castle during the medieval period (*see:* http://www.rcahms.gov.uk/).

Although the "killing team" sent after Bruce is my invention, at this time there would have been plenty of enemies and resistance to a Bruce kingship—even in the part of Scotland he controlled north of the Tay. The factions and blood feuds had been going on for years, and the supporters of the MacDougalls and Comyns would not have given up so easily. Indeed, as I alluded to in the book, John of Lorn was still causing trouble out west and trying to make a return to Scotland.

The inspiration for Bruce's axe-in-the-forehead injury was taken from a dent over the left brow found in a cast made of what is believed to be his skull.

Whether the recurring illness that first struck Bruce in the winter of 1307 on his campaign north was scurvy, leprosy, or something else (syphilis is also hypothesized) is all conjecture. But there is some support for leprosy—which might have been contracted at a later date—found in facial anomalies of the skull.

The inspiration for Gregor MacGregor's arrow was Henry V, who at the age of sixteen was said to have had an arrowhead removed from just below his eye at a depth of six inches(!) by a presumably highly skilled medieval surgeon.

The derivation of "keep your friends close and your enemies closer" is unknown, although it is sometimes attributed to an ancient Chinese general.

A few minor notes: Dun Raith is my made-up name for the unnamed ancient Norse structure that predated what is now Castle Leod, and Loch Glascarnoch, where the royal party camps, is actually a later-date man-made loch.

As always, please visit www.monicamccarty.com for picture books of some of the places mentioned in this book, extended Author's Notes, deleted scenes, and more.

Read on for an excerpt from

THE RECRUIT

by Monica McCarty

Published by Ballantine Books

Kenneth was in his element, enjoying every minute of his moment in the sun. He'd been born for this. Fighting. Competing. Winning. Aye, most of all winning.

It had taken him years of hard work, determination, and pulling himself out of the mud more times than he wanted to remember, but he was on the cusp of achieving what he'd wanted: to be the best.

One more event to go and a place in Bruce's secret army would be his. He was going to do this, he could feel it. He exulted in the cheers of the crowd, knowing they could feel it too. Fate and destiny had joined forces behind him, and nothing was going to stand in his way. For the first time, there would be no one in front of him. Tomorrow, after the wrestling event, he would be named champion.

He'd already achieved something no man had ever done before, winning all five weapon events. In one more sign that fate was with him, he'd won the archery contest. It had taken the shot of his life to defeat John MacGregor, but he'd done so by less than a quarter of an inch.

He wished he could have seen MacKay's face. After to-morrow there would be no doubt that he deserved to take his place among the best warriors in Scotland in Bruce's secret army, and his former rival wasn't going to be able to do a damned thing to stop it.

Kenneth glanced up to the king's pavilion, pleased to see Bruce clapping along with the rest.

That's when he saw her. His wee voyeur.

He'd found himself looking for her more than once over the past few days—four, he realized—and had begun to wonder whether he'd imagined her. But nay, there she was, sitting serenely and inauspiciously at the end of the king's platform with Alexander MacKenzie and his wife. Was she one of Lady Margaret's attendants, then?

Solving the mystery should have been enough to put the matter behind him. Right now he should only be thinking of one thing: tomorrow's contest. He shouldn't be wondering what it would be like to be the one to cut those too-tight laces of hers and release some of the passion she had bottled up tightly beneath the austere facade.

Hell, he knew there were men who fantasized about debauching a nun, he just hadn't thought he was one of them. But he couldn't deny the fierce hum that ran through his veins when he thought about ripping off that shapeless black gown that she donned like armor to reveal the wanton he'd glimpsed hiding beneath that fade-into-the-background facade.

He wanted to make her gasp. Wanted to see her lips part and color flood to her cheeks when he touched her. He wanted to be the one to make her shatter for the first time.

To his surprise, when he caught her gaze, he found himself nodding to her. Acknowledging in some way that he hadn't forgotten her. He'd never singled out a woman so publicly—or done anything that could be construed as romantic—and the gesture took him aback.

Although he doubted anyone else had noticed, she did.

He could have seen her eyes widen from halfway across Scotland, let alone the fifty or so paces that separated them. He was more amused than surprised when she immediately ducked behind the man in front of her. But if she thought she could escape him so easily, she was mistaken.

He amended his earlier decision. Hell, he'd worked hard. He could afford to relax and enjoy a little pre-victory celebration. He wanted her, and waiting no longer seemed necessary.

He started toward her, but he'd barely exited the arena before he found his path blocked by the first of many well-wishers. He heard some form of "Sir Kenneth, you were magnificent" from the female contingent, and "Bloody impressive fighting, Sutherland" from the male.

After working so hard to get here, he should have been savoring every minute of this; it was what he'd always wanted. But instead he found himself impatiently scanning the platform and stairs where he'd last seen the lass. But the crowd was too thick and the lass too small for him to pick her out.

He finally managed to extract himself. Threading his way to the base of the stairs, he caught a glimpse of black in the sea of colorful silk moving away from him. He smiled, thinking it ironic that her plain clothing, which he suspected was meant to hide, was what identified her.

He would have gone after her, but Lady Moira caught him first. "Congratulations, Sir Kenneth, on yet another victory. Were you by chance looking for someone?" she batted her eyelashes so aggressively that he was tempted to ask whether she had something in her eye. Normally, such coquetry amused him, but right now he found it vaguely annoying.

His mouth tightened as he saw his prey slipping away.

Moira stood with Lady Elizabeth Lindsay, who seemed amused by her companion's efforts. Lady Elizabeth was reputed to be devoted to her husband, and nothing Kenneth had seen suggested the contrary. She was friendly and polite, but nothing more. Which suited him just fine. Although she was a beautiful woman, she was shrewd, stubborn, and opinionated. He didn't envy Lindsay the headache. Challenges were for the battlefield, not the bedchamber.

"We are all trying to figure it out," Lady Elizabeth said.

"Figure what out?" he asked, glancing over her shoulder, trying to keep his eye on her.

"Who the nod was for," Lady Elizabeth said.

He looked at her, barely hiding his surprise. "Nod?"

"Aye, it created quite a stir. The ladies seated around me were all quite sure you were nodding to them," Lady Elizabeth said with a smile.

Ah hell, he guessed it had been more noticeable than he realized. Kenneth hid his reaction behind a wicked smile. "I was," he said.

Lady Moira nearly yelped with pleasure, clapping her hands together. "I knew it, to whom?"

"I'll leave that to you to find out," he said with a playful wink. "Now, if you'll excuse me. I see my sister, and I need to have her patch me up so I'll be ready for tomorrow's competition."

It was only partially a lie. The blow he'd taken across the ribs was starting to throb beneath his habergeon. The shirt of mail offered scant protection against the impact of steel on bone. He suspected he had a fairly nasty bruise brewing. He would see Helen to fix it up, but *after* he caught up with his little nun, who was weaving her way through the crowd at nearly a run in her effort to avoid him.

She was only running from the inevitable. Almost as certain as he was that he would win tomorrow, Kenneth was certain that before the night was out, he would have her under him. Or perhaps on top of him.

He felt a pleasant tightening in his groin just thinking about it.

She'd just passed through the gate into the castle when he saw her stop and turn.

"Mary, wait!" he heard someone—a woman—say. He turned, recognizing the speaker as Lady Margaret MacKenzie. "Where are you going in such a rush?"

Mary. He should have guessed. A common, unremarkable name that would draw no attention—just like the rest of her. He was only a few feet away, but she hadn't seen him yet. "I think the sun—"

She stopped suddenly. Her eyes widening and mouth caught in an O of surprise as she saw him. On such a severe countenance, it shouldn't have been so adorable. He found himself smiling.

In the sunlight, without the lens hiding half her face, he got his first really good look at her. Her hair was still hidden beneath an ugly black veil and wimple, her gown was still boxy and shapeless, her skin was still pale, her features were still too sharp—especially her cheekbones which stuck out prominently over sunken cheeks—and there was still an overall gray, ghostlike quality to her, but on closer scrutiny he knew his instincts had been right. The hint of prettiness and intentional obscuring of beauty was even more obvious in the stark light of day.

There was no hiding her eyes, and they were spectacular. Round and overlarge in her hollow-cheeked face, they were a remarkable greenish blue, and framed by thick, long lashes that seemed incongruously soft on such an otherwise brittle exterior. Her mouth, too, was soft and full, with a sensual dip that made him think of a bow on a package he wanted to unwrap.

As soon as their eyes met, she instinctively dropped her gaze, as if hiding her eyes from his view.

Hiding. That's exactly what she was doing. The question was why and from what.

"Lady Mary, Lady Margaret," he said, approaching the two women with a bow.

Lady Margaret turned on him with a gasp. She gaped at him, and then at Mary. "You've met?"

He grinned, seeing the blush rise to Mary's cheeks.

"Briefly," she said tightly. The lass really needed to relax. She was pulled as tight as a bowstring.

"Not too briefly," he corrected, unable to stop himself from teasing her. He liked seeing the color in her cheeks. "I'm looking forward to furthering our acquaintance. I hope you are not bored with the Games already? Perhaps they are not *exciting* enough for you?"

He knew he was being horrible, but he couldn't help teasing her.

She wasn't shy, though. Her eyes flashed at him in outrage.

"Oh, it was exciting, wasn't it, Mary?" Lady Margaret interposed.

He thought she nodded, but her jaw was clenched so tight it was hard to tell. "I'm sure Sir Kenneth has heard enough accolades for the day, Margaret. He doesn't need to hear them from us."

She gave him a smile that made him frown. She had a way of making it sound unflattering. He was used to reading a certain amount of feminine admiration in a woman's gaze, but with her there was only cool challenge. He didn't think he liked it.

"There is still the sword dance to be held this afternoon. If Lady Margaret doesn't object, I would be happy to escort you."

Lady Margaret looked at him in surprise. "Why would I object?"

"No!" Lady Mary said over her. Her blush deepened as she realized she'd spoken too harshly. "I mean, I regret that I must return to the castle. I'm feeling unwell."

Lady Margaret became immediately concerned. She put her hand on Mary's arm. "Is that why you rushed off?" She laid the back of her hand across her forehead. "You do look flushed."

Mary nodded, not looking in his direction. Probably to avoid his quirked brow. "I think the sun was too much for me."

Lady Margaret turned to him. "Mary has just recovered from an illness. This was the first time she's had a chance to see the Games all week."

"Is that so?" he drawled.

She couldn't avoid looking at him any longer. He could see a flash of anger in her blue-green eyes that reminded him of sun glinting on the sea. He hadn't expected so much spirit from such a quiet exterior, and his intrigue grew.

"Aye, I've been very unwell." He swore he could see her chin stiffen, challenging him to disagree with her.

"My sister is a healer. If you like, I could send her to you."

Her mouth tightened, hearing his challenge. "That is very kind of you, but I'm sure that will not be necessary. I think I just need to lie down."

"Lying down sounds like a wonderful idea."

Though there was nothing suggestive in his voice, he knew she'd understood when he heard her sharp intake of breath.

She was outraged, as no doubt she should be. But he could also see by the delicate flutter of her pulse below a surprisingly velvety-soft–looking cheek that she was more intrigued than she wanted to let on.